POSITIVELY
izzy

TERRI LIBENSON

PUFFIN BOOKS

UK | USA | Canada | Ireland | Australia
India | New Zealand | South Africa

Puffin Books is part of the Penguin Random House group of companies
whose addresses can be found at global.penguinrandomhouse.com.

www.penguin.co.uk   www.puffin.co.uk   www.ladybird.co.uk

Penguin
Random House
UK

First published in the USA by Balzer + Bray, an imprint of HarperCollins Publishers, 2018
Published in Great Britain by Puffin Books 2018

001

Typography by Terri Libenson and Katie Fitch
Printed in Great Britain by Clays Ltd, St Ives plc

A CIP catalogue record for this book is available from the British Library

ISBN: 978-0-141-37232-7

All correspondence to:
Puffin Books
Penguin Random House Children's
80 Strand, London WC2R 0RL

To all you readers, who should never be branded as anything except "awesome"

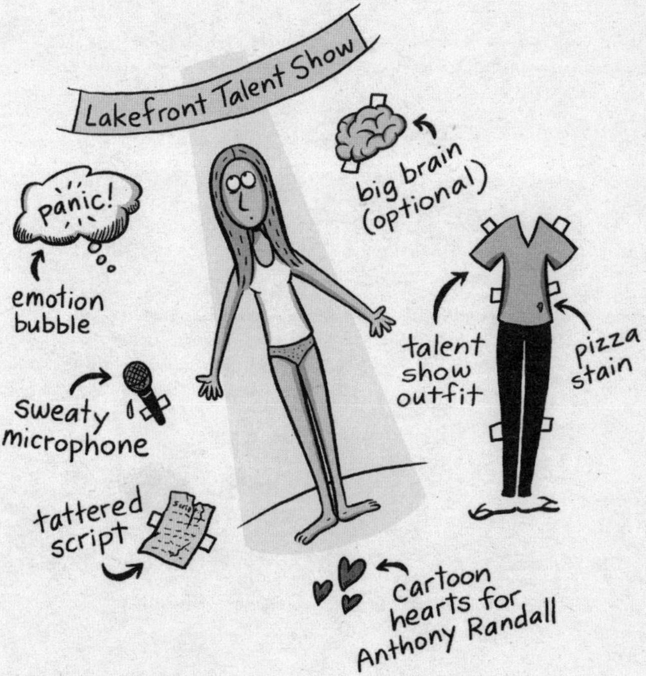

Lakefront Talent Show
panic!
emotion bubble
big brain (optional)
talent show outfit
pizza stain
sweaty microphone
tattered script
cartoon hearts for Anthony Randall

PROLOGUE

Brianna

I don't like labels. I just want to make that clear up front. And middle school is full of labels.

gossip girls
yakka yak
the jock
BRAPP
class clown
idiot
squilch

Let's be real. People aren't just one thing. Trouble is, unless you're friends with someone, you don't really know **them**, only what they're known **for**.

Take my best friend. She's known for being a great artist. And that's good. But she's so quiet, no one knows she's also sweet and funny and even kind of wacky (she has wacky parents, so that's kind of a given).

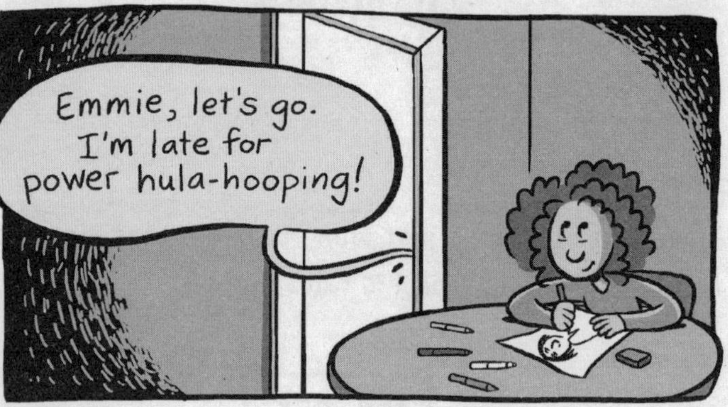
Emmie, let's go. I'm late for power hula-hooping!

Me? Well . . .

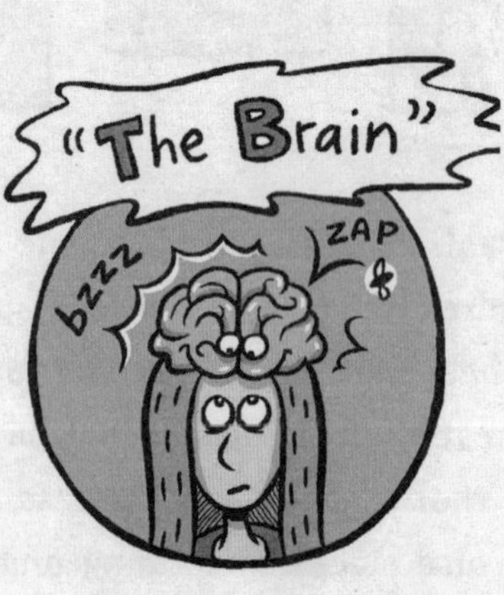
"The Brain"
bzzz
ZAP

Yeah. Ever since I moved here in kindergarten. I wouldn't even mind that label so much if . . . well, if people could look past it a little.

It's like being typecast as an actor . . . a role you're known for. That's all people expect or even want of you, 'cause it's safe.

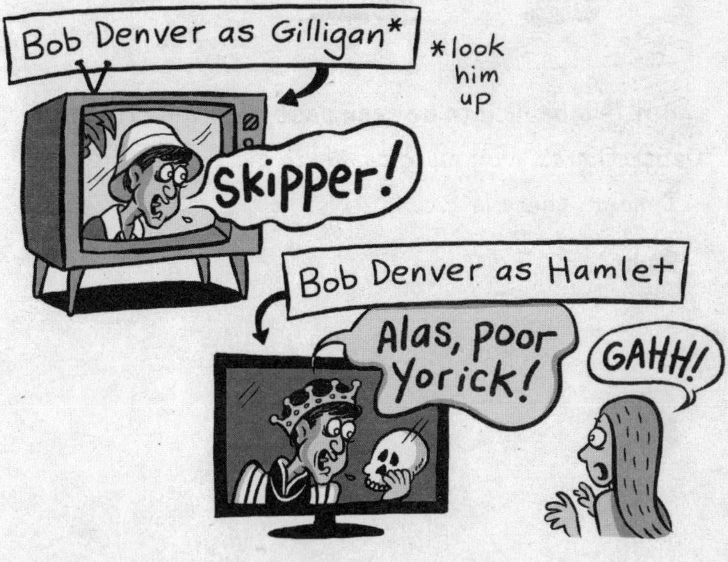
Bob Denver as Gilligan*
*look him up
Skipper!
Bob Denver as Hamlet
Alas, poor Yorick!
GAHH!

. Don't get me wrong. I like being smart. I wouldn't want to change that by flunking out or something. Then I'd be known for something **worse.**

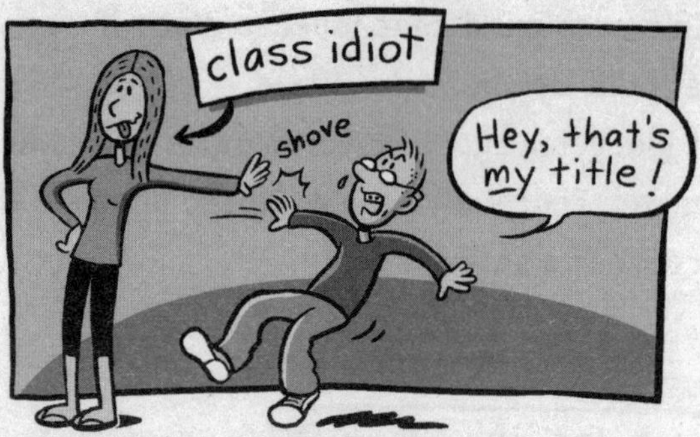
class idiot
shove
Hey, that's my title!

But it'd be nice to be seen past my brains for once. 'Cause there's way more to me!

I mean, there is . . .

Right?

IZZY

First of all, let's get the name thing out of the way. My older sister, Danielle, started calling me Izzy when we were little. Not because my real name is Isabelle or Isabella or anything. It's because of a knock-knock joke that I made up and repeated over and over to anyone I'd meet.

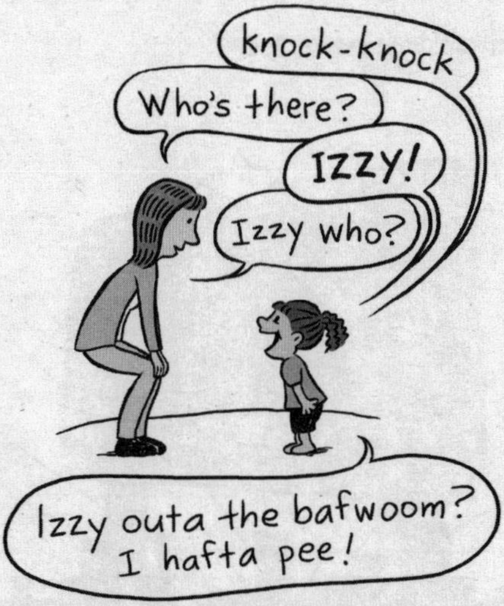
knock-knock
Who's there?
IZZY!
Izzy who?
Izzy outa the bafwoom? I hafta pee!

My mom thought the name was cute and started calling me Izzy too. Then Ashley did. Then my classmates did. So it stuck. I barely remember my real name.

Sophie? Emma? Ed?

The name even grew on me. Now I kinda like it. Some people are born with a name that suits them, and others—well, they have to grow into theirs or get a new one, you know? My mom always said I look more like an Izzy than my real name, so it all makes sense. It's a great stage name, too.

IZZY SILVER

I'm the middle child. My older sister, Danielle, is a sophomore in high school and my younger sister, Ashley, is in sixth grade.

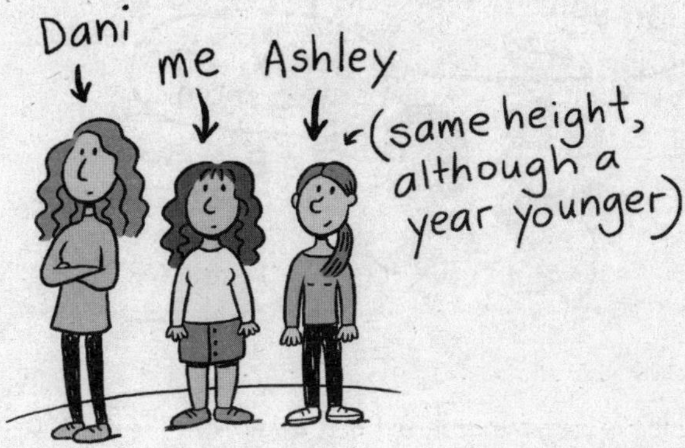
Dani
me
Ashley
(same height, although a year younger)

Dani is smart, practical, and very, very bossy. She's good at getting stuff done.

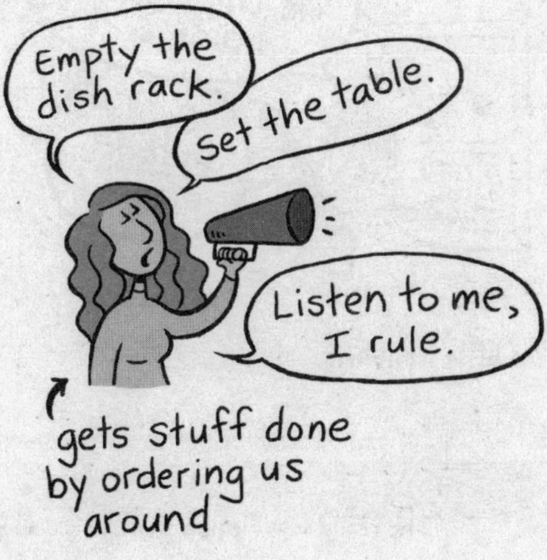
Empty the dish rack.
Set the table.
Listen to me, I rule.
gets stuff done by ordering us around

Not only is Dani bossy, but she's mega-smart too. That and being the oldest make her think **she's** our mother.

Do your homework, Izzy.

Honey, I'm the mom.

But she's right, Izzy. Do your homework.

Ashley is the youngest and gets away with the most. Probably 'cause she has a way of "turning lemons into lemonade,"* as my mom says.

It's raining and we can't go on a picnic?

Cool— indoor picnic!

Yeah, it's a little irritating.

*she really says "lemon shandy" . . . whatever that is.

But Ash is so sweet, even I can't resist her. Well, usually. We're only fourteen months apart ("Irish twins," although we're not Irish and not twins). We have similar minds and like to use our imaginations—mainly by making up plays and acting them out. Or pretending we're characters from our favorite TV shows.

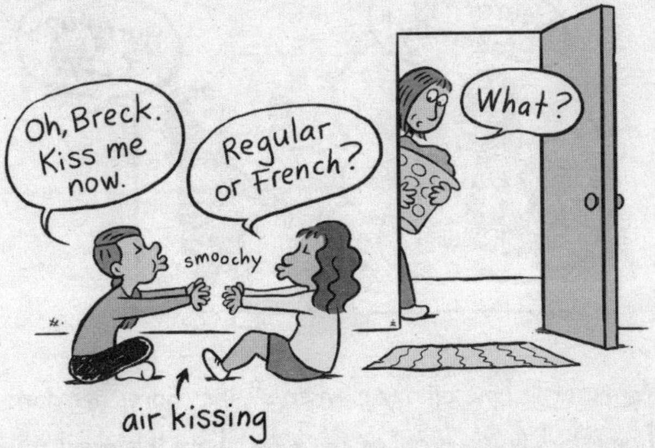
Oh, Breck. Kiss me now.
Regular or French?
What?
smoochy
air kissing

My mom is an ER nurse and raises us alone. Since she works odd shifts in a hospital and is gone a lot, my sisters and I have a ton of chores we're responsible for.

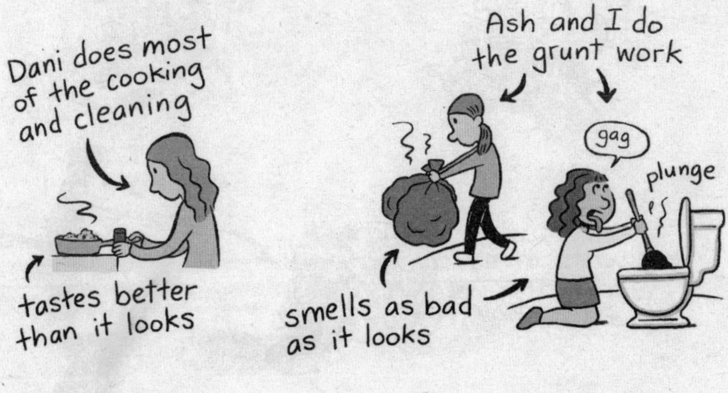
Dani does most of the cooking and cleaning
tastes better than it looks
Ash and I do the grunt work
gag
plunge
smells as bad as it looks

"Obedient Ash" doesn't mind the chores. Well, she doesn't complain, anyway. Sometimes I don't even mind, but mostly it's really boring or gross and I have to pretend I'm doing something more exciting to make the time go faster.

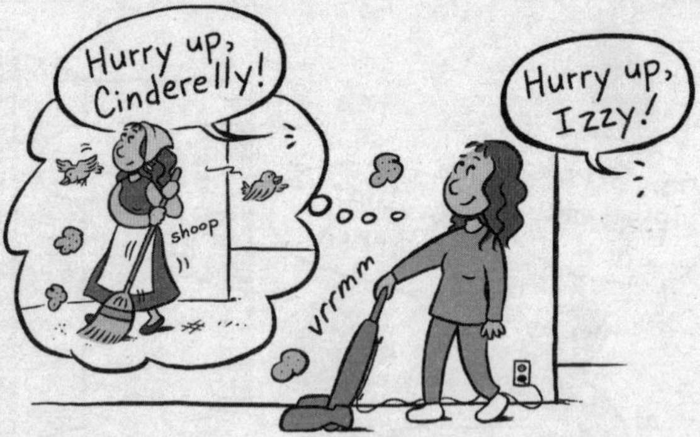
Hurry up, Cinderelly!
shoop
Hurry up, Izzy!
vrrmm

My favorite time of day is when all the chores are done and my homework (yuck) is out of the way. I have this great ritual.

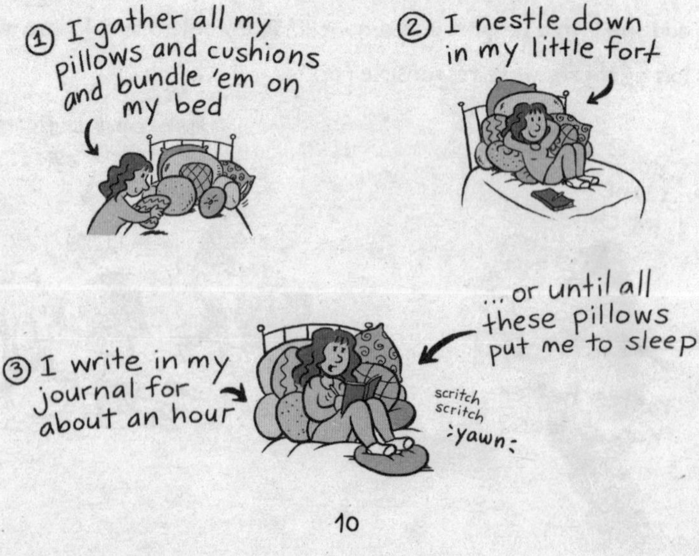
① I gather all my pillows and cushions and bundle 'em on my bed
② I nestle down in my little fort
③ I write in my journal for about an hour
... or until all these pillows put me to sleep
scritch
scritch
:yawn:

I write about my life (so far), stories I make up, and if I'm feeling especially artsy . . . I doodle.

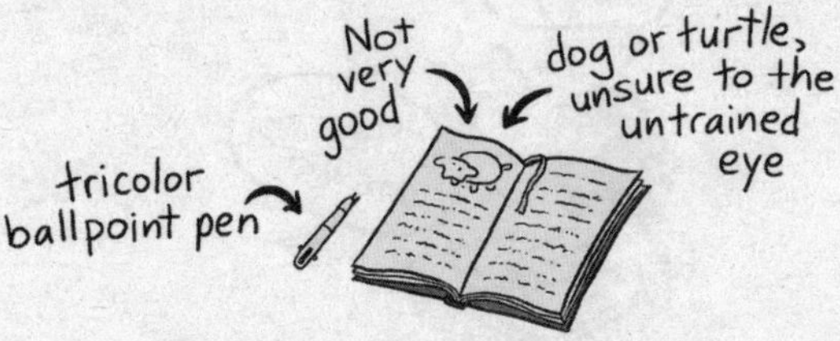
Not very good
dog or turtle, unsure to the untrained eye
tricolor ballpoint pen

I'd rather do that than read like Dani or watch TV like Ashley (who doesn't study as hard as Dani but still gets decent grades!).

My grades aren't so great, which bugs my mom. She wishes I'd pay more attention in school. I wish I would, too, but there are so many more interesting things that run through my head than come out of my teachers' mouths.

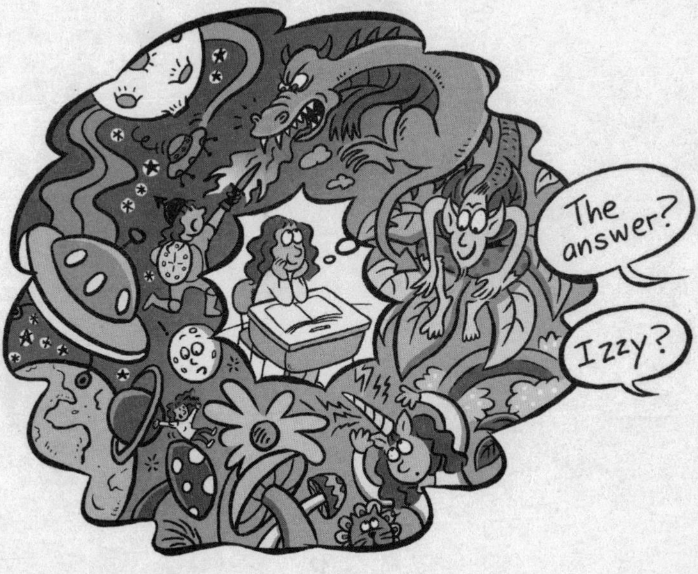
The answer?
Izzy?

Yeah, I know I could do better if I tried.

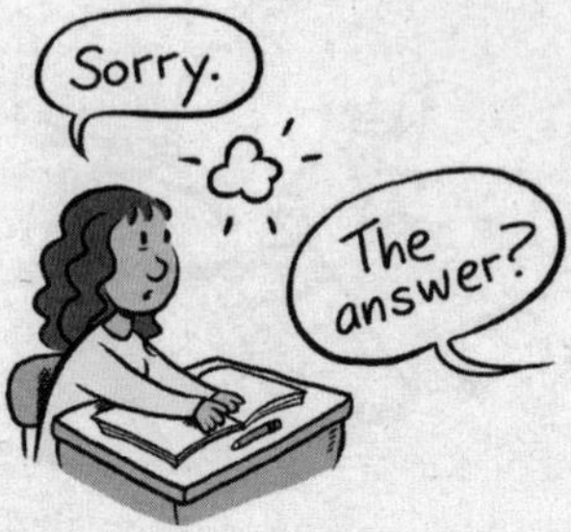
Sorry.
The answer?

Or . . . to be totally, completely, **ginormously** honest . . .

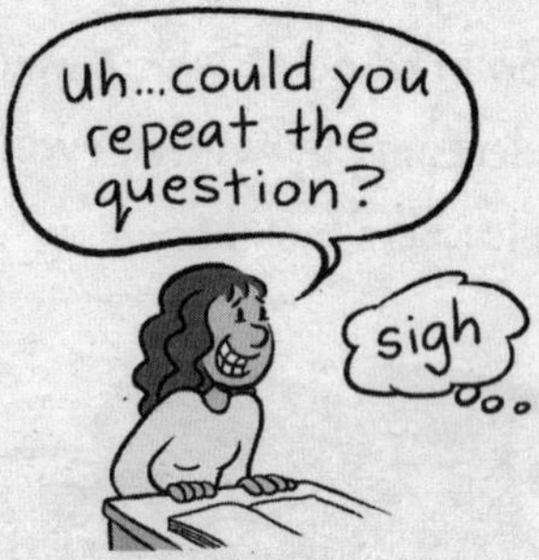
Uh...could you repeat the question?
sigh

. . . cared.

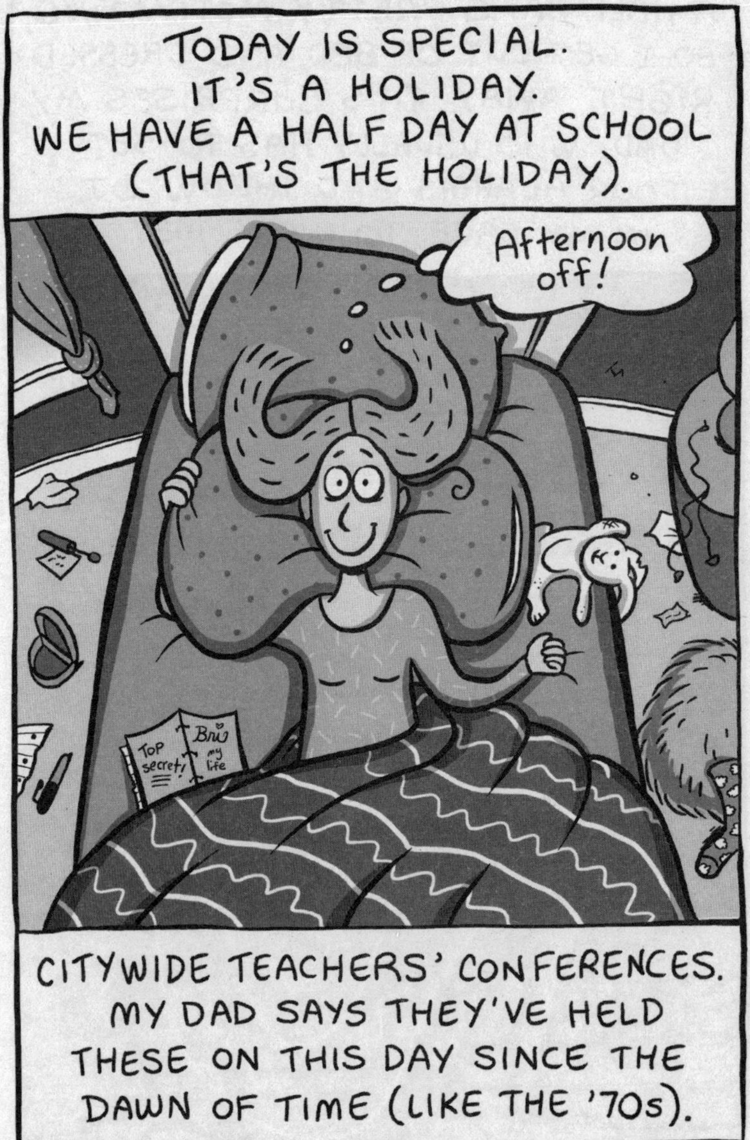
TODAY IS SPECIAL.
IT'S A HOLIDAY.
WE HAVE A HALF DAY AT SCHOOL
(THAT'S THE HOLIDAY).
Afternoon off!
Top secret!
Bri
my life
CITYWIDE TEACHERS' CONFERENCES.
MY DAD SAYS THEY'VE HELD
THESE ON THIS DAY SINCE THE
DAWN OF TIME (LIKE THE '70s).

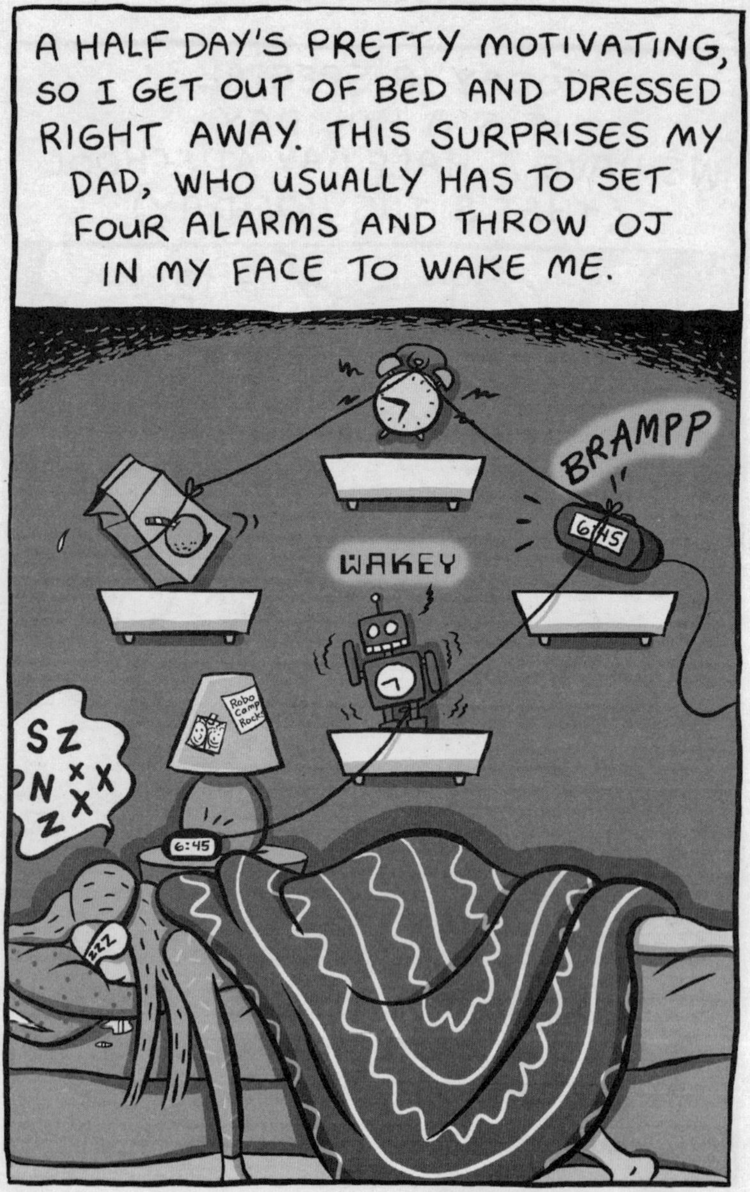
A HALF DAY'S PRETTY MOTIVATING, SO I GET OUT OF BED AND DRESSED RIGHT AWAY. THIS SURPRISES MY DAD, WHO USUALLY HAS TO SET FOUR ALARMS AND THROW OJ IN MY FACE TO WAKE ME.
BRAMPP
WAKEY
Robo Camp Rocks
6:45

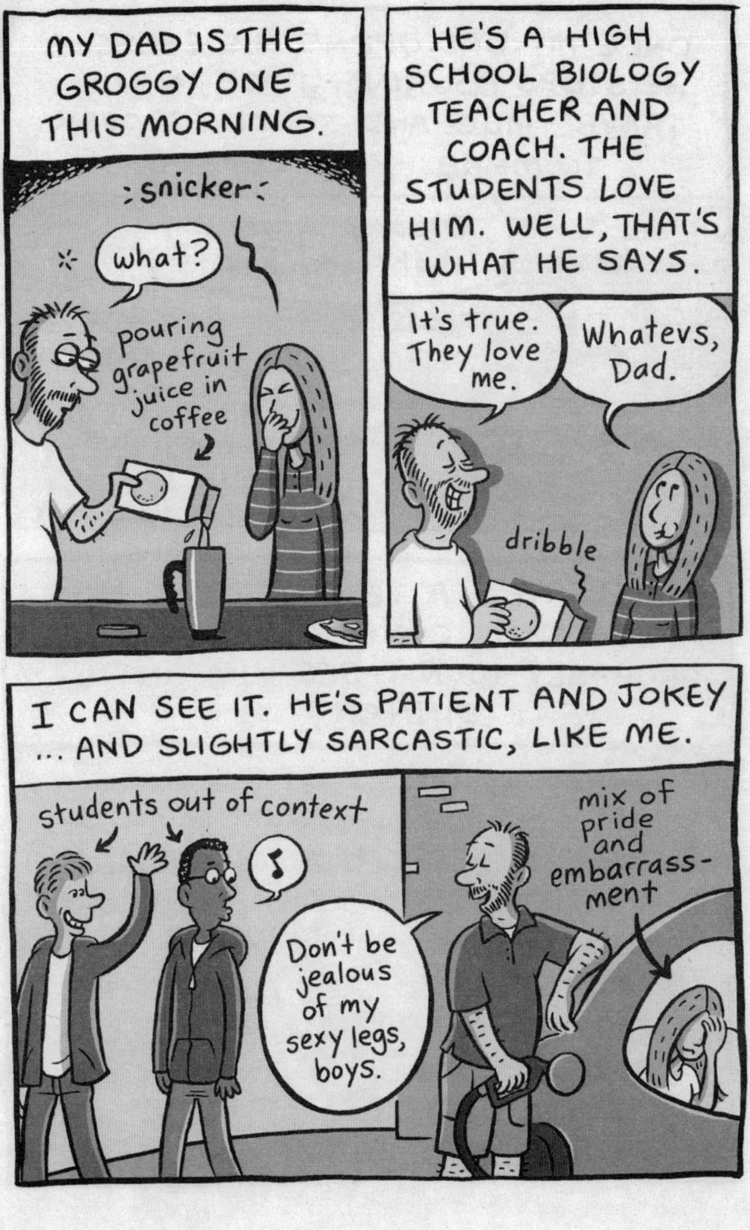
MY DAD IS THE GROGGY ONE THIS MORNING.
:snicker:
what?
pouring grapefruit juice in coffee
HE'S A HIGH SCHOOL BIOLOGY TEACHER AND COACH. THE STUDENTS LOVE HIM. WELL, THAT'S WHAT HE SAYS.
It's true. They love me.
Whatevs, Dad.
dribble
I CAN SEE IT. HE'S PATIENT AND JOKEY ... AND SLIGHTLY SARCASTIC, LIKE ME.
students out of context
Don't be jealous of my sexy legs, boys.
mix of pride and embarrass-ment

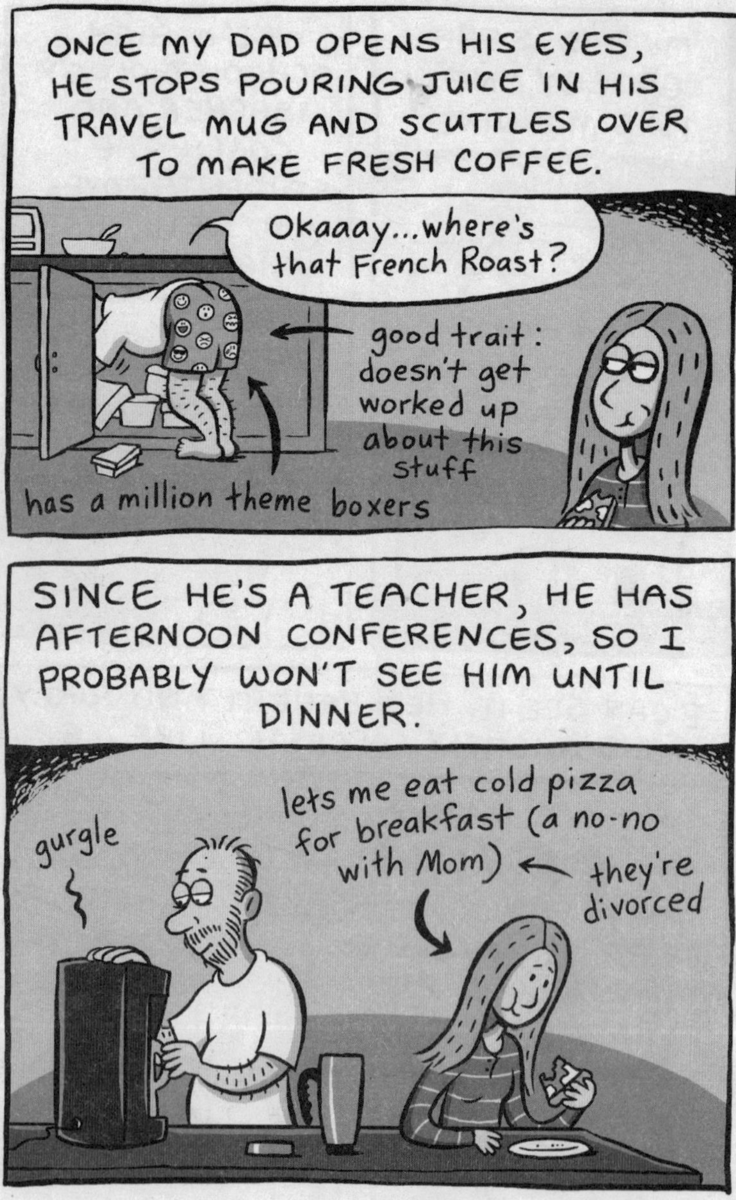
ONCE MY DAD OPENS HIS EYES, HE STOPS POURING JUICE IN HIS TRAVEL MUG AND SCUTTLES OVER TO MAKE FRESH COFFEE.
Okaaay...where's that French Roast?
good trait: doesn't get worked up about this stuff
has a million theme boxers
SINCE HE'S A TEACHER, HE HAS AFTERNOON CONFERENCES, SO I PROBABLY WON'T SEE HIM UNTIL DINNER.
gurgle
lets me eat cold pizza for breakfast (a no-no with Mom)
they're divorced

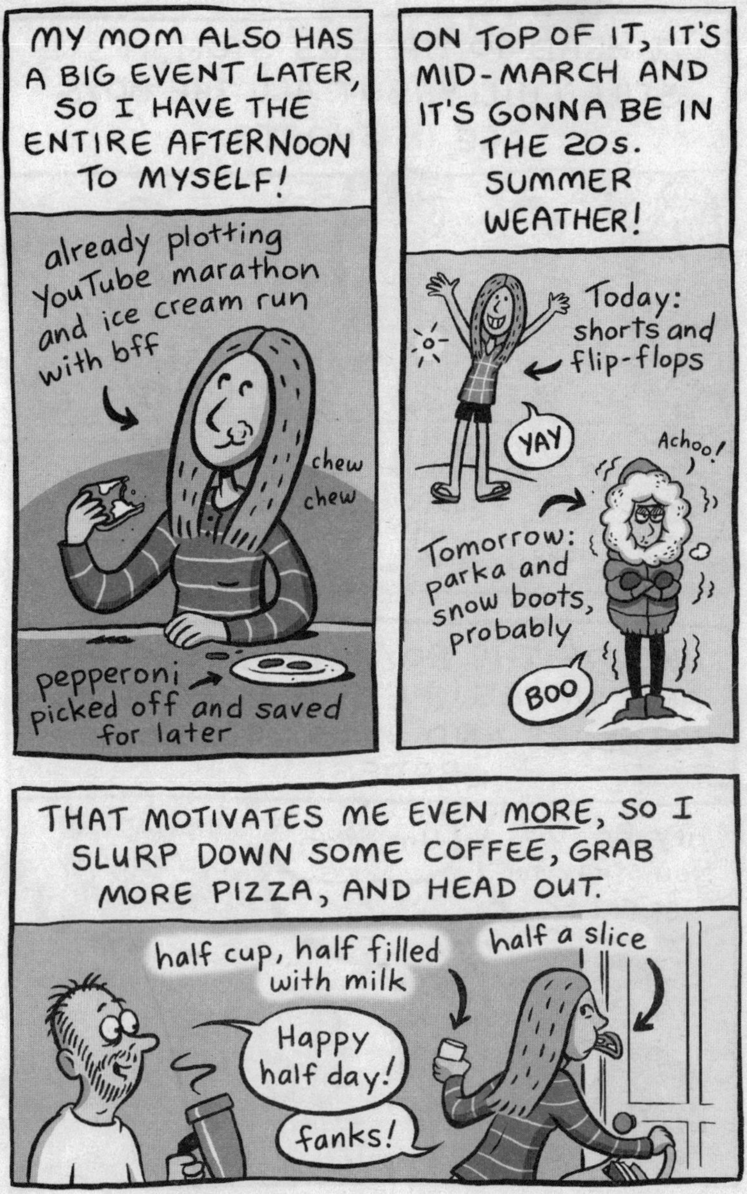
MY MOM ALSO HAS A BIG EVENT LATER, SO I HAVE THE ENTIRE AFTERNOON TO MYSELF!
already plotting YouTube marathon and ice cream run with bff
chew
chew
pepperoni picked off and saved for later
ON TOP OF IT, IT'S MID-MARCH AND IT'S GONNA BE IN THE 20s. SUMMER WEATHER!
Today: shorts and flip-flops
YAY
Achoo!
Tomorrow: parka and snow boots, probably
BOO
THAT MOTIVATES ME EVEN MORE, SO I SLURP DOWN SOME COFFEE, GRAB MORE PIZZA, AND HEAD OUT.
half cup, half filled with milk
half a slice
Happy half day!
fanks!

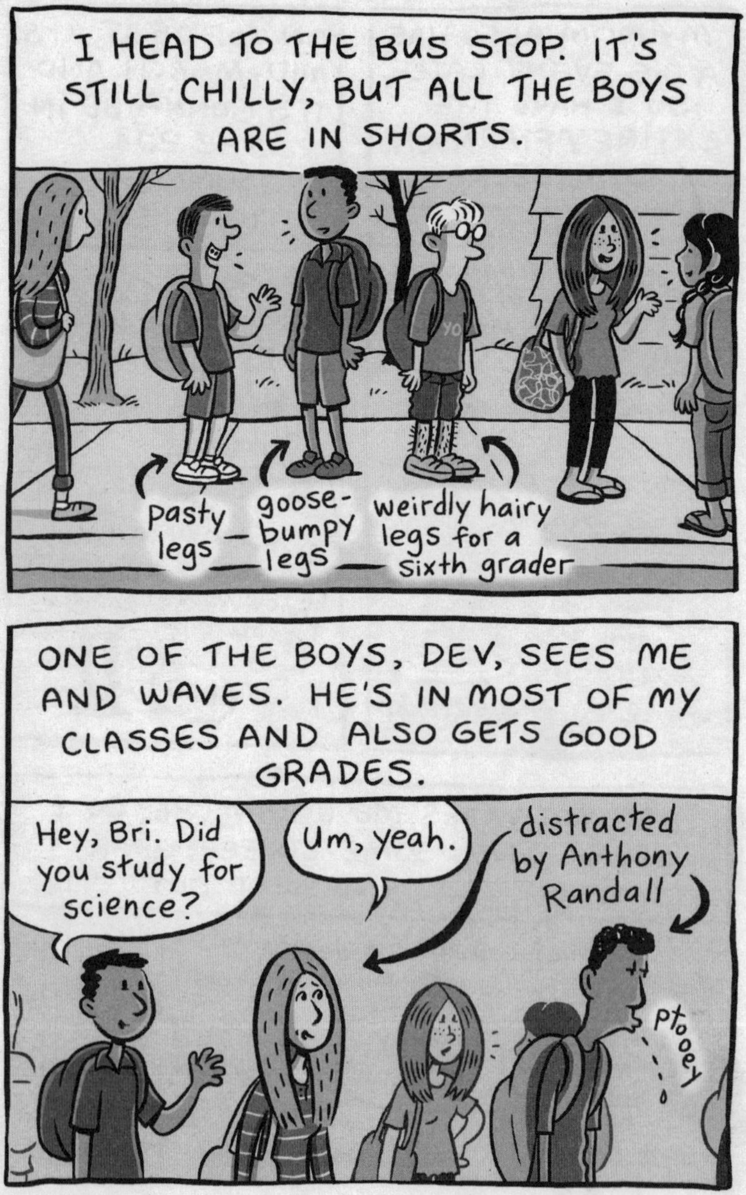
I HEAD TO THE BUS STOP. IT'S STILL CHILLY, BUT ALL THE BOYS ARE IN SHORTS.
pasty legs
goose-bumpy legs
weirdly hairy legs for a sixth grader
ONE OF THE BOYS, DEV, SEES ME AND WAVES. HE'S IN MOST OF MY CLASSES AND ALSO GETS GOOD GRADES.
Hey, Bri. Did you study for science?
Um, yeah.
distracted by Anthony Randall
Ptooey

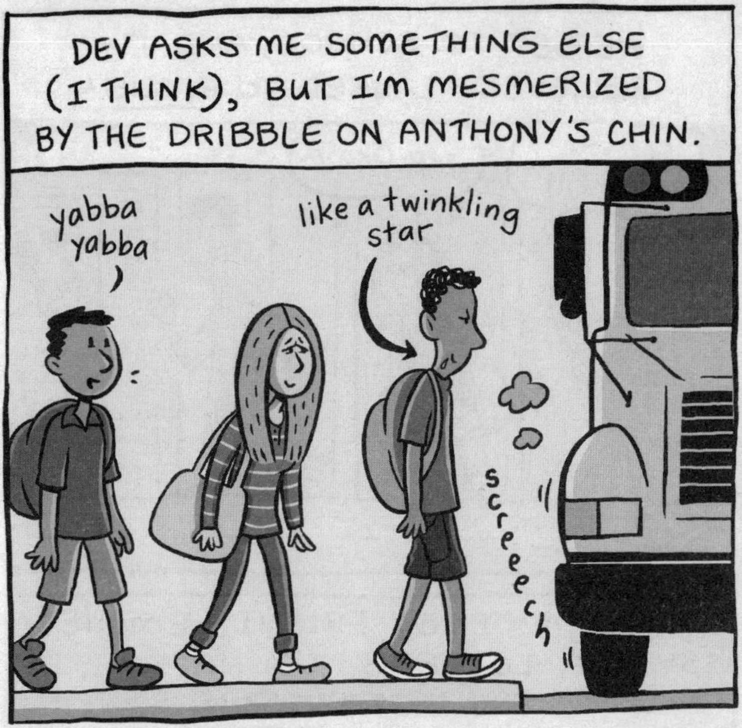
DEV ASKS ME SOMETHING ELSE (I THINK), BUT I'M MESMERIZED BY THE DRIBBLE ON ANTHONY'S CHIN.
yabba yabba
like a twinkling star
screeech

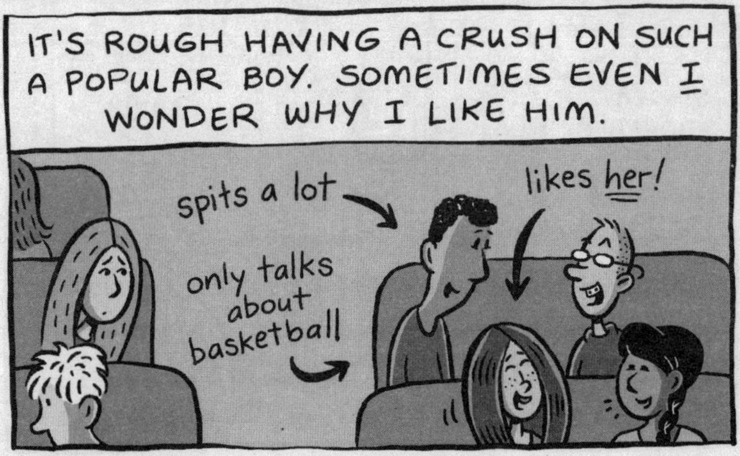
IT'S ROUGH HAVING A CRUSH ON SUCH A POPULAR BOY. SOMETIMES EVEN I WONDER WHY I LIKE HIM.
spits a lot
only talks about basketball
likes her!

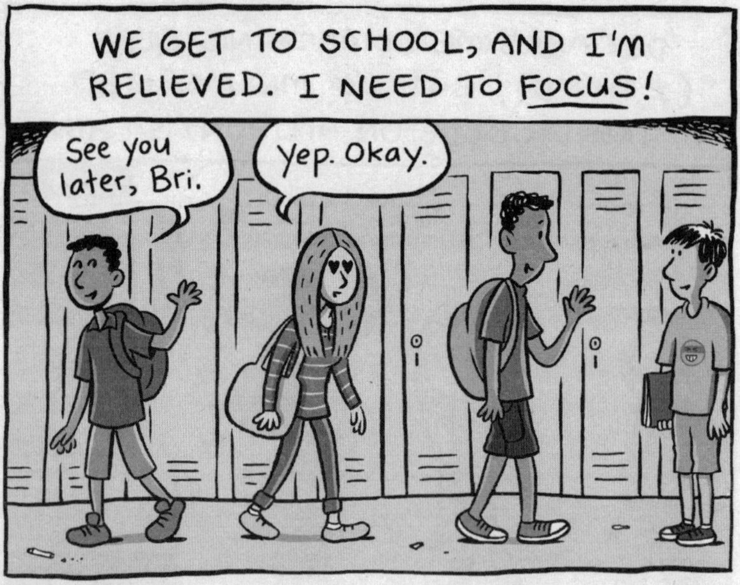
WE GET TO SCHOOL, AND I'M RELIEVED. I NEED TO FOCUS!
See you later, Bri.
Yep. Okay.

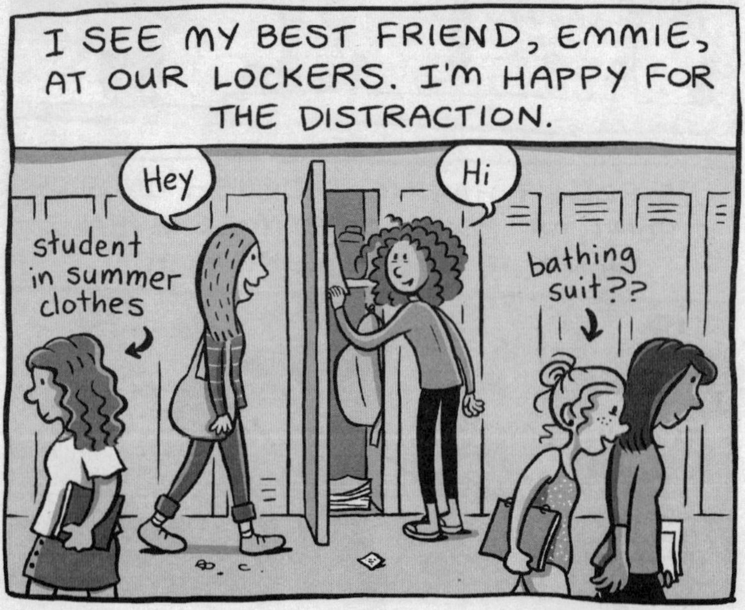
I SEE MY BEST FRIEND, EMMIE, AT OUR LOCKERS. I'M HAPPY FOR THE DISTRACTION.
Hey
Hi
student in summer clothes
bathing suit??

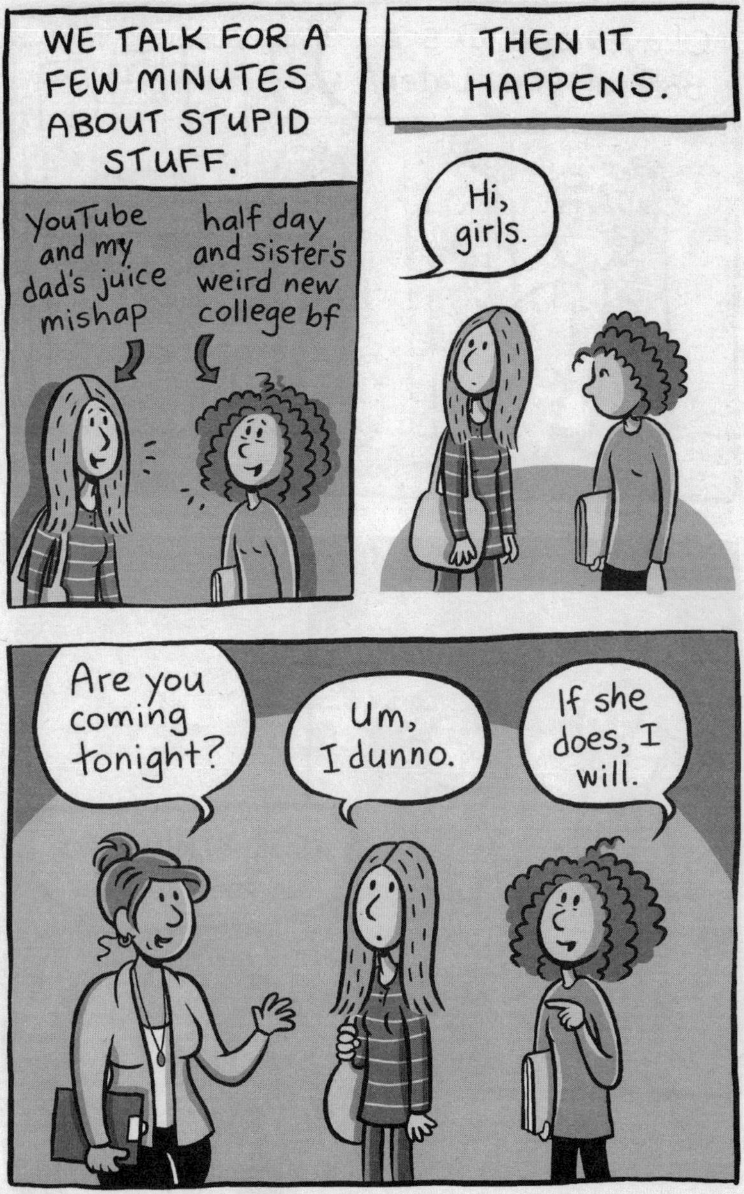
WE TALK FOR A FEW MINUTES ABOUT STUPID STUFF.
YouTube and my dad's juice mishap
half day and sister's weird new college bf
THEN IT HAPPENS.
Hi, girls.
Are you coming tonight?
Um, I dunno.
If she does, I will.

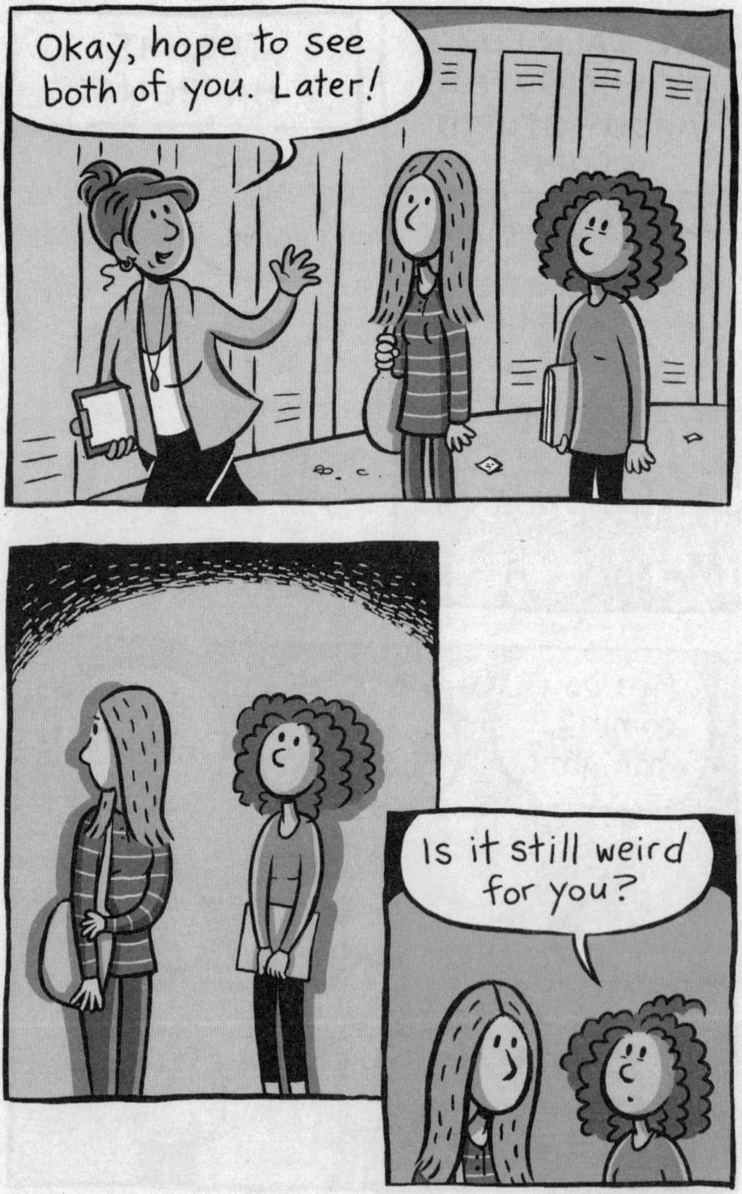
Okay, hope to see both of you. Later!
Is it still weird for you?

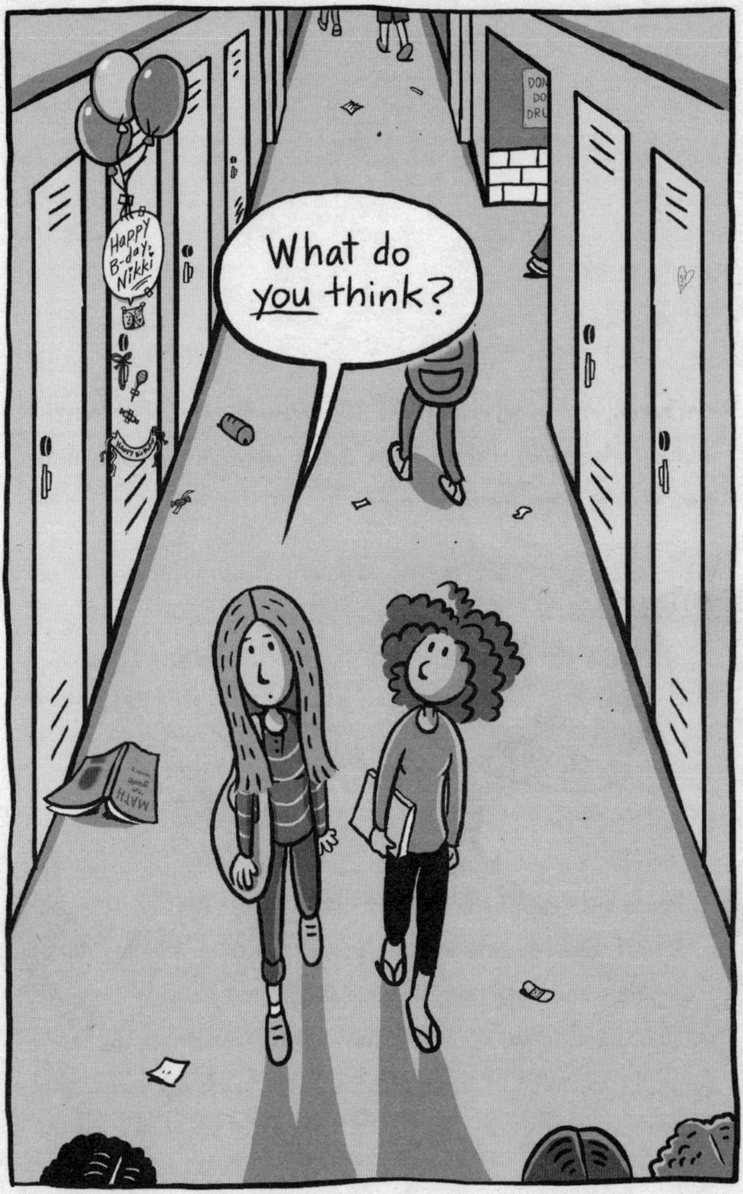
What do you think?
Happy B-day, Nikki
MATH

IZZY

I'm barely able to get out of bed. It's unusually warm for March, and my window is cracked open. Sooo relaxing. Well, it is until Dani shrieks from the other room.

Hurry up! You've gotta take out the trash before school.

← Dani

←delicious breeze

Sigh

Looks like Ash has already gotten up. Show-off.

I have about twenty minutes before we catch the bus. First, I scribble some stuff (mostly complaints about Dani) in my journal. I'm about to put my book down when I remember the weird dream I had, and I jot that down too. I like to use my dreams for inspiration. Maybe someday they'll make great sci-fi movie plots!

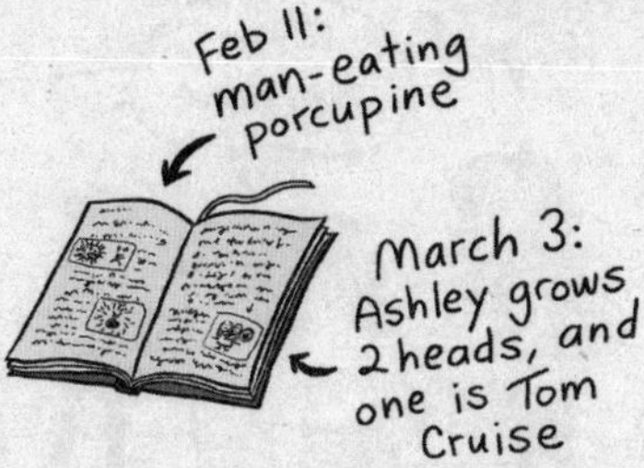
Feb 11:
man-eating
porcupine
March 3:
Ashley grows
2 heads, and
one is Tom
Cruise

Now I'm running late, so I quickly get dressed, run a comb through my snaggy hair, and stumble into our tiny kitchen. I start to scarf down some cereal.

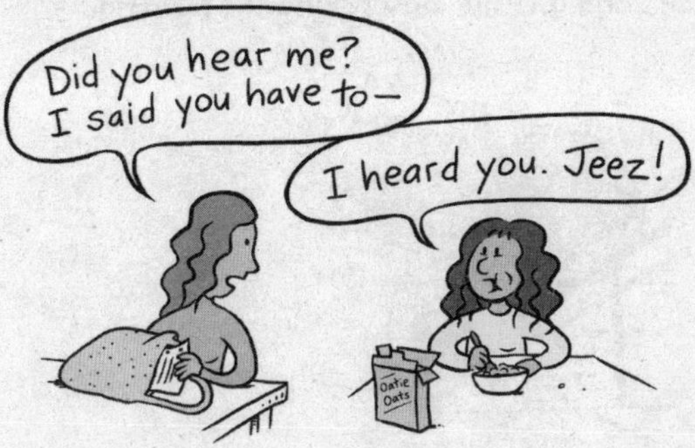
Did you hear me?
I said you have to—
I heard you. Jeez!
Oatie Oats

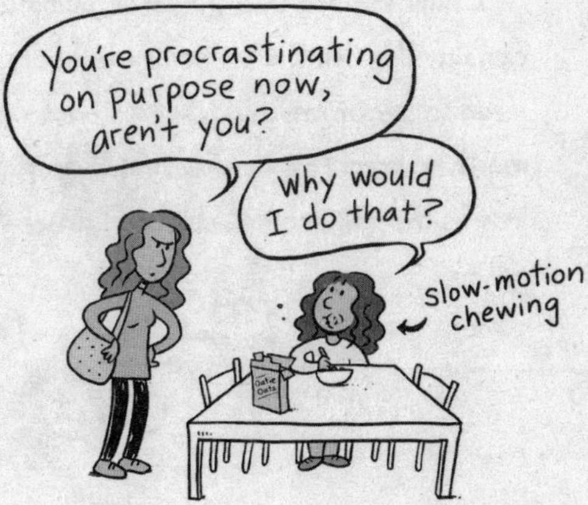
You're procrastinating on purpose now, aren't you?
Why would I do that?
slow-motion chewing

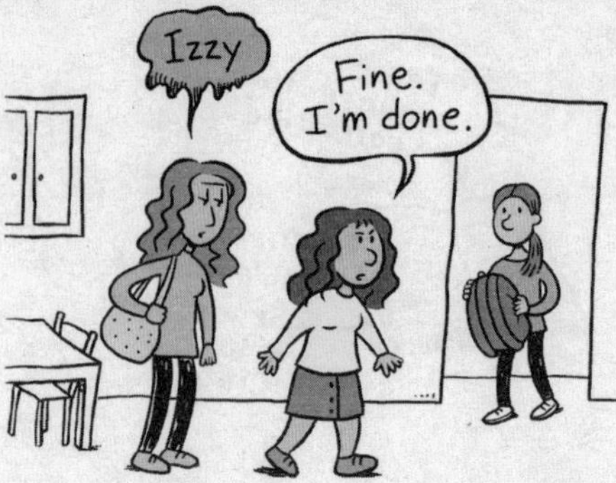
Izzy
Fine.
I'm done.

I quickly grab all the garbage bags in the apartment and dump them into a heavier, monster-sized one. I haul it—not so gently—down the back stairs and into the alley behind the building.

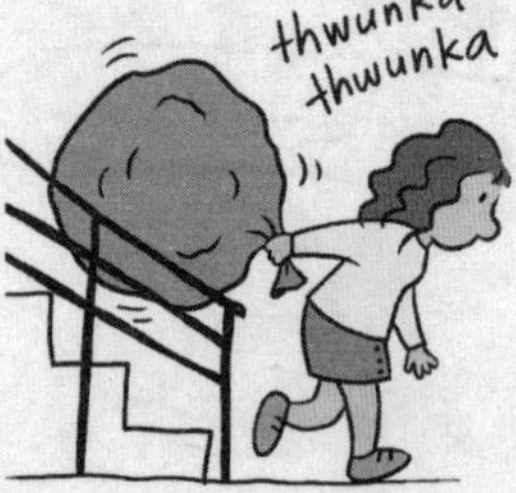
thwunka
thwunka

I hurl the bag into the large Dumpster in the alley and then climb up the stairs. I see some neighbors in the windows. I don't mean to spy or anything, but it's hard not to notice people chewing their breakfast or watering their plants. Once I even saw a lady in the bathroom. I still can't unsee it.

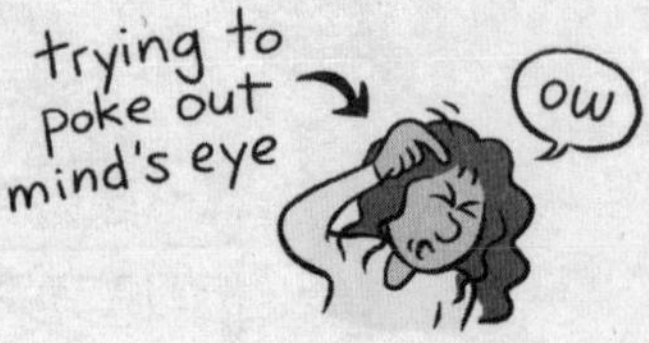
trying to
poke out
mind's eye
OW

Sometimes I make up stuff about the people in the building.

Yeah, that lady, Mrs. Wodaski, is a retired spy. She smiles to hide the fact that she was once a lethal gun-for-hire.

I race back upstairs to our apartment. Just in time. Ash is waiting for me at the front door. Dani must've just left. Good—I'm tired of her being on my case.

We only have half a day today. Citywide teachers' conferences or something. Ash and I are pretty pumped. We head out.

We live in a pretty big apartment complex. It's across from a cemetery. That always freaks people out when they visit for the first time, but it's actually kinda peaceful. Sometimes Ash and I go there to hang out. We like to make up stories about the people buried there. Yeah, I know that sounds creepy, but we give them **really** good stories.

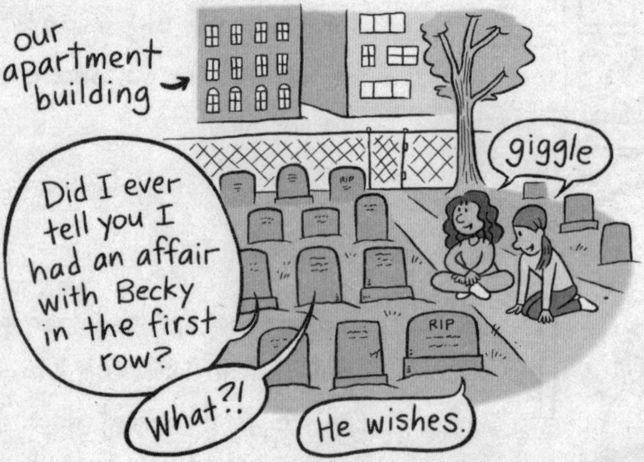
our apartment building
giggle
Did I ever tell you I had an affair with Becky in the first row?
What?!
He wishes.

My mom, the ER nurse, has this dark joke that many of her patients now live across the street from us.

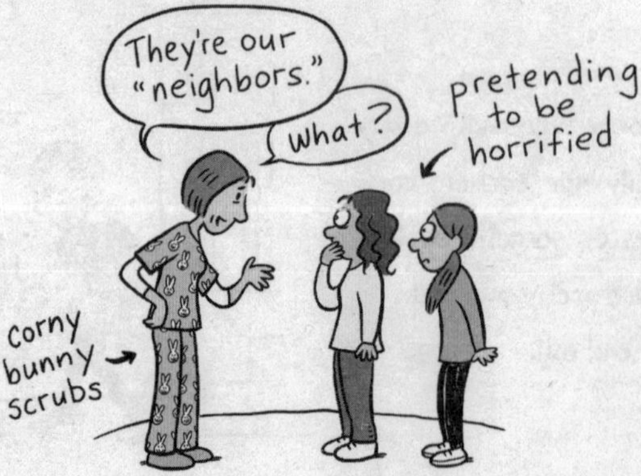
They're our "neighbors."
What?
pretending to be horrified
corny bunny scrubs

My mom is a weird combination of funny and a worrywart. She worries all the time. She especially worries about me, which is kinda odd, considering I'm the middle kid and middle kids tend to go unnoticed.

Then again, I'm a bit of a "special case."

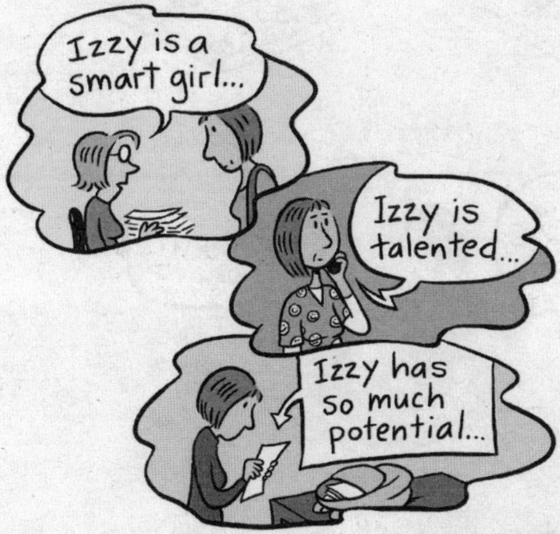
Izzy is a smart girl...
Izzy is talented...
Izzy has so much potential...

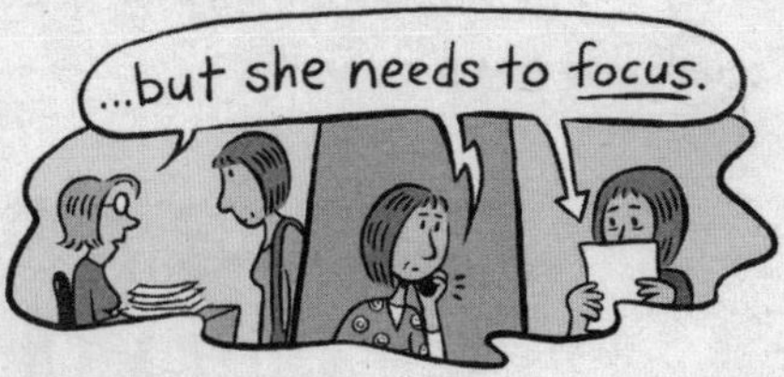
...but she needs to focus.

Focus is a word teachers use about me a lot.

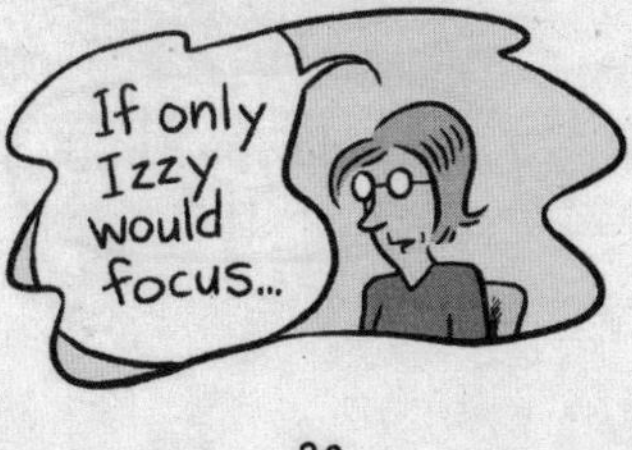
If only Izzy would focus...

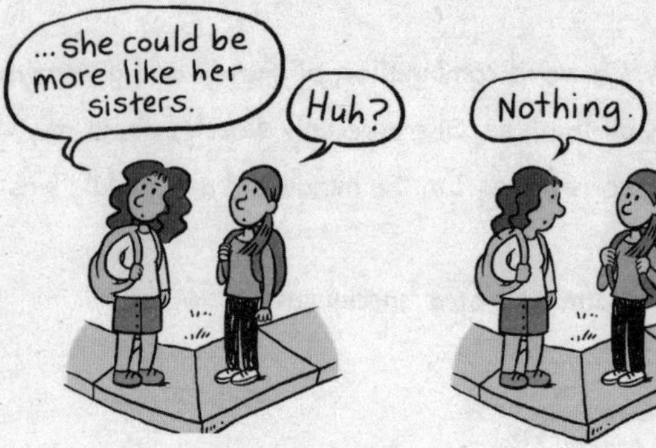
...she could be more like her sisters.
Huh?
Nothing.

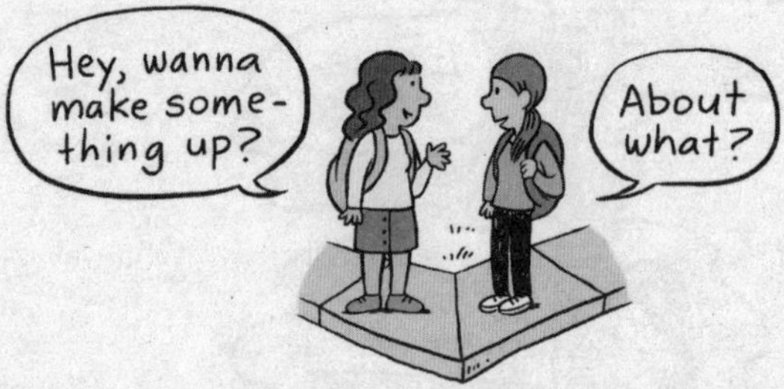
Hey, wanna make some-thing up?
About what?

A city bus passes, leaving a cloud of thick, smelly smog. We cough and fan it away.

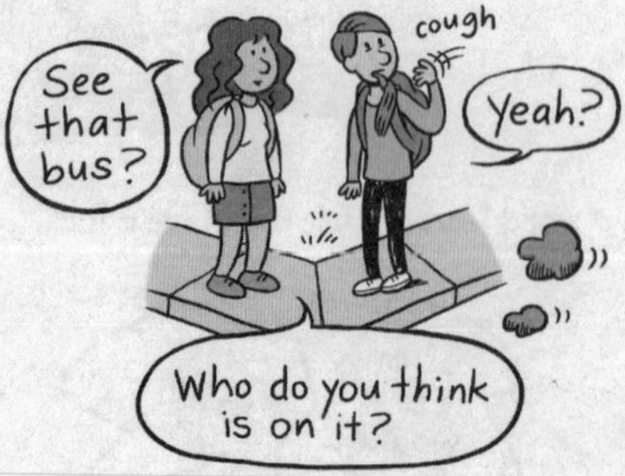
See that bus?
cough
Yeah?
Who do you think is on it?

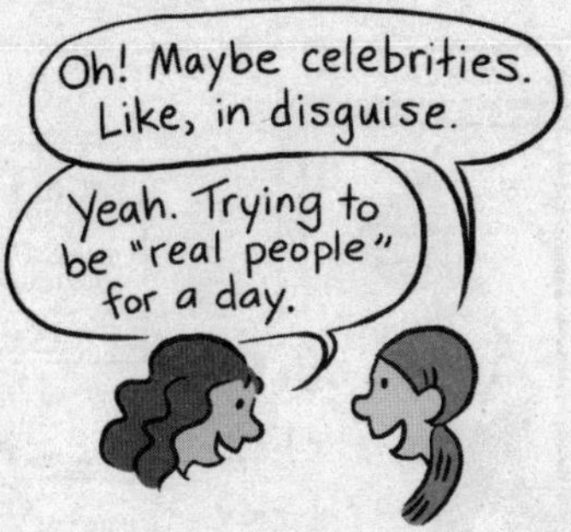
Oh! Maybe celebrities. Like, in disguise.
Yeah. Trying to be "real people" for a day.

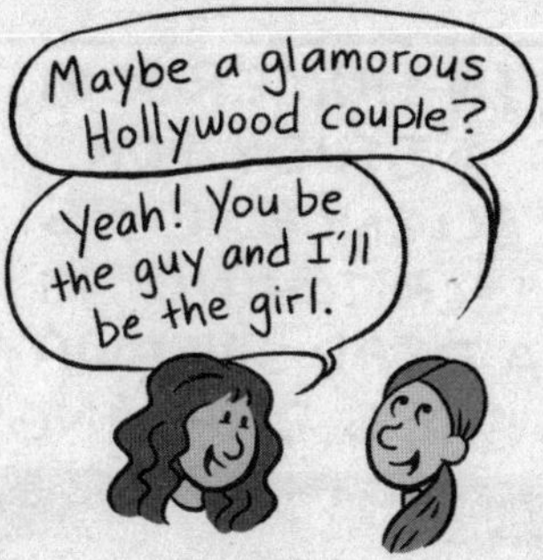
Maybe a glamorous Hollywood couple?
Yeah! You be the guy and I'll be the girl.

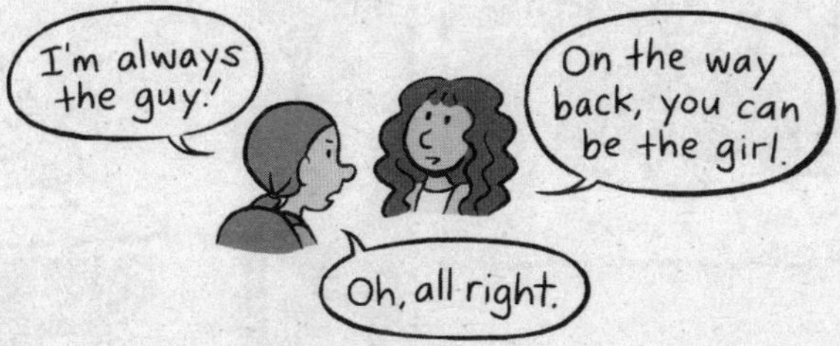
I'm always the guy!
On the way back, you can be the girl.
Oh, all right.

Before we know it, we're lost in our heads and the school bus pulls up.

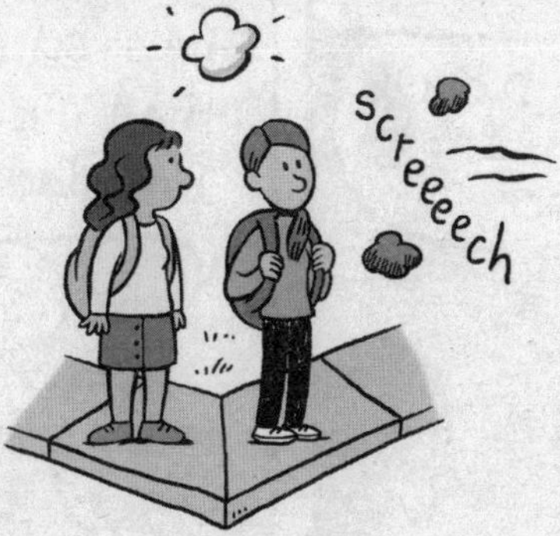
Screeeeech

And now, back to reality.

Brianna

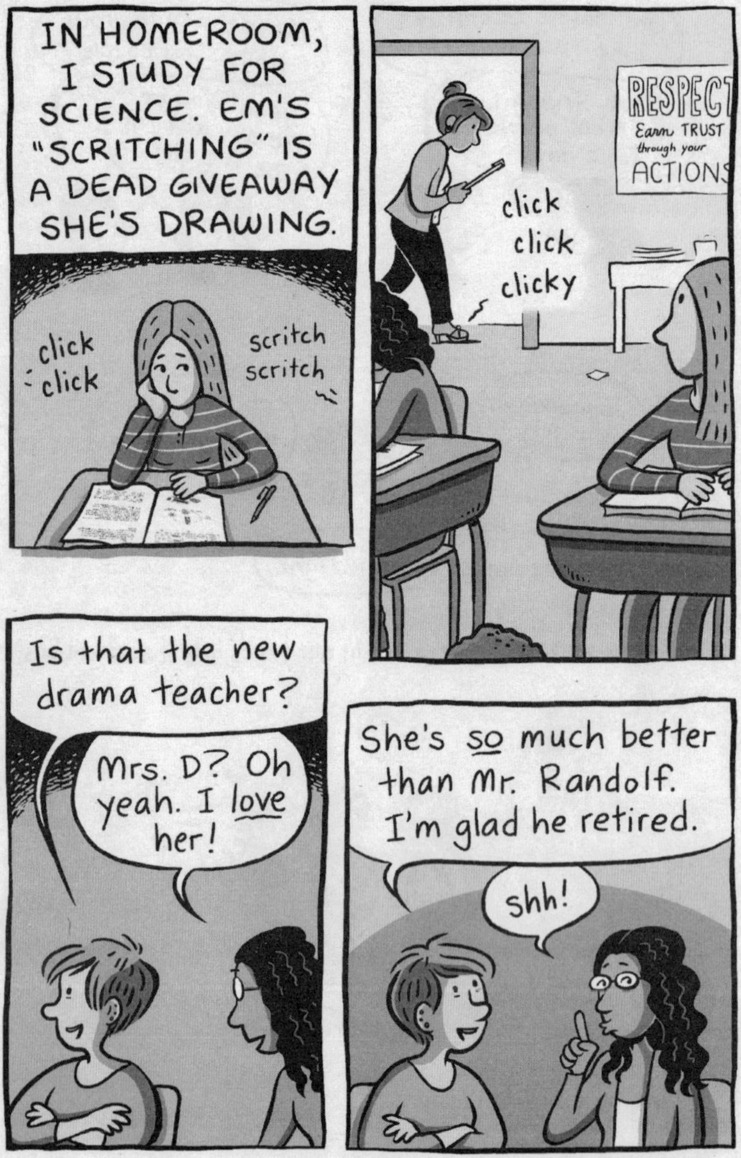
IN HOMEROOM, I STUDY FOR SCIENCE. EM'S "SCRITCHING" IS A DEAD GIVEAWAY SHE'S DRAWING.
click click
scritch scritch
RESPECT
Earn TRUST through your ACTIONS
click click clicky
Is that the new drama teacher?
Mrs. D? Oh yeah. I love her!
She's so much better than Mr. Randolf. I'm glad he retired.
shh!

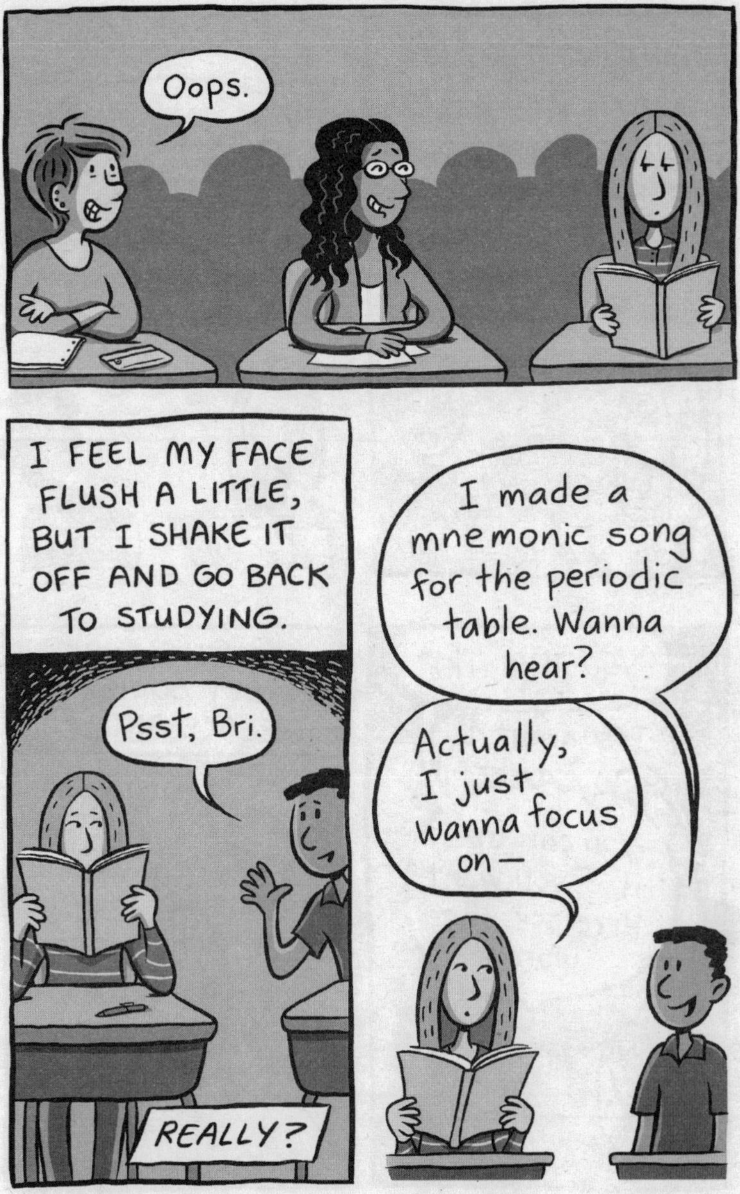
Oops.
I FEEL MY FACE FLUSH A LITTLE, BUT I SHAKE IT OFF AND GO BACK TO STUDYING.
Psst, Bri.
REALLY?
I made a mnemonic song for the periodic table. Wanna hear?
Actually, I just wanna focus on—

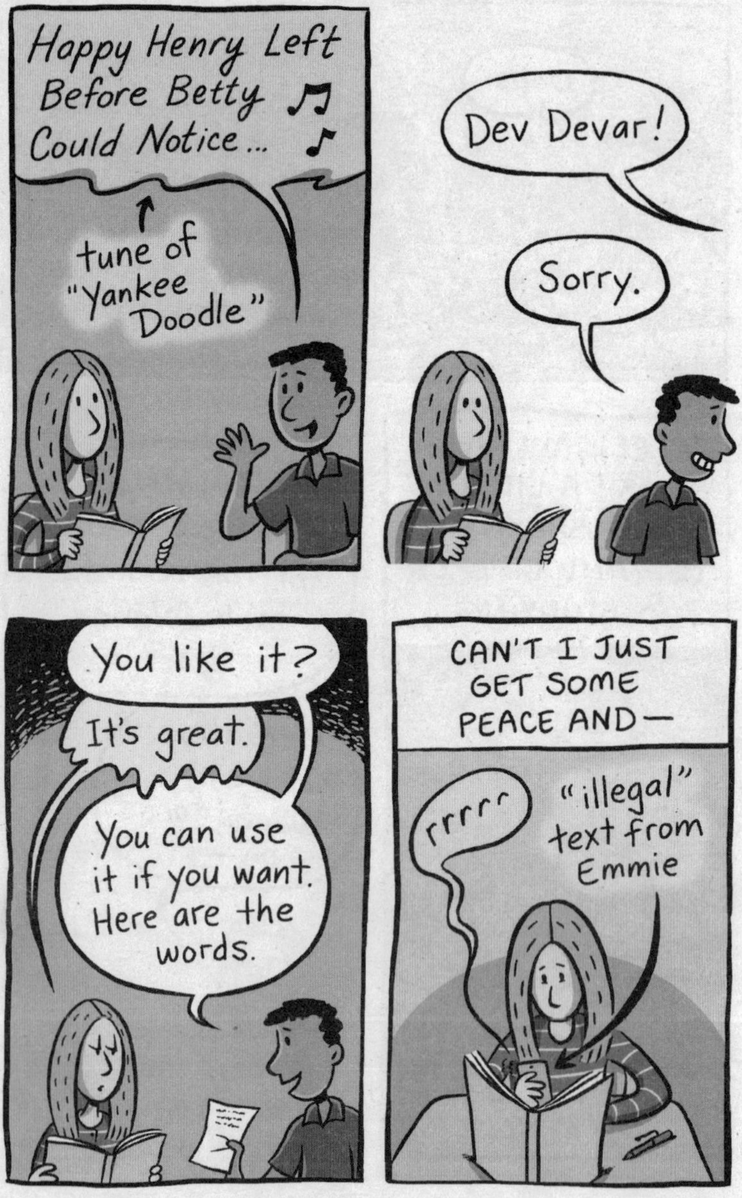
Happy Henry Left Before Betty Could Notice ...
tune of "Yankee Doodle"
Dev Devar!
Sorry.
You like it?
It's great.
You can use it if you want. Here are the words.
CAN'T I JUST GET SOME PEACE AND—
rrrrr
"illegal" text from Emmie

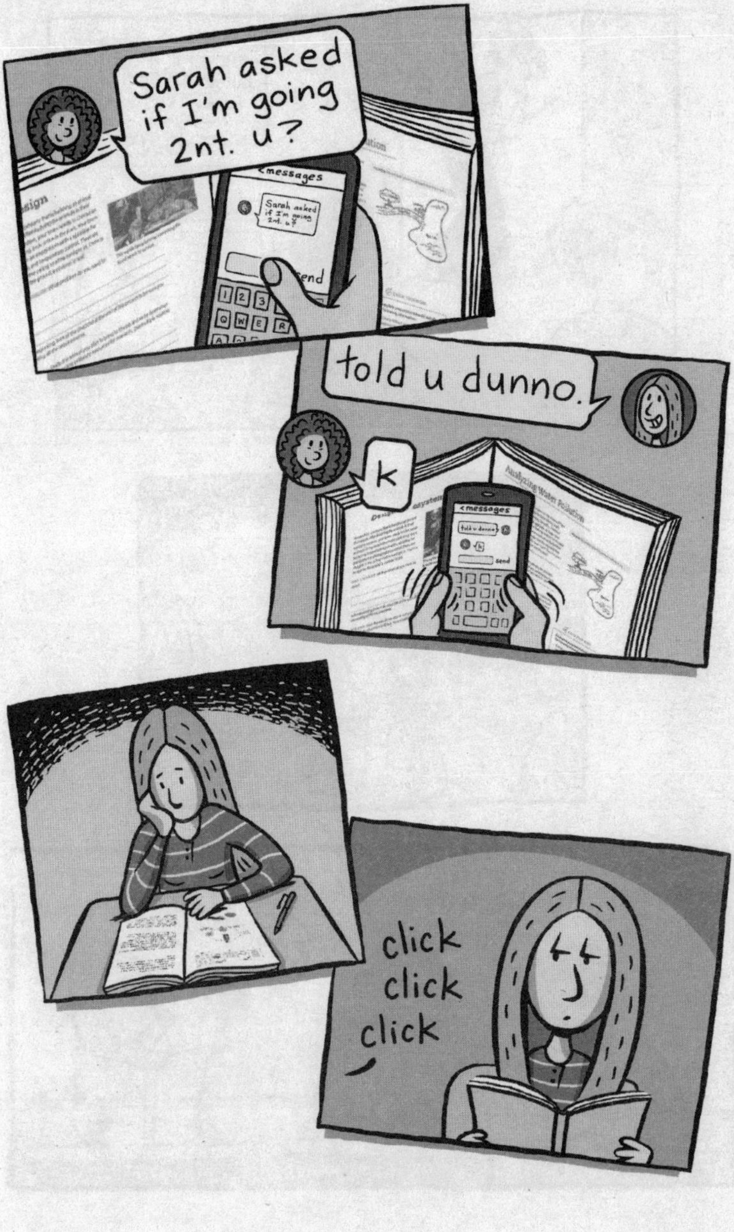
Sarah asked if I'm going 2nt. u?
told u dunno.
k
click
click
click

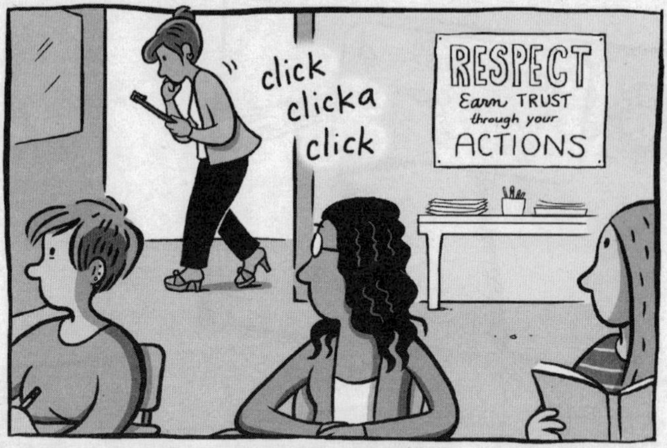
click
clicka
click
RESPECT
Earn TRUST
through your
ACTIONS

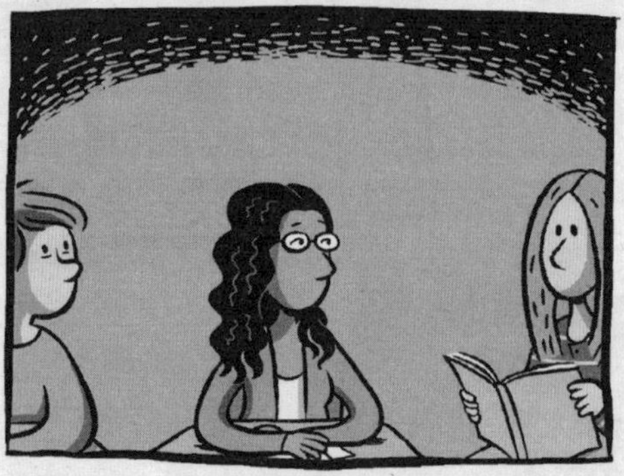

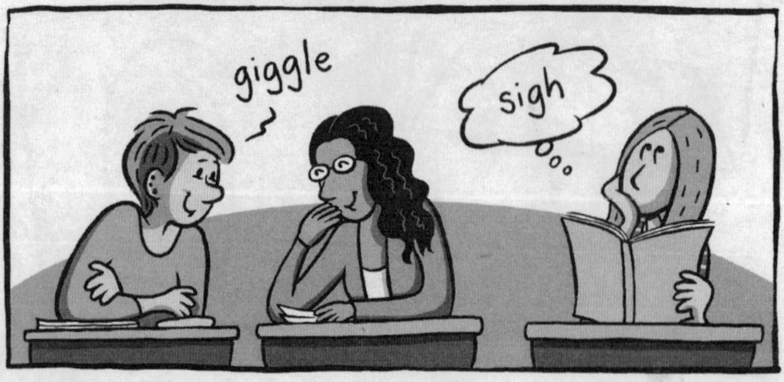
giggle
sigh

IZZY

Ash and I get to school and separate. I head to my locker. I notice a bunch of posters for tonight's talent show hanging on the wall.

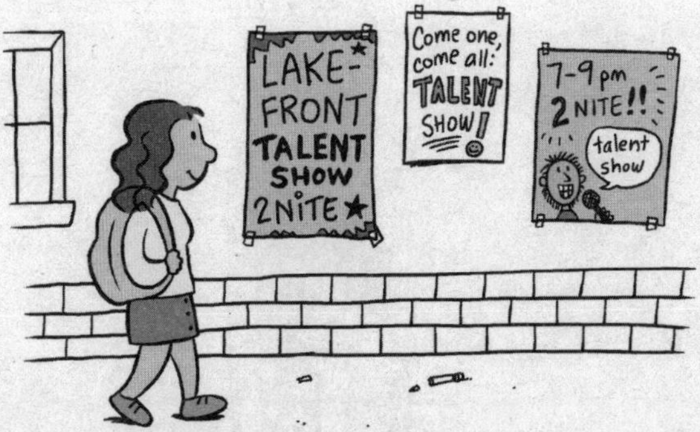
LAKE-FRONT TALENT SHOW 2NITE
Come one, come all: TALENT SHOW!
7-9 pm 2 NITE!!
talent show

Spoiler: I made about half of them.

I'm in drama club, and we're the ones hosting the show. I'm so, so (SO) excited! Ash and I made up a three-minute skit, and I'm going to perform it. It started out as a dialogue, but Ash chickened out, so now it's a monologue. I think it's funnier as a one-woman show, anyway.

I've practiced every day for the past month, but right now I'm inwardly running through my lines. I want this down **pat**.

Standing like a statue

Okay, got it.

I put away my backpack and take out my books. I head to registration, passing a group of loud girls.

One of them is Becca, my old elementary school friend. We were **really** good friends. But things kinda changed last year.

In grade school, I had three close friends: Hannah, Gabi, and Becca. We hung out all the time. At recess, we used to hide under the big slide and talk, or we'd color with chalk on the cracked sidewalk.

lopsided flower

deranged eyeball

After fifth grade, Hannah's parents moved across town and decided to send her to private school.

Then Gabi's dad lost his job, and they had to move in with her grandparents in a different state.

As for Becca . . . we hung out in the beginning of sixth grade but eventually drifted apart. Without the other two, we felt a little weird together. Plus, she joined choir and made new friends.

So that left me without a best friend this year. It's okay, I do have other friends, especially in drama club. But there's no one I'm as close to. These days I'm what my mom calls "in between friends." She says it happens to a lot of kids in middle school. Even Dani agrees.

My friend groups switched in eighth grade.

And I have totally new friends now.

Middle school sucks.

Uh... thanks.

I hope they're right.

I continue walking to registration. Once I get there, I take a seat and proceed to daydream the period away.

glamour bus couple

Miss Silver?

Afterward, I head to science, where I continue my daydreaming (or self-contemplating, if I want to sound more school-ish). I'm pretty bad at science.

You hit on the BUS DRIVER?!

She's my secret wife!

PUNCH

glamour bus couple now involved in tabloid scandal

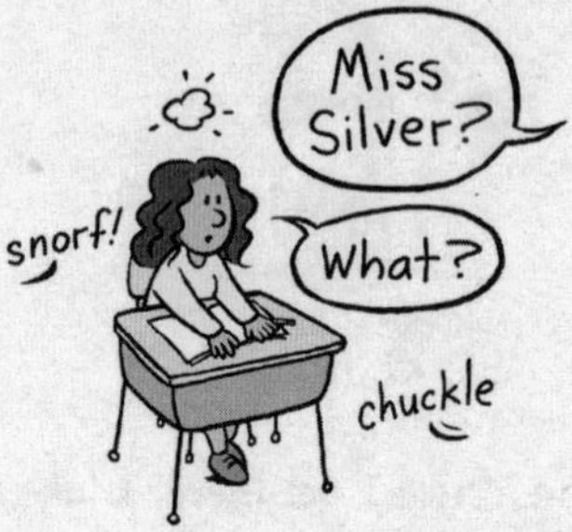
Miss Silver?
snorf!
What?
chuckle

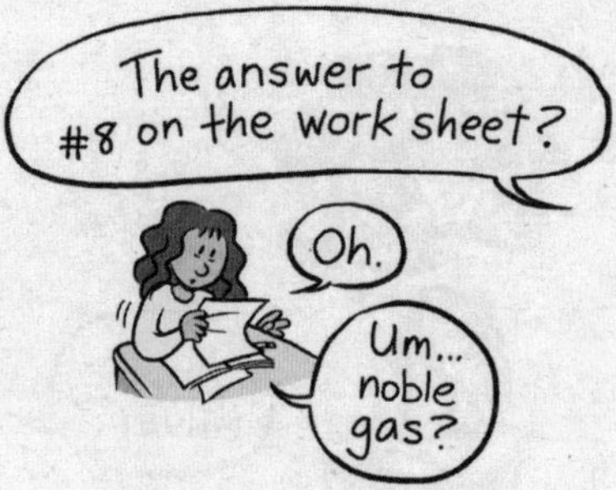
The answer to #8 on the work sheet?
Oh.
Um... noble gas?

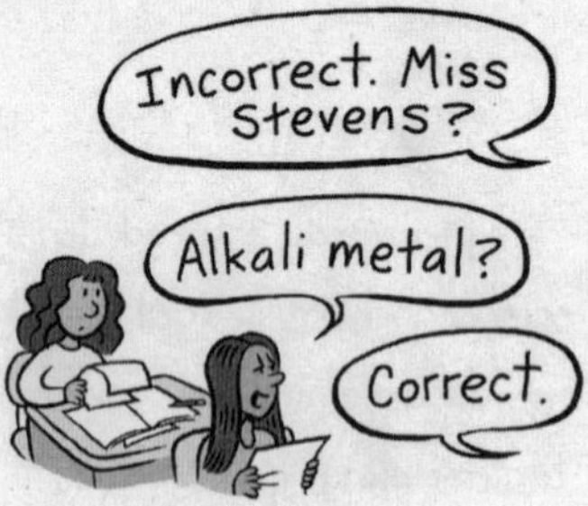
Incorrect. Miss Stevens?
Alkali metal?
Correct.

Some kids are good at every class, like Jessica Stevens. I guess I'm pretty right-brained.

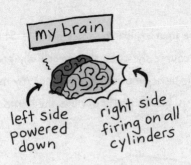

my brain

left side
powered
down

right side
firing on all
cylinders

I like creative writing, art, and
drama. It shows in my grades. It's
like someone drew a dividing line in
the middle of my report card.

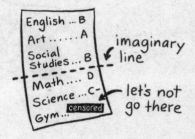

English ... B
Art ...... A
Social
Studies ... B
Math .... D
Science ... C-
Gym ... censored

imaginary
line

let's not
go there

I try to pay attention to Ms. Bloom, but her voice is so bland,
I feel like I'm listening to the hum of an electric fan.

RMMMMMM

ZZZZZ

43

I wish I were smarter, like my sister Danielle. She gets straight As. I mean, of course she does; she's practically perfect in every way (not to quote Disney movies or anything). My mom tries hard not to compare us, but it's pretty obvious she thinks Dani has it all together.

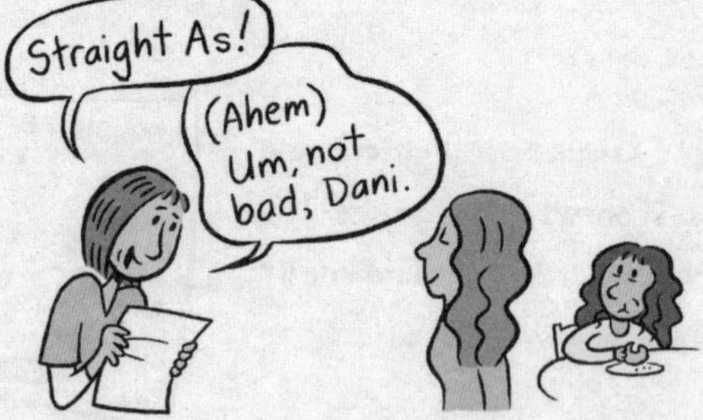
Straight As!
(Ahem) Um, not bad, Dani.

But what's really frustrating is that Ashley gets away with murder. I guess it's third child syndrome or something. She does well in school, unlike me, but she's no Danielle.

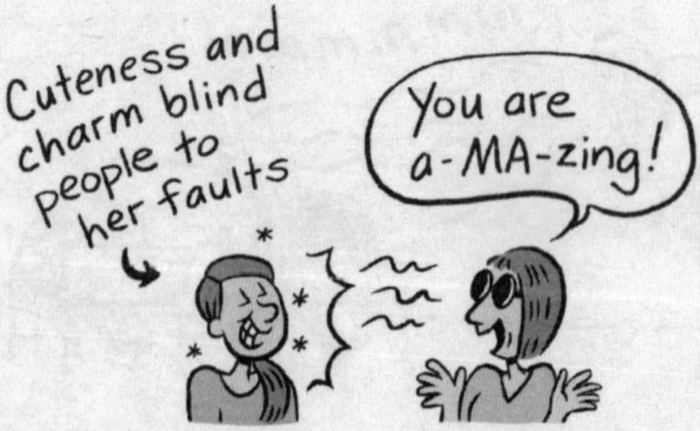
Cuteness and charm blind people to her faults
You are a-MA-zing!

Anyway, back to class. What was I doing again?

Right! Focus!

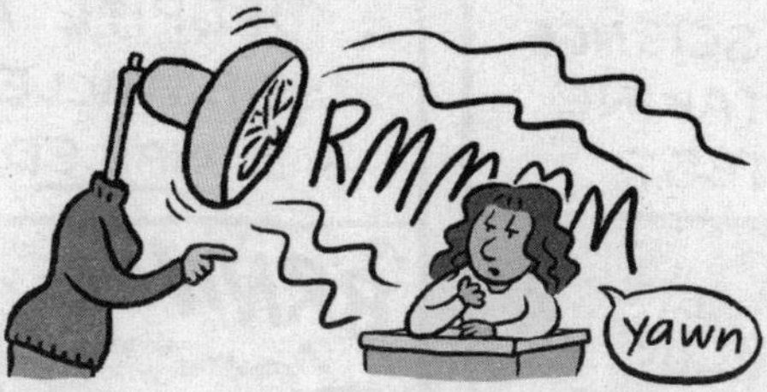
RMMMMM
yawn

I start thinking (sleepily) about the talent show. It starts at seven. I have to be back at school by five for rehearsal, and then Mrs. D is ordering pizza before the show.

I start to run through my lines again (partly to stay awake). The scene is really funny. And stalker-y. In it, I'm following a boy home from school without his noticing me. I'm hiding behind things, like a shed, a mailbox, and some other stuff (Ash and I spent **days** in the art room, making 'em out of foam core) . . . and all along I'm talking about the boy and all the ways I like him, and—

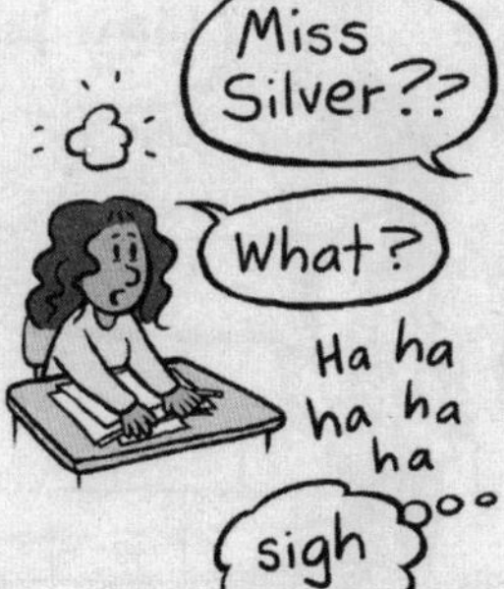
Miss Silver??
What?
Ha ha ha ha ha
sigh

oops.

Brianna

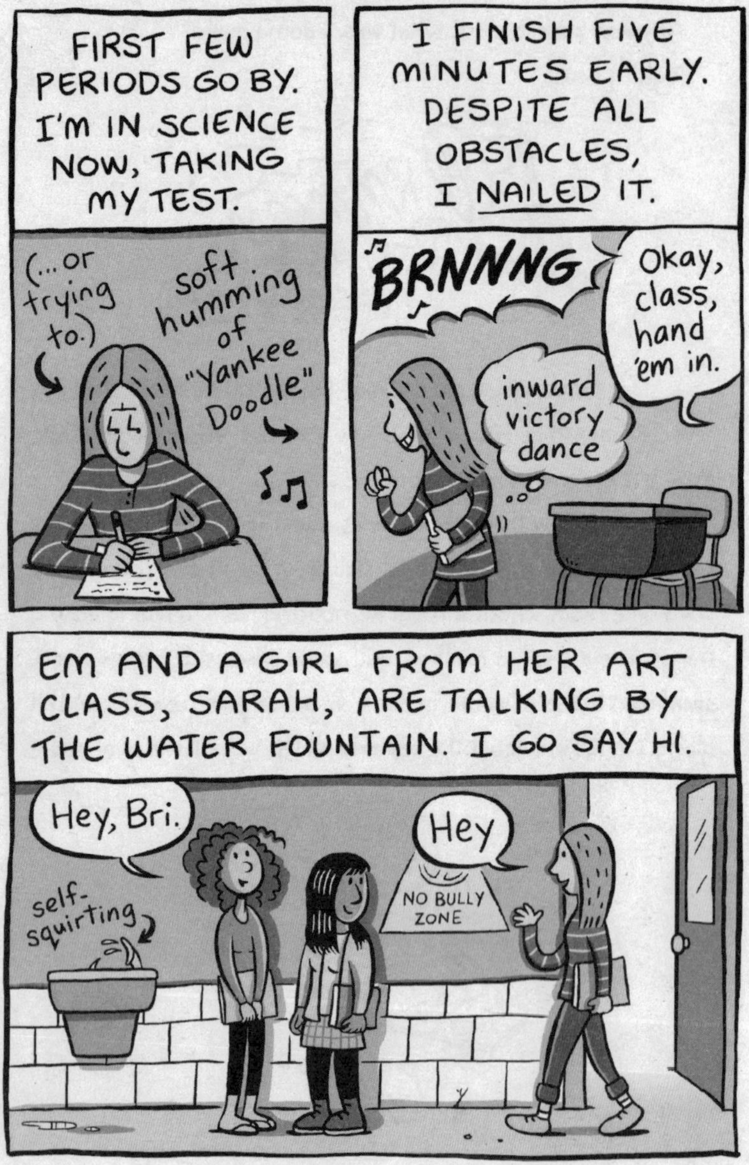

FIRST FEW PERIODS GO BY. I'M IN SCIENCE NOW, TAKING MY TEST.
(...or trying to.)
soft humming of "Yankee Doodle"
I FINISH FIVE MINUTES EARLY. DESPITE ALL OBSTACLES, I NAILED IT.
BRNNNG
Okay, class, hand 'em in.
inward victory dance
EM AND A GIRL FROM HER ART CLASS, SARAH, ARE TALKING BY THE WATER FOUNTAIN. I GO SAY HI.
Hey, Bri.
Hey
self-squirting
NO BULLY ZONE

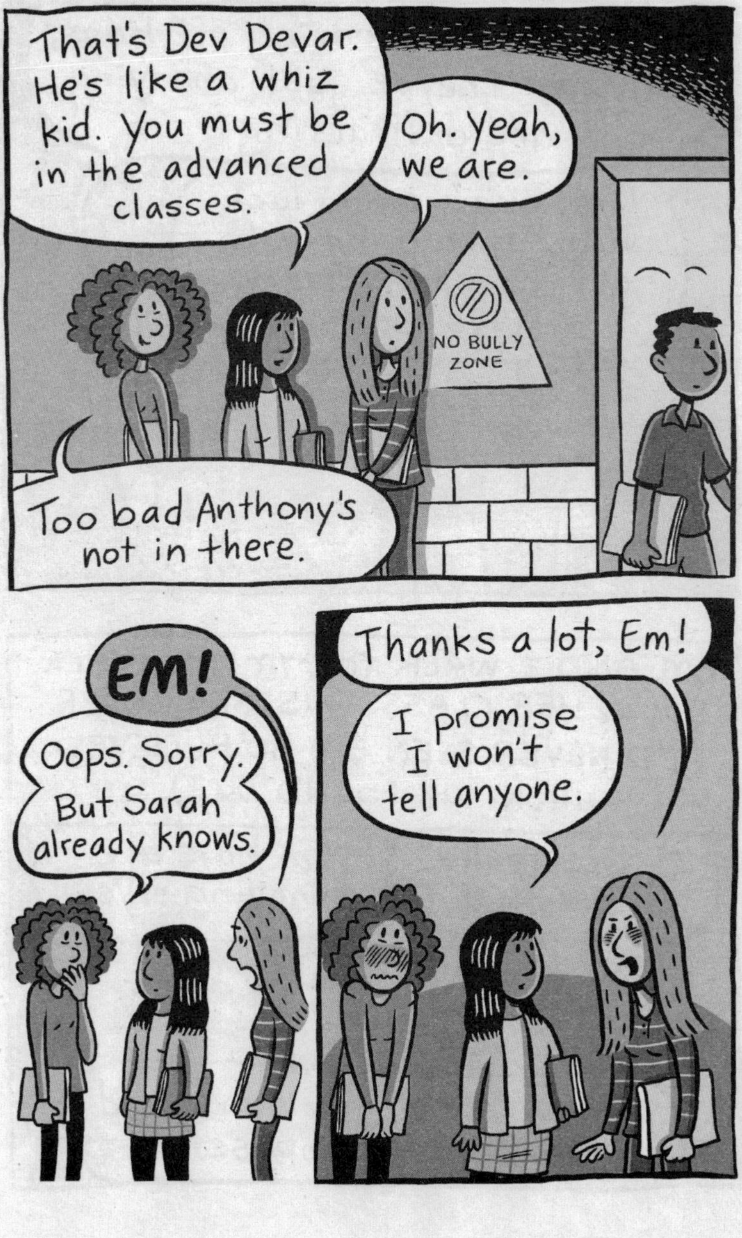
That's Dev Devar. He's like a whiz kid. You must be in the advanced classes.
Oh. Yeah, we are.
NO BULLY ZONE
Too bad Anthony's not in there.
EM!
Oops. Sorry. But Sarah already knows.
Thanks a lot, Em!
I promise I won't tell anyone.

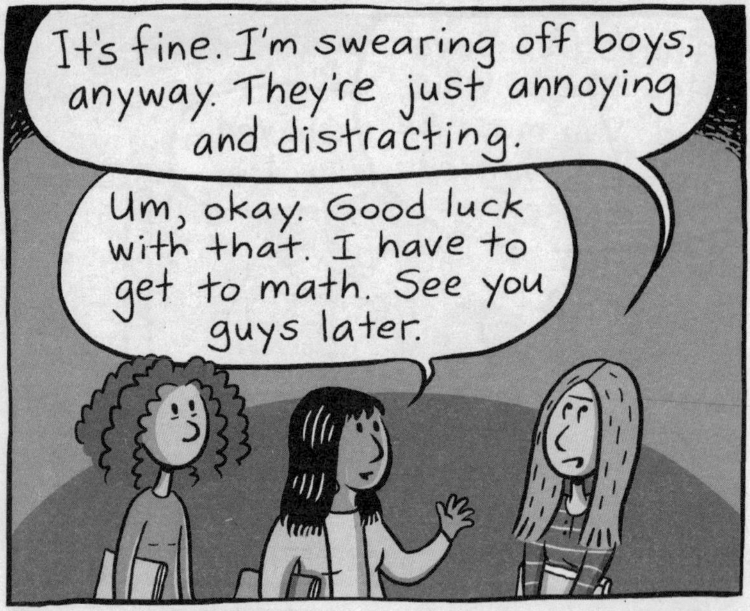
It's fine. I'm swearing off boys, anyway. They're just annoying and distracting.
Um, okay. Good luck with that. I have to get to math. See you guys later.

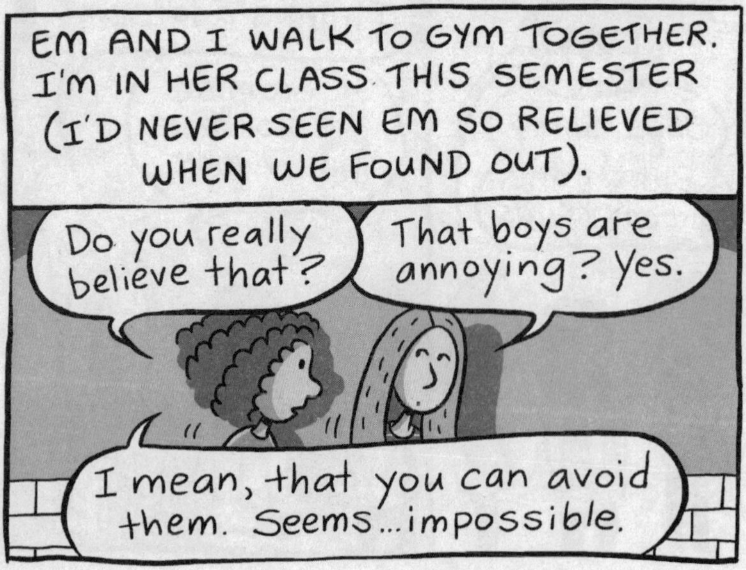
EM AND I WALK TO GYM TOGETHER. I'M IN HER CLASS THIS SEMESTER (I'D NEVER SEEN EM SO RELIEVED WHEN WE FOUND OUT).
Do you really believe that?
That boys are annoying? Yes.
I mean, that you can avoid them. Seems...impossible.

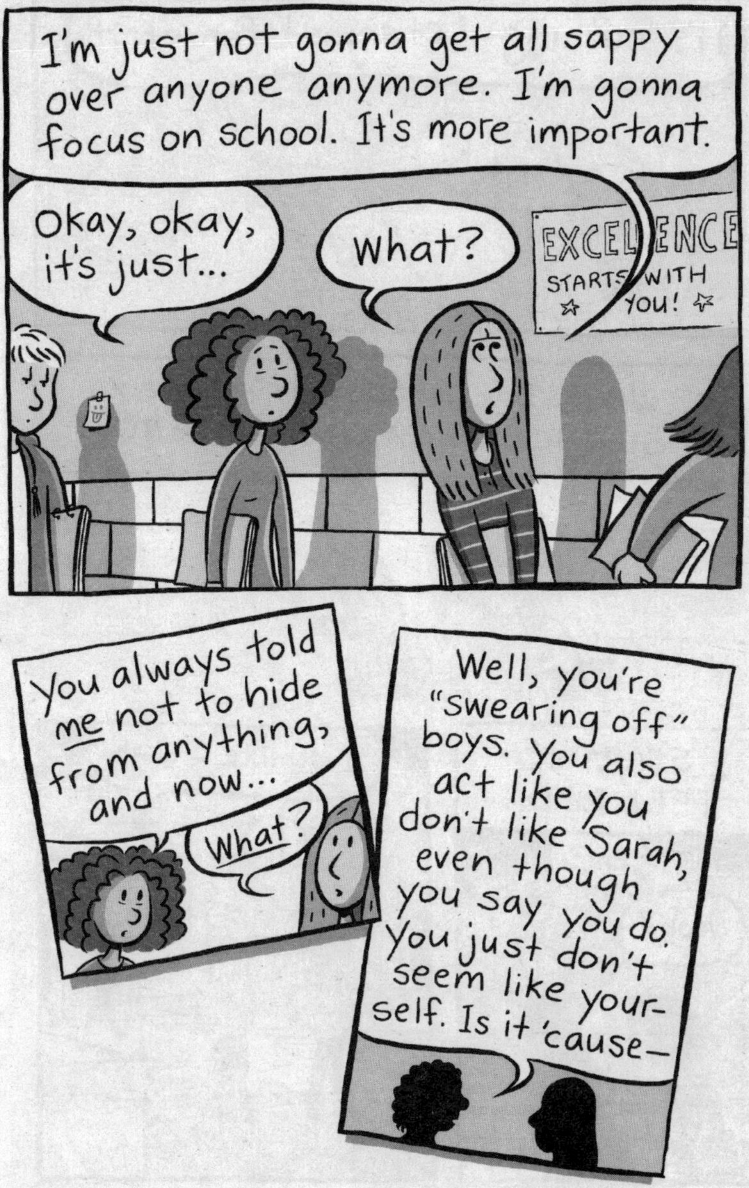
I'm just not gonna get all sappy over anyone anymore. I'm gonna focus on school. It's more important.
Okay, okay, it's just...
What?
EXCELLENCE STARTS WITH YOU!
You always told me not to hide from anything, and now...
What?
Well, you're "swearing off" boys. You also act like you don't like Sarah, even though you say you do. You just don't seem like yourself. Is it 'cause—

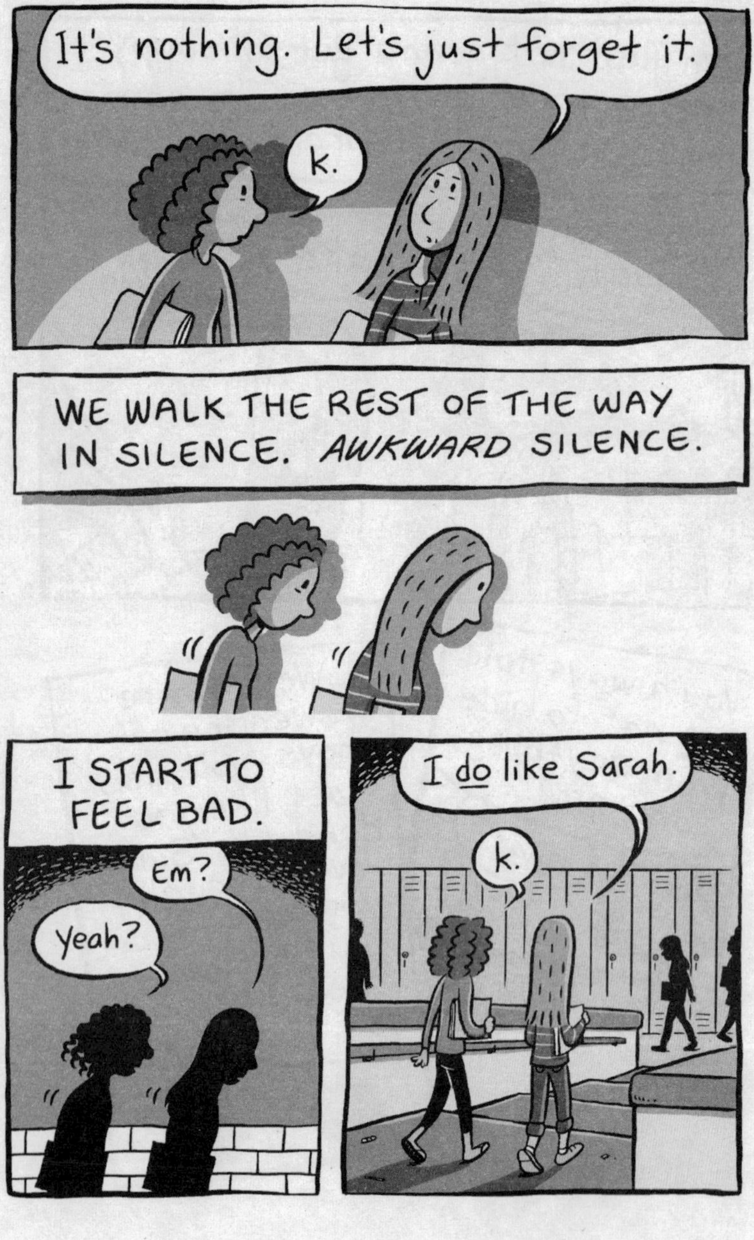

It's nothing. Let's just forget it.
k.
WE WALK THE REST OF THE WAY IN SILENCE. *AWKWARD* SILENCE.
I START TO FEEL BAD.
Em?
Yeah?
I do like Sarah.
k.

IZZY

I have two more classes to get through. English and math. I like English. Well, compared to math, anyway. The teacher, Miss Gelb, is so nice. Problem is, even though I like reading and writing, I still get average grades here. The only time I did really well was when we were asked to write our papers in the style of a play. I've been making up plays since I was six, so that kinda came naturally. I wrote a scene Ash and I made up last year about a little girl going to an amusement park with her mom for the first time. I got an A+ and a note from Miss Gelb.

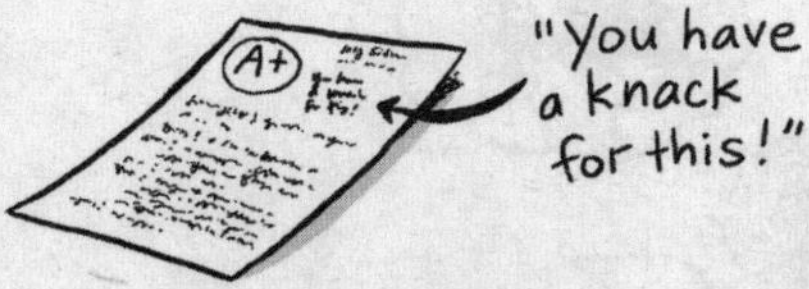
A+
"You have a knack for this!"

Today we're getting back last week's test papers on sentence structure. I have a knot in my stomach even before I see mine.

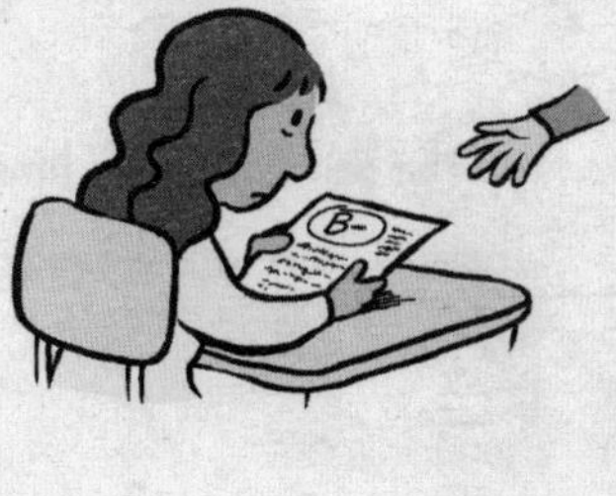
B-

Yeah, not so surprising. There's a little note under my grade. Miss Gelb is big on notes.

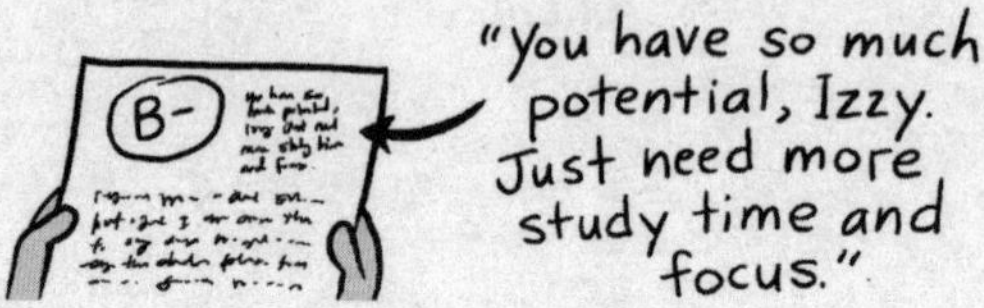
B-
"You have so much potential, Izzy. Just need more study time and focus."

There's that word again.

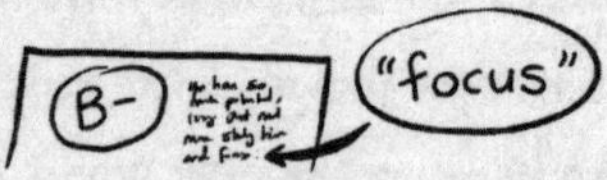
B-
"focus"

Thing is, I know they're right. Half the time, I just don't care. I know I **should** care, but I'd rather be doing things I like to do. Like the talent show.

I cannot WAIT!

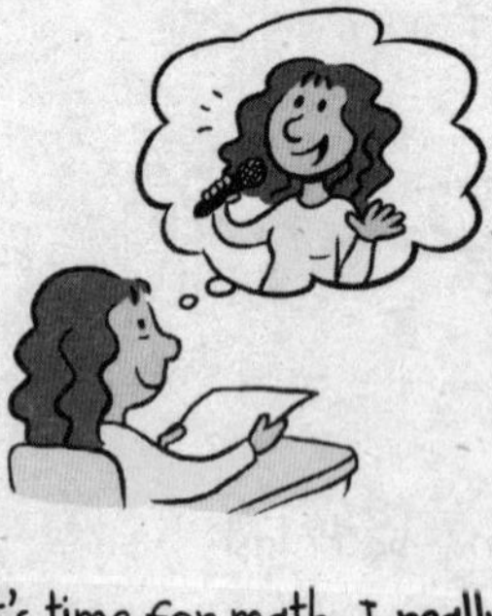

The bell signals it's time for math. I **really** take my time getting there. I have a test today and I didn't study. I **kind of** know the material, but . . .

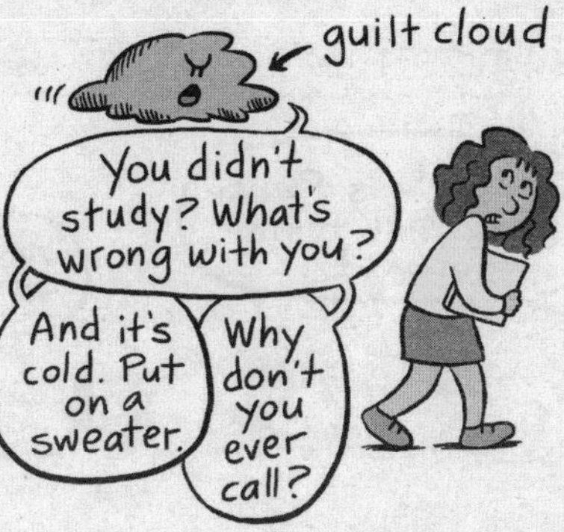
guilt cloud
You didn't study? What's wrong with you?
And it's cold. Put on a sweater.
Why don't you ever call?

I sit down. Teacher's not here yet. I hear someone whispering behind me.

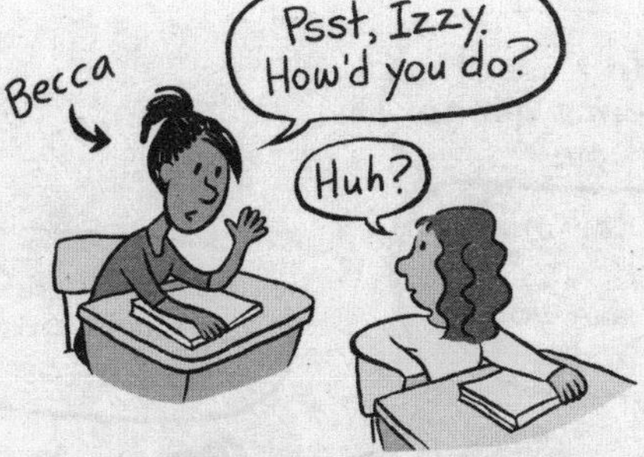
Becca
Psst, Izzy. How'd you do?
Huh?

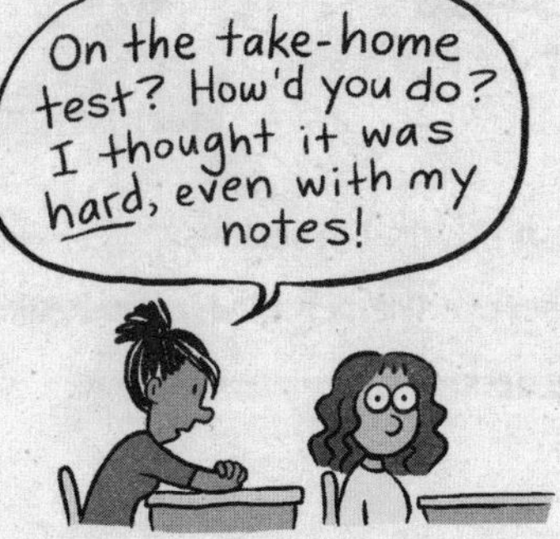
On the take-home test? How'd you do? I thought it was hard, even with my notes!

Uh-oh . . .

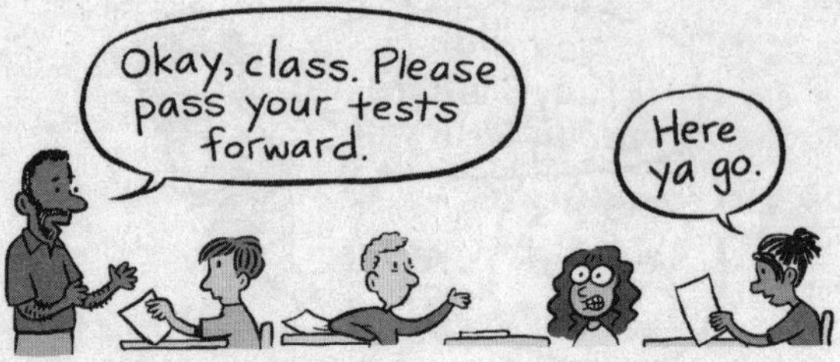
Okay, class. Please pass your tests forward.
Here ya go.

OHNONONONO!

Take-home test? I thought that was a study guide!

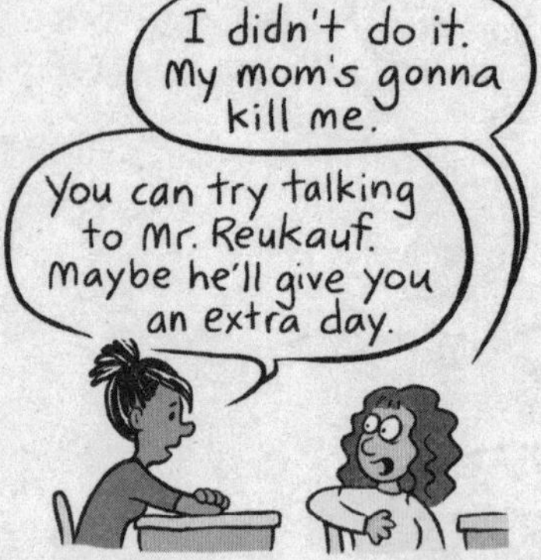
I didn't do it. My mom's gonna kill me.
You can try talking to Mr. Reukauf. Maybe he'll give you an extra day.

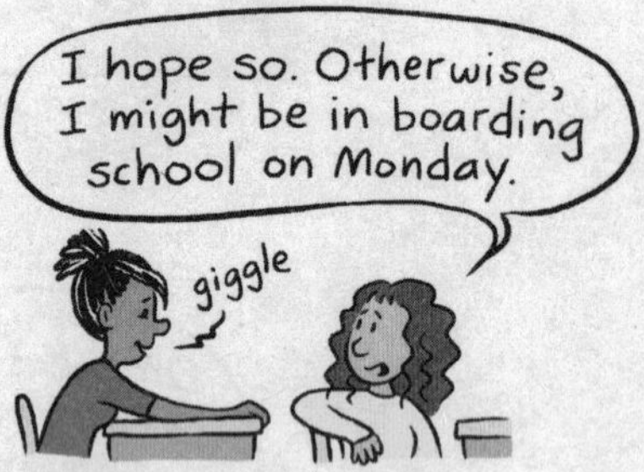
I hope so. Otherwise, I might be in boarding school on Monday.
giggle

Huh. She doesn't think I'm serious.

Five minutes before the bell rings, Mr. Reukauf motions for me to come to his desk.

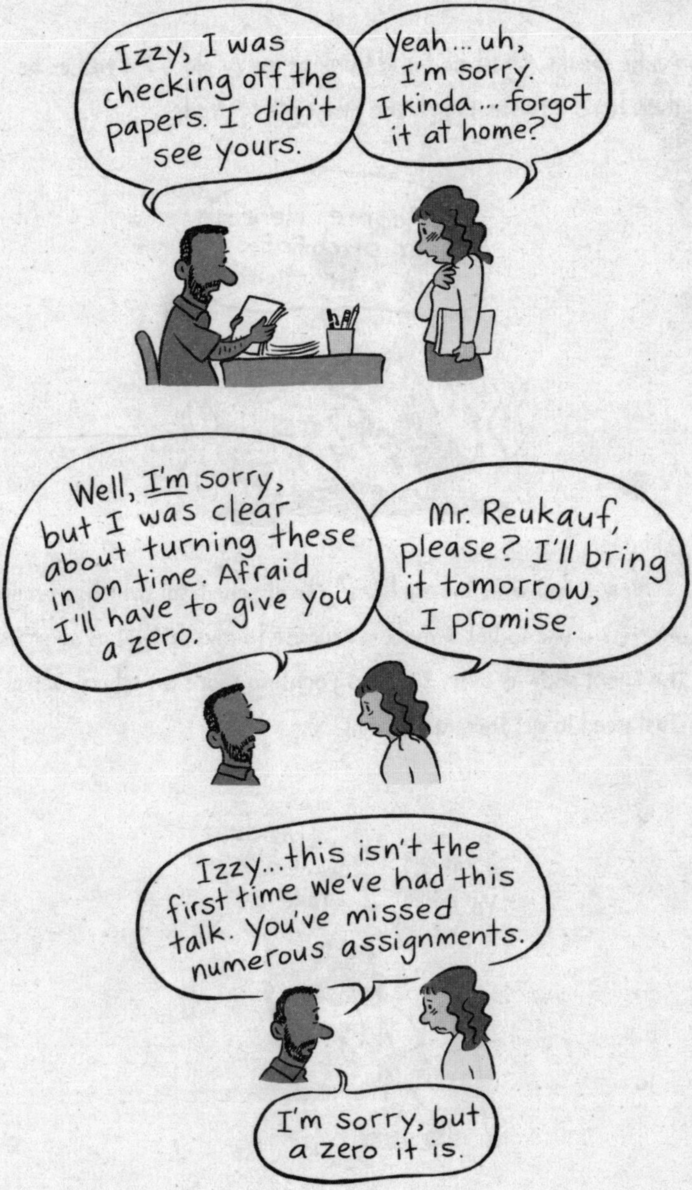
Izzy, I was checking off the papers. I didn't see yours.
Yeah... uh, I'm sorry. I kinda ... forgot it at home?
Well, I'm sorry, but I was clear about turning these in on time. Afraid I'll have to give you a zero.
Mr. Reukauf, please? I'll bring it tomorrow, I promise.
Izzy...this isn't the first time we've had this talk. You've missed numerous assignments.
I'm sorry, but a zero it is.

As he speaks, I just nod and think of every place I'd rather be than here. France. Egypt. The fiery pits of Hades.

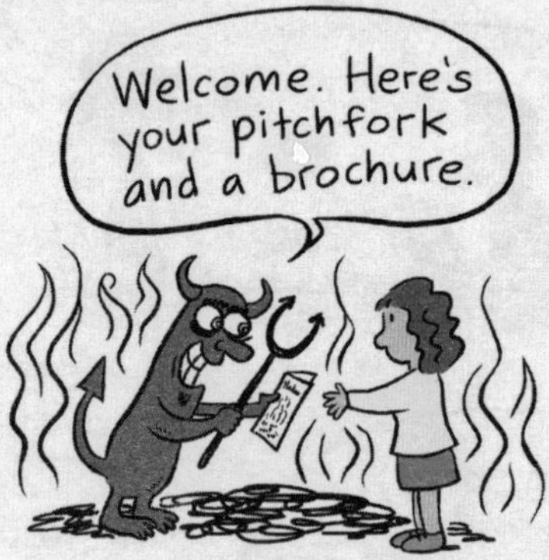
Welcome. Here's your pitchfork and a brochure.

Now I just wish I were home. Or at rehearsal (which is really where I'd like to be). I make a promise to myself that as soon as the talent show is over, I'll start focusing more on school. I will. Just need to get through today.

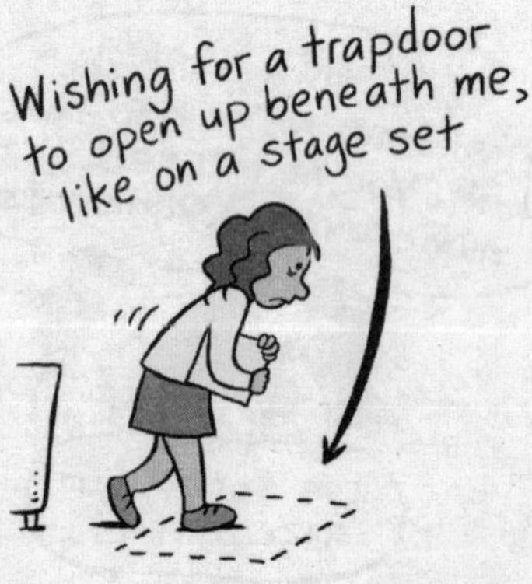
Wishing for a trapdoor to open up beneath me, like on a stage set

Luckily, the bell rings and Mr. Reukauf excuses me. My cheeks are on fire. So happy to get out of there.

After I grab my backpack from my locker, I meet up with Ashley. We walk out together. Everybody is super-excited about the half day, pushing and shoving to get as far away from school as possible.

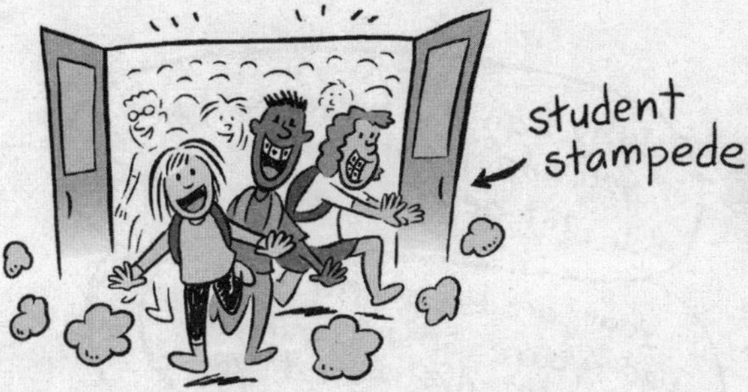
student stampede

Ash is also excited, and she talks about going to get ice cream after our chores. My stomach both dances and lurches at the same time. I just nod dumbly and find a seat on the bus.

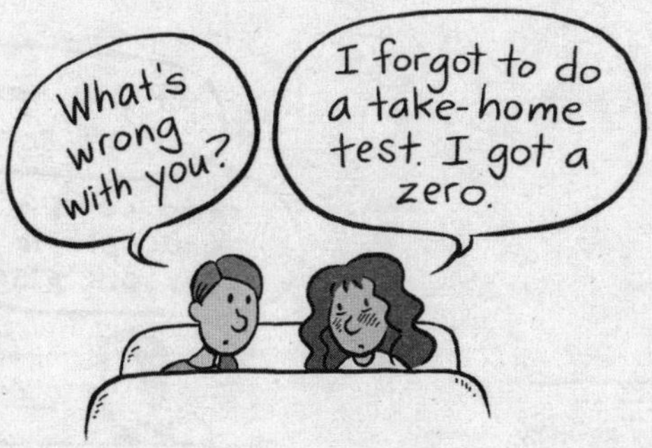
What's wrong with you?
I forgot to do a take-home test. I got a zero.

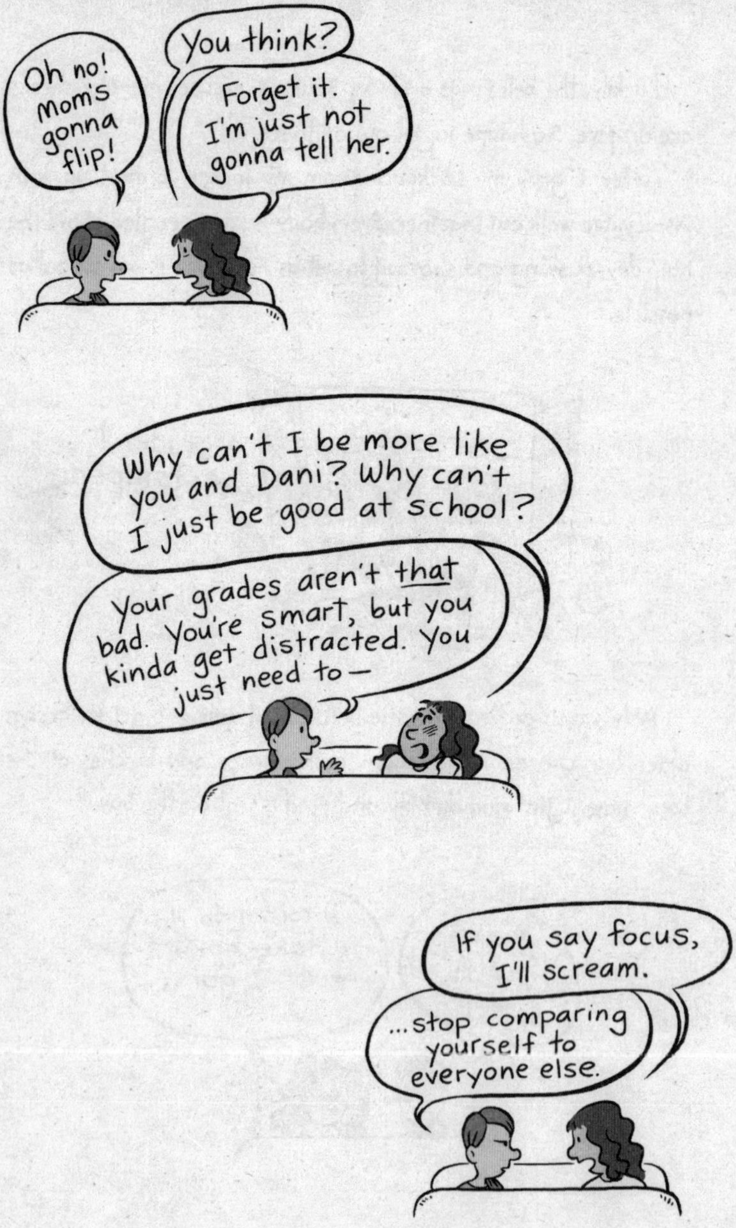
Oh no! Mom's gonna flip!
You think?
Forget it. I'm just not gonna tell her.
Why can't I be more like you and Dani? Why can't I just be good at school?
Your grades aren't that bad. You're smart, but you kinda get distracted. You just need to—
If you say focus, I'll scream.
...stop comparing yourself to everyone else.

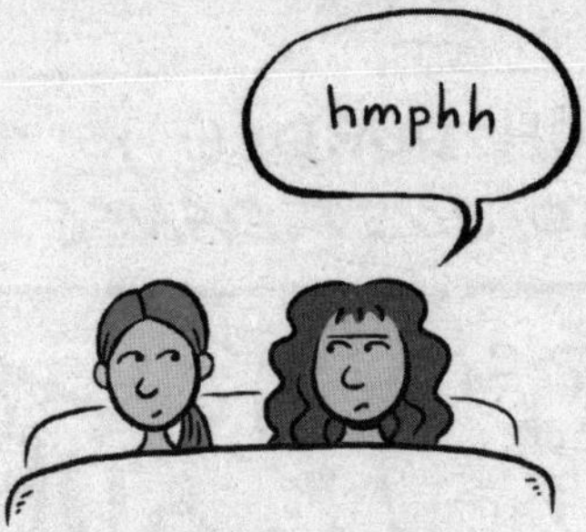
hmphh

Stupid, smart little sister.

The bus starts to shake violently. They haven't fixed the potholes yet. For once, I don't notice. I don't even feel like distracting myself with made-up games.

I just want to be someone else.

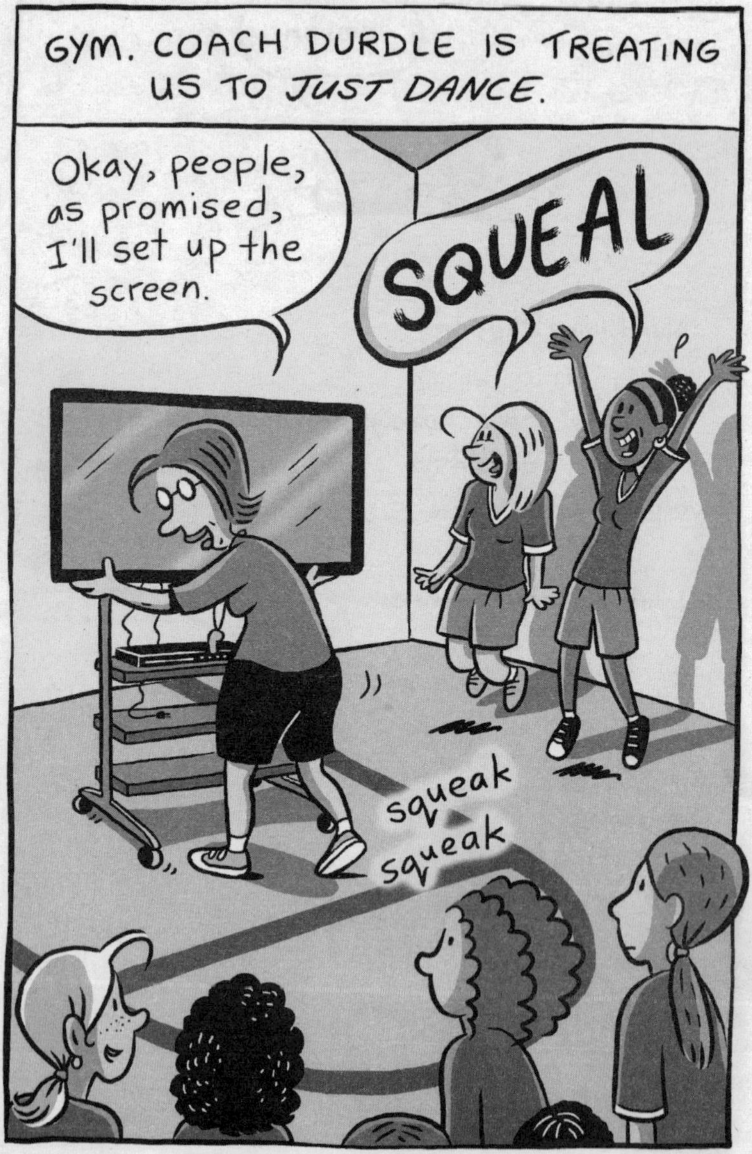
GYM. COACH DURDLE IS TREATING US TO *JUST DANCE*.
Okay, people, as promised, I'll set up the screen.
SQUEAL
squeak
squeak

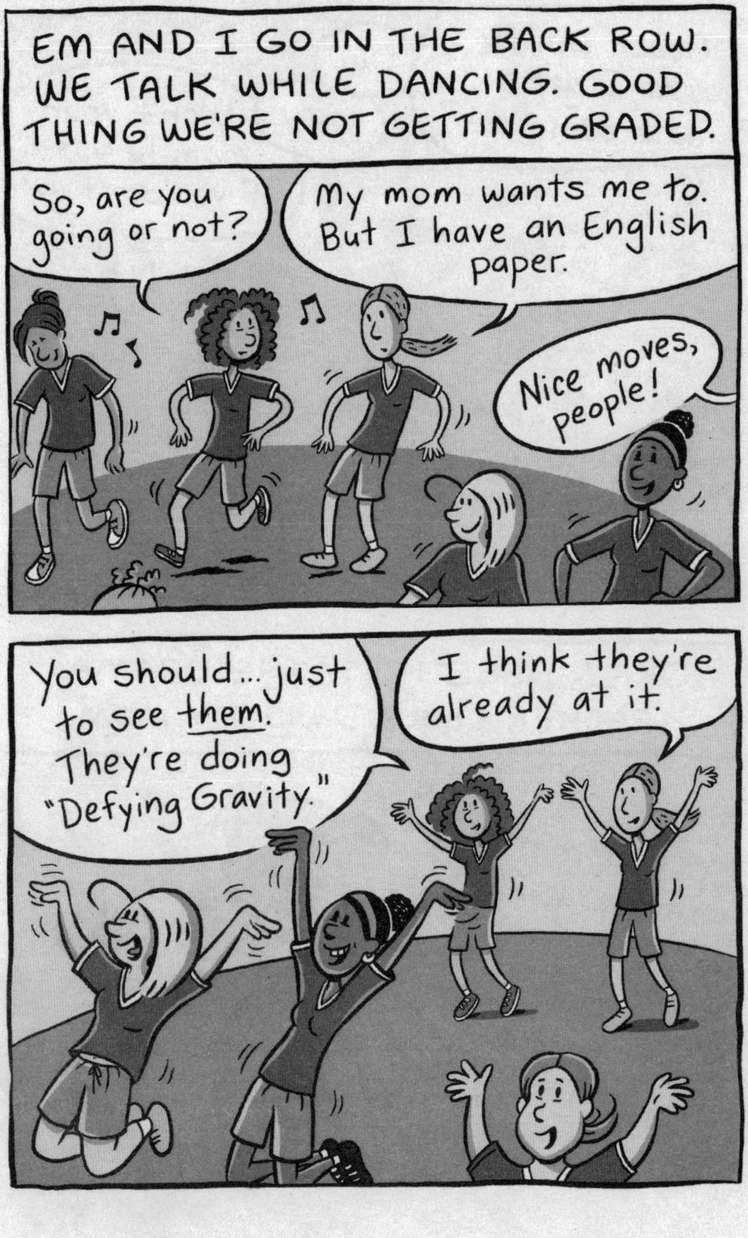
EM AND I GO IN THE BACK ROW. WE TALK WHILE DANCING. GOOD THING WE'RE NOT GETTING GRADED.
So, are you going or not?
My mom wants me to. But I have an English paper.
Nice moves, people!
Em
You should... just to see them. They're doing "Defying Gravity."
I think they're already at it.

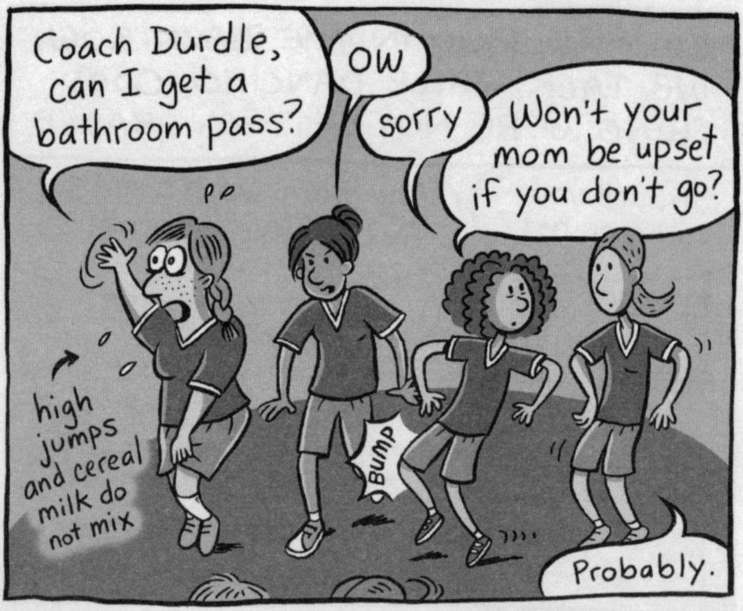
Coach Durdle, can I get a bathroom pass?
OW
sorry
Won't your mom be upset if you don't go?
high jumps and cereal milk do not mix
BUMP
Probably.

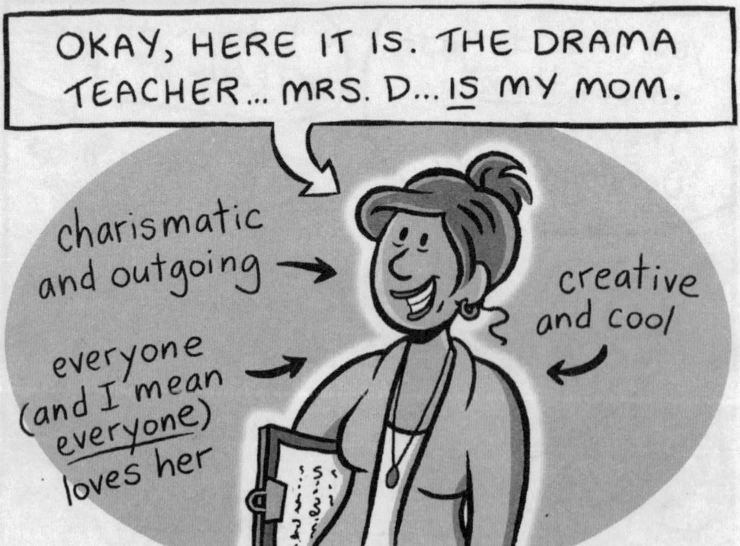
OKAY, HERE IT IS. THE DRAMA TEACHER... MRS. D... IS MY MOM.
charismatic and outgoing
creative and cool
everyone (and I mean everyone) loves her

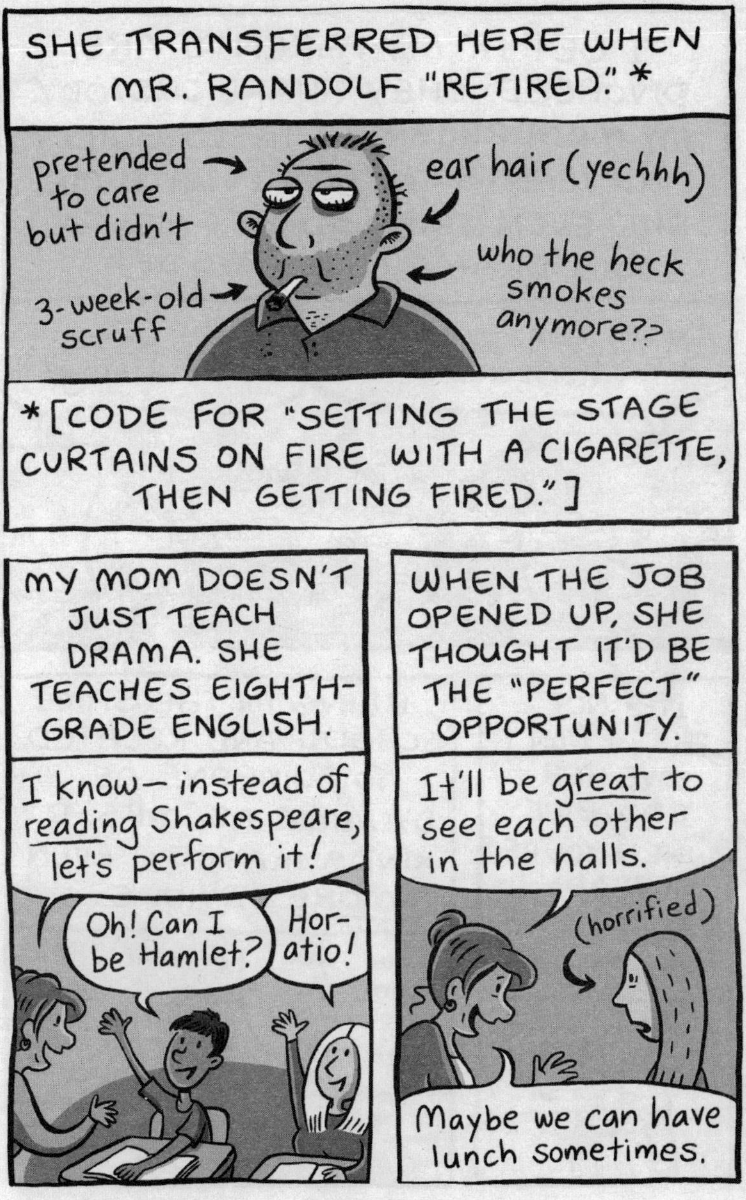
SHE TRANSFERRED HERE WHEN MR. RANDOLF "RETIRED."*
pretended to care but didn't
ear hair (yechhh)
who the heck smokes anymore??
3-week-old scruff
*[CODE FOR "SETTING THE STAGE CURTAINS ON FIRE WITH A CIGARETTE, THEN GETTING FIRED."]
MY MOM DOESN'T JUST TEACH DRAMA. SHE TEACHES EIGHTH-GRADE ENGLISH.
I know— instead of reading Shakespeare, let's perform it!
Oh! Can I be Hamlet?
Hor-atio!
WHEN THE JOB OPENED UP, SHE THOUGHT IT'D BE THE "PERFECT" OPPORTUNITY.
It'll be great to see each other in the halls.
(horrified)
Maybe we can have lunch sometimes.

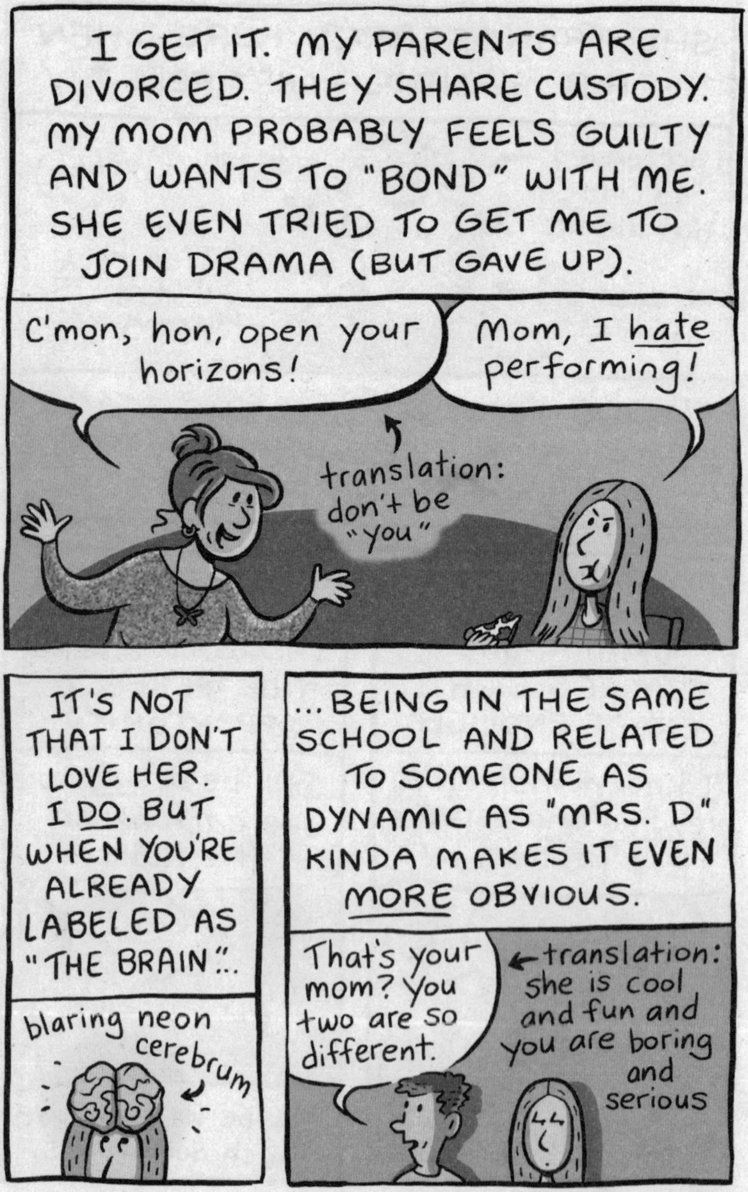

I GET IT. MY PARENTS ARE DIVORCED. THEY SHARE CUSTODY. MY MOM PROBABLY FEELS GUILTY AND WANTS TO "BOND" WITH ME. SHE EVEN TRIED TO GET ME TO JOIN DRAMA (BUT GAVE UP).
C'mon, hon, open your horizons!
Mom, I hate performing!
translation: don't be "you"
IT'S NOT THAT I DON'T LOVE HER. I DO. BUT WHEN YOU'RE ALREADY LABELED AS "THE BRAIN"...
blaring neon cerebrum
...BEING IN THE SAME SCHOOL AND RELATED TO SOMEONE AS DYNAMIC AS "MRS. D" KINDA MAKES IT EVEN MORE OBVIOUS.
That's your mom? You two are so different.
translation: she is cool and fun and you are boring and serious

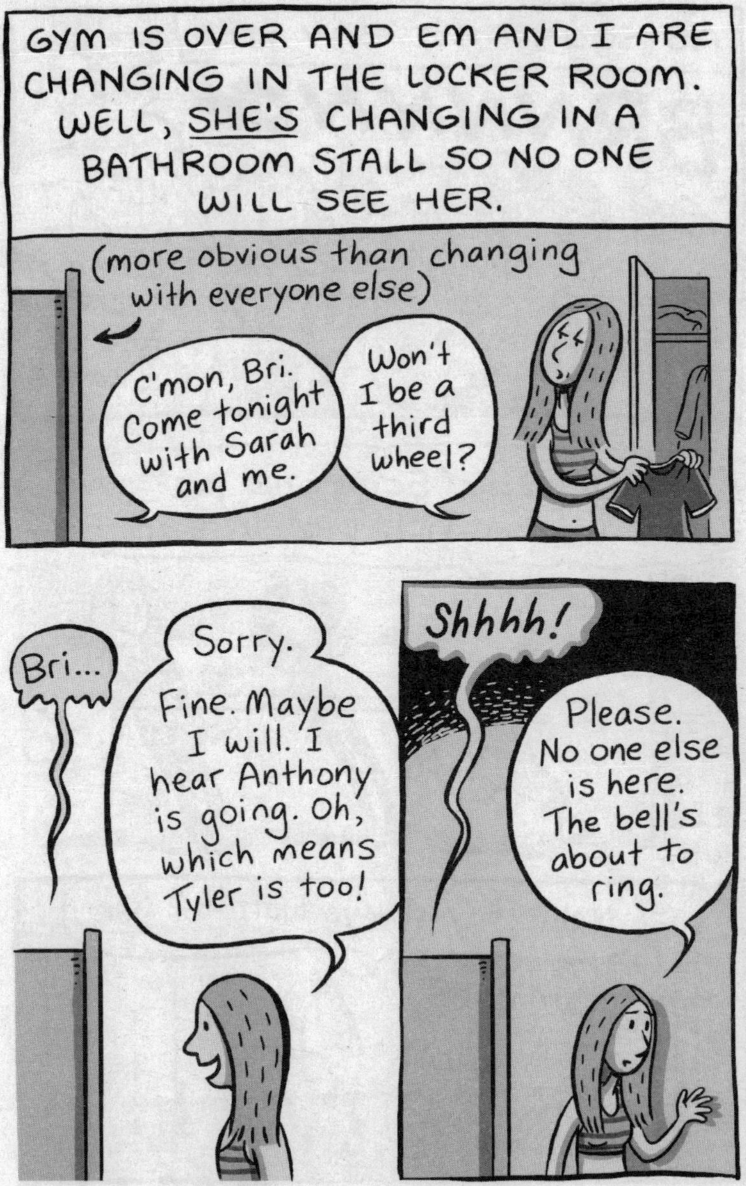
GYM IS OVER AND EM AND I ARE CHANGING IN THE LOCKER ROOM. WELL, SHE'S CHANGING IN A BATHROOM STALL SO NO ONE WILL SEE HER.
(more obvious than changing with everyone else)
C'mon, Bri. Come tonight with Sarah and me.
Won't I be a third wheel?
Bri...
Sorry.
Fine. Maybe I will. I hear Anthony is going. Oh, which means Tyler is too!
Shhhh!
Please. No one else is here. The bell's about to ring.

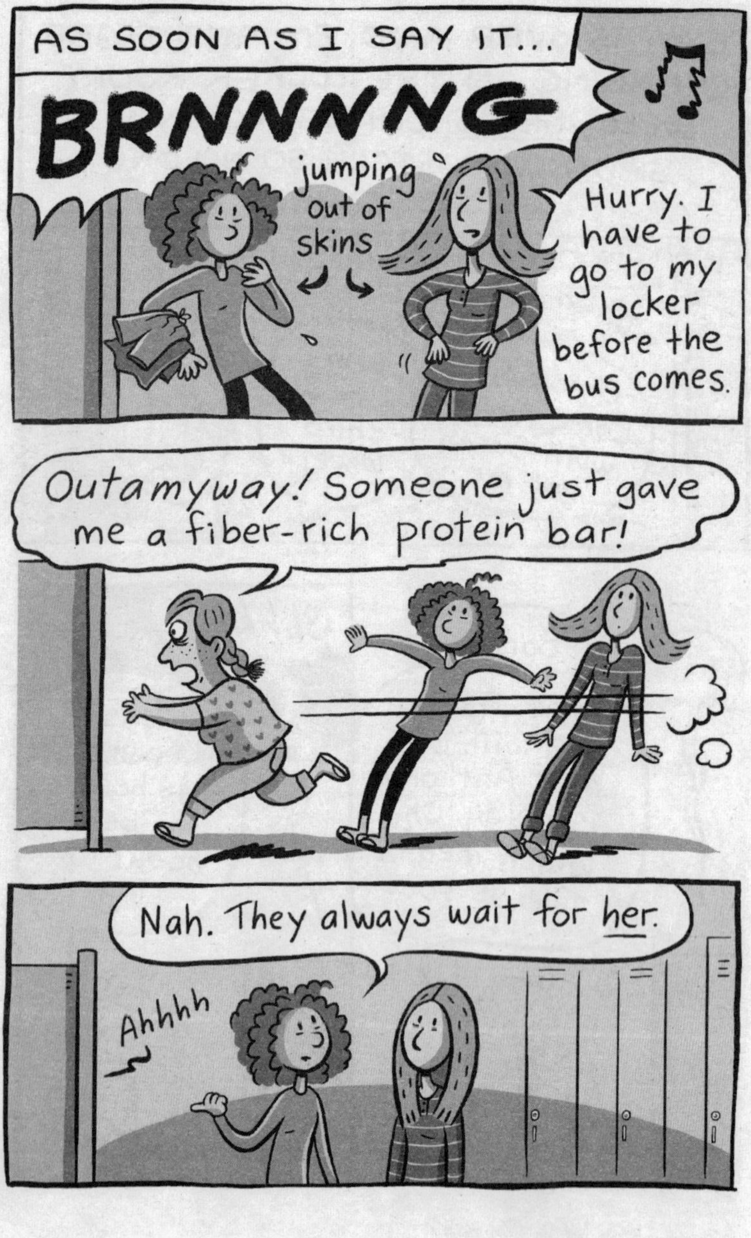
AS SOON AS I SAY IT...
BRNNNNG
jumping out of skins
Hurry. I have to go to my locker before the bus comes.
Outamyway! Someone just gave me a fiber-rich protein bar!
Nah. They always wait for her.
Ahhhh

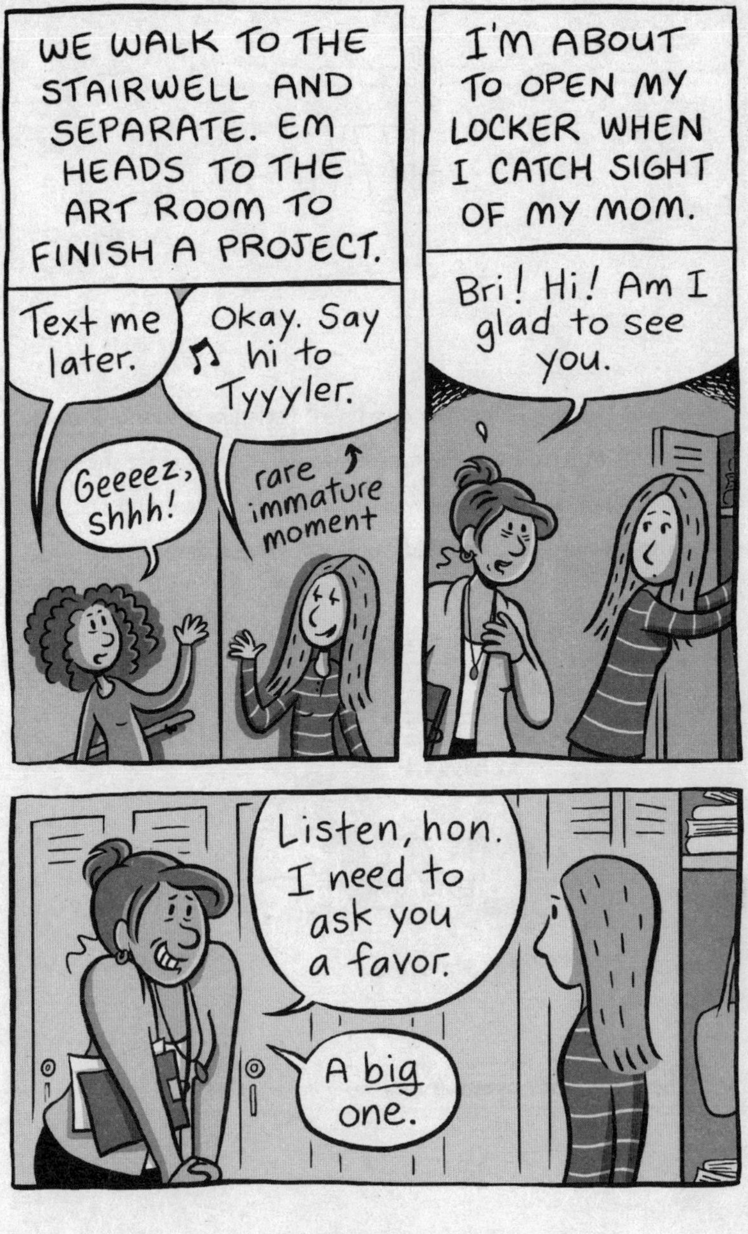
WE WALK TO THE STAIRWELL AND SEPARATE. EM HEADS TO THE ART ROOM TO FINISH A PROJECT.
I'M ABOUT TO OPEN MY LOCKER WHEN I CATCH SIGHT OF MY MOM.
Text me later.
Okay. Say ♫ hi to Tyyyler.
Geeeez, shhh!
rare immature moment
Bri! Hi! Am I glad to see you.
Listen, hon. I need to ask you a favor.
A big one.

IZZY

Ash and I arrive home. The apartment feels like a sauna. I can't believe it's March. I assume my mom is still at work since she's not around. Dani, who came home at the same time we did, cranks up the window unit and we huddle around it like a campfire.

wrrrnnnnn

→ unearthly hum we're all used to

Ahhhhhh

↑ craving s'mores

The front door opens. Mom.

groceries

normal scrubs

She throws me a look. Uh-oh.

Izzy, could you come in the kitchen, please?

gulp

Not sure what's going on, but I don't like it. My mom, who's normally pretty chill, looks like she's trying to keep from wringing my neck.

So...I discovered this when I was cleaning up the kitchen earlier.

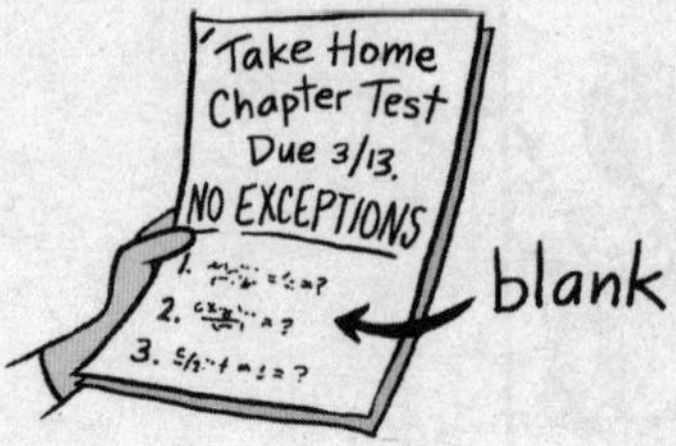
Take Home
Chapter Test
Due 3/13.
NO EXCEPTIONS
blank

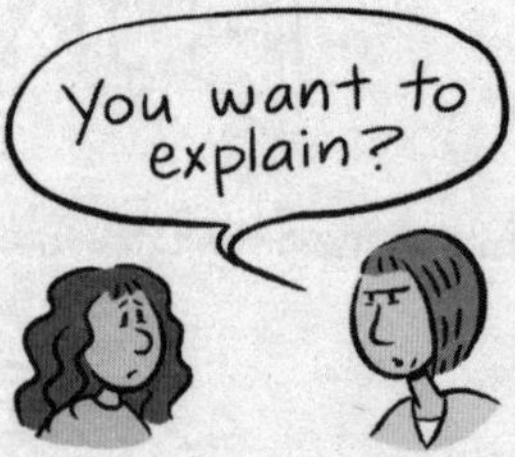
You want to explain?

I say nothing.
Survival technique.

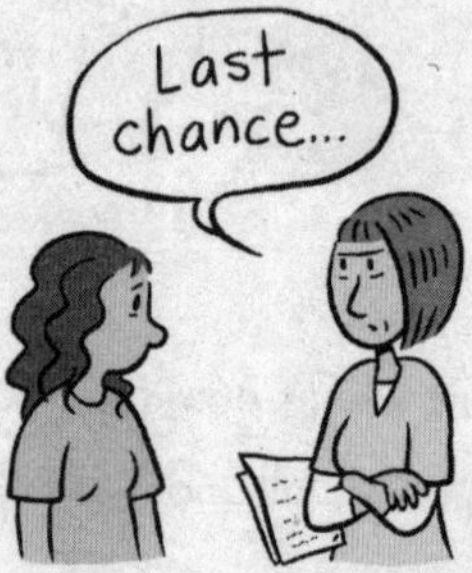
Last chance...

Nope.

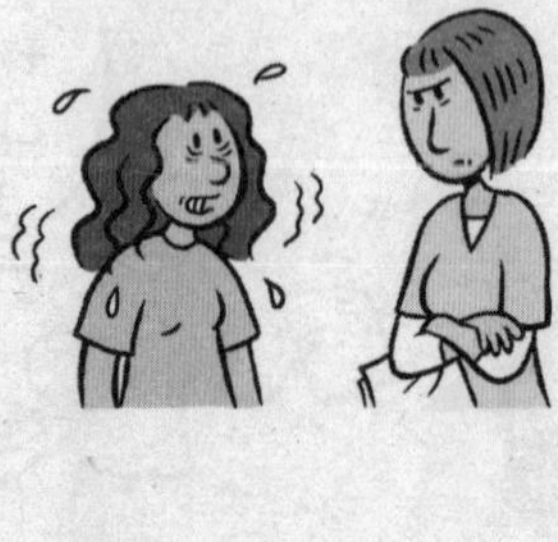

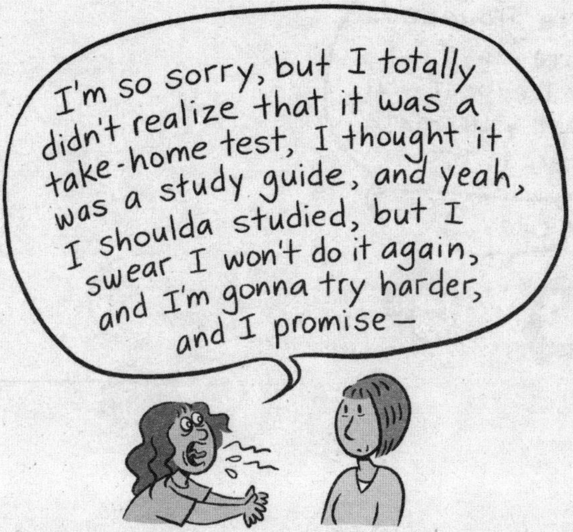
I'm so sorry, but I totally didn't realize that it was a take-home test, I thought it was a study guide, and yeah, I shoulda studied, but I swear I won't do it again, and I'm gonna try harder, and I promise—

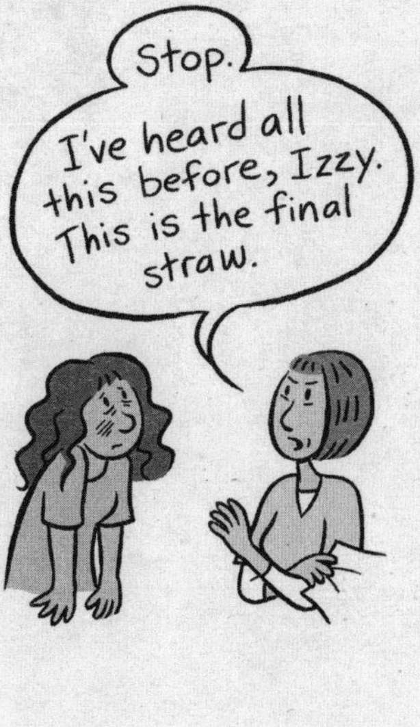
Stop.
I've heard all this before, Izzy. This is the final straw.

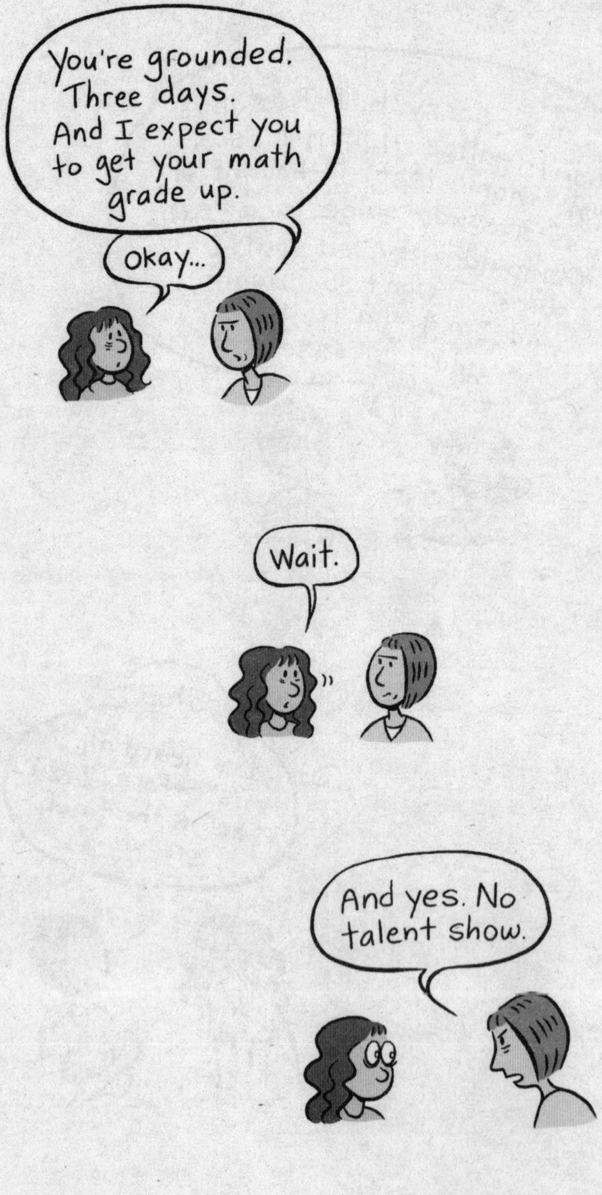
You're grounded. Three days. And I expect you to get your math grade up.
Okay...
Wait.
And yes. No talent show.

NOOOOOOOOOOOOOOOOOOOOOOOOOOOOOOOOOOOO
OOOOOOOOOOOOOOOOOOO!

 But...

No negotiating. I had a long shift last night and I need rest. I'm going back to bed.

M-o-o-o-m, I'm s-sorry. But it's not fair. I worked so h-hard...

I'm sorry, too, Izzy. But I'm not budging.

teardrop tidal wave

Even through my tears, I can see she means business. This is so unfair!!

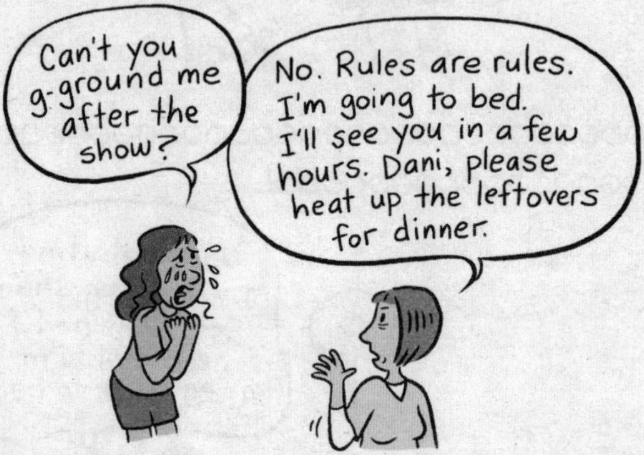
Can't you g-ground me after the show?
No. Rules are rules. I'm going to bed. I'll see you in a few hours. Dani, please heat up the leftovers for dinner.

I feel like I can't breathe. The **one** thing that makes me happy and I'm good at, and she took it away.

I run past her and my sisters, into my room. I slam the door. HARD.

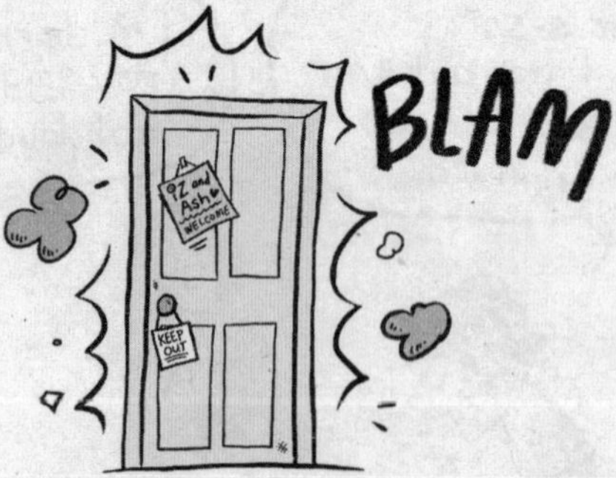
BLAM
KEEP OUT

I hear Dani through the thin walls.

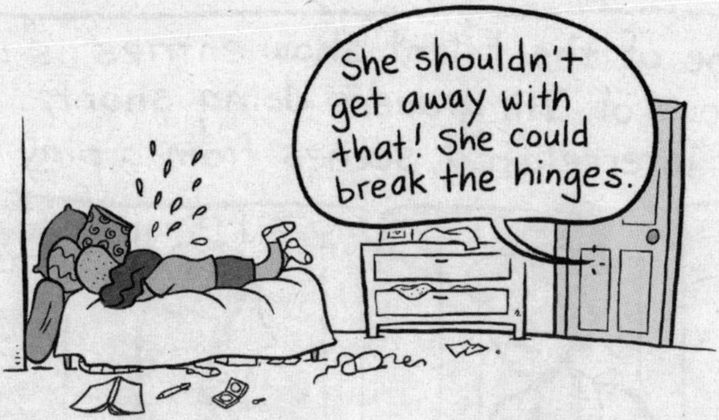

She shouldn't get away with that! She could break the hinges.

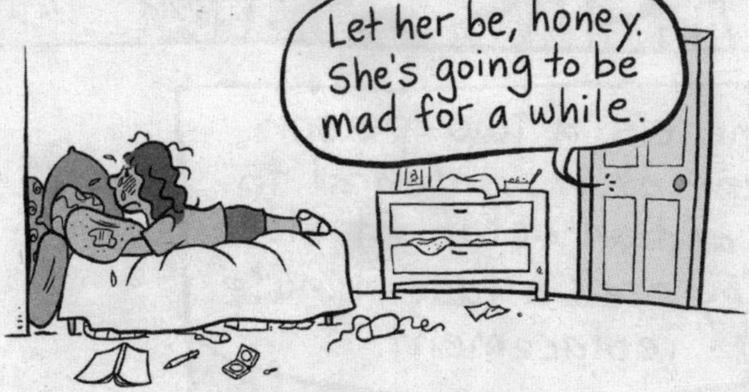

Let her be, honey. She's going to be mad for a while.

Oh, you can say **that** again.

Brianna

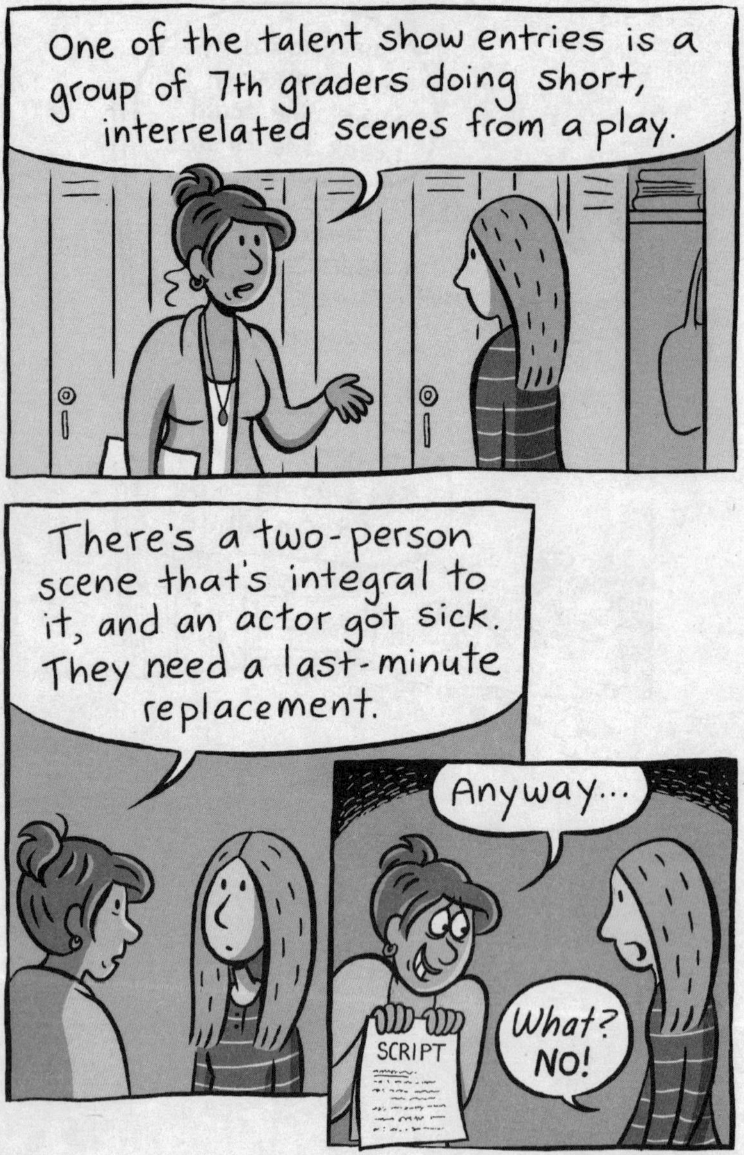
One of the talent show entries is a group of 7th graders doing short, interrelated scenes from a play.
There's a two-person scene that's integral to it, and an actor got sick. They need a last-minute replacement.
Anyway...
SCRIPT
What? NO!

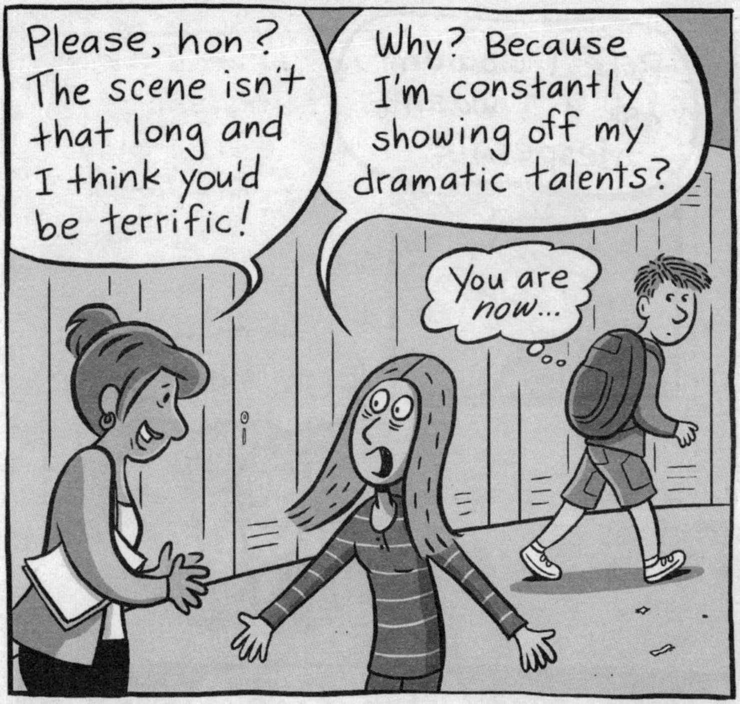
Please, hon? The scene isn't that long and I think you'd be terrific!
Why? Because I'm constantly showing off my dramatic talents?
You are *now*...

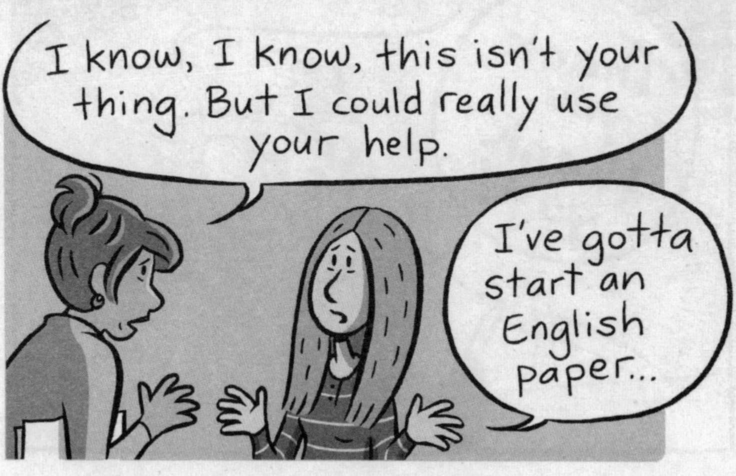
I know, I know, this isn't your thing. But I could really use your help.
I've gotta start an English paper...

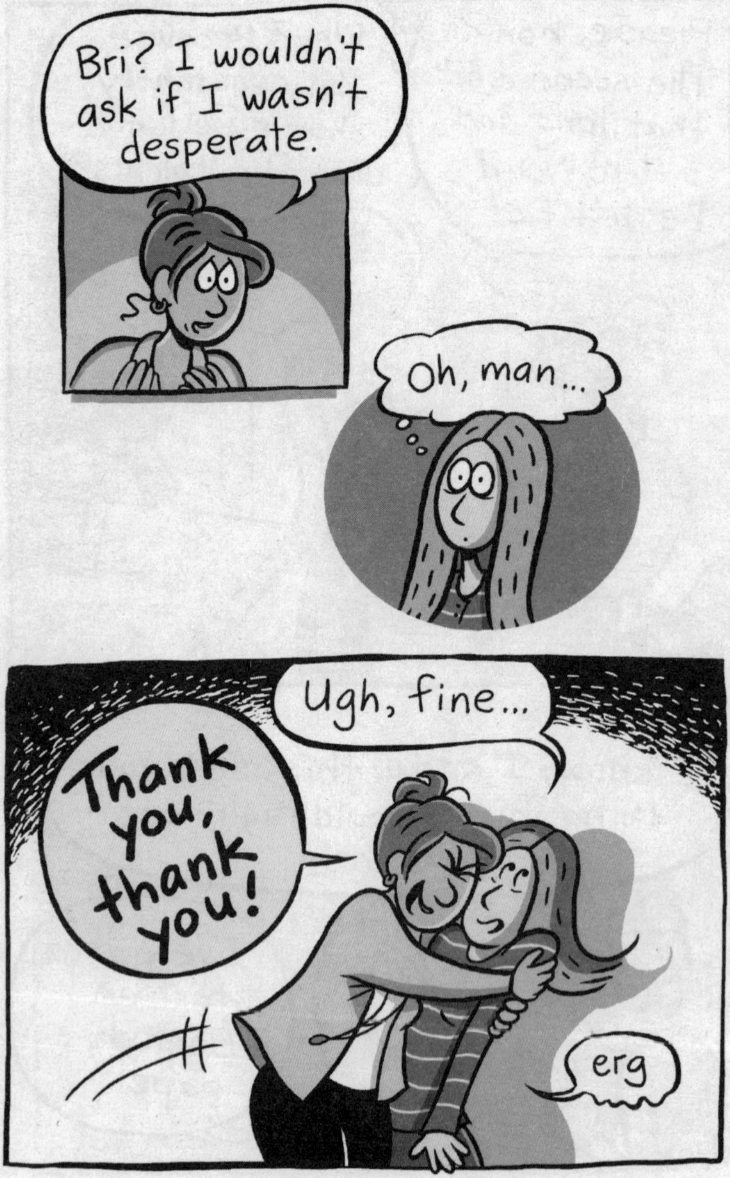
Bri? I wouldn't ask if I wasn't desperate.
Oh, man...
Ugh, fine...
Thank you, thank you!
erg

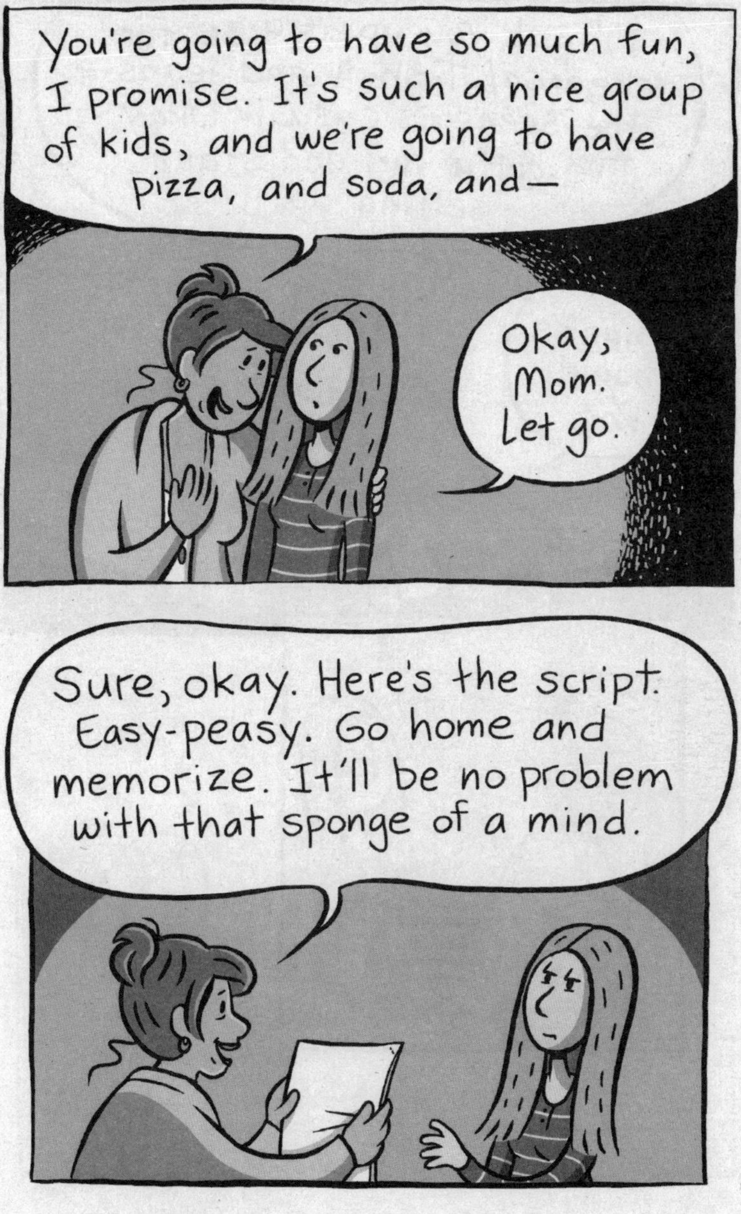
You're going to have so much fun, I promise. It's such a nice group of kids, and we're going to have pizza, and soda, and—
Okay, Mom. Let go.
Sure, okay. Here's the script. Easy-peasy. Go home and memorize. It'll be no problem with that sponge of a mind.

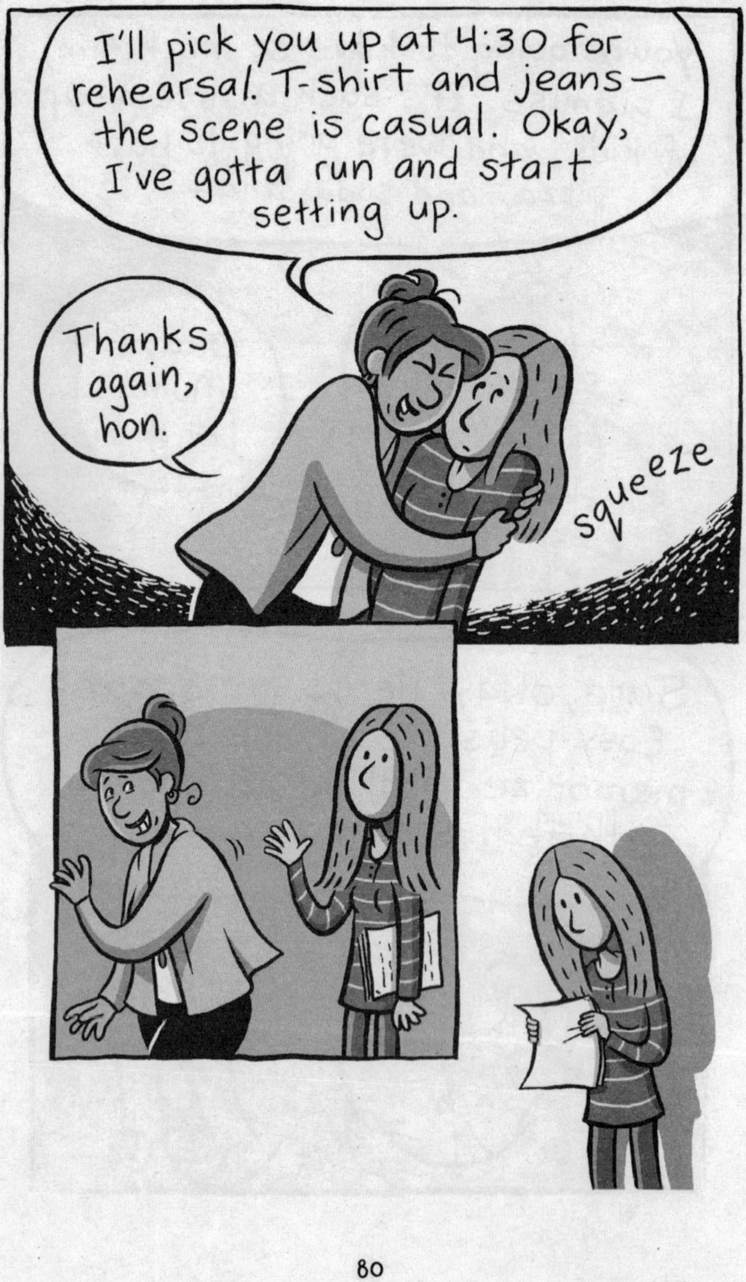
I'll pick you up at 4:30 for rehearsal. T-shirt and jeans—the scene is casual. Okay, I've gotta run and start setting up.
Thanks again, hon.
squeeze

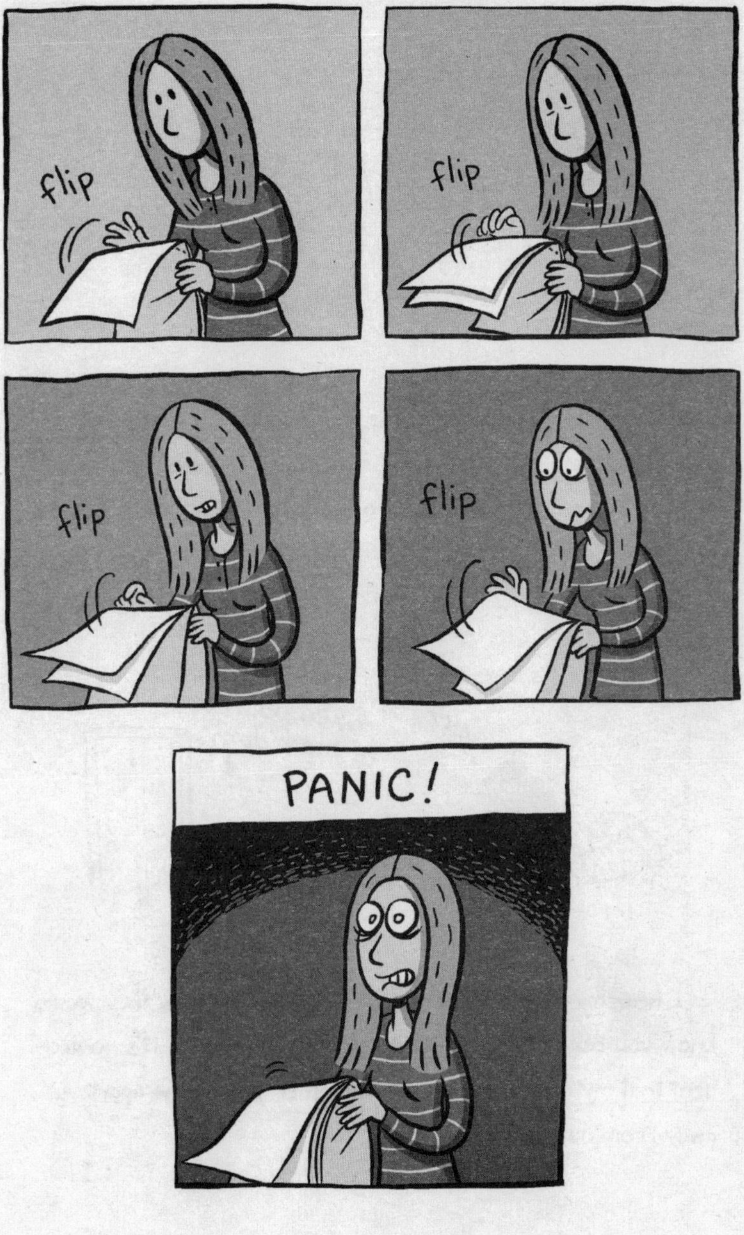
flip
flip
flip
flip
PANIC!

IZZY

I sit on my bed and stare at the wall numbly. I mean, why not? There's nothing better to do. I don't need to rehearse. I don't need to pick out performance clothes (okay, I had 'em picked out a month ago).

So I stare.

sniff

fixed point of staredom

I hear my sisters whispering. You'd think by now they would know you can hear everything through these walls. It's no accident that my mom's room is on the other side of the apartment, away from ours.

She brought it on herself.
But it's not fair, Dani. Izzy's really, really good. And she practiced so much.
Maybe she should've paid as much attention in class.
Well, I'm gonna try to cheer her up.
KNOCK KNOCK
Go away, Ashley.
It's my room, too. Let me in.

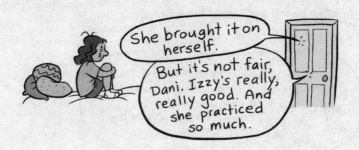

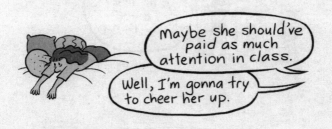

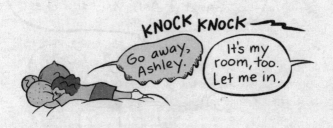

Rats. She has a point. I lift myself off the bed like an old lady with rattly bones, and I open the door.

I know what you're trying to do, but it won't work. When Mom makes up her mind, that's it. So I'm just gonna be grumpy for the rest of my life.

It's not the rest of your life. It's a one-time thing.

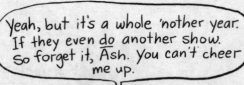

Yeah, but it's a whole 'nother year. If they even <u>do</u> another show. So forget it, Ash. You can't cheer me up.

Okay, fine.

We sit in silence for a minute. Suddenly Ashley brightens and grabs my arm.

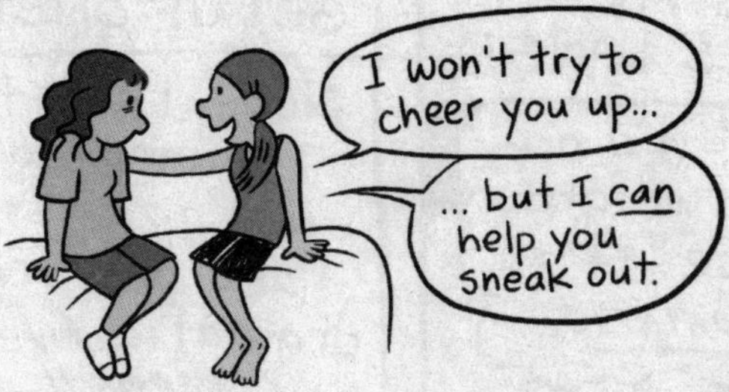
I won't try to cheer you up...
... but I can help you sneak out.

Brianna

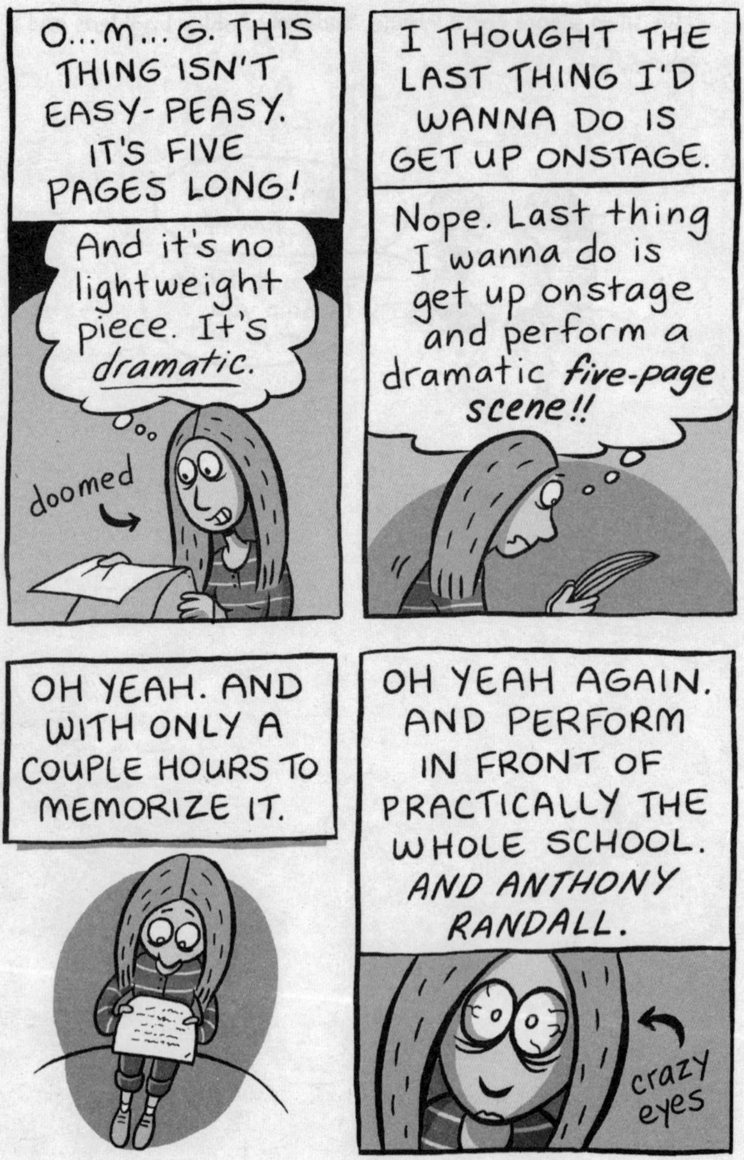
O...M...G. THIS THING ISN'T EASY-PEASY. IT'S FIVE PAGES LONG!
And it's no lightweight piece. It's dramatic.
doomed
I THOUGHT THE LAST THING I'D WANNA DO IS GET UP ONSTAGE.
Nope. Last thing I wanna do is get up onstage and perform a dramatic five-page scene!!
OH YEAH. AND WITH ONLY A COUPLE HOURS TO MEMORIZE IT.
OH YEAH AGAIN. AND PERFORM IN FRONT OF PRACTICALLY THE WHOLE SCHOOL. AND ANTHONY RANDALL.
crazy eyes

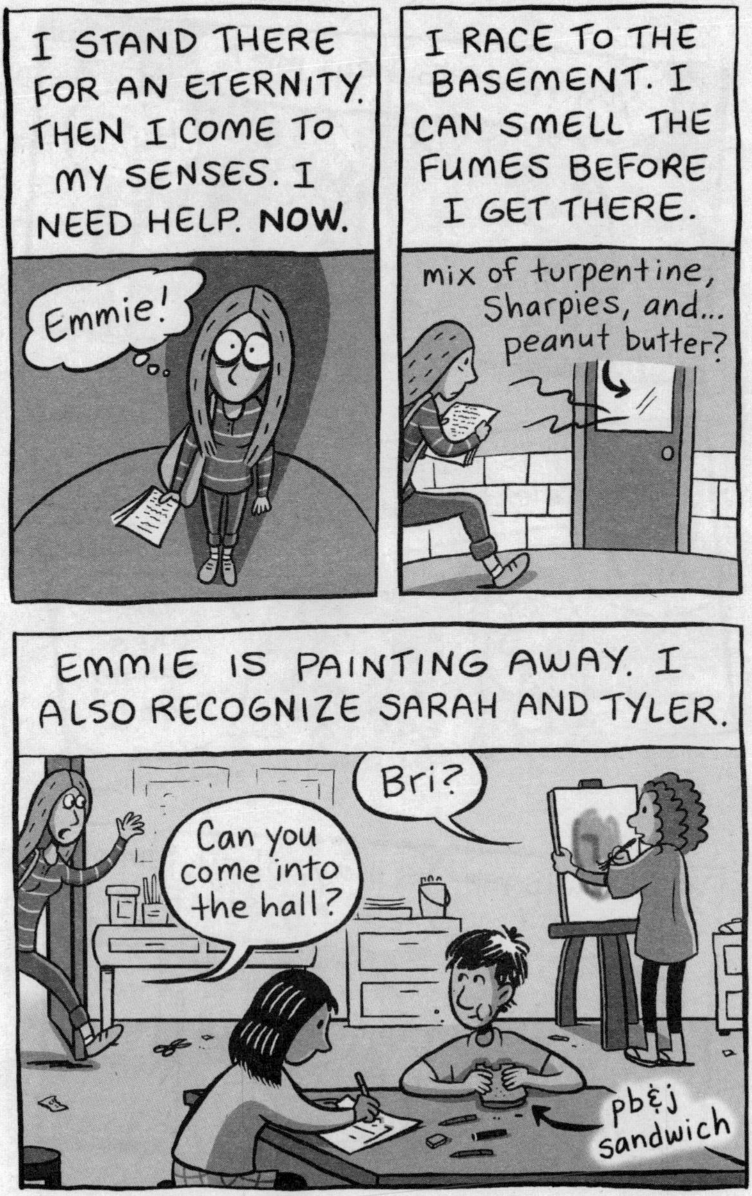
I STAND THERE FOR AN ETERNITY. THEN I COME TO MY SENSES. I NEED HELP. NOW.
Emmie!
I RACE TO THE BASEMENT. I CAN SMELL THE FUMES BEFORE I GET THERE.
mix of turpentine, Sharpies, and... peanut butter?
EMMIE IS PAINTING AWAY. I ALSO RECOGNIZE SARAH AND TYLER.
Bri?
Can you come into the hall?
pb&j sandwich

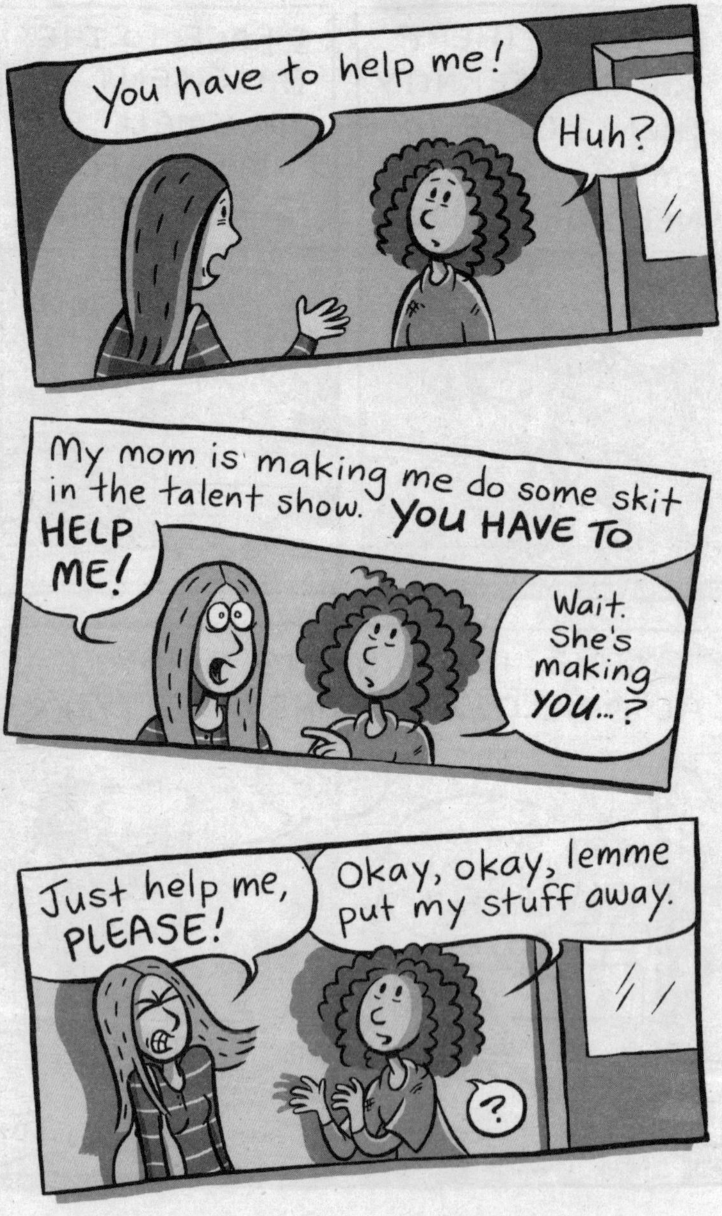
You have to help me!
Huh?
My mom is making me do some skit in the talent show. YOU HAVE TO HELP ME!
Wait. She's making YOU...?
Just help me, PLEASE!
Okay, okay, lemme put my stuff away.
?

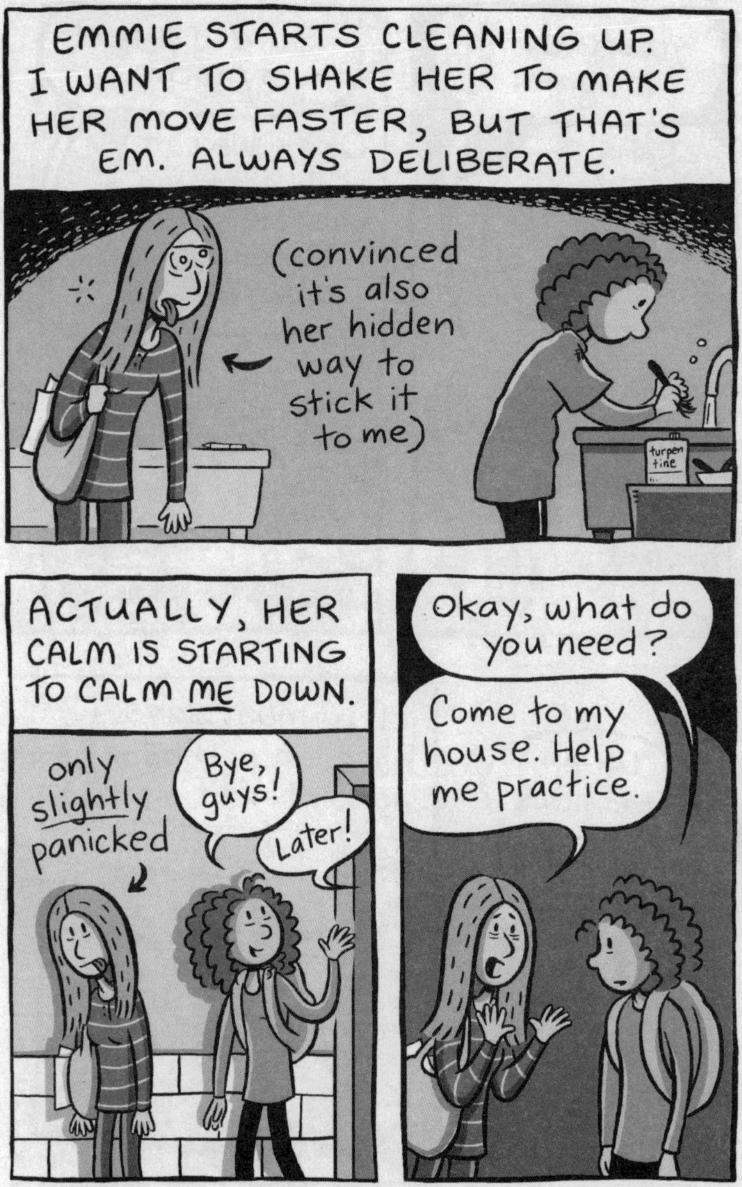
EMMIE STARTS CLEANING UP. I WANT TO SHAKE HER TO MAKE HER MOVE FASTER, BUT THAT'S EM. ALWAYS DELIBERATE.
(convinced it's also her hidden way to stick it to me)
turpentine
ACTUALLY, HER CALM IS STARTING TO CALM ME DOWN.
only slightly panicked
Bye, guys!
Later!
Okay, what do you need?
Come to my house. Help me practice.

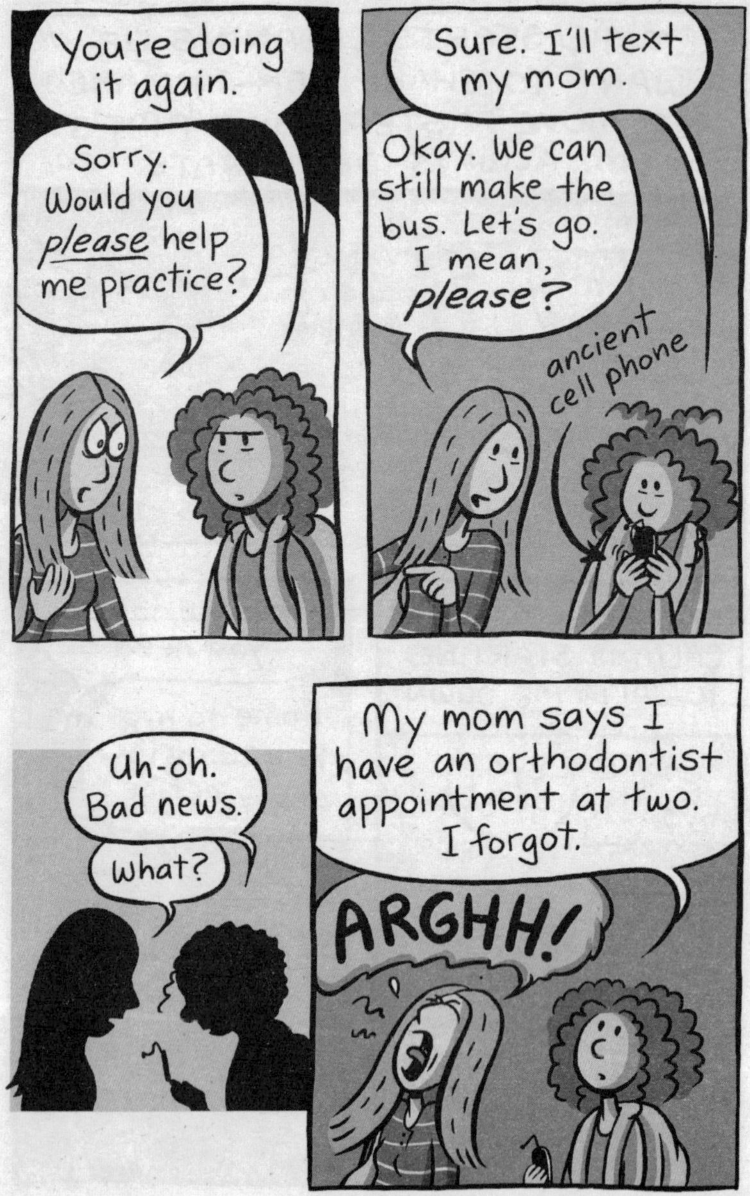
You're doing it again.
Sorry. Would you please help me practice?
Sure. I'll text my mom.
Okay. We can still make the bus. Let's go. I mean, please?
ancient cell phone
Uh-oh. Bad news.
What?
My mom says I have an orthodontist appointment at two. I forgot.
ARGHH!

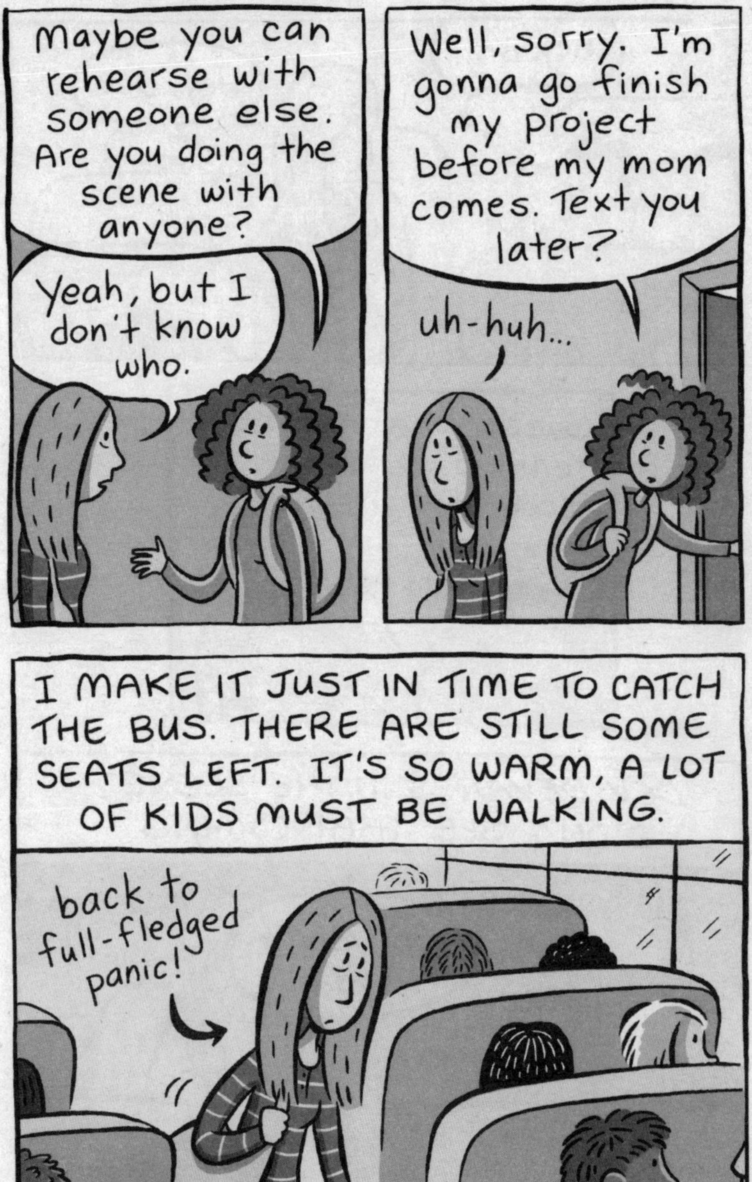
Maybe you can rehearse with someone else. Are you doing the scene with anyone?
Yeah, but I don't know who.
Well, sorry. I'm gonna go finish my project before my mom comes. Text you later?
uh-huh...
I MAKE IT JUST IN TIME TO CATCH THE BUS. THERE ARE STILL SOME SEATS LEFT. IT'S SO WARM, A LOT OF KIDS MUST BE WALKING.
back to full-fledged panic!

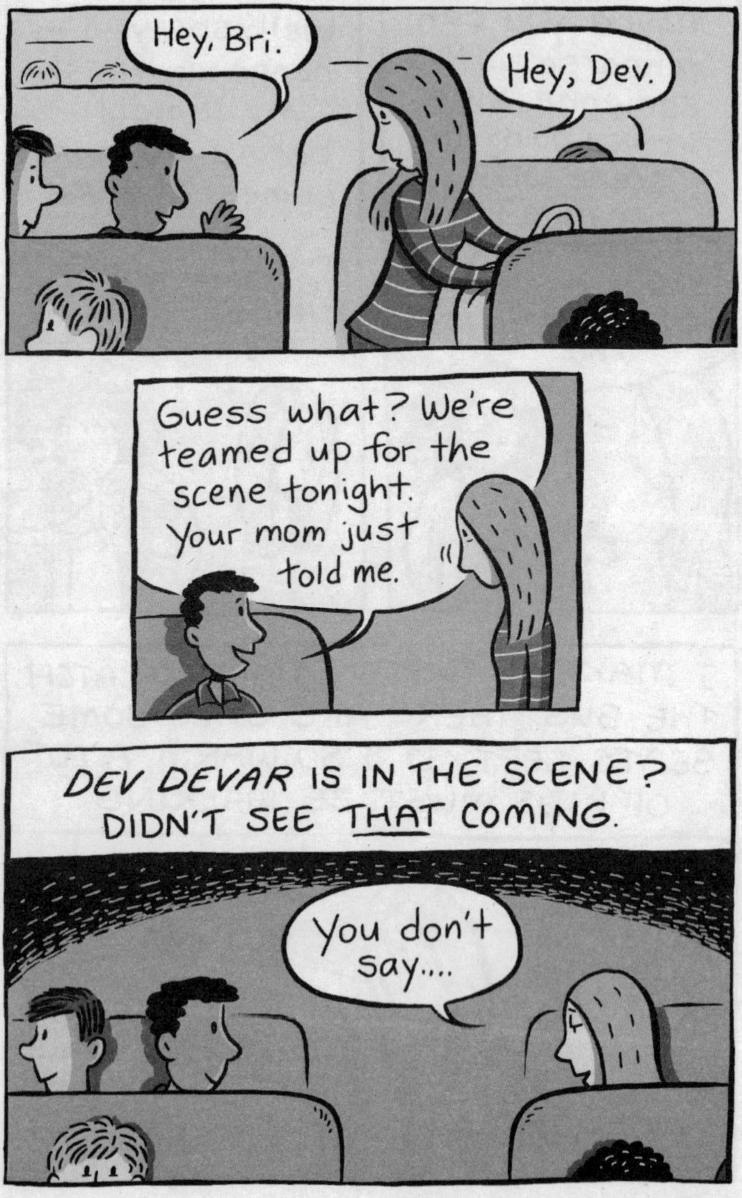
Hey, Bri.
Hey, Dev.
Guess what? We're teamed up for the scene tonight. Your mom just told me.
DEV DEVAR IS IN THE SCENE? DIDN'T SEE THAT COMING.
You don't say....

IZZY

I look at Ashley like she's grown three heads.

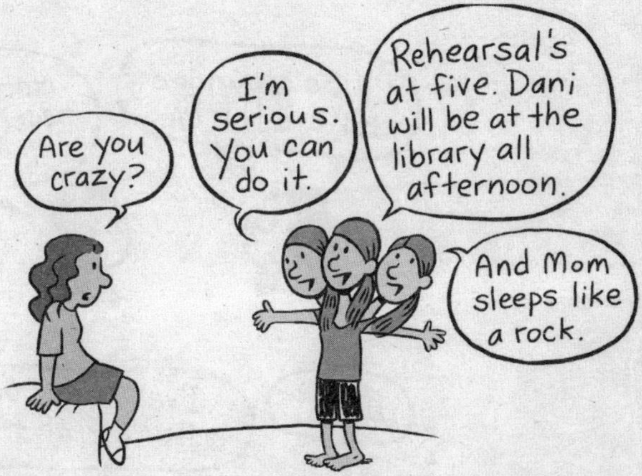
Are you crazy?
I'm serious. You can do it.
Rehearsal's at five. Dani will be at the library all afternoon.
And Mom sleeps like a rock.

It's true. Our mom could sleep through an earthquake—especially after a long shift. My heart starts pounding. Oh man, I want to do it. Still . . . I may not be the best kid at school, but I've never done anything . . . well, like **this**.

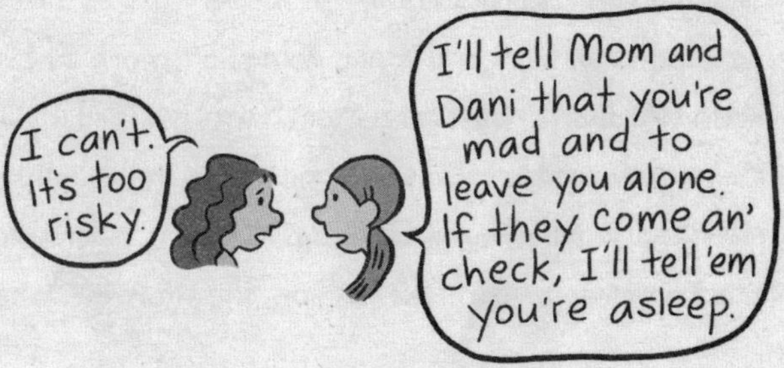
I can't. It's too risky.
I'll tell Mom and Dani that you're mad and to leave you alone. If they come an' check, I'll tell 'em you're asleep.

Oh wow. This could work. Then again, what if someone at the show sees me perform and tells my mom? Doubtful. Mom barely knows any of the parents, she works so much.

And what if Dani finds out? Would she snitch? If I get caught . . .

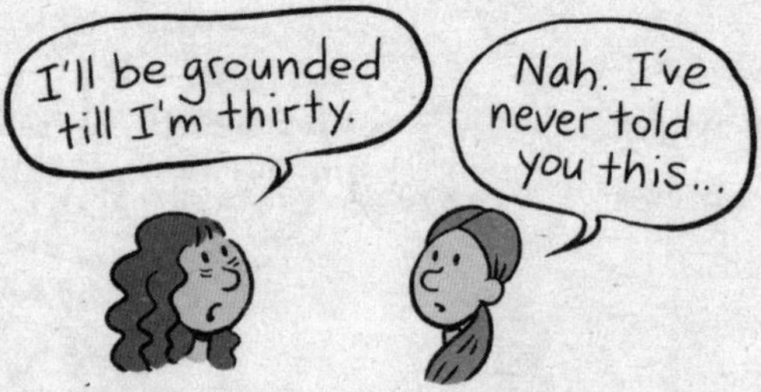
I'll be grounded till I'm thirty.
Nah. I've never told you this...

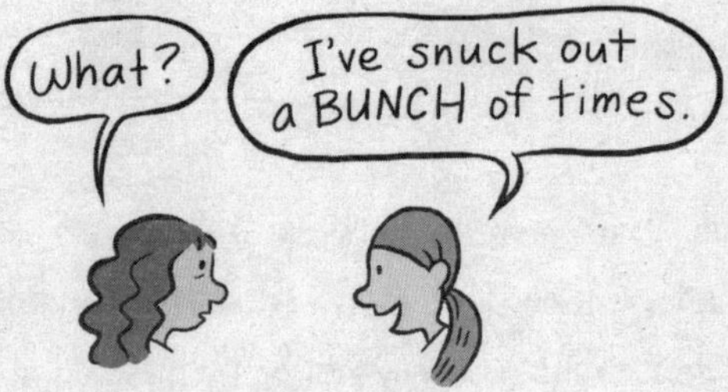
What?
I've snuck out a BUNCH of times.

I laugh. I can't help it. I know Ash sneaks out. She leaves when Mom's asleep or at work and Dani is doing homework. She goes to her friend Meghan's house (who Mom thinks is a "bad influence") and they sneak-read her dad's dirty magazines in the bathroom. I know this 'cause Dani found out from Meghan's older sister and told me. In weird, un-Dani-like fashion, she swore me to secrecy.

I think it's partly 'cause Meghan's sister didn't want her to snitch (and take away **her** reading fun) and because . . . well, no one wants to take Ashley down. Not even Dani.

Ash is looking at me funny.

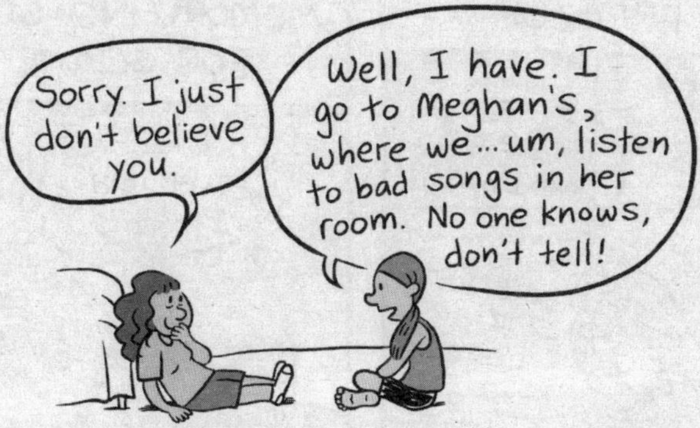

Sorry. I just don't believe you.
Well, I have. I go to Meghan's, where we... um, listen to bad songs in her room. No one knows, don't tell!

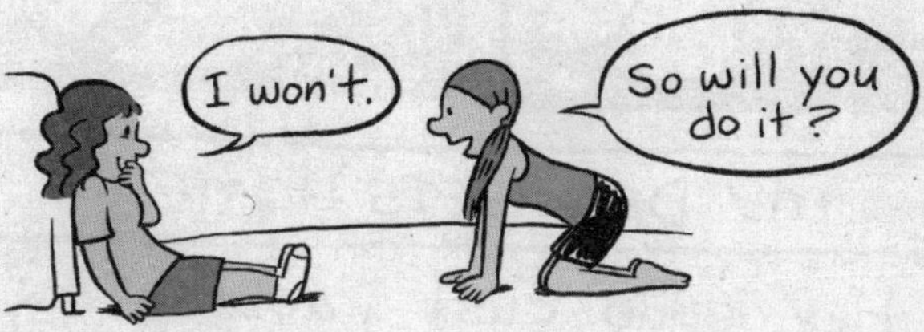

I won't.
So will you do it?

I think about it for a minute.

Actually, I've already made up my mind.

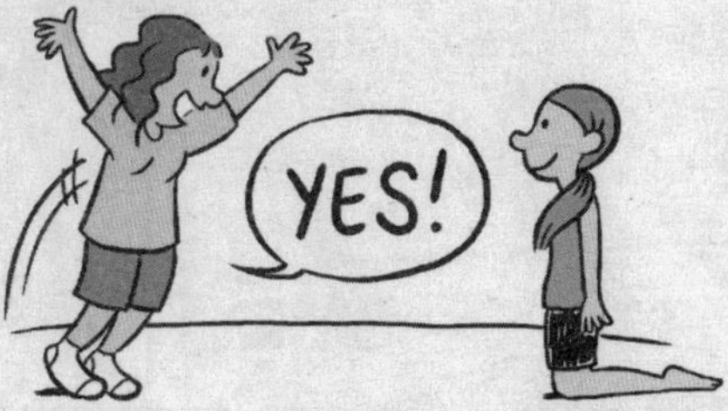

YES!

Brianna

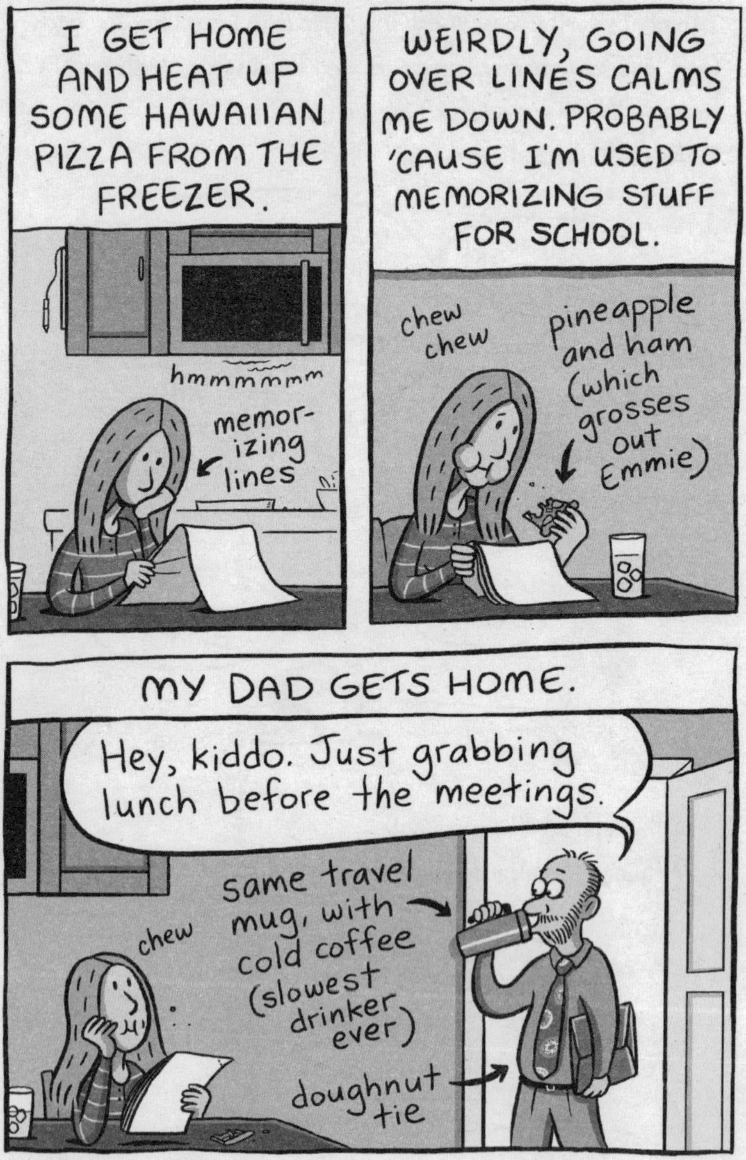
I GET HOME AND HEAT UP SOME HAWAIIAN PIZZA FROM THE FREEZER.
hmmmmmm
memor-izing lines
WEIRDLY, GOING OVER LINES CALMS ME DOWN. PROBABLY 'CAUSE I'M USED TO MEMORIZING STUFF FOR SCHOOL.
chew chew
pineapple and ham (which grosses out Emmie)
MY DAD GETS HOME.
Hey, kiddo. Just grabbing lunch before the meetings.
same travel mug, with cold coffee (slowest drinker ever)
chew
doughnut tie

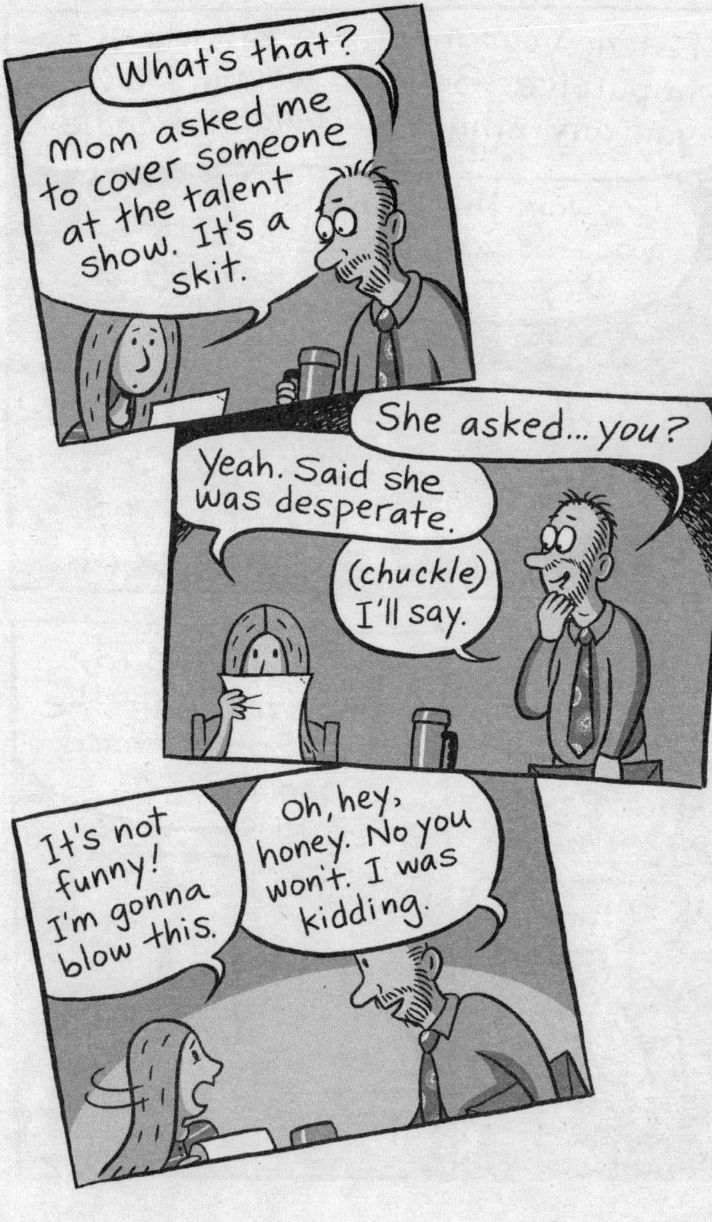
What's that?
Mom asked me to cover someone at the talent show. It's a skit.
She asked... you?
Yeah. Said she was desperate.
(chuckle) I'll say.
It's not funny! I'm gonna blow this.
Oh, hey, honey. No you won't. I was kidding.

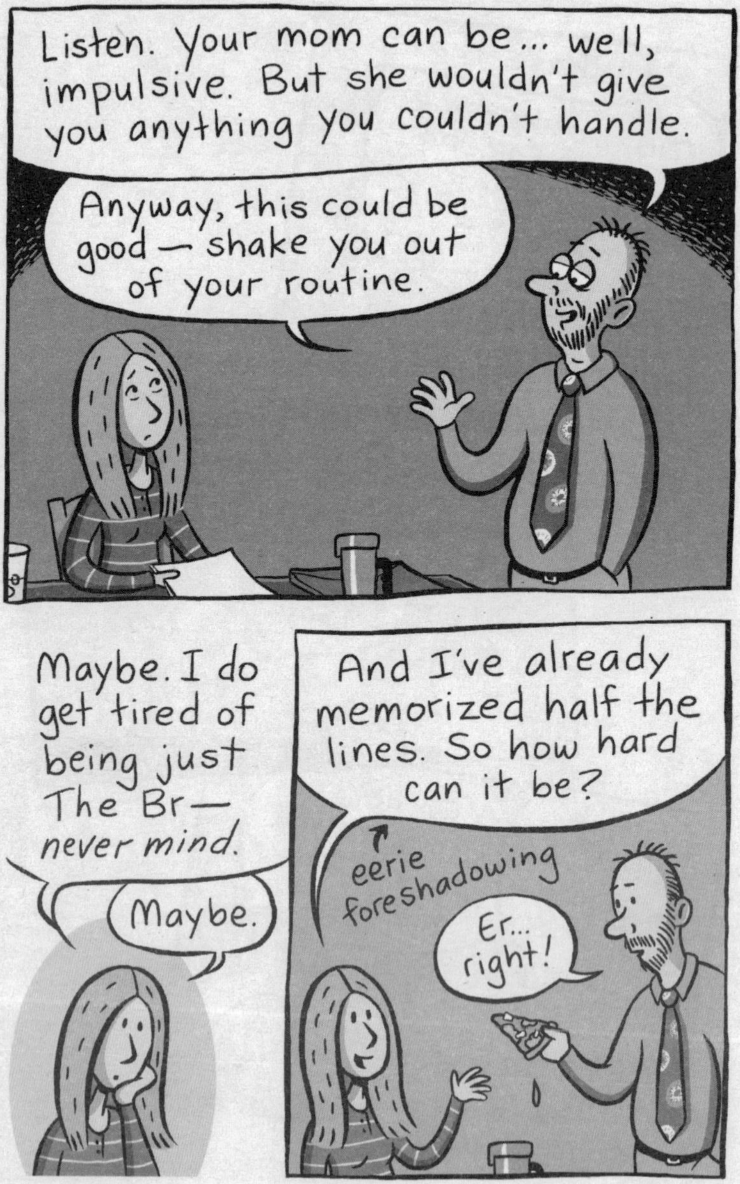
Listen. Your mom can be... well, impulsive. But she wouldn't give you anything you couldn't handle.
Anyway, this could be good — shake you out of your routine.
Maybe. I do get tired of being just The Br— never mind.
Maybe.
And I've already memorized half the lines. So how hard can it be?
eerie foreshadowing
Er... right!

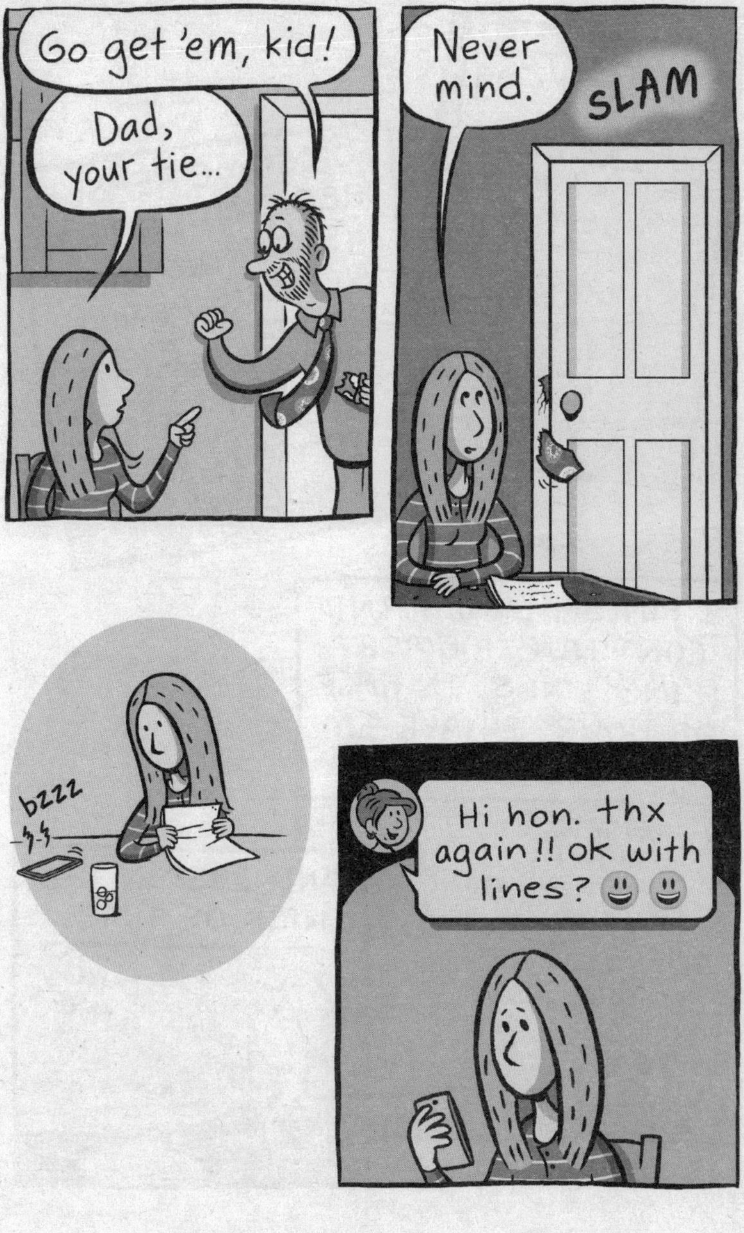

Go get 'em, kid!
Dad, your tie...
Never mind.
SLAM
bzzz
Hi hon. thx again!! ok with lines? 😃 😃

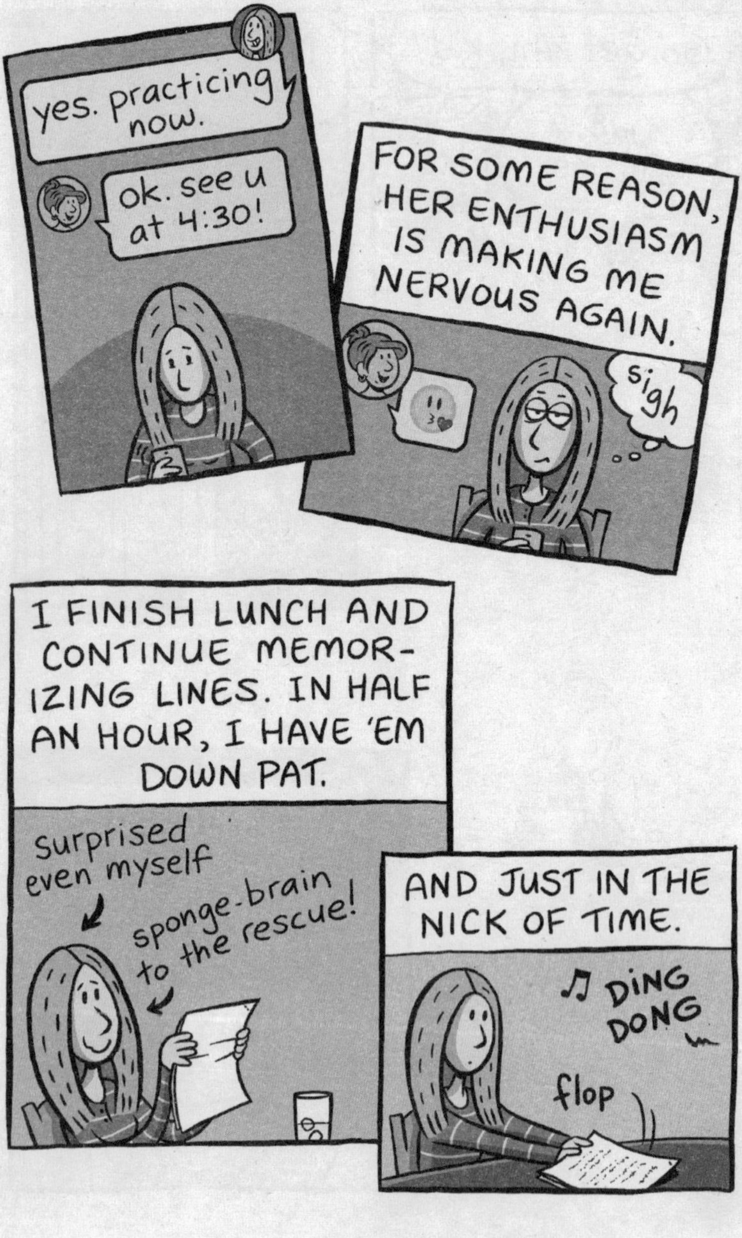
yes. practicing now.
ok. see u at 4:30!
FOR SOME REASON, HER ENTHUSIASM IS MAKING ME NERVOUS AGAIN.
sigh
I FINISH LUNCH AND CONTINUE MEMOR-IZING LINES. IN HALF AN HOUR, I HAVE 'EM DOWN PAT.
surprised even myself
sponge-brain to the rescue!
AND JUST IN THE NICK OF TIME.
♫ DING DONG
flop

IZZY

It's late afternoon when I ~~tiptoe in terror from~~ leave the apartment.

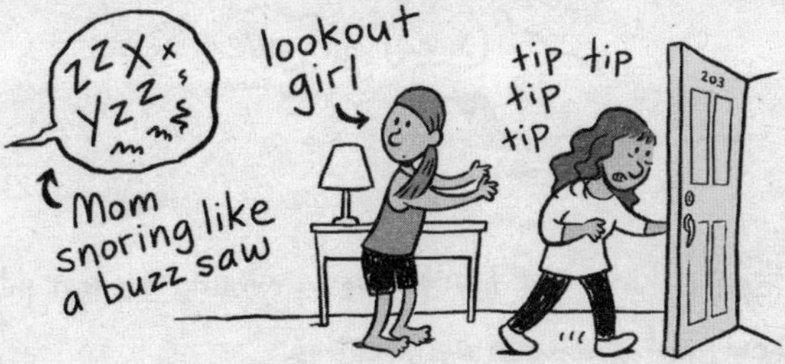

ZZX x
YZZ
lookout
girl
tip tip
tip
tip
203
Mom
snoring like
a buzz saw

I quickly and quietly head down the empty back stairwell, through a side door into the courtyard, and down the narrow path that runs along the side of the building. My heart is pounding so hard, I'm afraid it'll burst out of my chest. I'm convinced if that happens, Mom will somehow find my ghost and ground her.

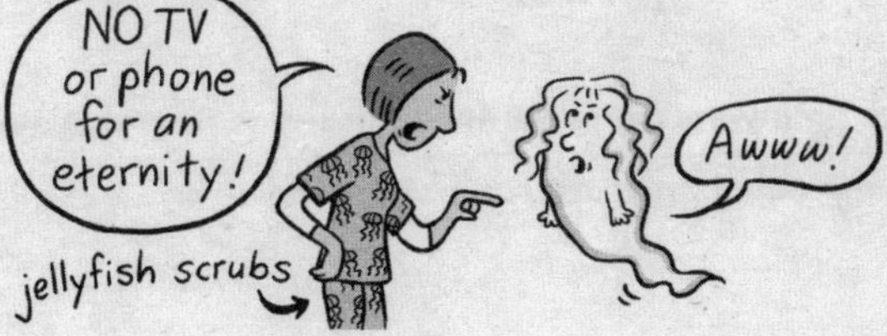

NO TV
or phone
for an
eternity!
Awww!
jellyfish scrubs

I made Ashley promise—no, **swear** up and down—that she would keep Mom and Dani away from our room. She even thought of little details, like turning on some music really low so it would seem like I was holed up, listening. Or maybe later taking a snack to me because "I refuse to come out."

Not only is my heart pounding, but my stomach is churning. I hate going behind my mom's back.

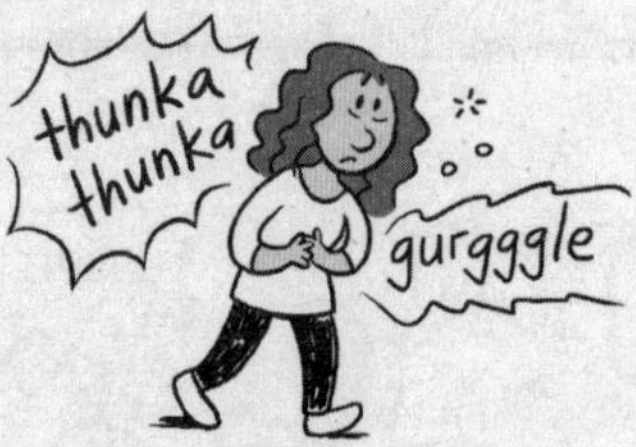
thunka thunka
gurgggle

But then I think: she didn't have to ground me tonight. She **knows** how much I've been wanting this.

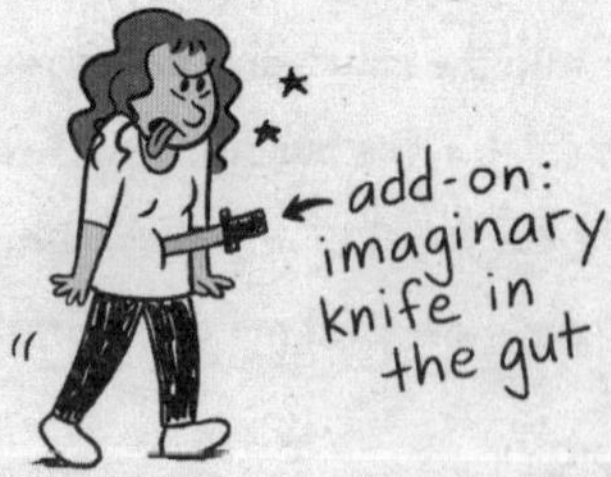
add-on: imaginary knife in the gut

I pick up my pace and cut through the cemetery to save time. It's like my old friends are rooting for me.

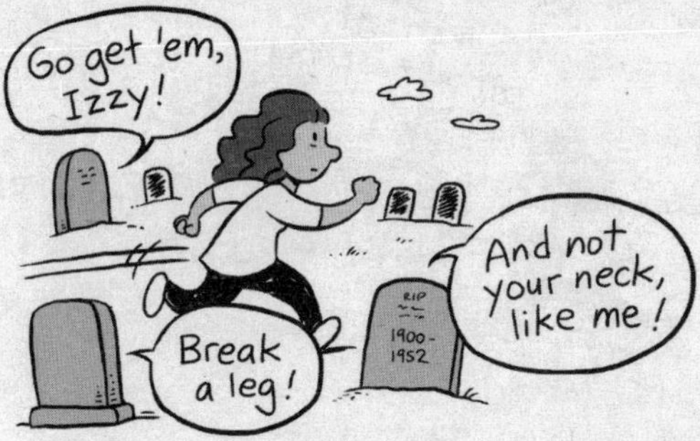
Go get 'em, Izzy!
And not your neck, like me!
RIP
1900-1952
Break a leg!

Once I'm out of there and round the corner, I breathe a little. Thankfully, Dani and the library are in the opposite direction.

It's not just warm out. It's **hot**. I pass my favorite ice cream place, Taystee's, and suddenly I'm craving a chocolate chip cone. I'm lactose intolerant, but that stuff's worth the gas.

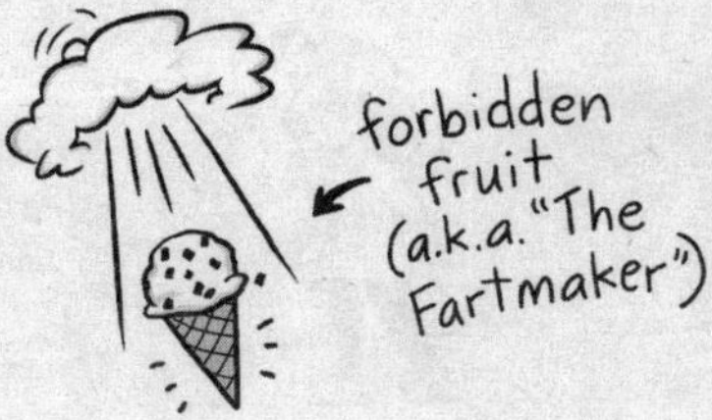
forbidden fruit (a.k.a. "The Fartmaker")

My grade school friends and I used to save our allowance and go to Taystee's every Friday after school. Even on cold days. I'd always get chocolate chip on a sugar cone. I miss that.

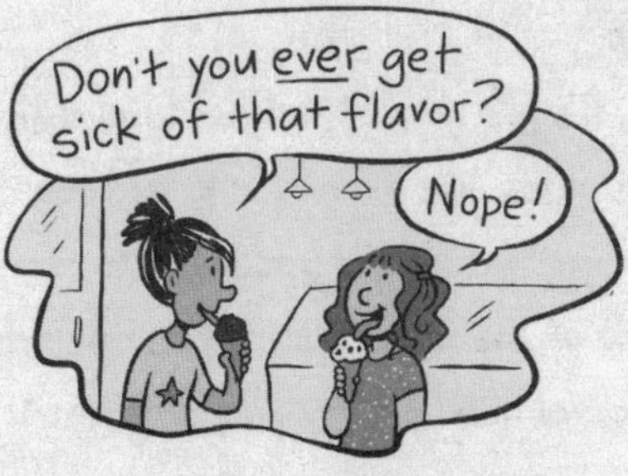
Don't you ever get sick of that flavor?
Nope!

I realize I'm slowing down thinking about ice cream, so I pick up the pace again.

Lakefront
Middle School

LAKEFRONT

(no lake)

Speaking of old times, I see Becca walking into the school with some other girls. At first, I'm surprised to see her, and then I realize she takes choir, so she's probably singing with some friends in the show.

There's a whole bunch of other kids trickling in. Some are from drama club, like me. As well as a bunch of popular kids who think they can sing. A few from band. And some I barely recognize (Lakefront is pretty big).

I walk in alone. At first, it's pretty quiet. I head toward the auditorium and hear some sounds, like furniture being moved. Mrs. D is already there, directing two eighth-grade boys to carry a dilapidated couch to the side of the stage. It drops on one side and the noise echoes all over. Not good for my pounding heart.

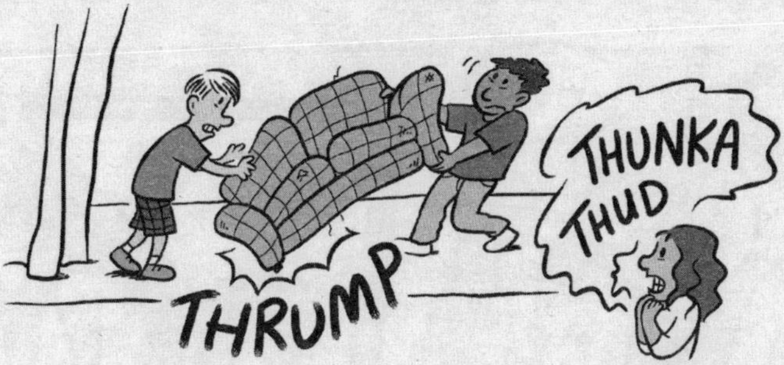
THRUMP
THUNKA THUD

I join a few drama club kids up front. Becca waves hello from across the aisle. We may not be best friends anymore, but at least she's still friendly.

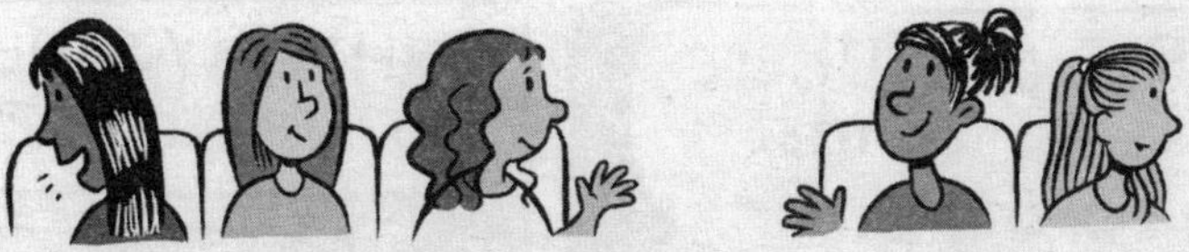

I wait quietly and try not to think about how I just snuck out. Funny—I'm not that nervous about getting onstage . . .

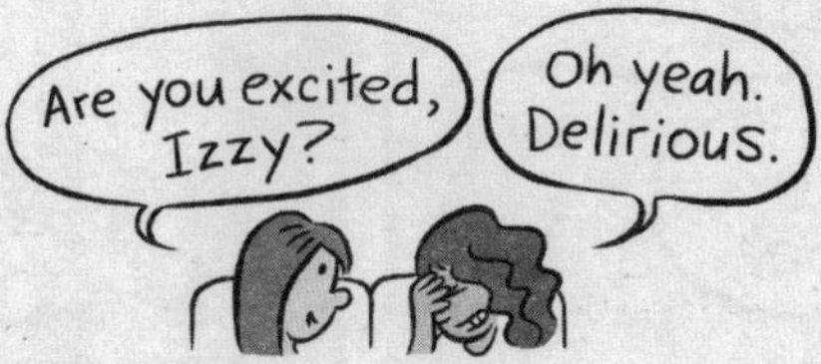
Are you excited, Izzy?
Oh yeah. Delirious.

. . . but I'm **freaked out** about that!

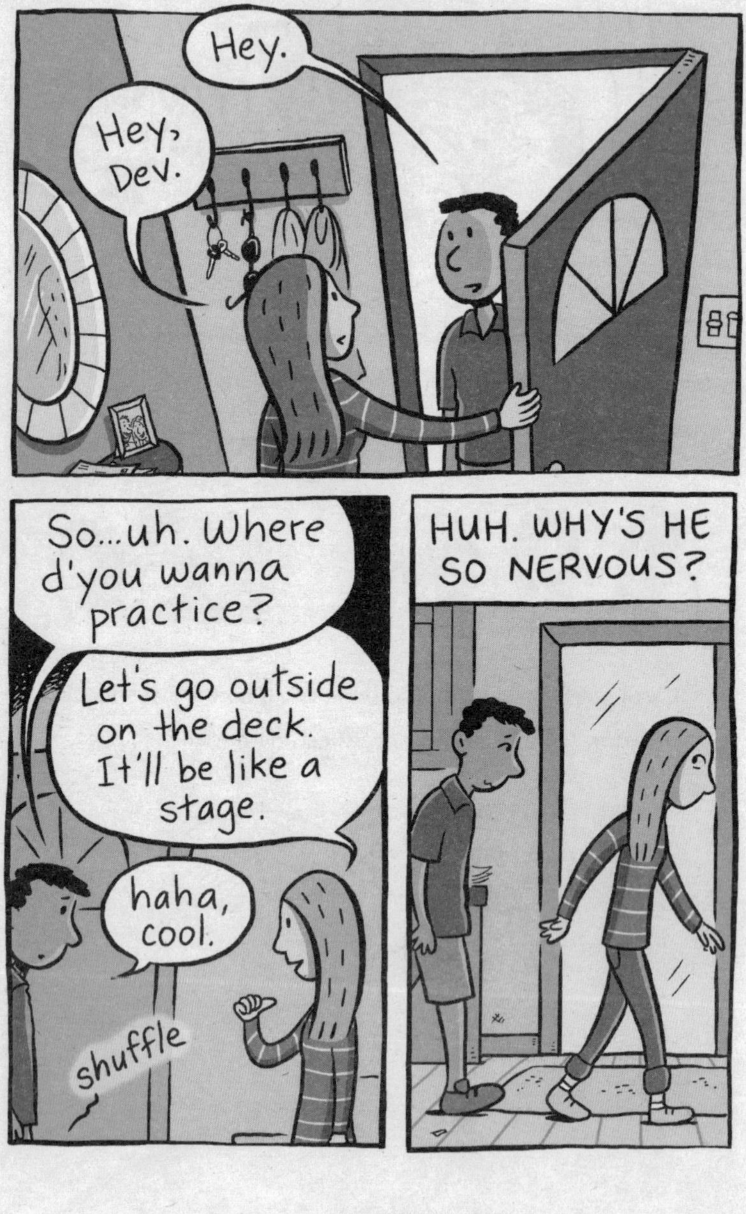
Hey.
Hey, Dev.
So...uh. Where d'you wanna practice?
Let's go outside on the deck. It'll be like a stage.
haha, cool.
shuffle
HUH. WHY'S HE SO NERVOUS?

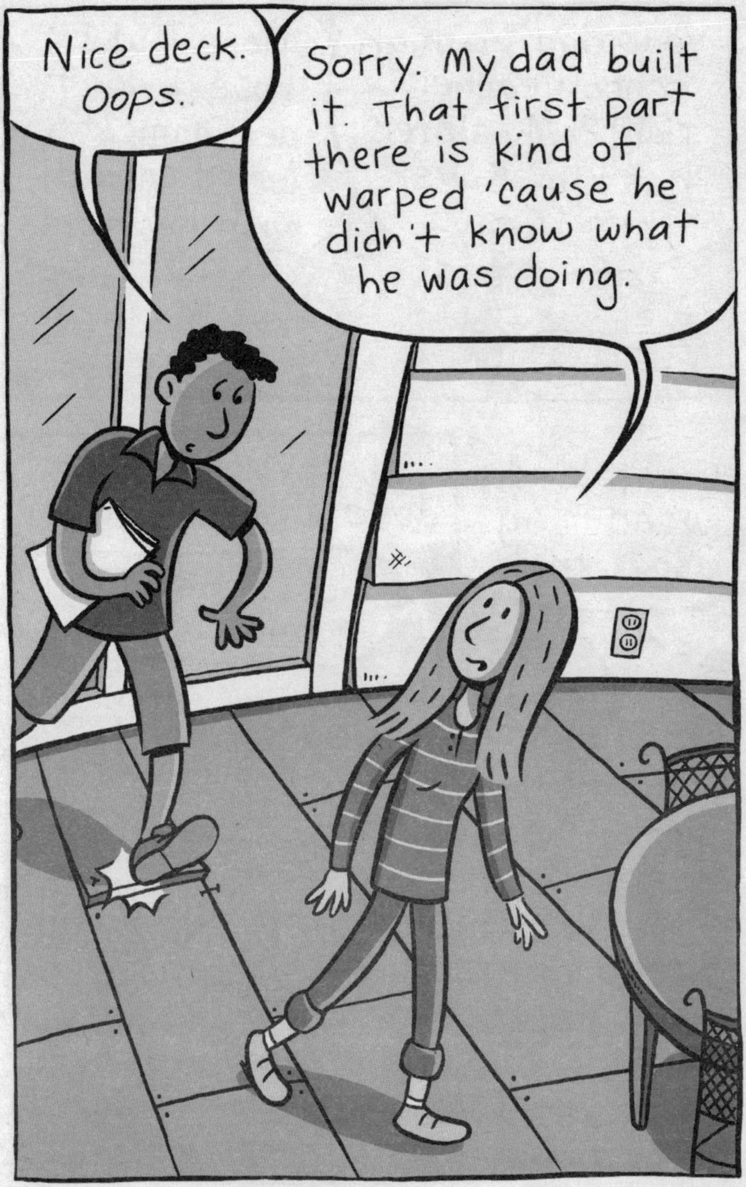
Nice deck. Oops.
Sorry. My dad built it. That first part there is kind of warped 'cause he didn't know what he was doing.

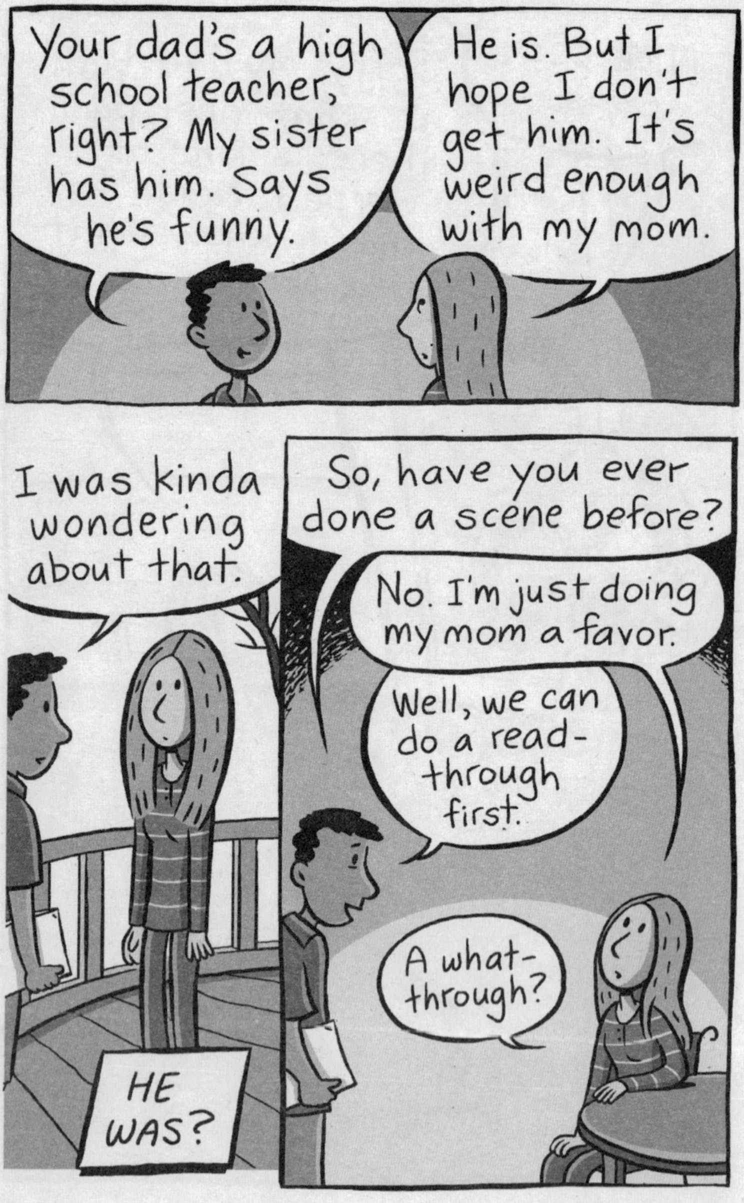
Your dad's a high school teacher, right? My sister has him. Says he's funny.
He is. But I hope I don't get him. It's weird enough with my mom.
I was kinda wondering about that.
HE WAS?
So, have you ever done a scene before?
No. I'm just doing my mom a favor.
Well, we can do a read-through first.
A what-through?

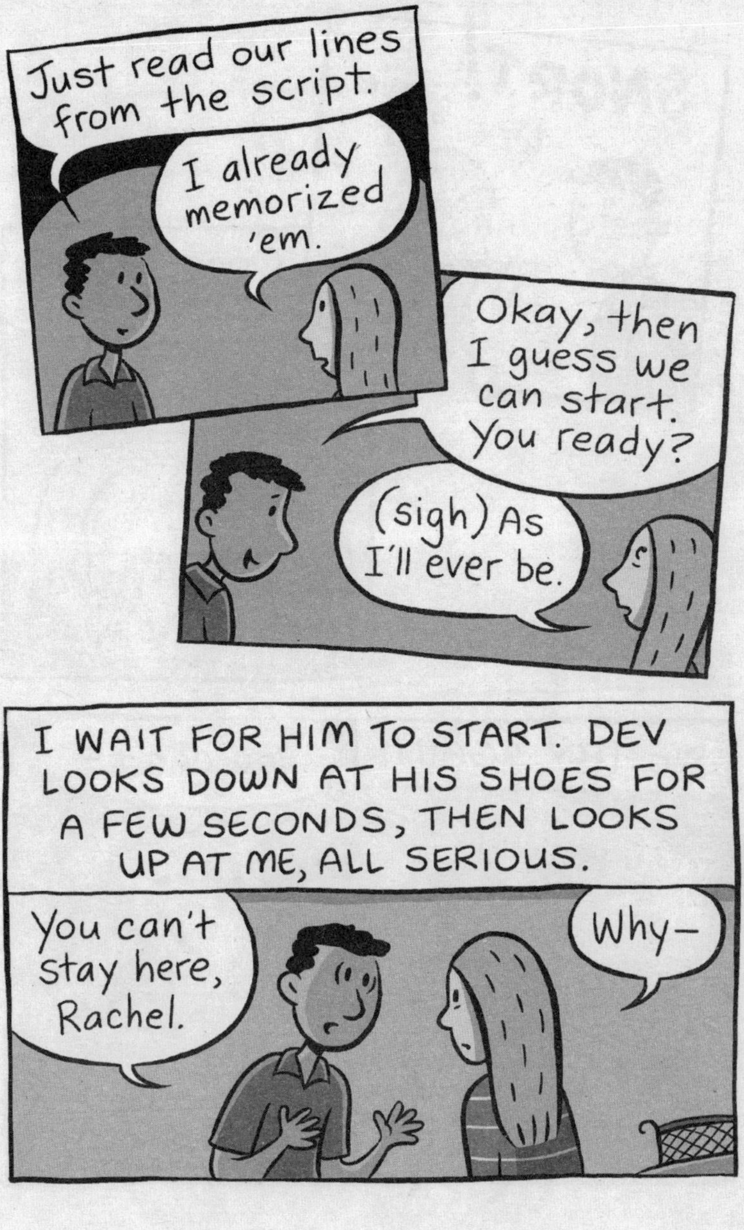
Just read our lines from the script.
I already memorized 'em.
Okay, then I guess we can start. You ready?
(sigh) As I'll ever be.
I WAIT FOR HIM TO START. DEV LOOKS DOWN AT HIS SHOES FOR A FEW SECONDS, THEN LOOKS UP AT ME, ALL SERIOUS.
You can't stay here, Rachel.
Why–

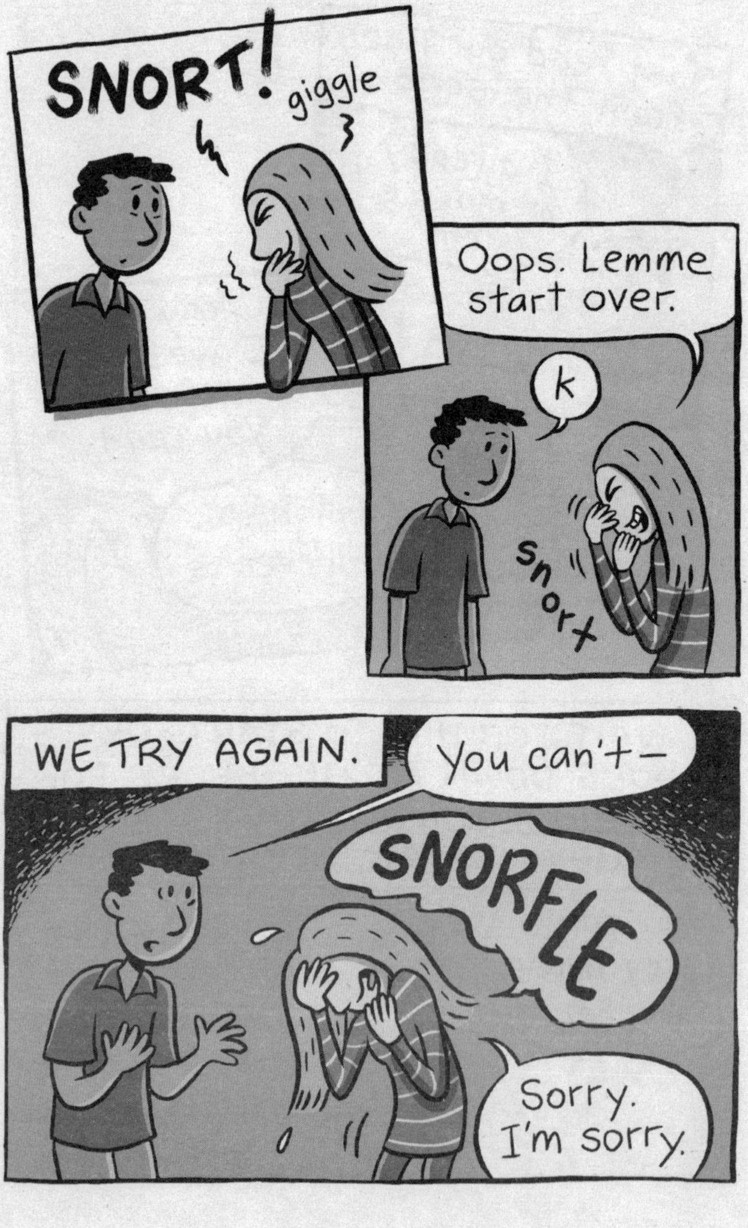
SNORT!
giggle
Oops. Lemme start over.
k
snort
WE TRY AGAIN.
You can't—
SNORFLE
Sorry. I'm sorry.

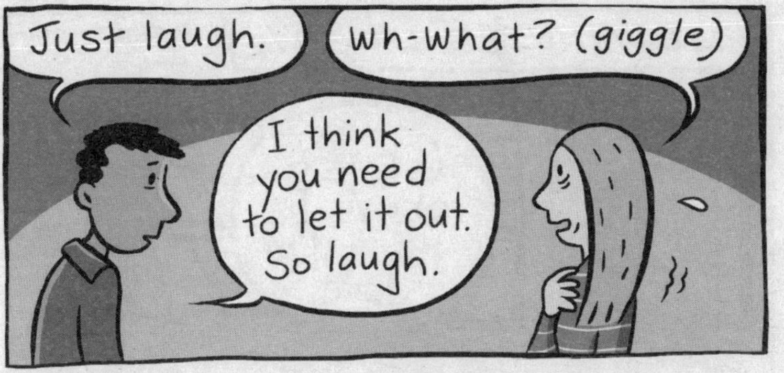
Just laugh.
Wh-What? (giggle)
I think you need to let it out. So laugh.

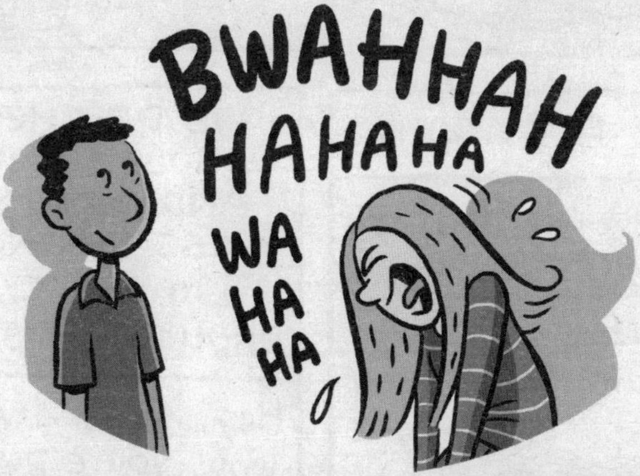
BWAHHAH
HAHAHA
WA
HA
HA

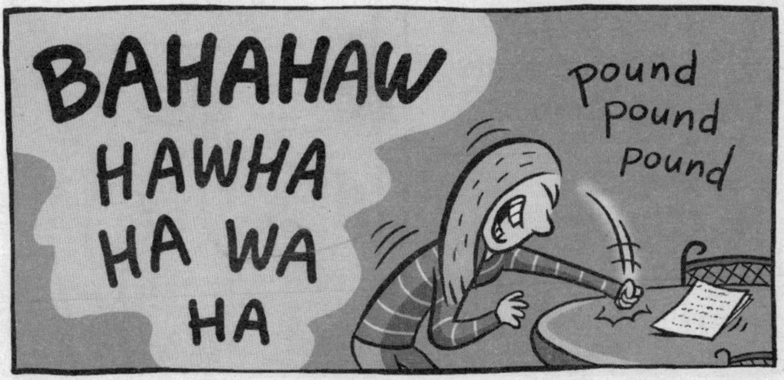
BAHAHAW
HAWHA
HA WA
HA
pound
pound
pound

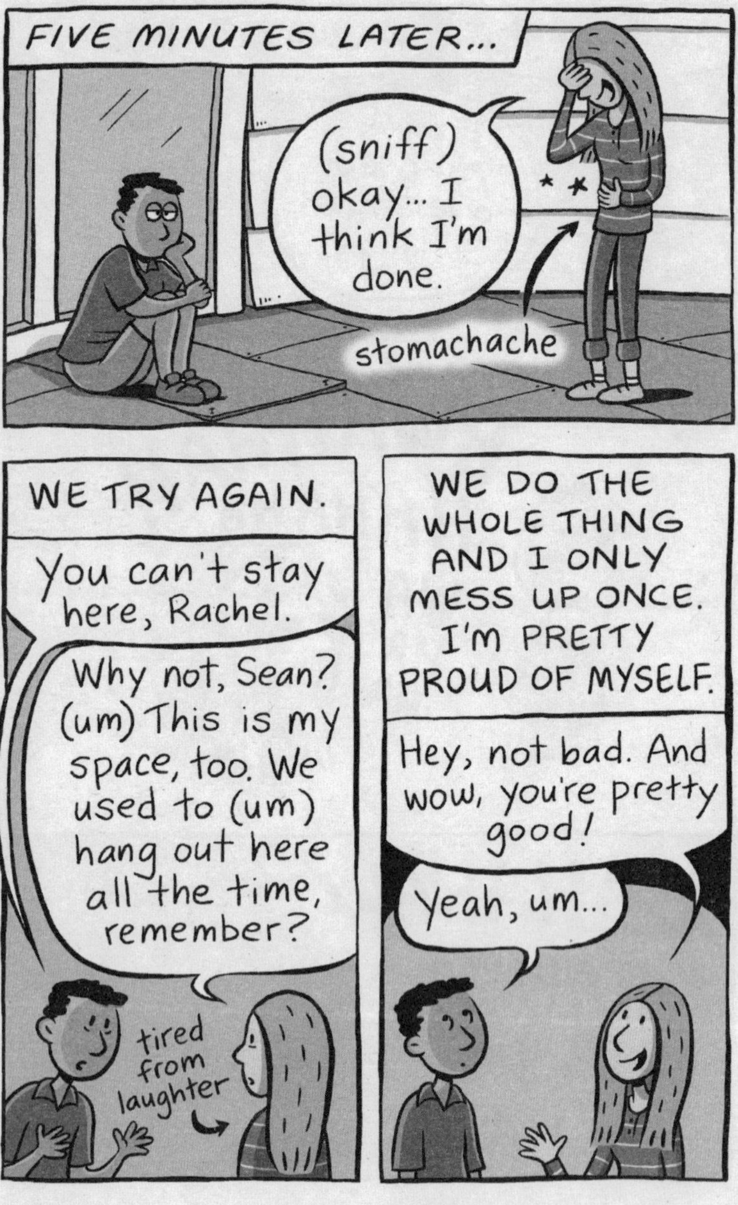
FIVE MINUTES LATER...
(sniff) okay... I think I'm done.
stomachache
WE TRY AGAIN.
You can't stay here, Rachel.
Why not, Sean? (um) This is my space, too. We used to (um) hang out here all the time, remember?
tired from laughter
WE DO THE WHOLE THING AND I ONLY MESS UP ONCE. I'M PRETTY PROUD OF MYSELF.
Hey, not bad. And wow, you're pretty good!
Yeah, um...

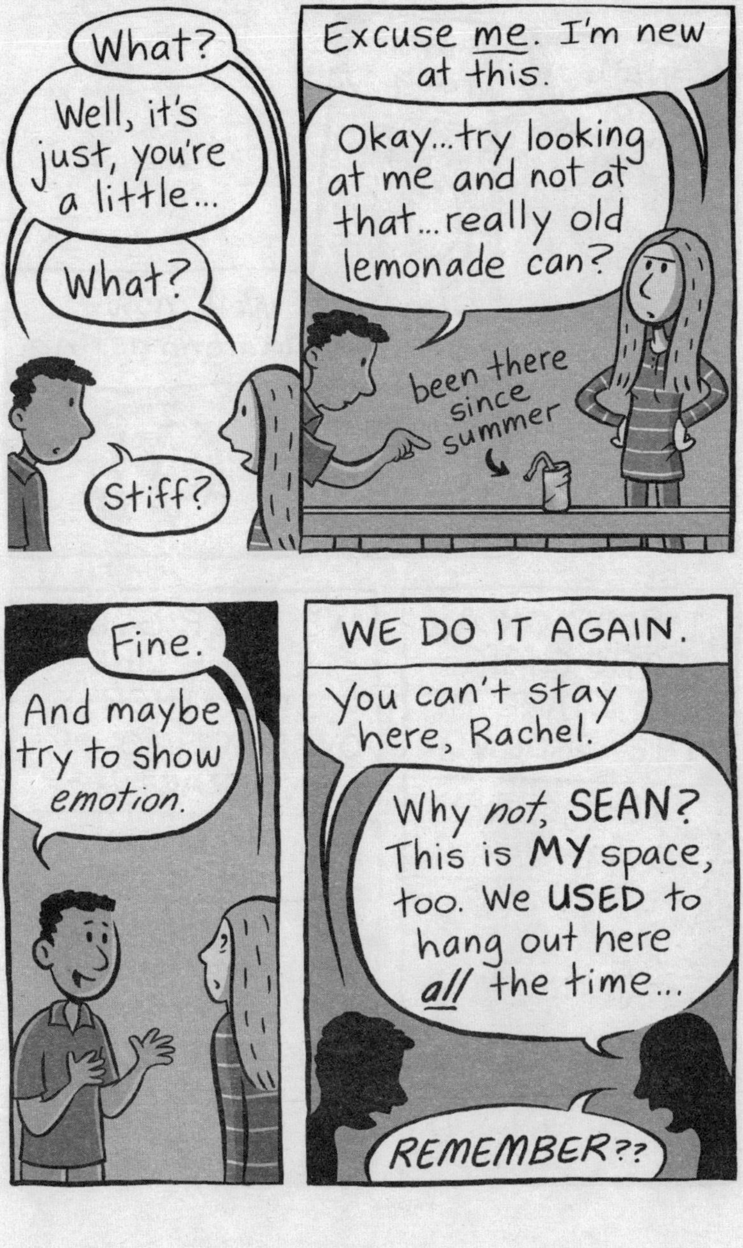
What?
Well, it's just, you're a little...
What?
Stiff?
Excuse me. I'm new at this.
Okay...try looking at me and not at that...really old lemonade can?
been there since summer
Fine.
And maybe try to show *emotion*.
WE DO IT AGAIN.
You can't stay here, Rachel.
Why *not*, SEAN? This is MY space, too. We USED to hang out here *all* the time...
REMEMBER??

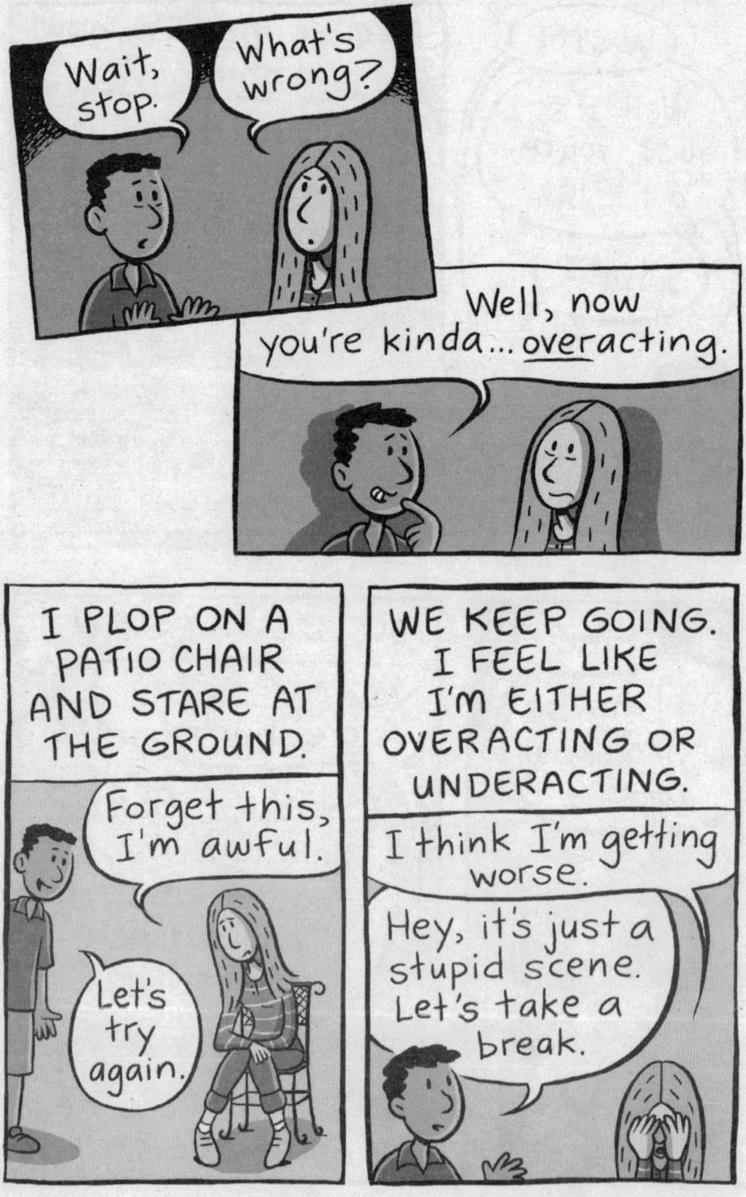

Wait, stop.
What's wrong?
Well, now you're kinda... overacting.
I PLOP ON A PATIO CHAIR AND STARE AT THE GROUND.
Forget this, I'm awful.
Let's try again.
WE KEEP GOING. I FEEL LIKE I'M EITHER OVERACTING OR UNDERACTING.
I think I'm getting worse.
Hey, it's just a stupid scene. Let's take a break.

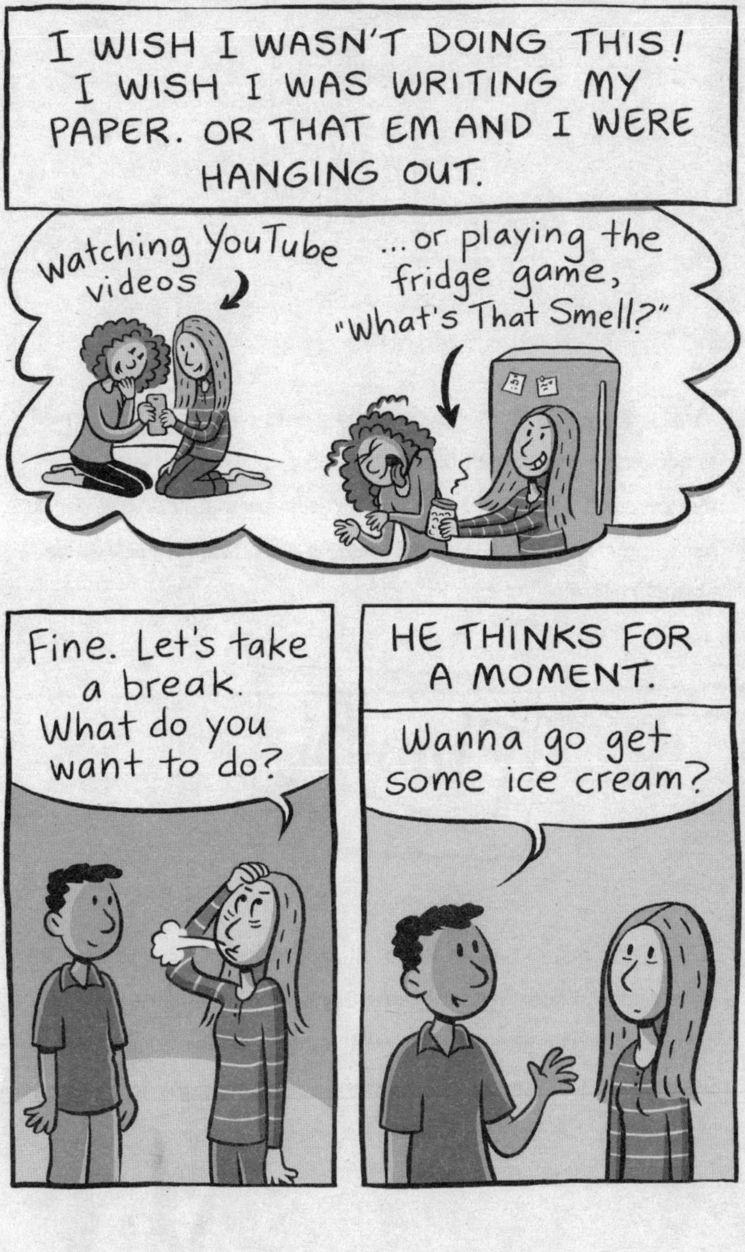
I WISH I WASN'T DOING THIS! I WISH I WAS WRITING MY PAPER. OR THAT EM AND I WERE HANGING OUT.
watching YouTube videos
...or playing the fridge game, "What's That Smell?"
Fine. Let's take a break. What do you want to do?
HE THINKS FOR A MOMENT.
Wanna go get some ice cream?

IZZY

Mrs. D gives us a quick welcome and passes out some photocopied programs so we can see the order. There are twenty-two performances, and I'm number five. I already knew this. I can sneak back home by eight. Ash and I made a plan. Two, in fact, in case plan A fails.

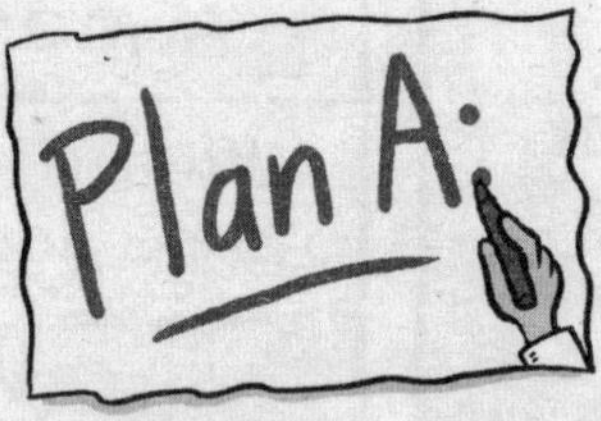
Plan A:

Ash will beg our mom to go out and get ice cream while Ash stays home to keep "me" company. Taystee's is in walking distance, and Mom never likes to walk outside alone in the evenings. So she'd take Dani. They do this a lot in the summer, and today **feels** like summer. While they're gone, I'd sneak back in.

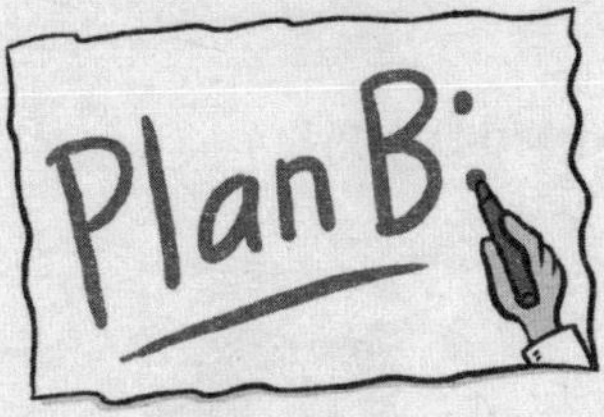
Plan B:

If they don't go for it, I'll hide in the courtyard toolshed until they're asleep. The shed's always open, even though the custodian is supposed to keep it locked. We used to play hide-and-seek in there or spy on the neighbors.

'Course, I could be in there for a while. . . .

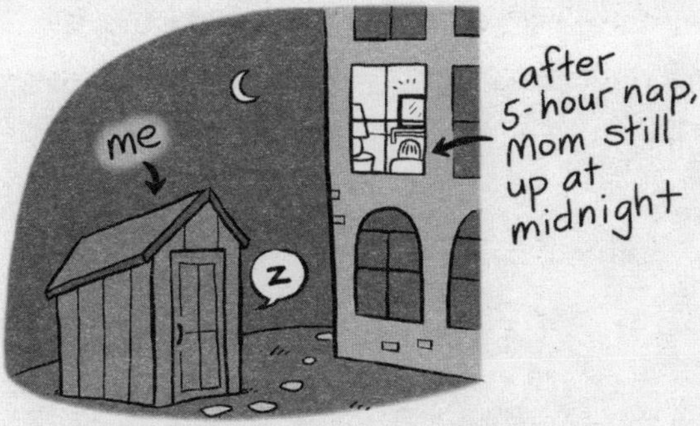
me
Z
after 5-hour nap, Mom still up at midnight

Mrs. D's amplified voice startles me out of my thoughts.

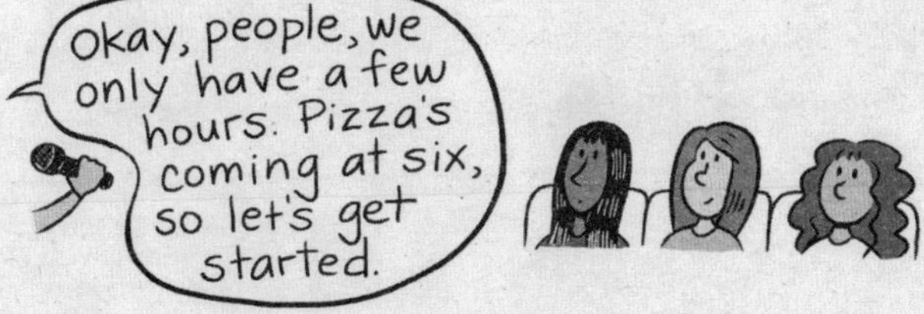
Okay, people, we only have a few hours. Pizza's coming at six, so let's get started.

My heart starts pounding again.

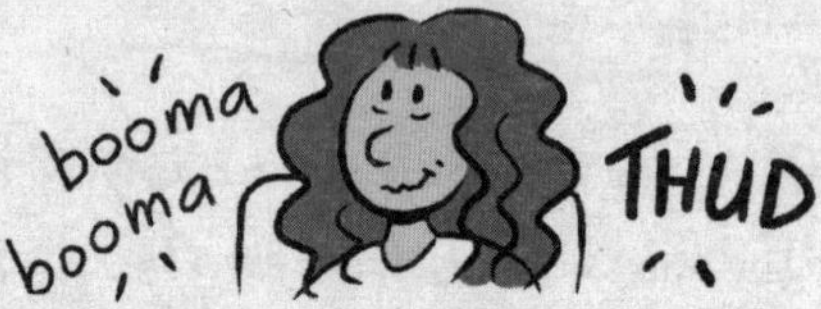
booma
booma
THUD

This time, it's from excitement.

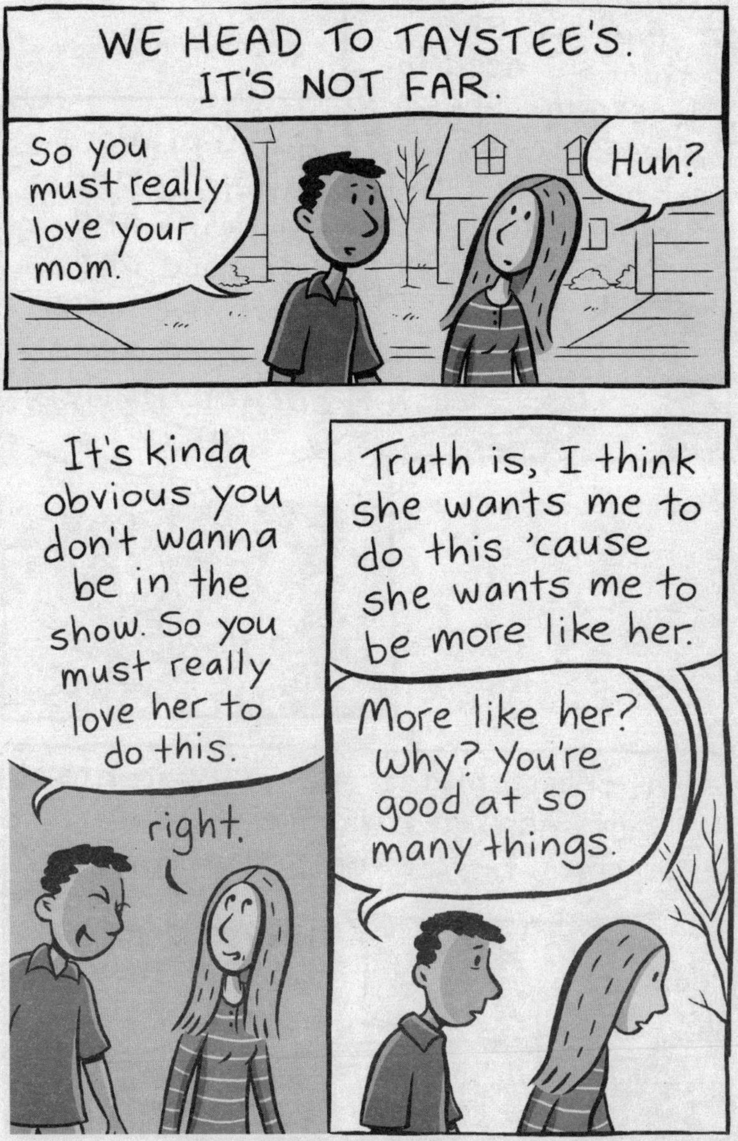
WE HEAD TO TAYSTEE'S. IT'S NOT FAR.
So you must really love your mom.
Huh?
It's kinda obvious you don't wanna be in the show. So you must really love her to do this.
right.
Truth is, I think she wants me to do this 'cause she wants me to be more like her.
More like her? Why? You're good at so many things.

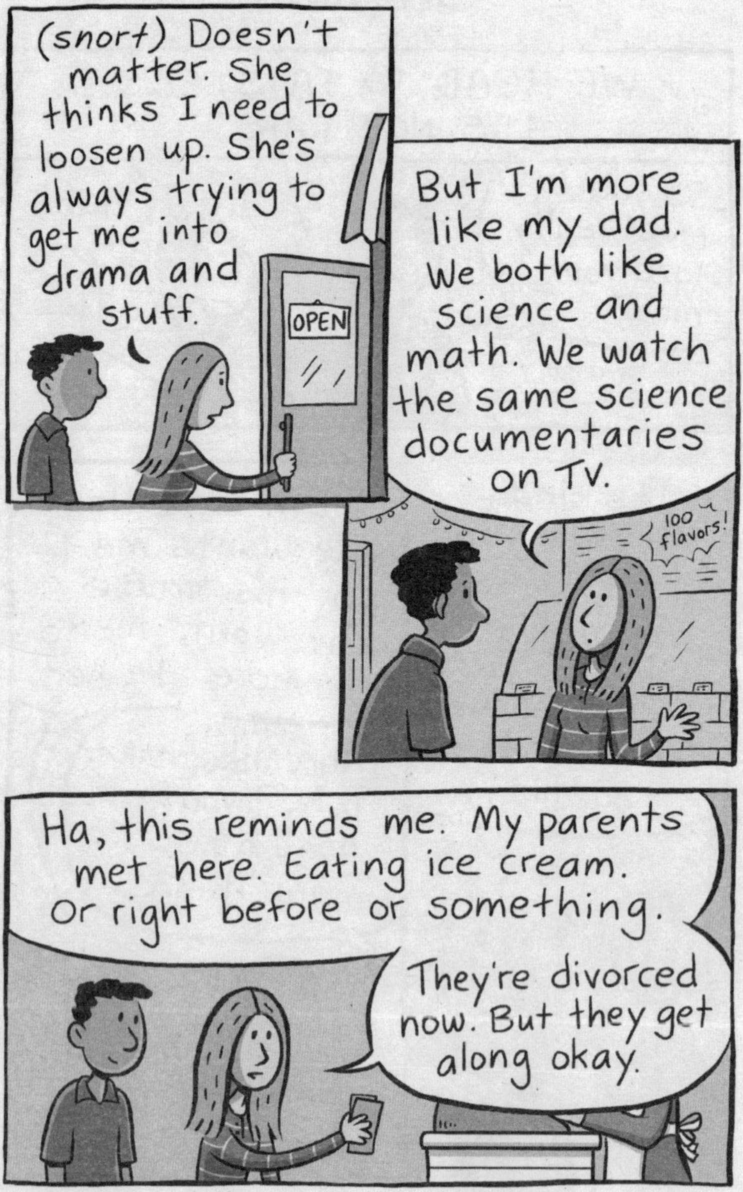
(snort) Doesn't matter. She thinks I need to loosen up. She's always trying to get me into drama and stuff.
OPEN
But I'm more like my dad. We both like science and math. We watch the same science documentaries on TV.
100 flavors!
Ha, this reminds me. My parents met here. Eating ice cream. Or right before or something.
They're divorced now. But they get along okay.

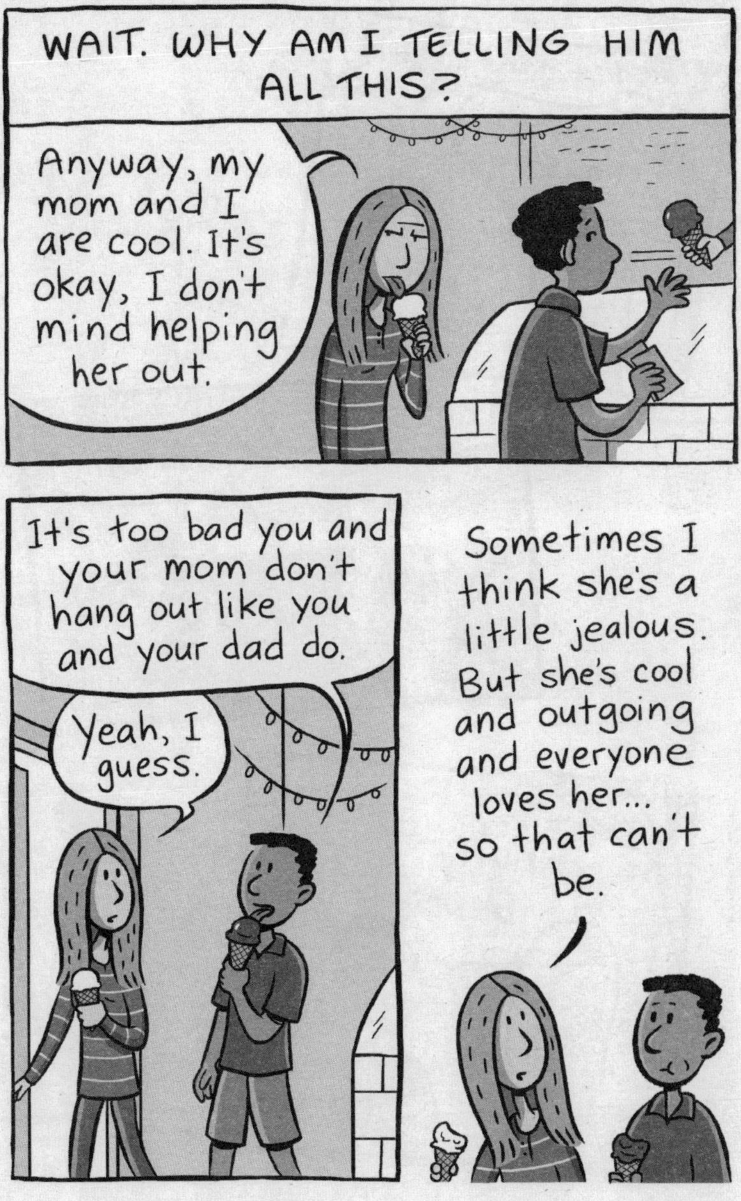

WAIT. WHY AM I TELLING HIM ALL THIS?
Anyway, my mom and I are cool. It's okay, I don't mind helping her out.
It's too bad you and your mom don't hang out like you and your dad do.
Yeah, I guess.
Sometimes I think she's a little jealous. But she's cool and outgoing and everyone loves her... so that can't be.

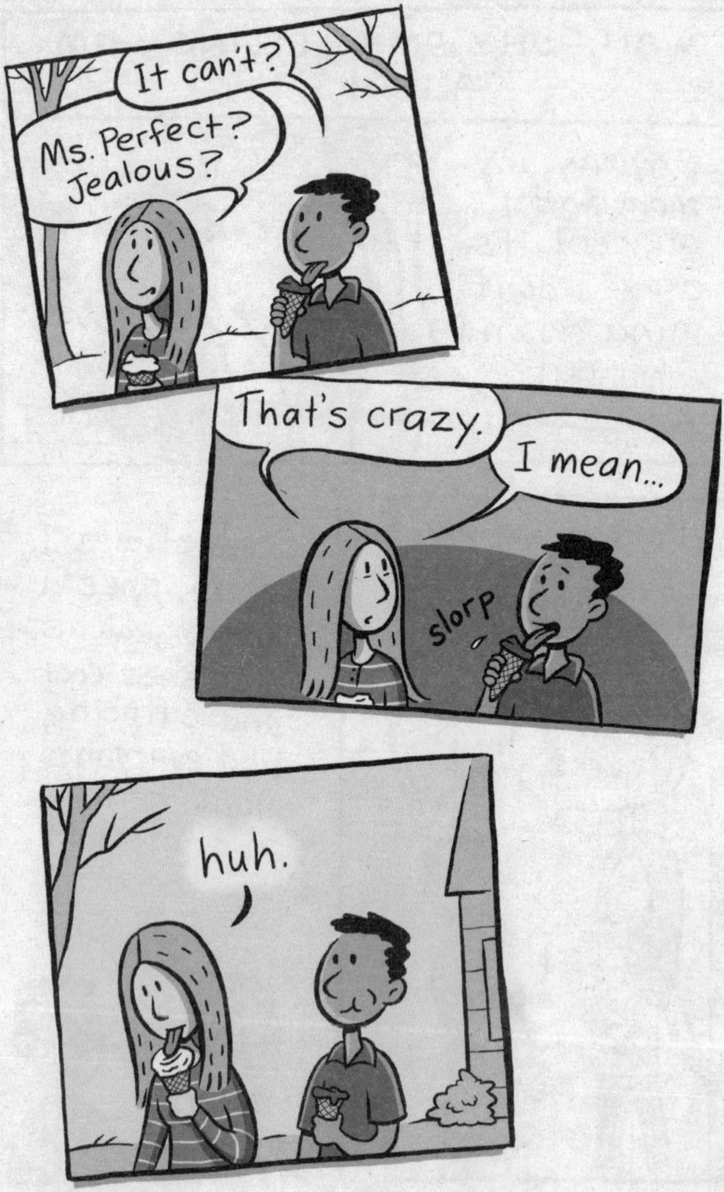
It can't?
Ms. Perfect? Jealous?
That's crazy.
I mean...
slorp
huh.

IZZY

Rehearsal. Mine goes pretty well. Gotta admit, I had a little stage fright at first—or **getting-caught** fright—but once I started the monologue, all my butterflies went away.

The only thing that went wrong was when I knocked over one of my props. But I caught it in time and didn't flub my lines.

I decide to take the prop to the art room while everyone else is rehearsing. I want to add an extra support on the bottom. There are usually some leftover wood blocks or foam core lying around.

One my way out, I hear a trumpet blast a way-out-of-tune note. They should really make a rule about not letting sixth graders do solos.

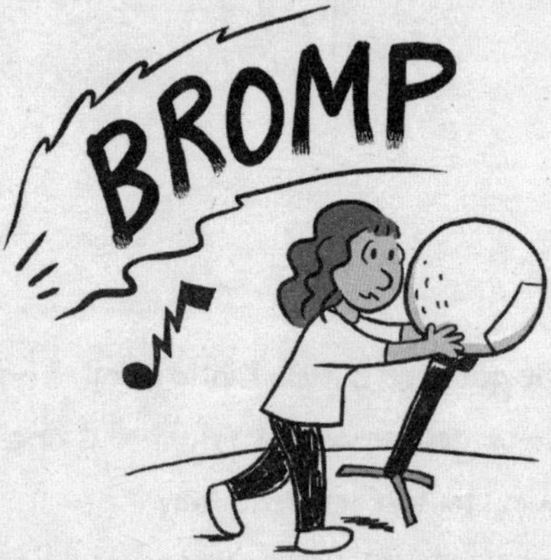
BROMP

I was a little worried everyone would think my skit was dumb, but I got a lot of laughs. Maybe Miss Gelb was right. . . . Maybe I do have a knack for this.

As I round the corner, I accidentally knock into someone getting a drink at the fountain.

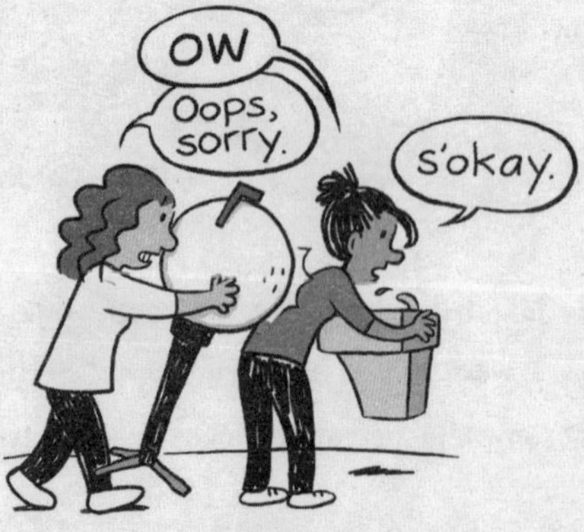
OW
Oops, sorry.
S'okay.

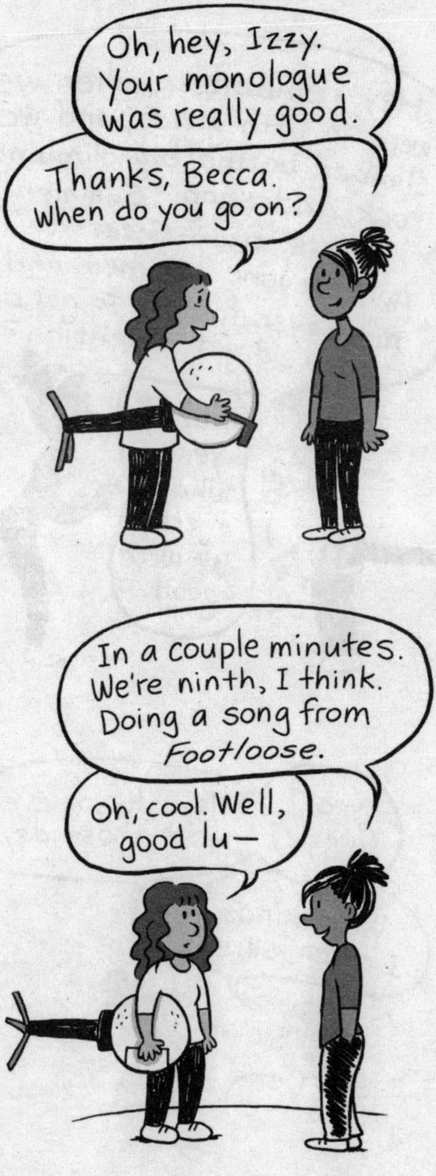
Oh, hey, Izzy. Your monologue was really good.
Thanks, Becca. When do you go on?
In a couple minutes. We're ninth, I think. Doing a song from *Footloose*.
Oh, cool. Well, good lu—

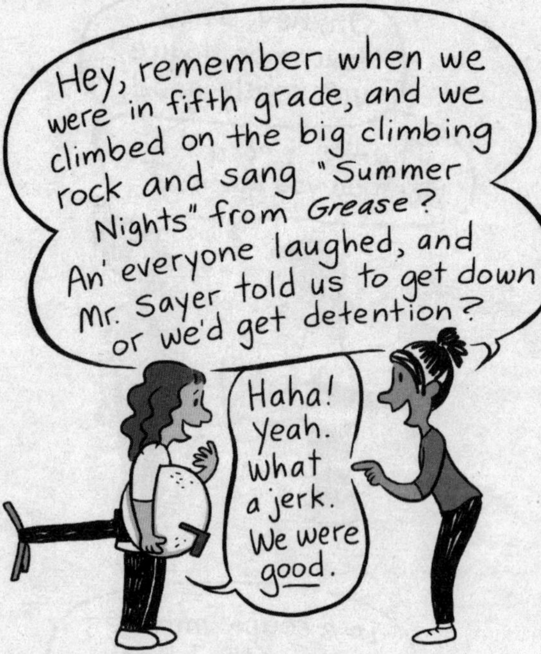
Hey, remember when we were in fifth grade, and we climbed on the big climbing rock and sang "Summer Nights" from *Grease*? An' everyone laughed, and Mr. Sayer told us to get down or we'd get detention?
Haha! Yeah. What a jerk. We were good.

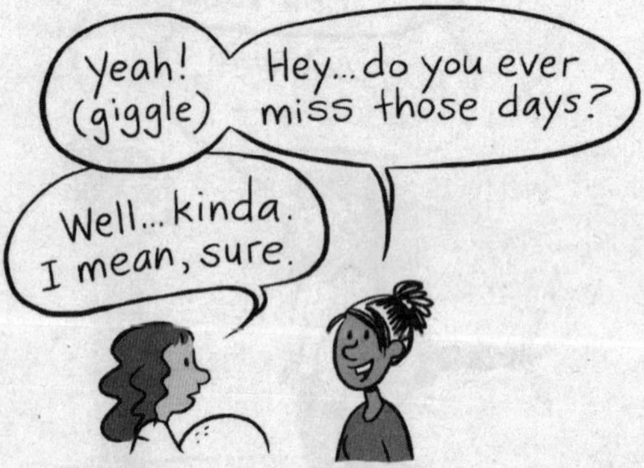
Yeah! (giggle)
Hey... do you ever miss those days?
Well... kinda. I mean, sure.

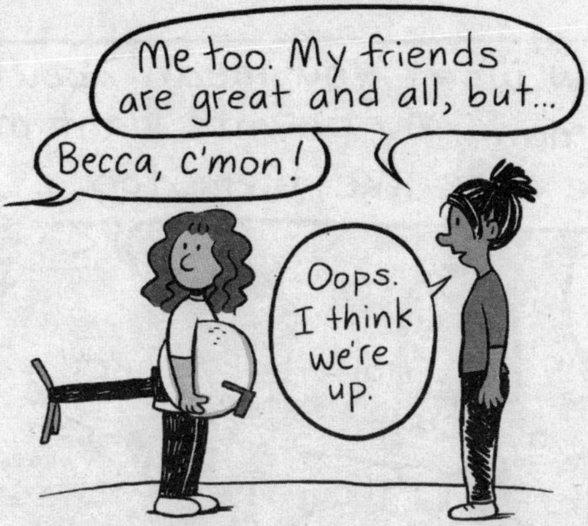
Me too. My friends are great and all, but...
Becca, c'mon!
Oops. I think we're up.

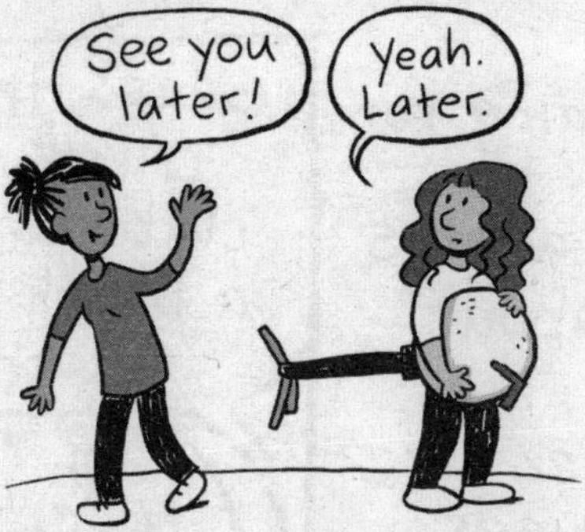
See you later!
Yeah. Later.

I make my way down the hall and down the stairs to the art room (which I smell long before I get there). I'm kinda shocked. I mean, I've missed Becca, like, a lot. I miss our friendship, our stupid pranks, our trips to the mall, and Taystee's. . . .

But I never thought she missed that stuff, too.

Brianna

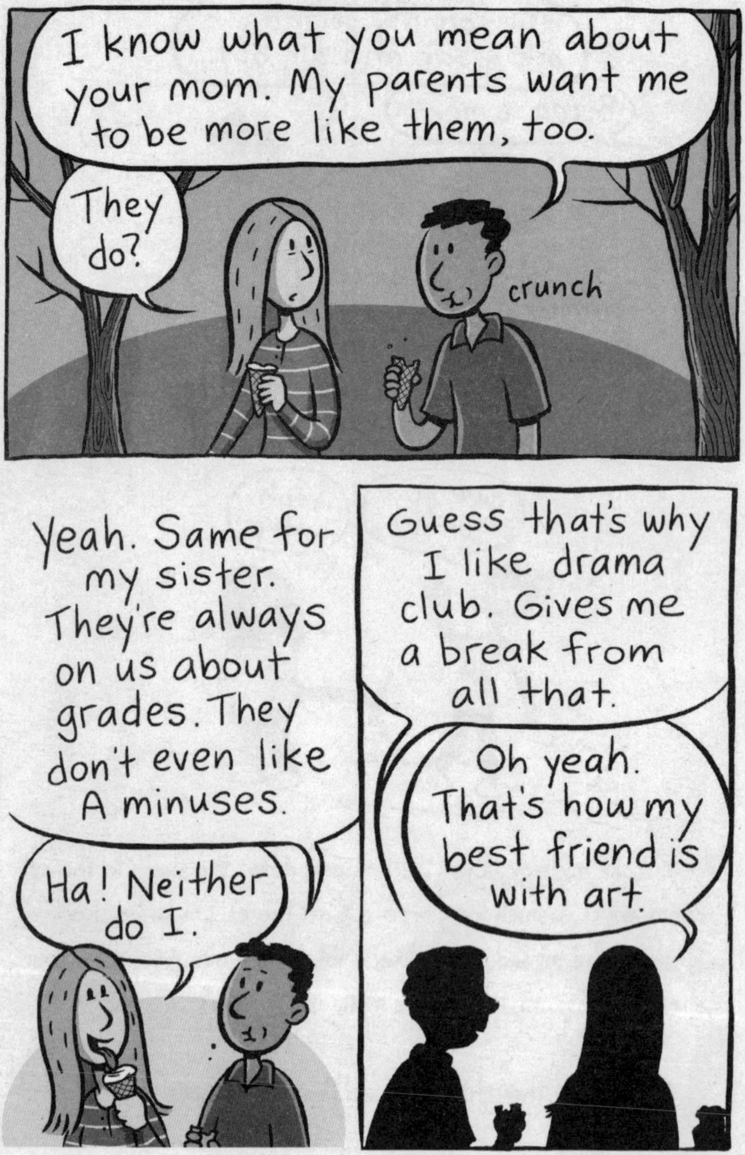
I know what you mean about your mom. My parents want me to be more like them, too.
They do?
crunch
Yeah. Same for my sister. They're always on us about grades. They don't even like A minuses.
Ha! Neither do I.
Guess that's why I like drama club. Gives me a break from all that.
Oh yeah. That's how my best friend is with art.

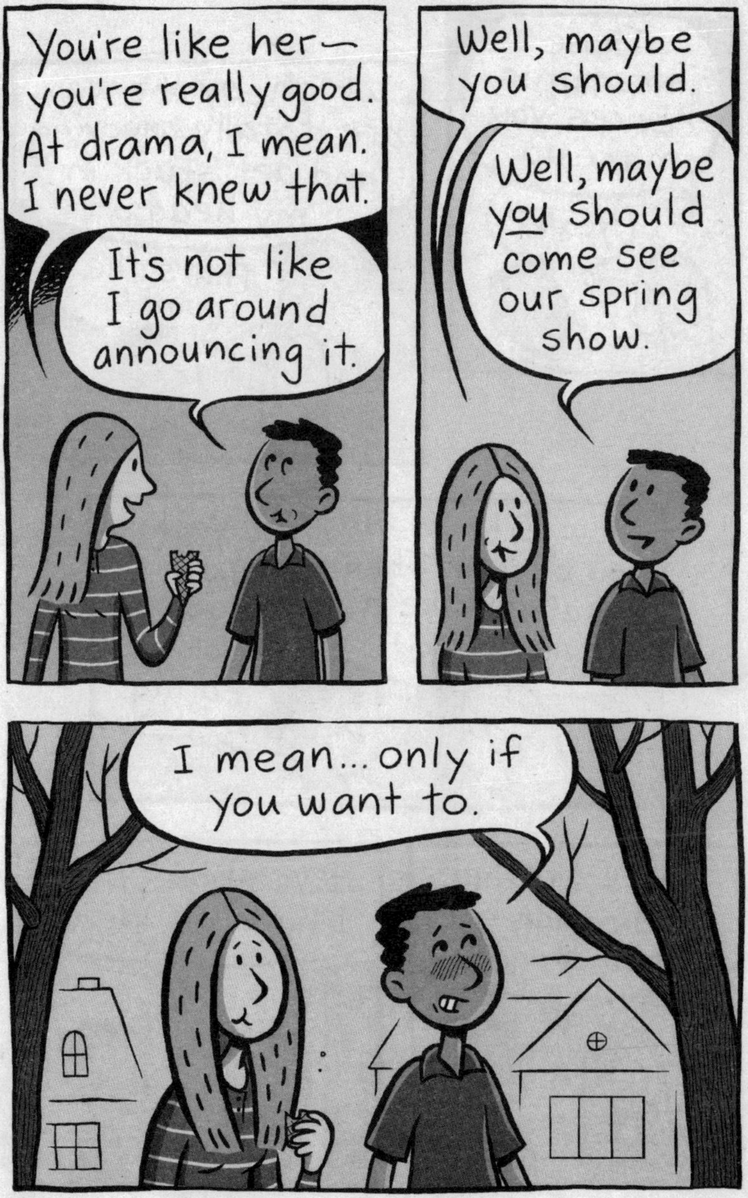
You're like her— you're really good. At drama, I mean. I never knew that.
It's not like I go around announcing it.
Well, maybe you should.
Well, maybe you should come see our spring show.
I mean... only if you want to.

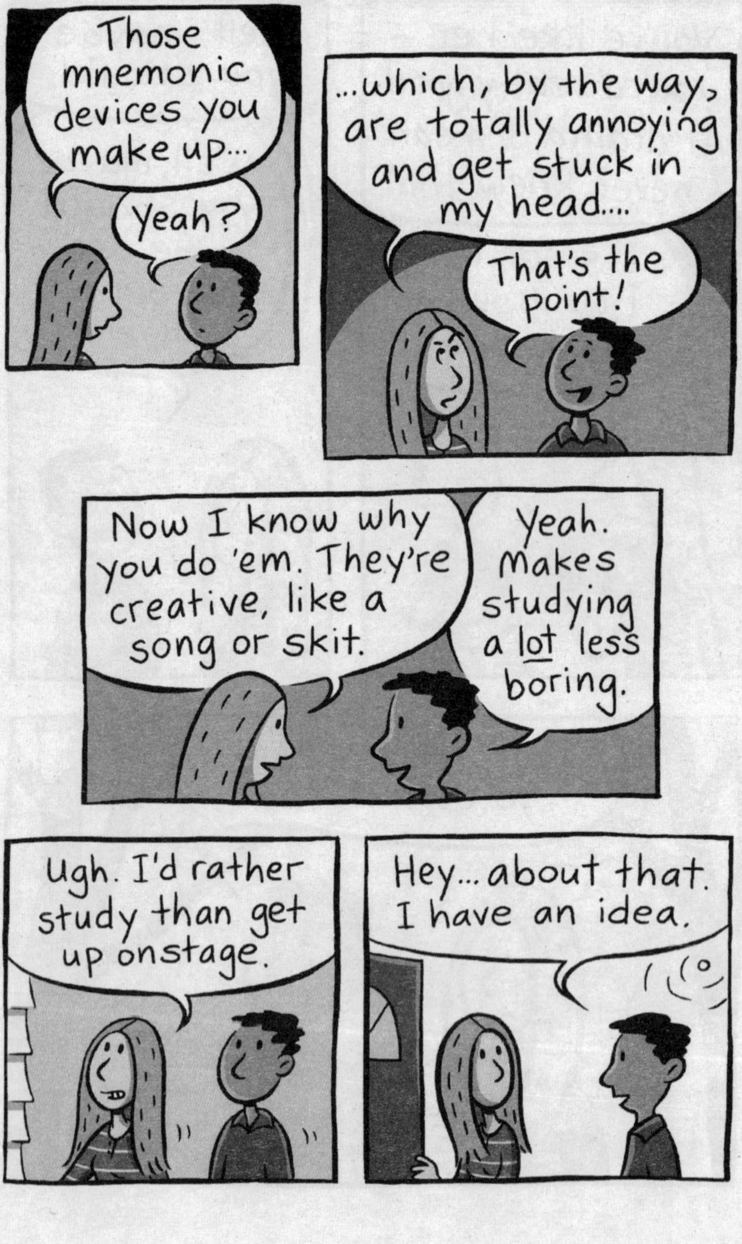
Those mnemonic devices you make up...
Yeah?
...which, by the way, are totally annoying and get stuck in my head....
That's the point!
Now I know why you do 'em. They're creative, like a song or skit.
Yeah. Makes studying a lot less boring.
Ugh. I'd rather study than get up onstage.
Hey... about that. I have an idea.

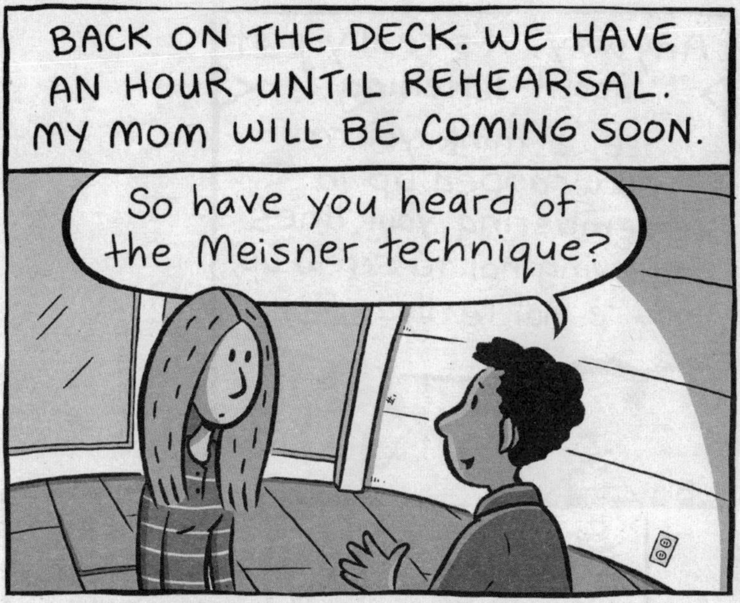
BACK ON THE DECK. WE HAVE AN HOUR UNTIL REHEARSAL. MY MOM WILL BE COMING SOON.
So have you heard of the Meisner technique?

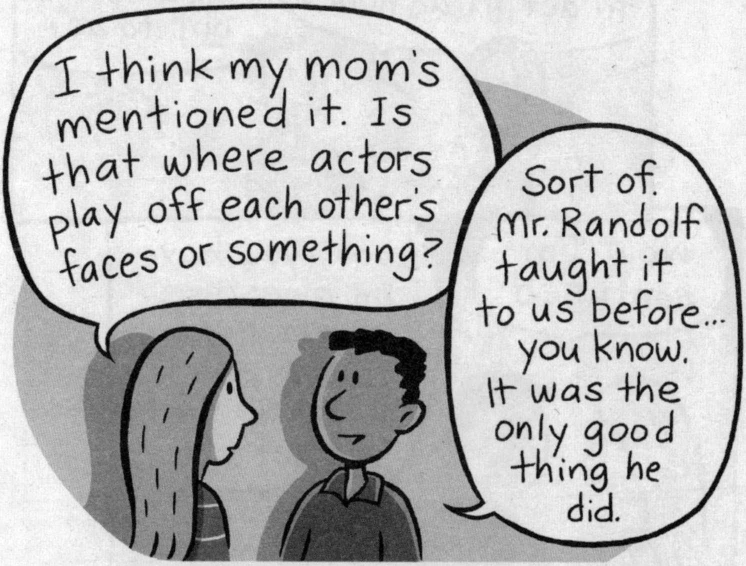
I think my mom's mentioned it. Is that where actors play off each other's faces or something?
Sort of. Mr. Randolf taught it to us before... you know. It was the only good thing he did.

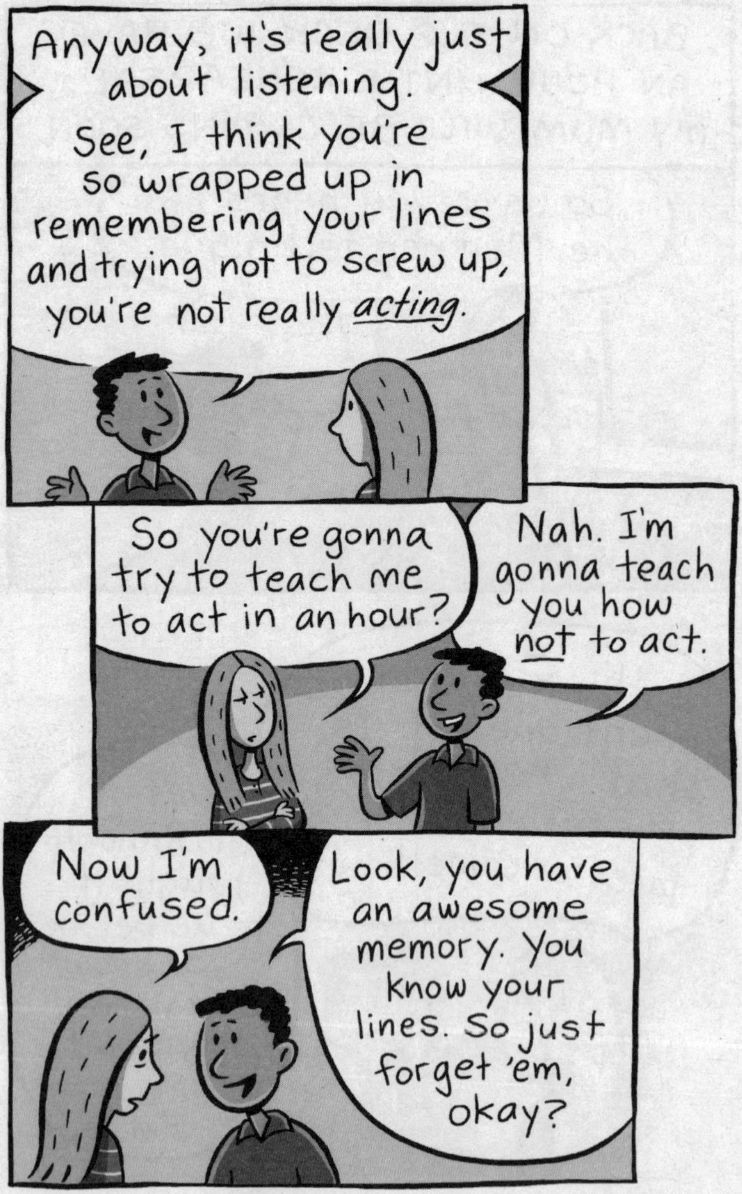
Anyway, it's really just about listening.
See, I think you're so wrapped up in remembering your lines and trying not to screw up, you're not really *acting*.
So you're gonna try to teach me to act in an hour?
Nah. I'm gonna teach you how *not* to act.
Now I'm confused.
Look, you have an awesome memory. You know your lines. So just forget 'em, okay?

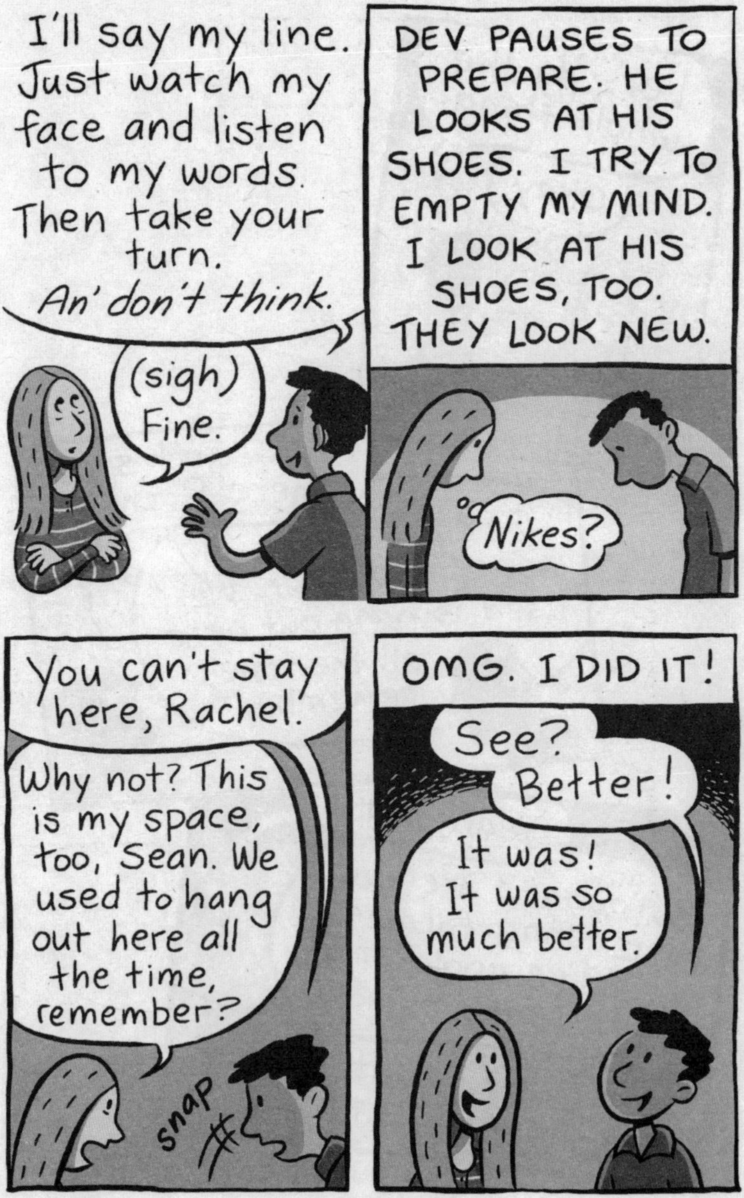
I'll say my line. Just watch my face and listen to my words. Then take your turn. An' don't think.
(sigh) Fine.
DEV. PAUSES TO PREPARE. HE LOOKS AT HIS SHOES. I TRY TO EMPTY MY MIND. I LOOK AT HIS SHOES, TOO. THEY LOOK NEW.
Nikes?
You can't stay here, Rachel.
Why not? This is my space, too, Sean. We used to hang out here all the time, remember?
snap
OMG. I DID IT!
See? Better!
It was! It was so much better.

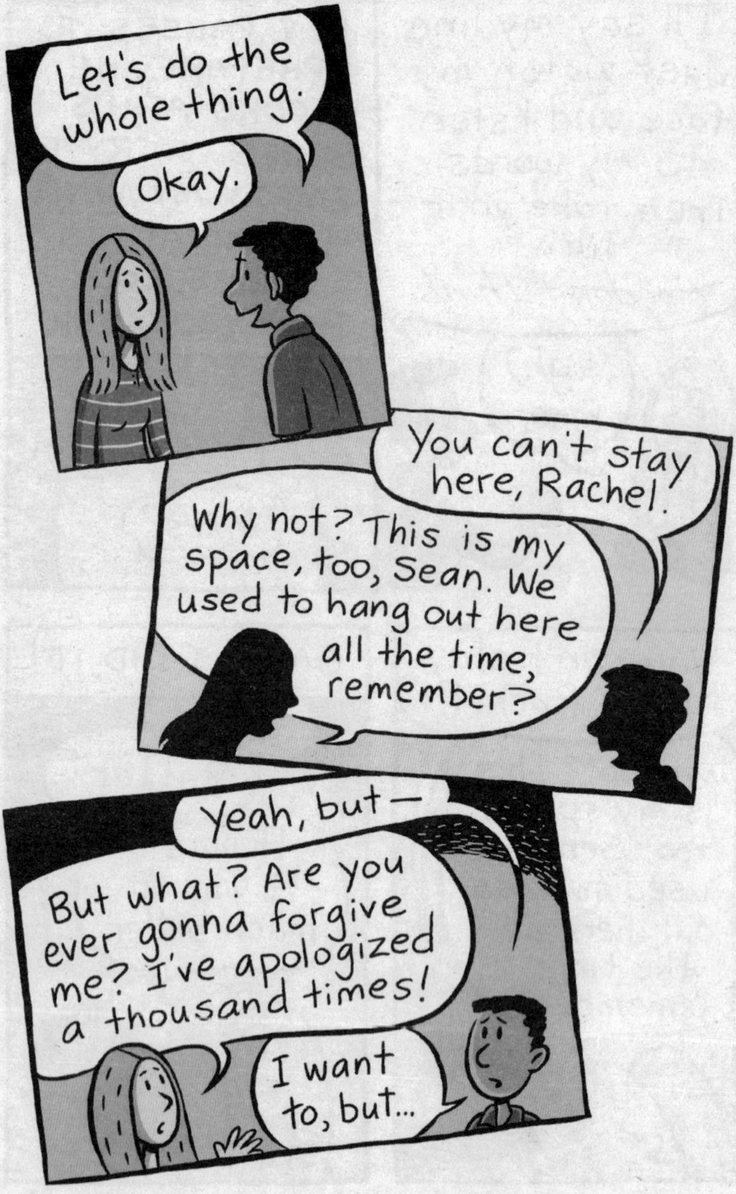
Let's do the whole thing.
Okay.
You can't stay here, Rachel.
Why not? This is my space, too, Sean. We used to hang out here all the time, remember?
Yeah, but—
But what? Are you ever gonna forgive me? I've apologized a thousand times!
I want to, but...

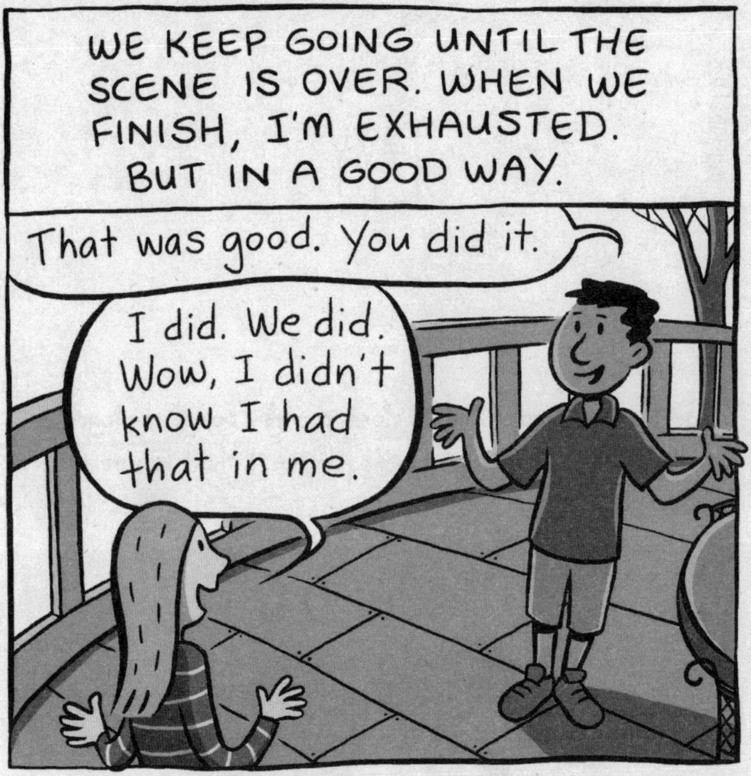
WE KEEP GOING UNTIL THE SCENE IS OVER. WHEN WE FINISH, I'M EXHAUSTED. BUT IN A GOOD WAY.
That was good. You did it.
I did. We did. Wow, I didn't know I had that in me.

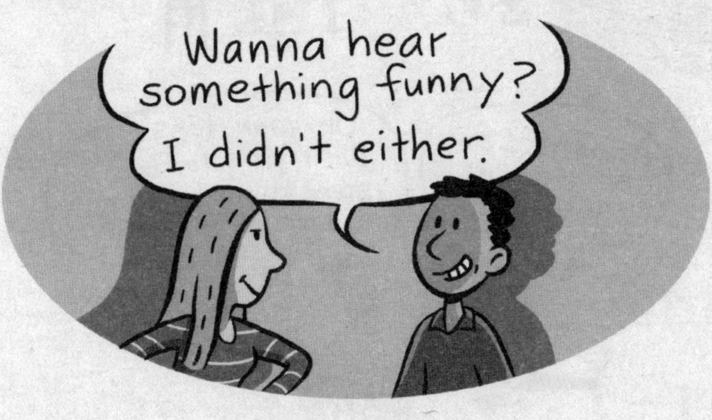
Wanna hear something funny? I didn't either.

IZZY

I get to the art room. I'm not alone. There's a boy gluing together a couple pieces of wood. He looks familiar. I think he's in eighth grade. Kinda cute.

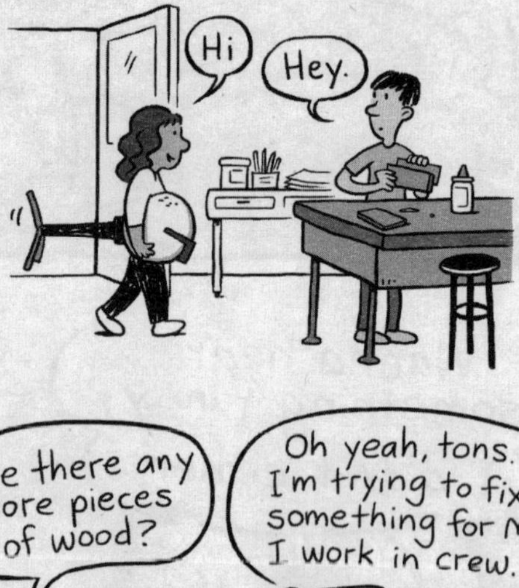
Hi
Hey.

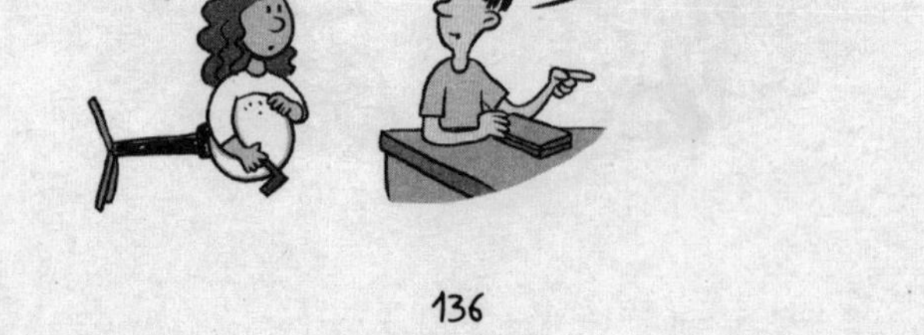
Are there any more pieces of wood?
Oh yeah, tons. I'm trying to fix something for Mrs. D. I work in crew.

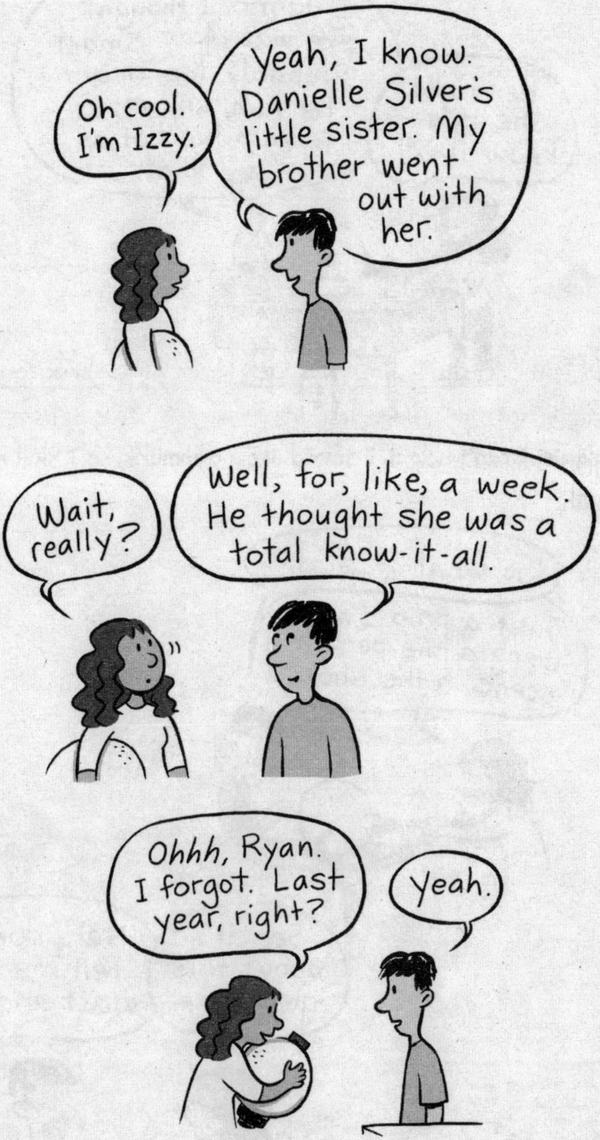
Oh cool. I'm Izzy.
Yeah, I know. Danielle Silver's little sister. My brother went out with her.
Wait, really?
Well, for, like, a week. He thought she was a total know-it-all.
Ohhh, Ryan. I forgot. Last year, right?
Yeah.

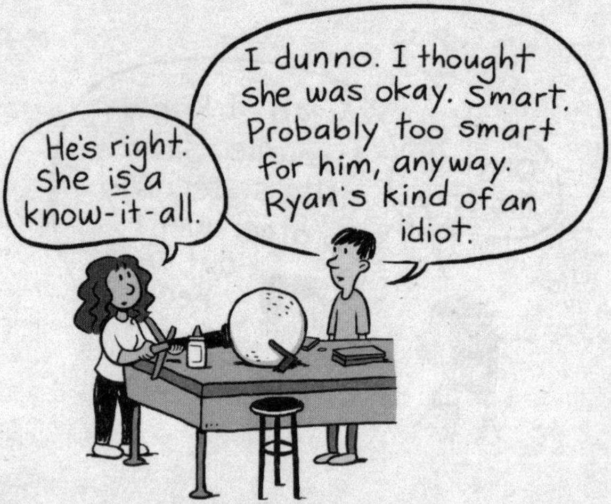
He's right. She is a know-it-all.
I dunno. I thought she was okay. Smart. Probably too smart for him, anyway. Ryan's kind of an idiot.

I giggle. I can't help it. I sound like a chipmunk, so I shut my mouth.

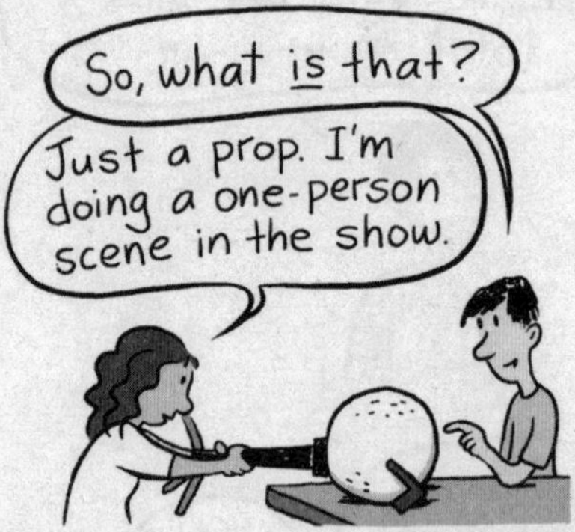
So, what is that?
Just a prop. I'm doing a one-person scene in the show.

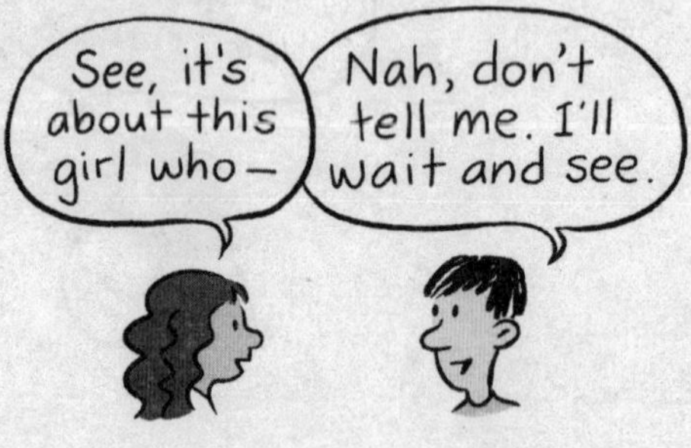
See, it's about this girl who—
Nah, don't tell me. I'll wait and see.

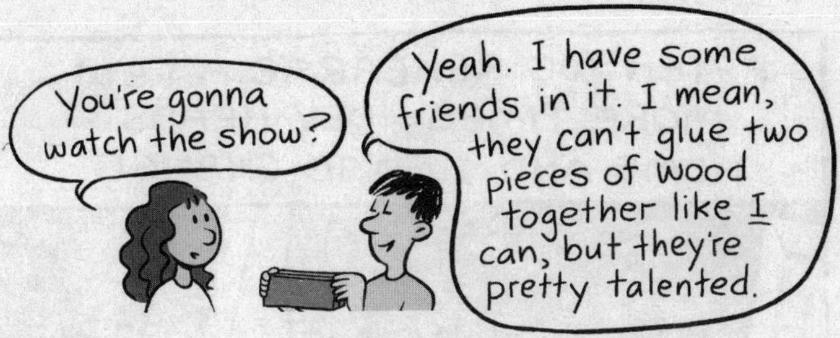
You're gonna watch the show?
Yeah. I have some friends in it. I mean, they can't glue two pieces of wood together like I can, but they're pretty talented.

I laugh. I like this guy.

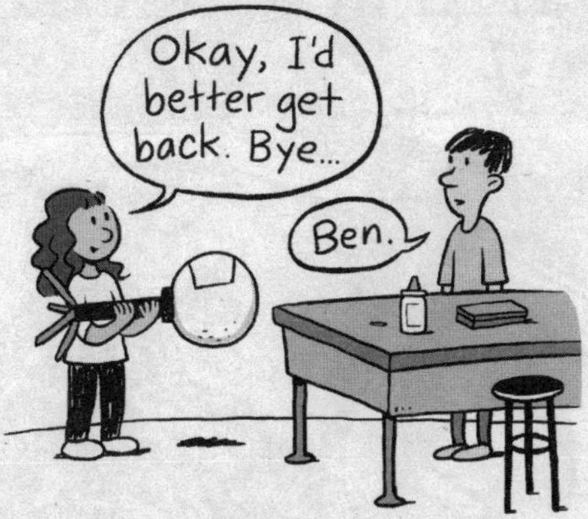
Okay, I'd better get back. Bye...
Ben.

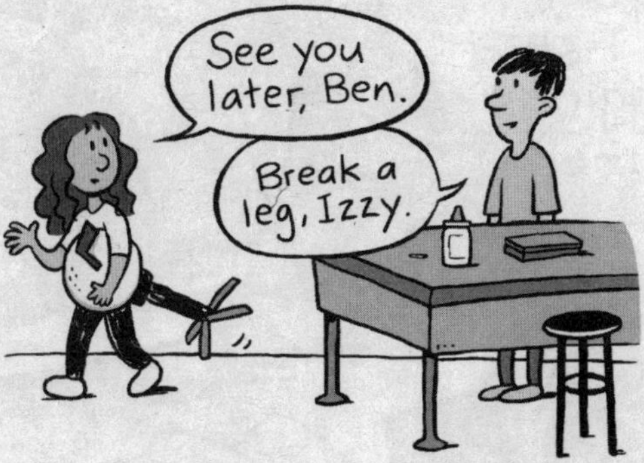
See you later, Ben.
Break a leg, Izzy.

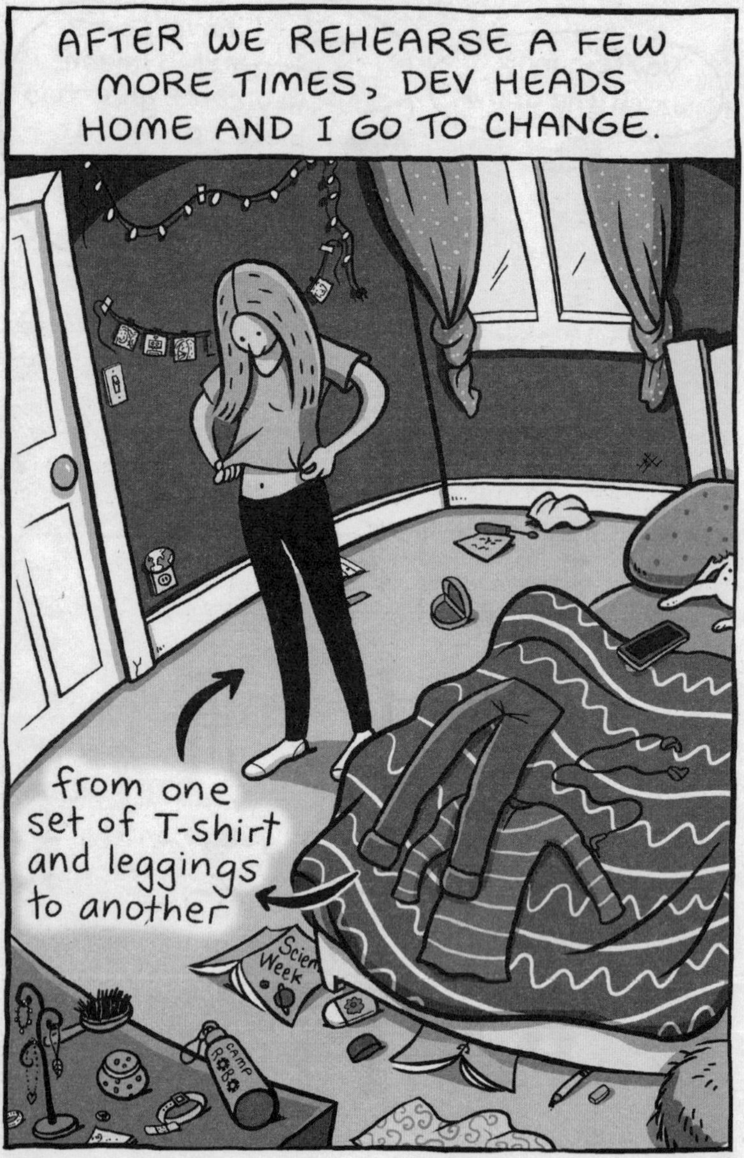
AFTER WE REHEARSE A FEW MORE TIMES, DEV HEADS HOME AND I GO TO CHANGE.
from one set of T-shirt and leggings to another

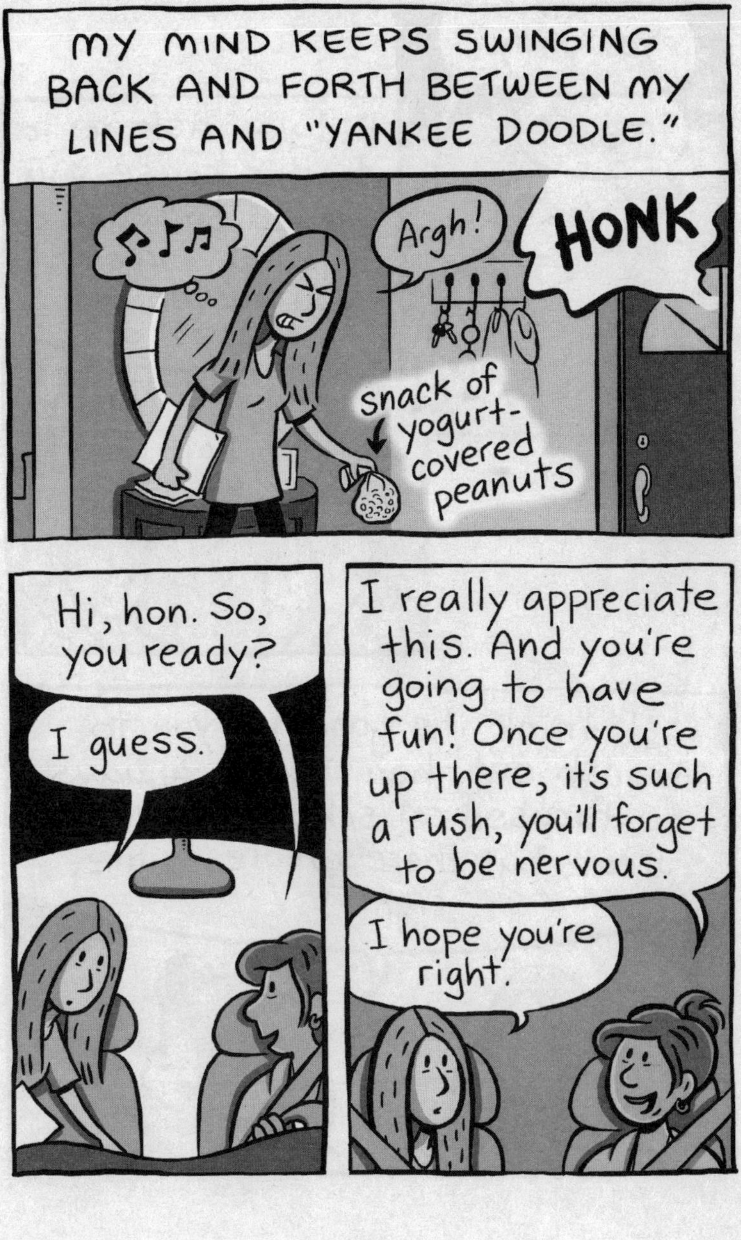
MY MIND KEEPS SWINGING BACK AND FORTH BETWEEN MY LINES AND "YANKEE DOODLE."
Argh!
HONK
snack of yogurt-covered peanuts
Hi, hon. So, you ready?
I guess.
I really appreciate this. And you're going to have fun! Once you're up there, it's such a rush, you'll forget to be nervous.
I hope you're right.

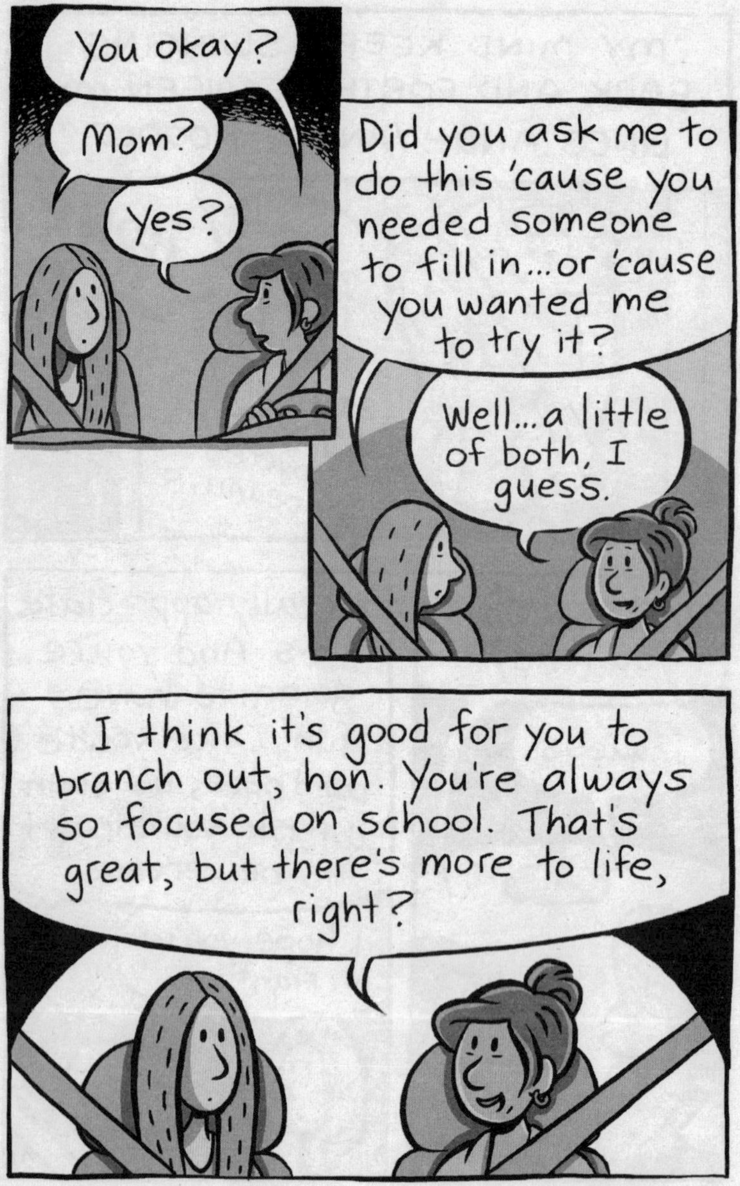
You okay?
Mom?
Yes?
Did you ask me to do this 'cause you needed someone to fill in...or 'cause you wanted me to try it?
Well...a little of both, I guess.
I think it's good for you to branch out, hon. You're always so focused on school. That's great, but there's more to life, right?

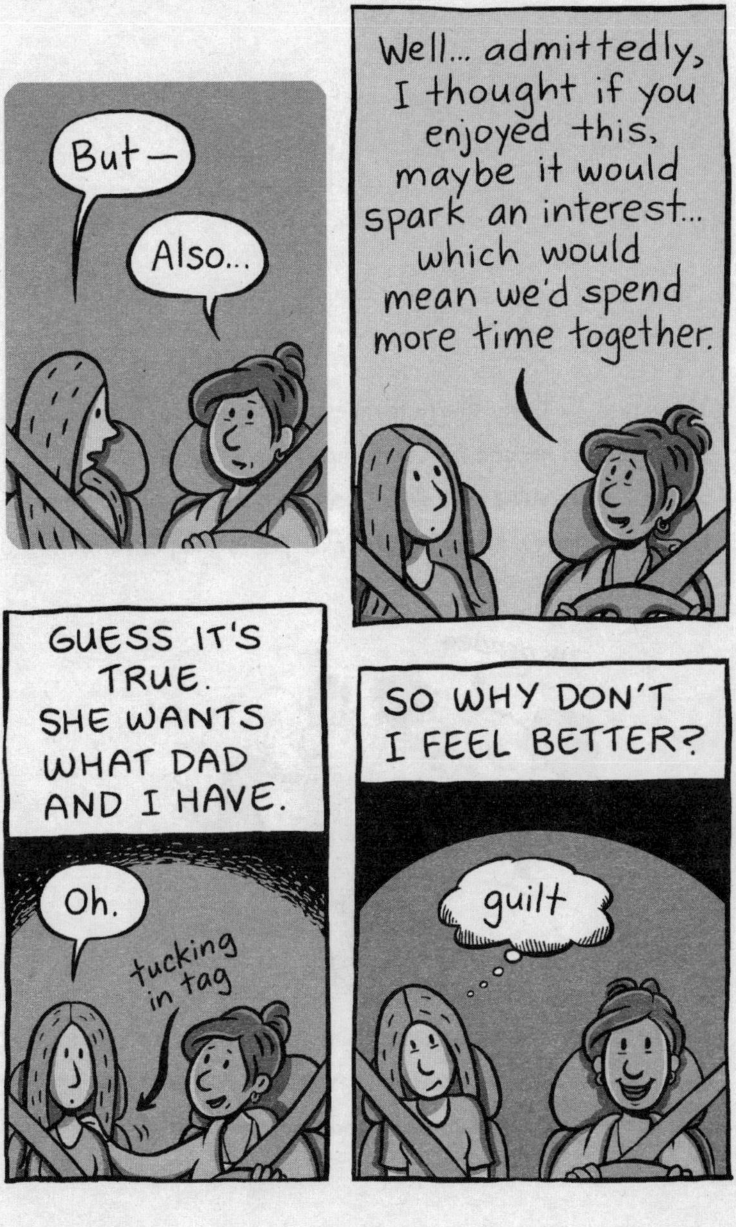
But—
Also...
Well... admittedly, I thought if you enjoyed this, maybe it would spark an interest... which would mean we'd spend more time together.
GUESS IT'S TRUE. SHE WANTS WHAT DAD AND I HAVE.
Oh.
tucking in tag
SO WHY DON'T I FEEL BETTER?
guilt

IZZY

It's almost six thirty (thirty minutes until showtime) and everyone's crowded around the big folding table in the back, grabbing pizza slices like vultures. I almost get knocked down by some band kid's tuba, which I'm sure he toted over just to snag extra room.

size of a 7th grader

I manage to grab a corner slice before I'm tuba-smacked again. I walk over to my drama friends. But then I see Becca heading to the auditorium seats, and I catch up with her instead.

Why not? It's a day of taking chances. Might as well see if she's interested in hanging out again.

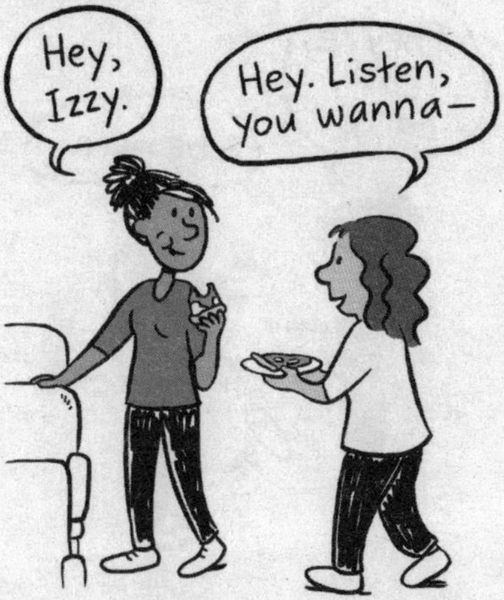
Hey, Izzy.
Hey. Listen, you wanna—

Her eyes suddenly glance at something behind me.

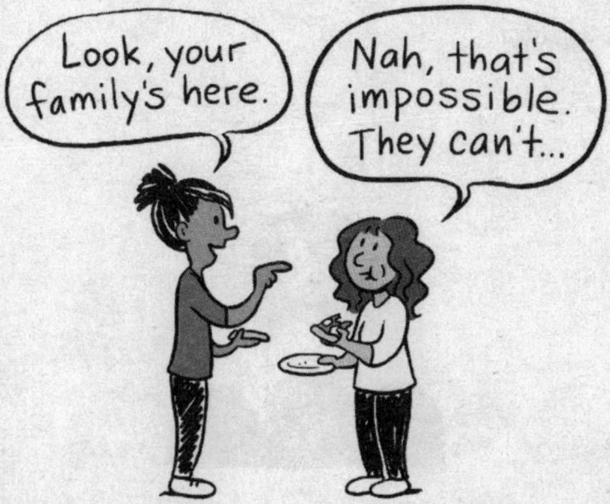
Look, your family's here.
Nah, that's impossible. They can't...

I glance back at the exit doors, and my stomach hits the floor.

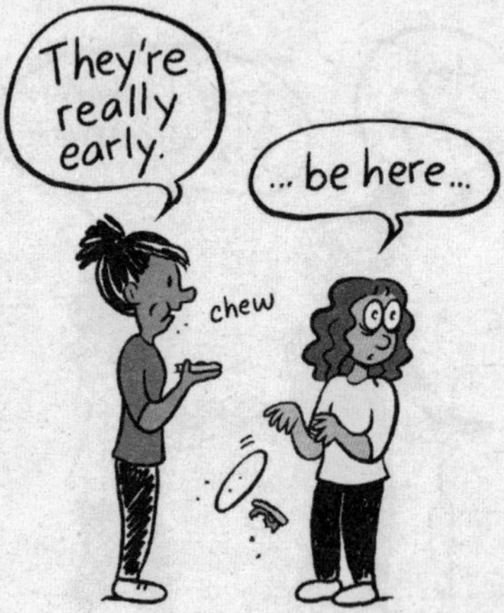
They're really early.
... be here...
chew

She's right.
(gulp)
It's my family!

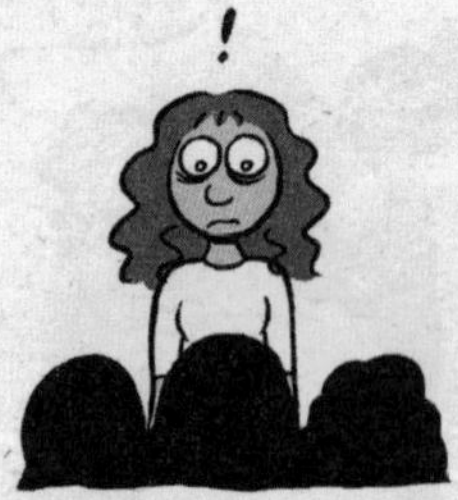
!

Brianna

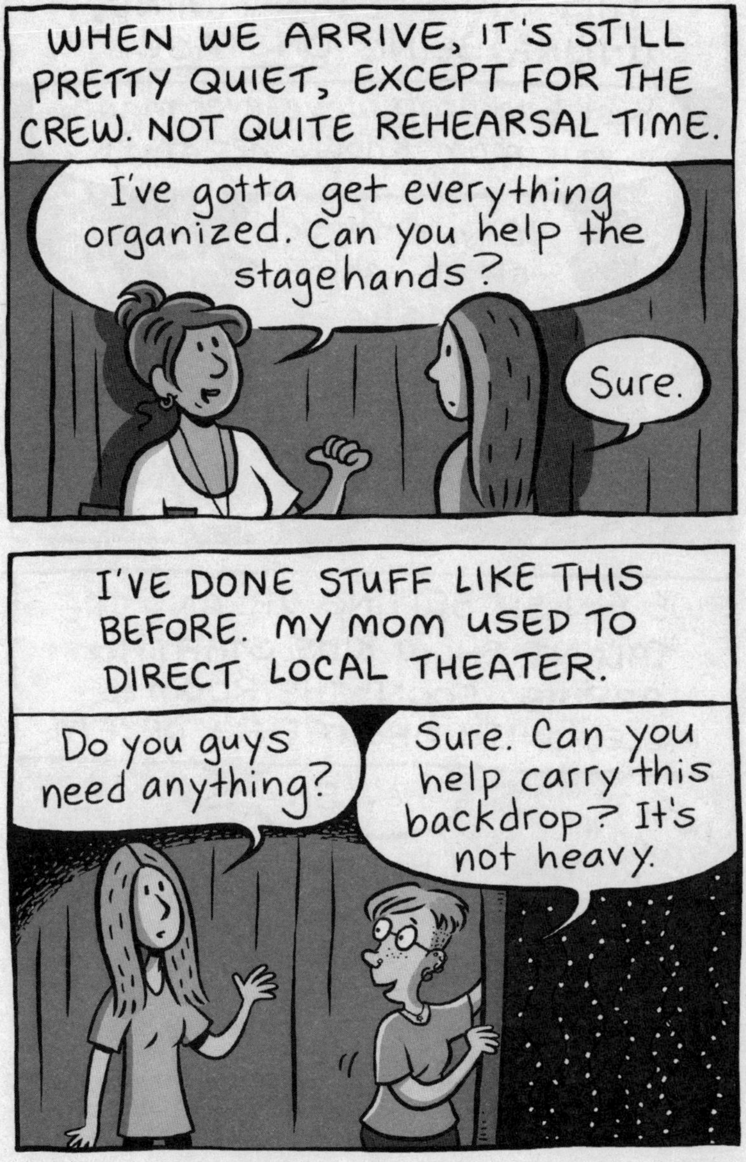

WHEN WE ARRIVE, IT'S STILL PRETTY QUIET, EXCEPT FOR THE CREW. NOT QUITE REHEARSAL TIME.
I've gotta get everything organized. Can you help the stagehands?
Sure.
I'VE DONE STUFF LIKE THIS BEFORE. MY MOM USED TO DIRECT LOCAL THEATER.
Do you guys need anything?
Sure. Can you help carry this backdrop? It's not heavy.

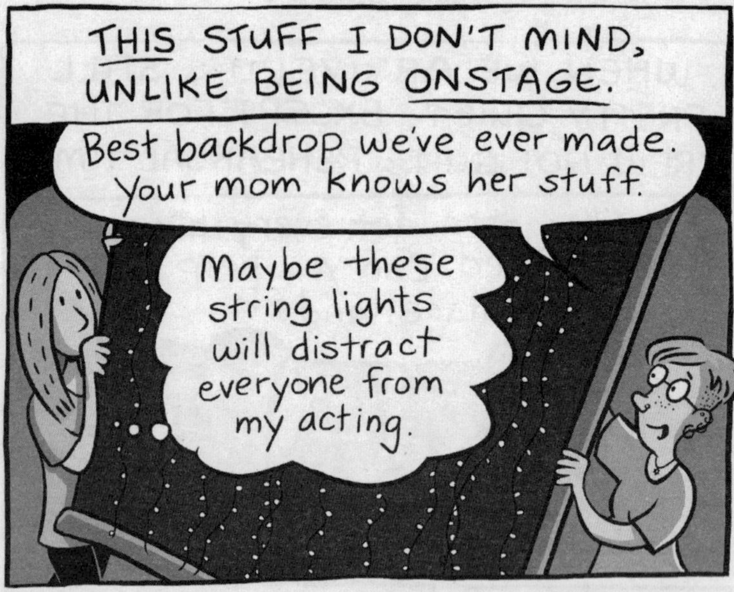
THIS STUFF I DON'T MIND, UNLIKE BEING ONSTAGE.
Best backdrop we've ever made. Your mom knows her stuff.
Maybe these string lights will distract everyone from my acting.

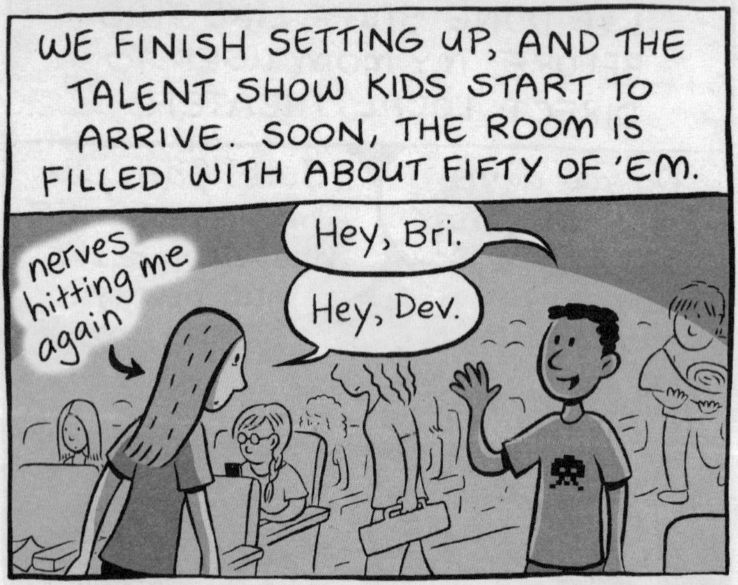
WE FINISH SETTING UP, AND THE TALENT SHOW KIDS START TO ARRIVE. SOON, THE ROOM IS FILLED WITH ABOUT FIFTY OF 'EM.
nerves hitting me again
Hey, Bri.
Hey, Dev.

WHAT AM I DOING HERE? I SHOULD BE BACK HOME, WRITING MY ENGLISH PAPER.

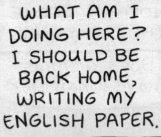

YOU KNOW, SOMETHING *FUN*.

MY MOM WELCOMES US AND PASSES OUT THE PROGRAMS. DEV AND I ARE NUMBER SIX.

gossip girls (should be interesting)

uh-oh, she's good!

WE'RE CALLED UP TO REHEARSE, IN ORDER. FIRST KID IS A FLUTE SOLO.

Maybe sixth graders shouldn't have solos.

threeeep!

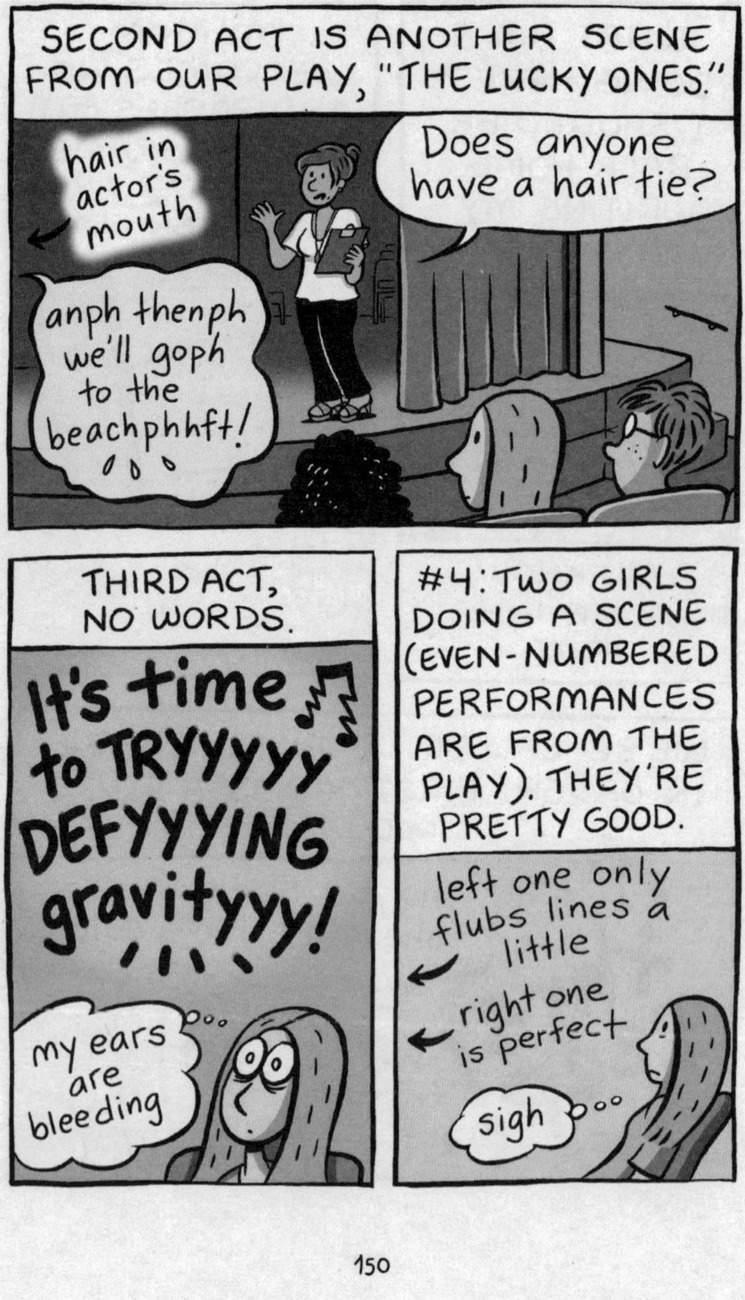
SECOND ACT IS ANOTHER SCENE FROM OUR PLAY, "THE LUCKY ONES."
hair in actor's mouth
anph thenph we'll goph to the beachphhft!
Does anyone have a hair tie?
THIRD ACT, NO WORDS.
It's time to TRYyyyy DEFYYYING gravityyy!
my ears are bleeding
#4: TWO GIRLS DOING A SCENE (EVEN-NUMBERED PERFORMANCES ARE FROM THE PLAY). THEY'RE PRETTY GOOD.
left one only flubs lines a little
right one is perfect
sigh

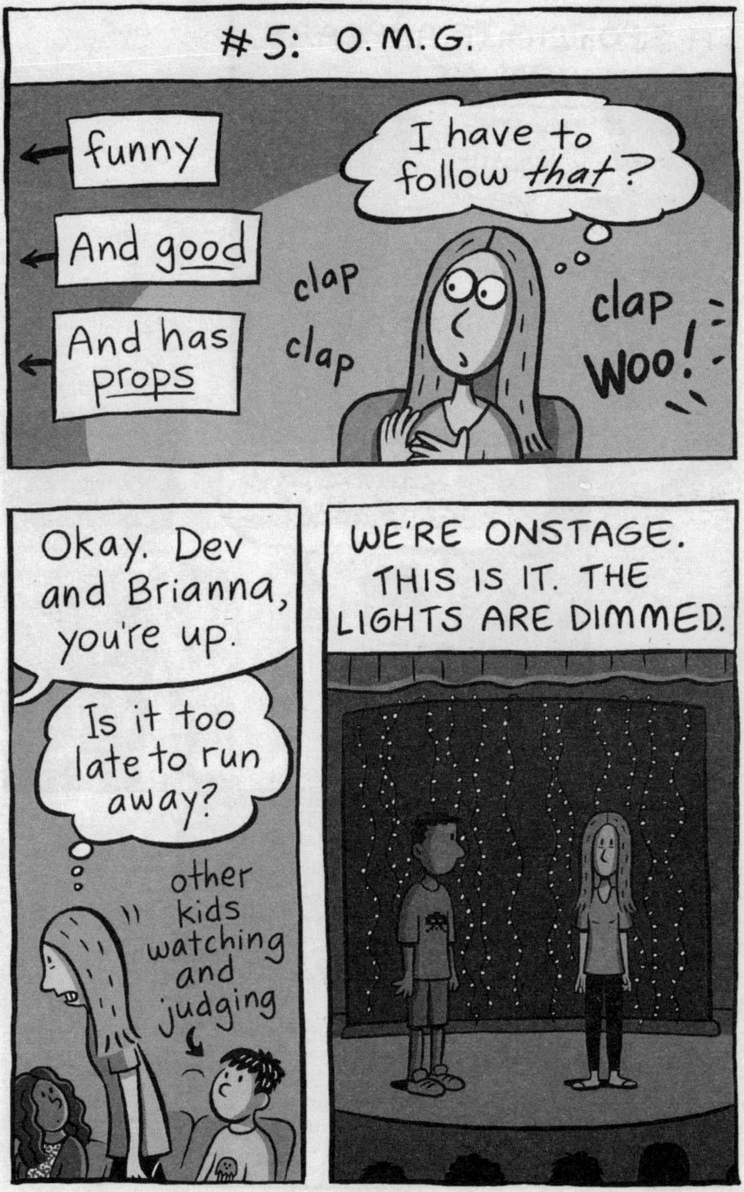
#5: O.M.G.
funny
And good
And has props
I have to follow that?
clap
clap
clap
WOO!
Okay. Dev and Brianna, you're up.
Is it too late to run away?
other kids watching and judging
WE'RE ONSTAGE. THIS IS IT. THE LIGHTS ARE DIMMED.

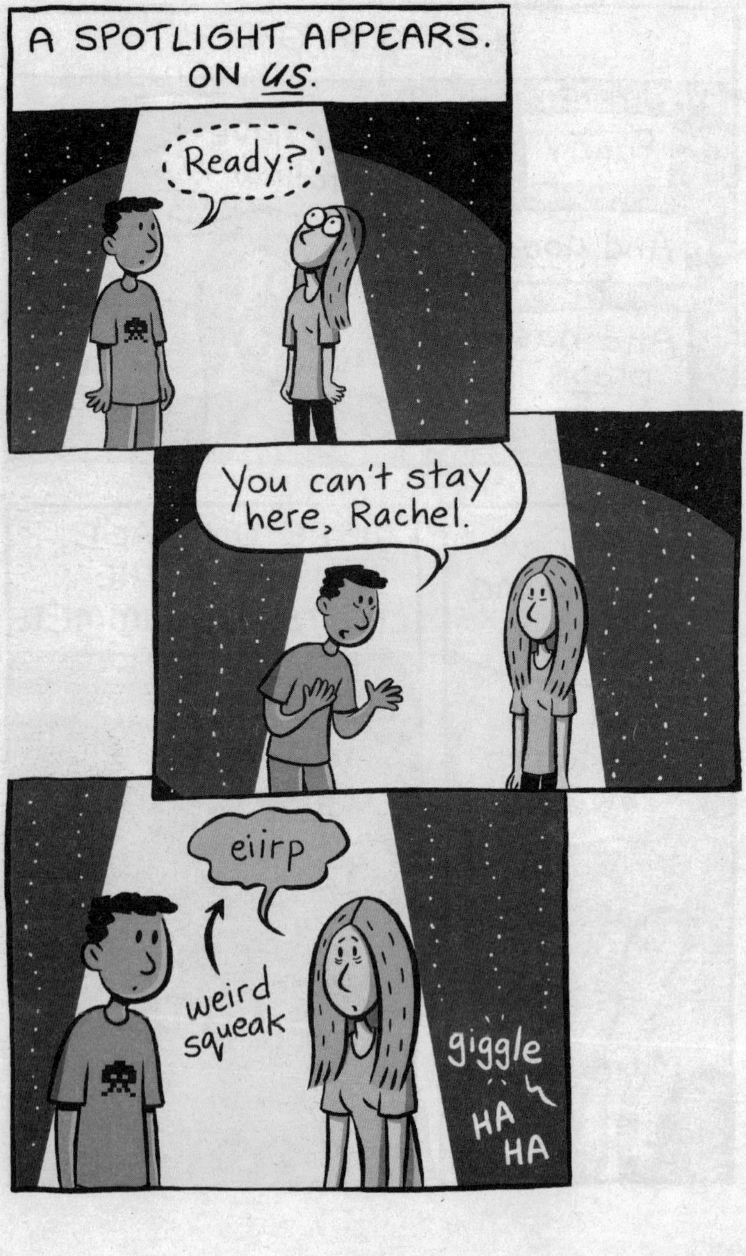
A SPOTLIGHT APPEARS.
ON US.
Ready?
You can't stay here, Rachel.
eiirp
weird squeak
giggle
HA
HA

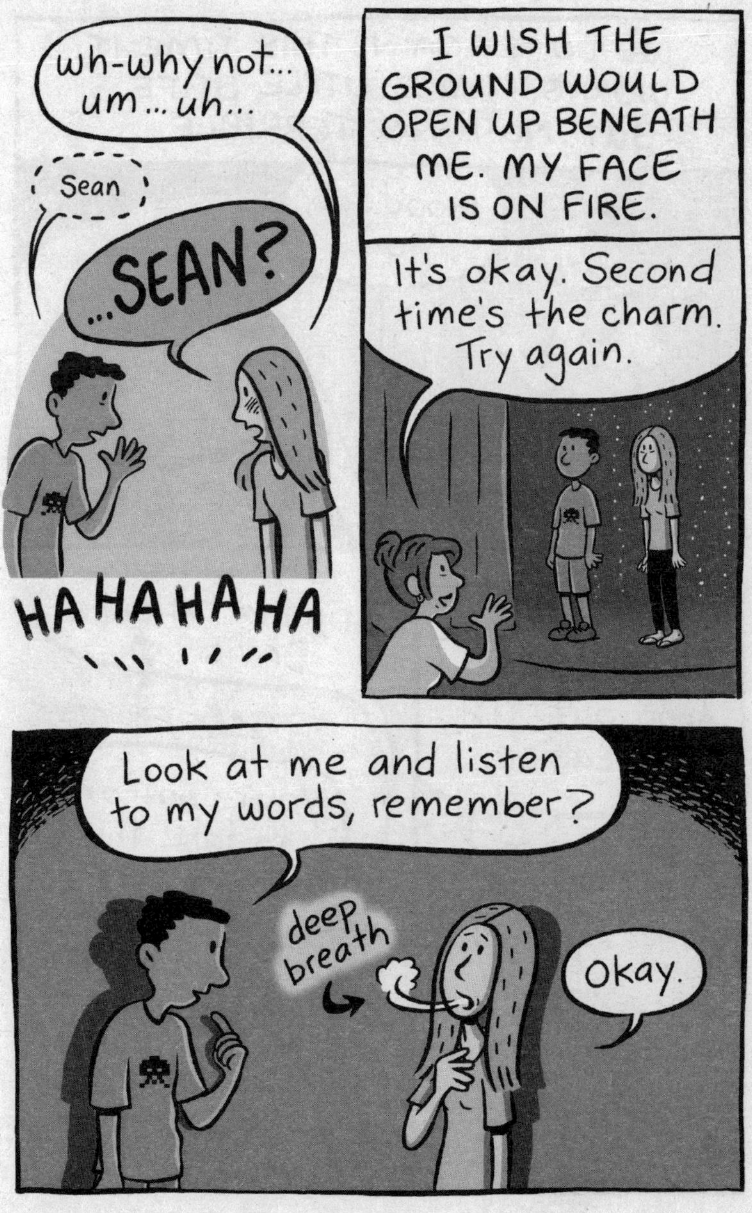
wh-why not... um... uh...
Sean
...SEAN?
HA HA HA HA HA
I WISH THE GROUND WOULD OPEN UP BENEATH ME. MY FACE IS ON FIRE.
It's okay. Second time's the charm. Try again.
Look at me and listen to my words, remember?
deep breath
Okay.

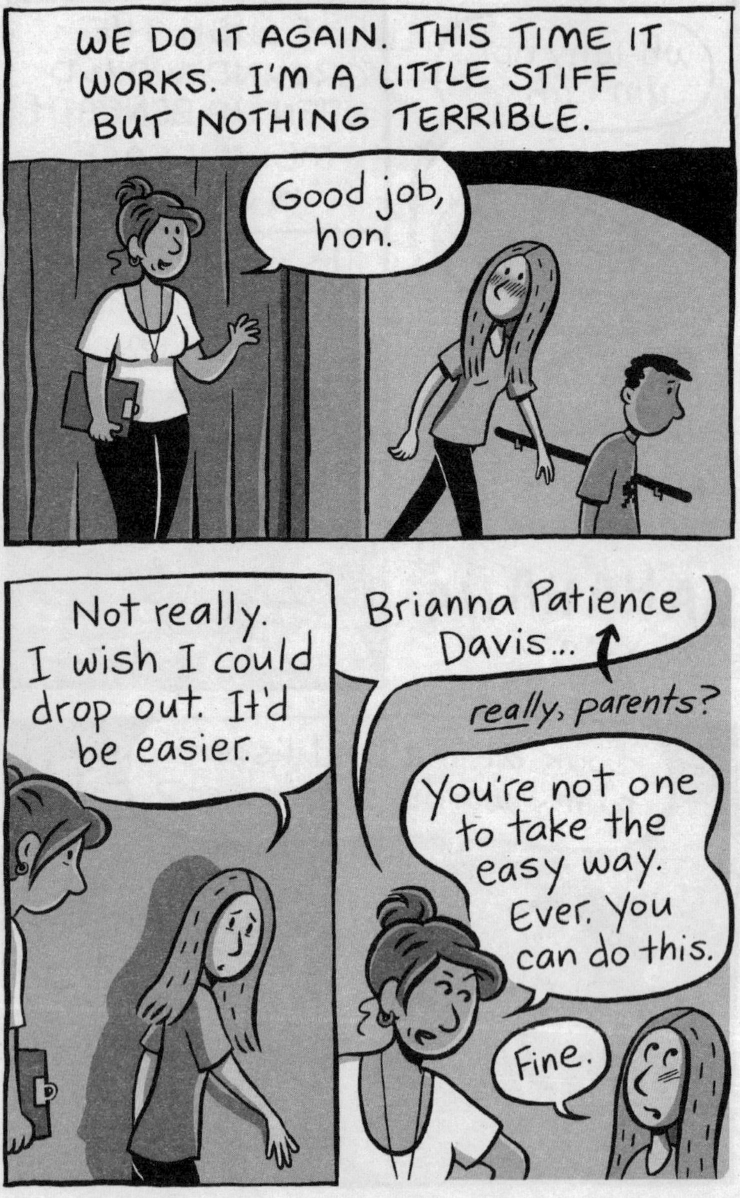
WE DO IT AGAIN. THIS TIME IT WORKS. I'M A LITTLE STIFF BUT NOTHING TERRIBLE.
Good job, hon.
Not really. I wish I could drop out. It'd be easier.
Brianna Patience Davis...
really, parents?
You're not one to take the easy way. Ever. You can do this.
Fine.

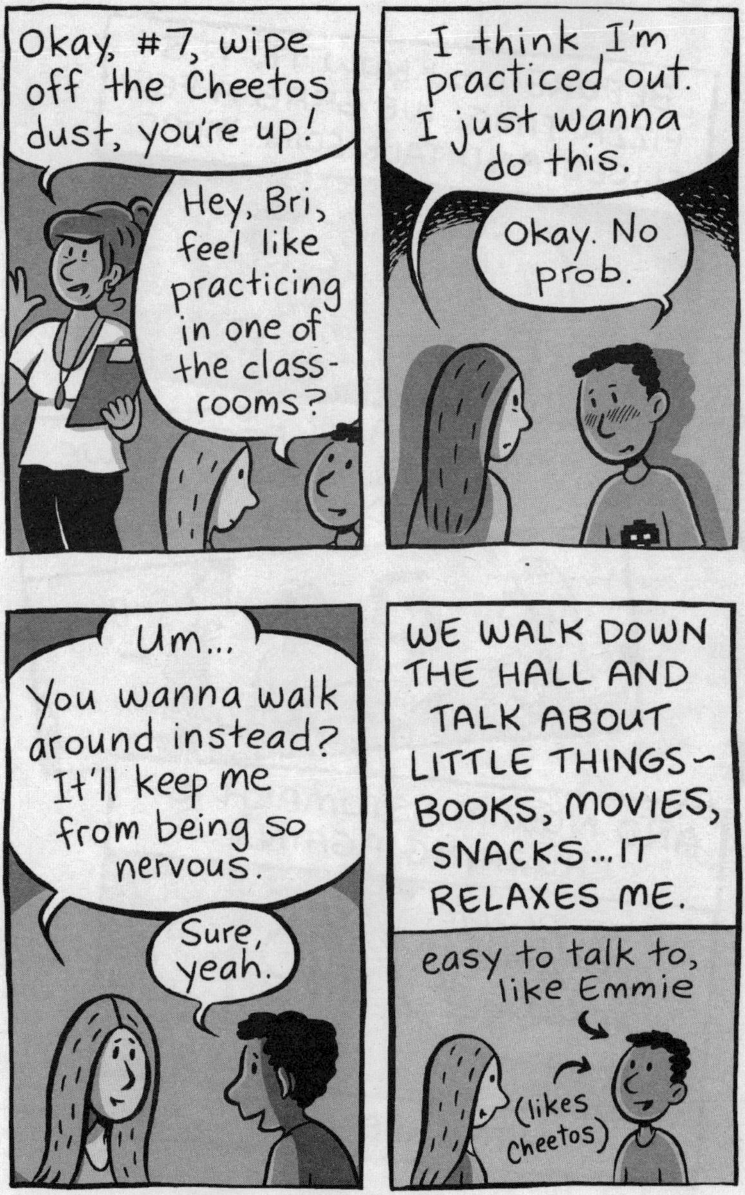
Okay, #7, wipe off the Cheetos dust, you're up!
Hey, Bri, feel like practicing in one of the class-rooms?
I think I'm practiced out. I just wanna do this.
Okay. No prob.
Um...
You wanna walk around instead? It'll keep me from being so nervous.
Sure, yeah.
WE WALK DOWN THE HALL AND TALK ABOUT LITTLE THINGS - BOOKS, MOVIES, SNACKS... IT RELAXES ME.
easy to talk to, like Emmie
(likes Cheetos)

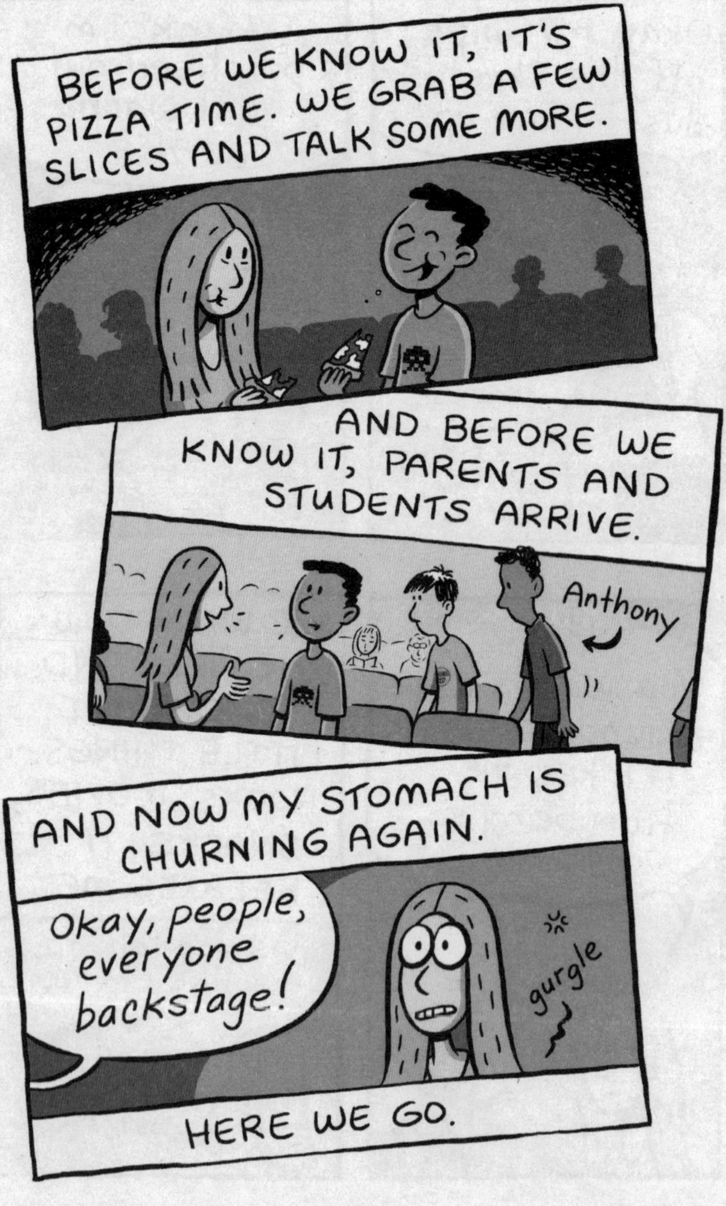
BEFORE WE KNOW IT, IT'S PIZZA TIME. WE GRAB A FEW SLICES AND TALK SOME MORE.
AND BEFORE WE KNOW IT, PARENTS AND STUDENTS ARRIVE.
Anthony
AND NOW MY STOMACH IS CHURNING AGAIN.
Okay, people, everyone backstage!
gurgle
HERE WE GO.

IZZY

I stand there with my jaw dropped to the floor. I guess it's joined my stomach.

jaw
stomach

My mom catches sight of me and glares. No, that's the wrong description. If a person could shoot flaming darts out of her eyeballs, **that's** how she looks at me.

weird forehead lines appearing out of nowhere
eyes of doom
grape-colored face

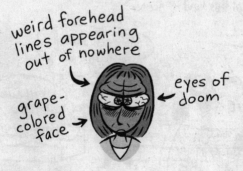

Oh man, I'm dead.

Then Ashley sees me. Her eyes are bright red. She gives me the most apologetic look a human can give. I feel so bad for her, I'm not even mad.

eyes of regret

Then I glance back at my mom and older sister and feel bad for me again.

erp

Before they have a chance to come over, I hurry toward them. I motion for them to follow me into an empty classroom, away from everyone else. Yeah, I'm into drama, but I really, **really** don't want this kind of scene.

Please don't kill me...

...till we get to this room.

My mom starts in.

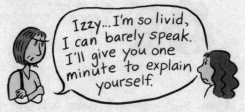

Izzy... I'm so livid, I can barely speak. I'll give you one minute to explain yourself.

For once, the impossible happens.
I'm speechless.

Mom, I told you. It's not Izzy's fault. I'm the one who—

I want to hear it from Izzy.

I take a deep, shaky breath and let it all out.

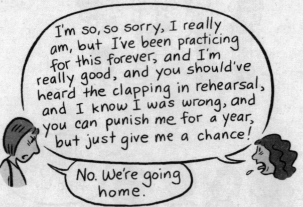

I'm so, so sorry, I really am, but I've been practicing for this forever, and I'm really good, and you should've heard the clapping in rehearsal, and I know I was wrong, and you can punish me for a year, but just give me a chance!

No. We're going home.

Ashley starts to cry. I swear she takes on other people's feelings so much, she should have multiple personalities.

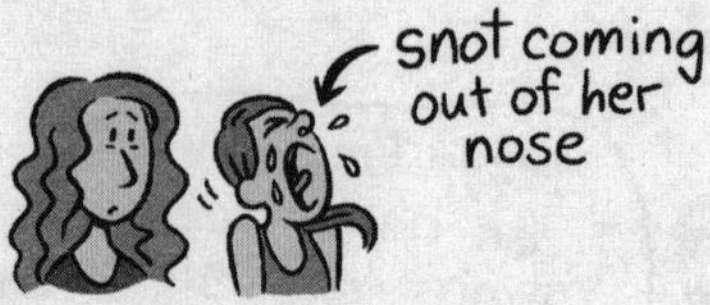
snot coming out of her nose

I glance at Dani. She's looking at Ashley. And starting to feel bad, I can tell. Dani looks back at me. That's when I lose it. Everyone's crying except my mom, who looks like she just wants to take a two-day nap.

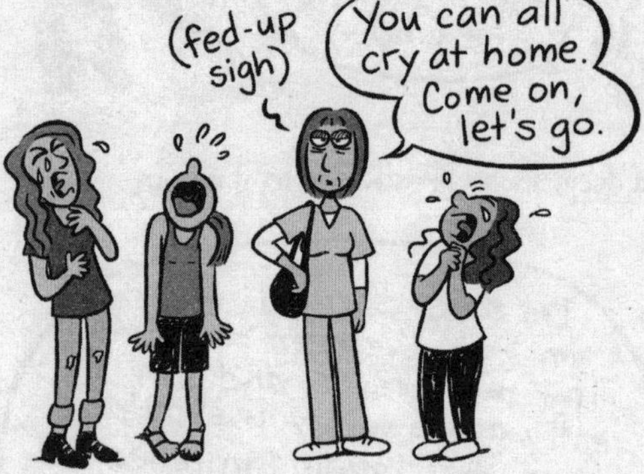
(fed-up sigh)
You can all cry at home. Come on, let's go.

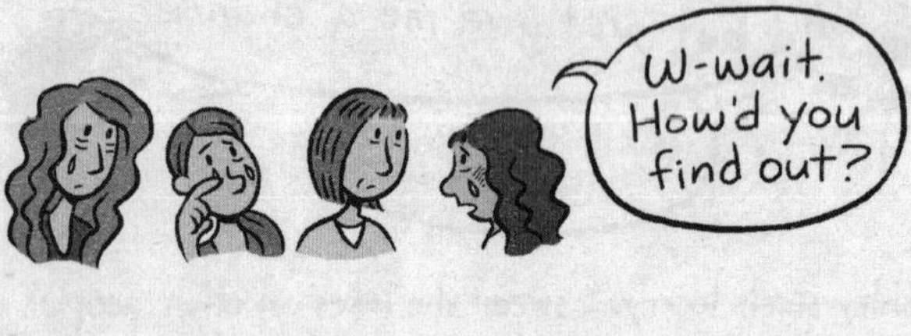
W-wait. How'd you find out?

I see Dani look away.

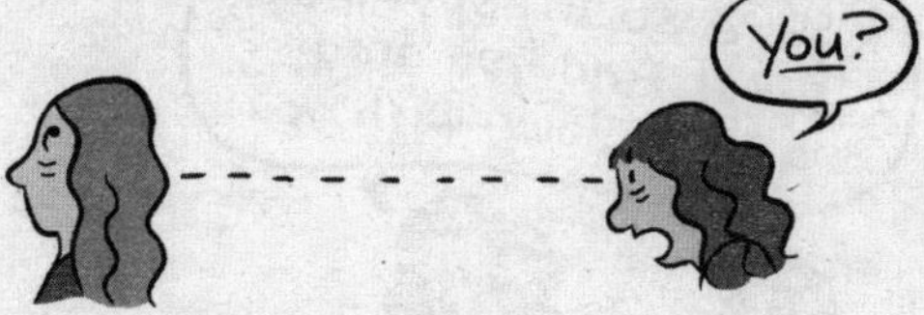
You?

She whirls around, her own eyes shooting darts. Scratch that. Bullets.

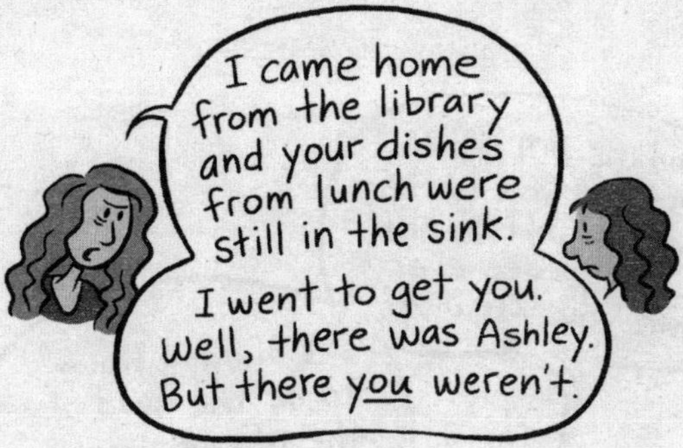
I came home from the library and your dishes from lunch were still in the sink.
I went to get you. Well, there was Ashley. But there you weren't.

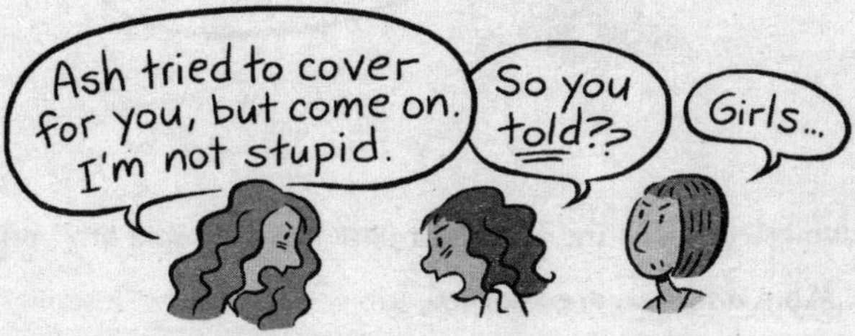
Ash tried to cover for you, but come on. I'm not stupid.
So you told??
Girls...

I was so mad! You're so irresponsible, Izzy! And you drag Ashley down with you.

She doesn't—

And it's NOT FAIR! Ash likes you better. And I'm left to pick up the pieces every time you screw up.

I always have to be the good one, the _responsible_ one. Or the _horrible_ one, to _you!_

I'm dumbstruck. It's the first time Dani has ever said anything like this. Mom and Ash are shocked, too.

Dani looks down.

I guess that was the last straw for me.

So yeah, I told.

I'm still pretty fired up. I also feel like I got socked in the gut. Her words hit. Hard.

oof!

Or the <u>horrible</u> one, to *you!*

But a strange thing happens. My anger starts to melt. Not all at once but kinda slowly, like dripping candle wax (okay, maybe quicker than that, but you get my point).

Actors and playwrights are supposed to put themselves in other people's shoes. I always try to do that. It's usually pretty easy for me. But never with Dani.

Usually Dani's so bossy and demanding that I can't see straight. But I don't think I've ever tried to look past all that.

For once, I try putting myself in her place.

Dani's the oldest. She's a bossy pain but tries to be responsible.

She makes sure the house is cleaned up, food's on the table, and homework's done.

All because Mom can't — she's busy trying to make a living.

And all **I've** ever done is make it harder for both of them. Even if I don't mean to.

Wow. What's that word that Miss Gelb had us define early in the year? **Epiphany.** I think I'm having one.

I take a deep breath and try to look my sister in the eye.

Then I say the most mature thing I've probably ever said in my life.

I'm sorry, Dani. You were right to be mad.

I think if she could faint from shock, she would. Instead, she stays quiet. But she smiles, a little.

My mom puts her arm around Dani's shoulders.

Sometimes I forget how much you all take on.

We'll work on that, okay?

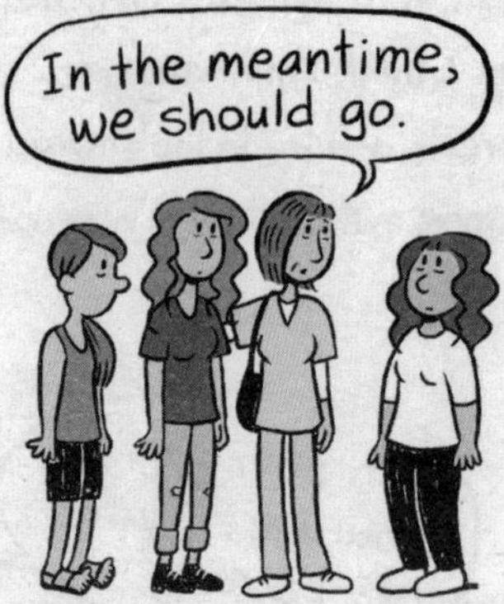
In the meantime, we should go.

I'm so disappointed, I'm unable to move. The talent show! But I'm also feeling pretty ashamed, so I force my feet toward the door.

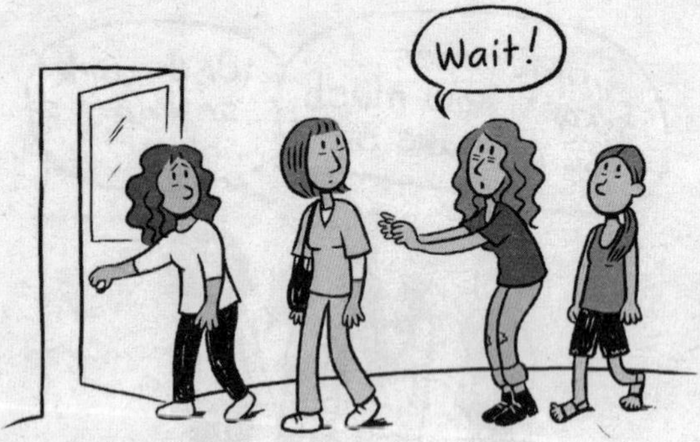
Wait!

Huh?

Brianna

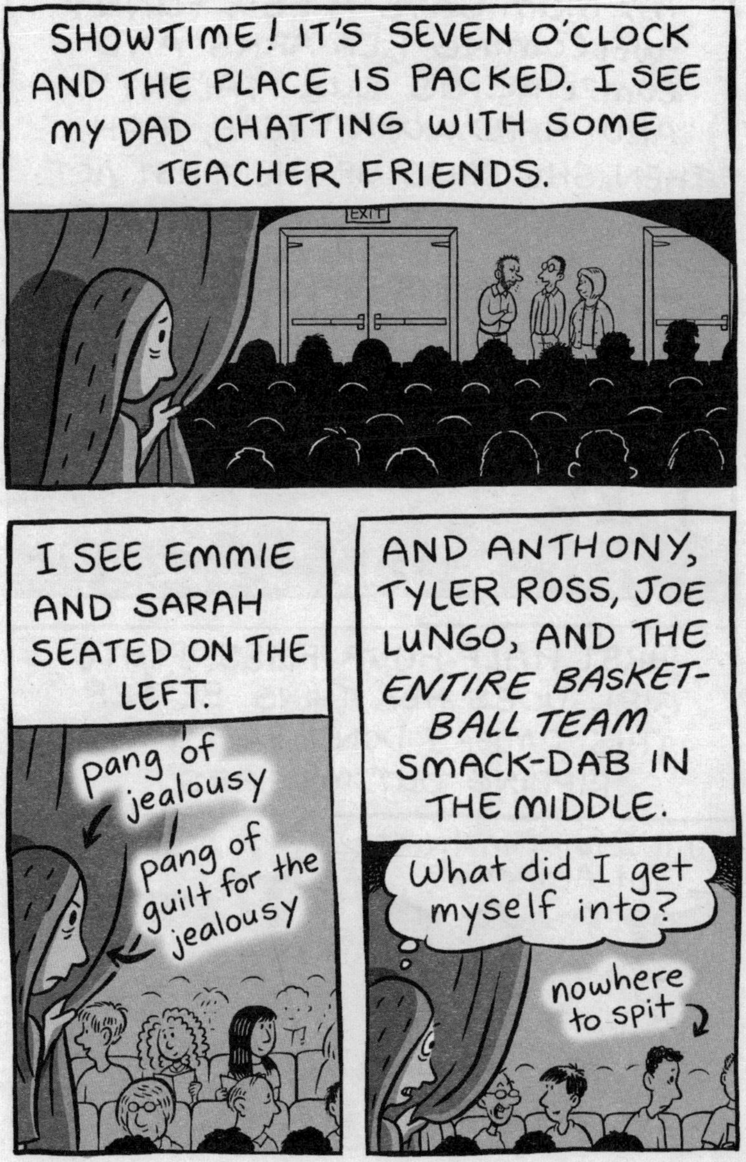
SHOWTIME! IT'S SEVEN O'CLOCK AND THE PLACE IS PACKED. I SEE MY DAD CHATTING WITH SOME TEACHER FRIENDS.
EXIT
I SEE EMMIE AND SARAH SEATED ON THE LEFT.
pang of jealousy
pang of guilt for the jealousy
AND ANTHONY, TYLER ROSS, JOE LUNGO, AND THE *ENTIRE BASKET-BALL TEAM* SMACK-DAB IN THE MIDDLE.
What did I get myself into?
nowhere to spit

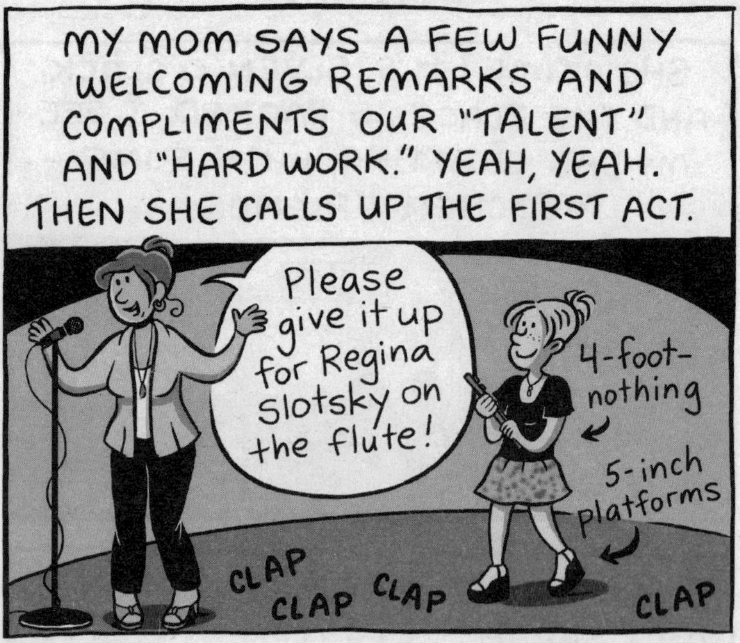
MY MOM SAYS A FEW FUNNY WELCOMING REMARKS AND COMPLIMENTS OUR "TALENT" AND "HARD WORK." YEAH, YEAH. THEN SHE CALLS UP THE FIRST ACT.
Please give it up for Regina Slotsky on the flute!
4-foot-nothing
5-inch platforms
CLAP
CLAP
CLAP
CLAP

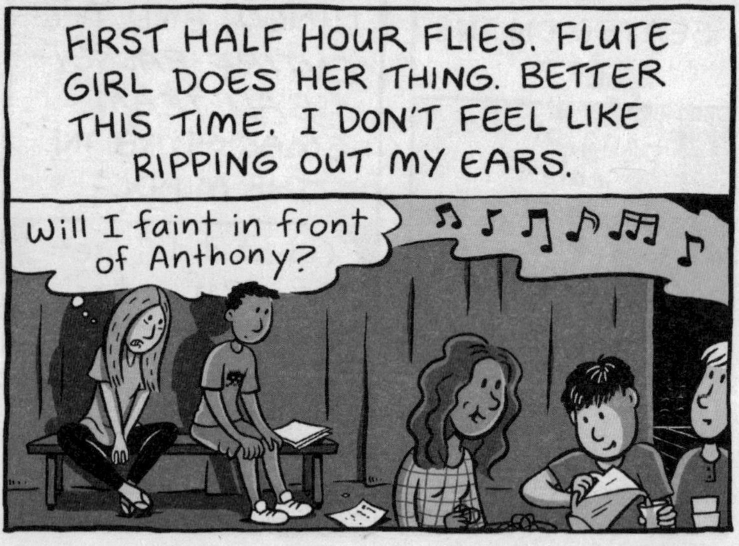
FIRST HALF HOUR FLIES. FLUTE GIRL DOES HER THING. BETTER THIS TIME. I DON'T FEEL LIKE RIPPING OUT MY EARS.
Will I faint in front of Anthony?

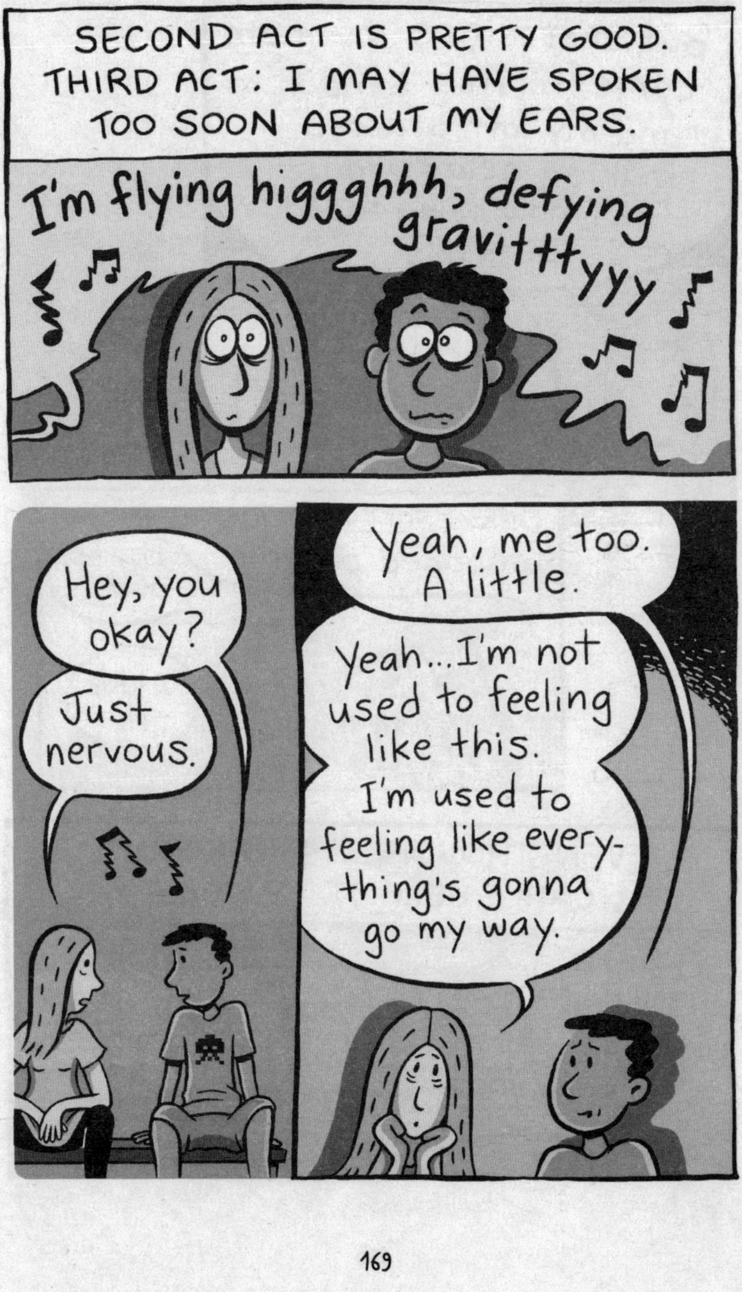
SECOND ACT IS PRETTY GOOD. THIRD ACT: I MAY HAVE SPOKEN TOO SOON ABOUT MY EARS.
I'm flying higgghhh, defying gravitttyyy
Hey, you okay?
Just nervous.
Yeah, me too. A little.
Yeah... I'm not used to feeling like this. I'm used to feeling like every-thing's gonna go my way.

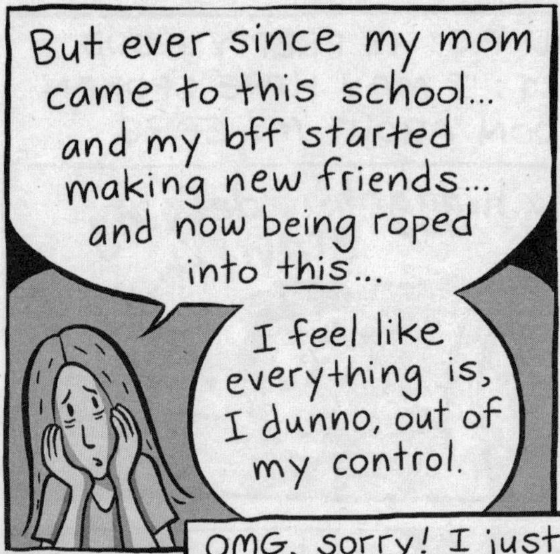
But ever since my mom came to this school... and my bff started making new friends... and now being roped into this...
I feel like everything is, I dunno, out of my control.

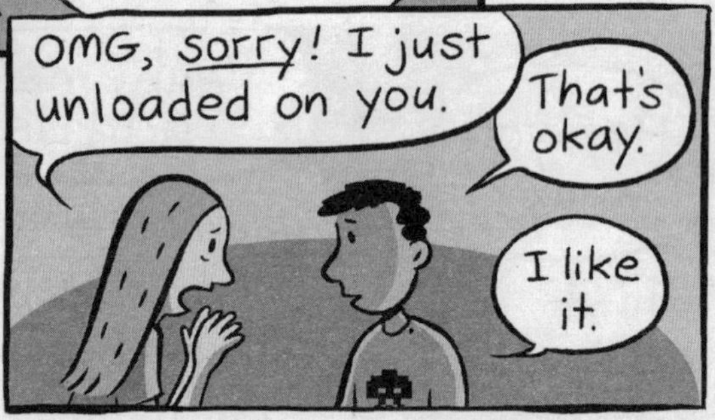
OMG, sorry! I just unloaded on you.
That's okay.
I like it.

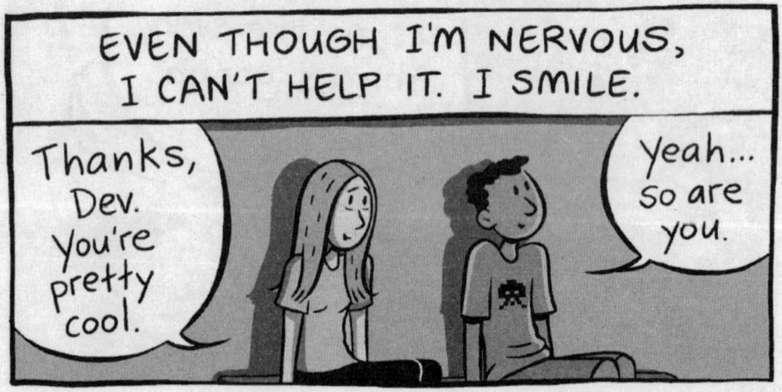
EVEN THOUGH I'M NERVOUS, I CAN'T HELP IT. I SMILE.
Thanks, Dev. You're pretty cool.
Yeah... so are you.

IZZY

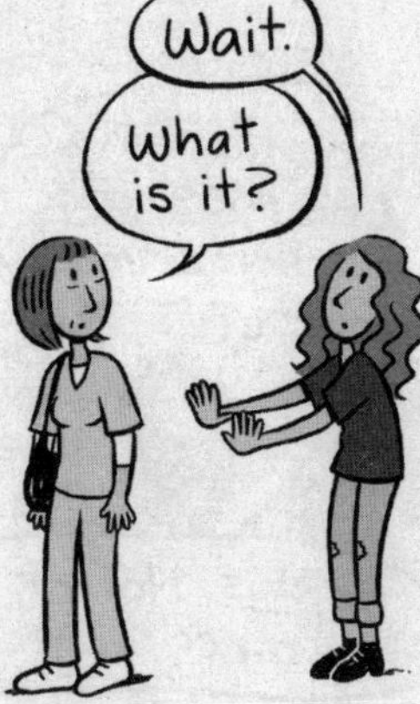
Wait.
What is it?

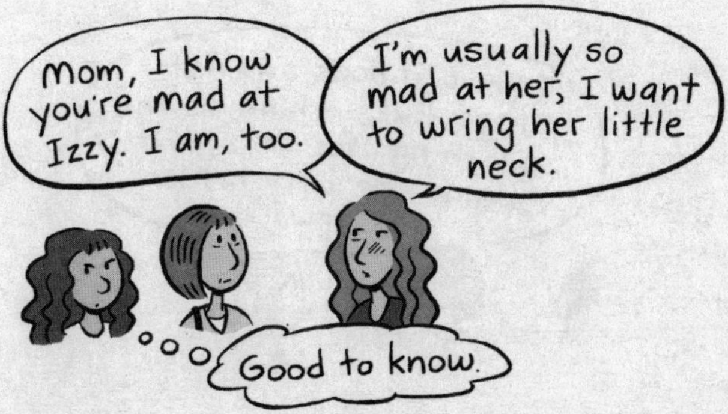
Mom, I know you're mad at Izzy. I am, too.
I'm usually so mad at her, I want to wring her little neck.
Good to know.

But she should be in the talent show.
What?
What?
She's been practicing forever. And she's good. I hear her sometimes.
She does?
She's worked really hard.
At this. Not at her other subjects.
I know it goes against all logic, but I think it's the right thing...for Izzy. And I think she'll try harder afterward.

My jaw is on the floor again. So is Ashley's.

Mom gives me a long look.

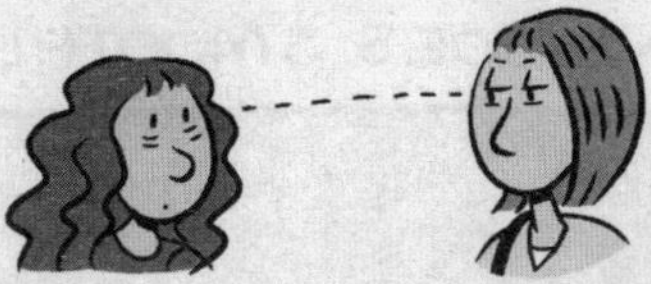

Her face softens a little.

The fiery darts disappear.

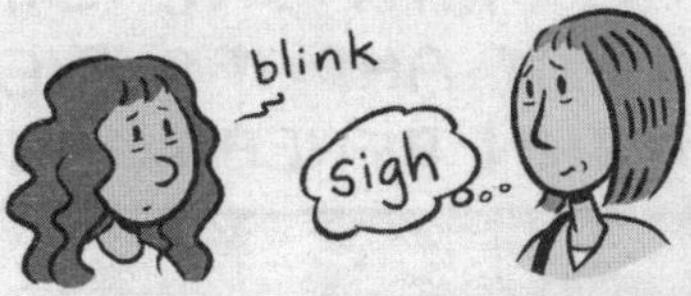
blink
sigh

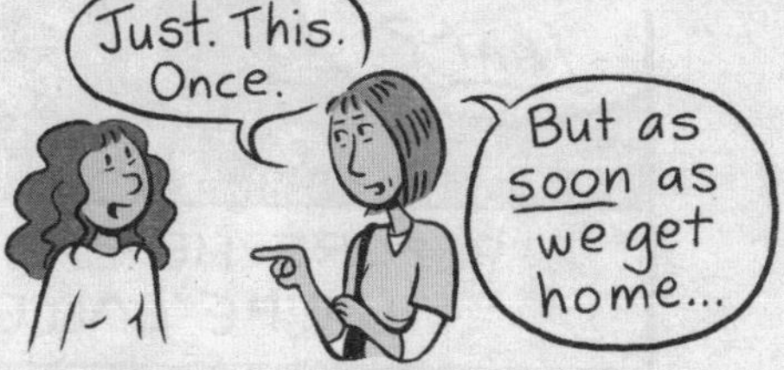
Just. This. Once.
But as soon as we get home...

I squeal and hug my mom so hard she almost falls over. Ash laughs and Dani snorts.

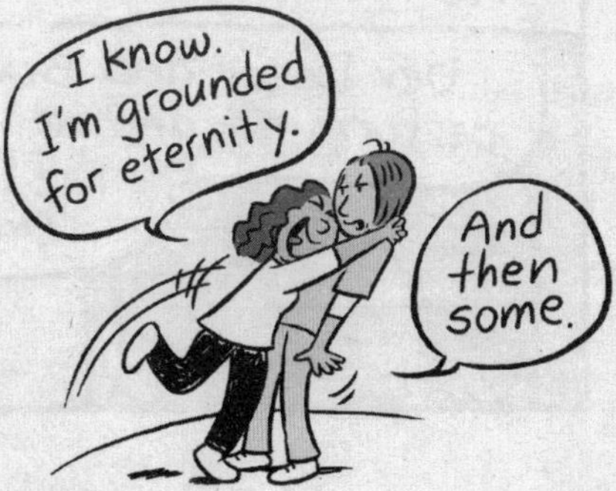
I know. I'm grounded for eternity.
And then some.

Brianna

DEV AND I WAIT THROUGH THE NEXT TWO ACTS. THE FOURTH ONE GOES SMOOTHLY.

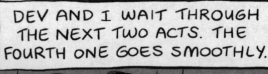

clap
clap
clap

I PEEK AT THE FIFTH ONE. GIRL DOES A SOLO ACT AND IT'S EVEN BETTER THAN IN REHEARSAL.

We have to follow *that?*

CLAP
CLAP
WOO!
yeah

BEFORE HE CAN RESPOND, WE'RE CALLED UP.

WE HEAD DOWNSTAGE AS MY MOM INTRODUCES US.

...Dev Devar and Brianna Davis performing another scene from "The Lucky Ones."

174

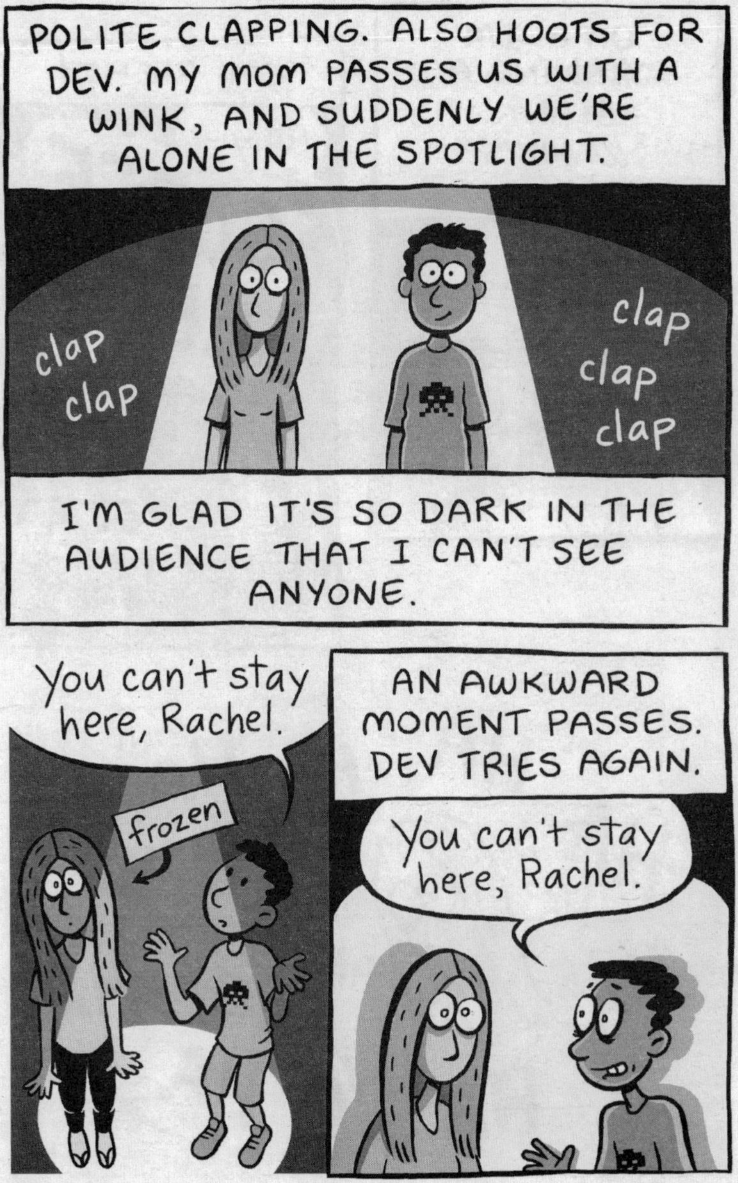
POLITE CLAPPING. ALSO HOOTS FOR DEV. MY MOM PASSES US WITH A WINK, AND SUDDENLY WE'RE ALONE IN THE SPOTLIGHT.
clap
clap
clap
clap
clap
I'M GLAD IT'S SO DARK IN THE AUDIENCE THAT I CAN'T SEE ANYONE.
You can't stay here, Rachel.
frozen
AN AWKWARD MOMENT PASSES. DEV TRIES AGAIN.
You can't stay here, Rachel.

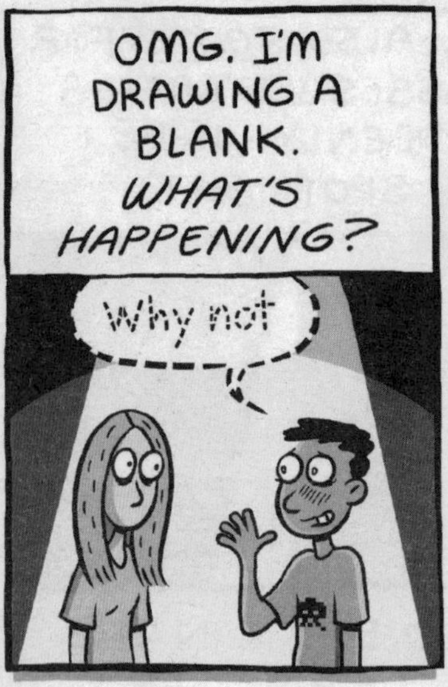
OMG. I'M DRAWING A BLANK. *WHAT'S HAPPENING?*
Why not

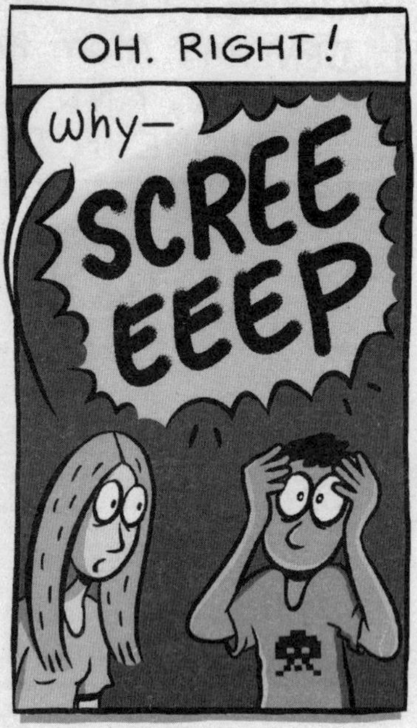
OH. RIGHT!
Why—
SCREE EEEP

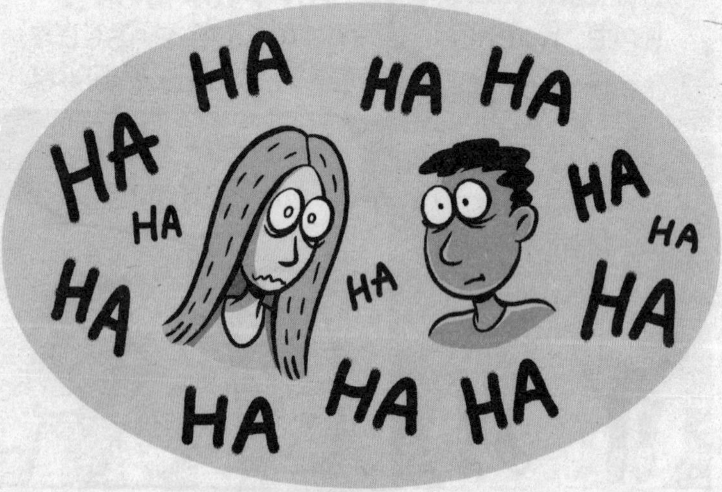
HA HA HA HA
HA HA HA HA HA HA HA HA HA HA HA

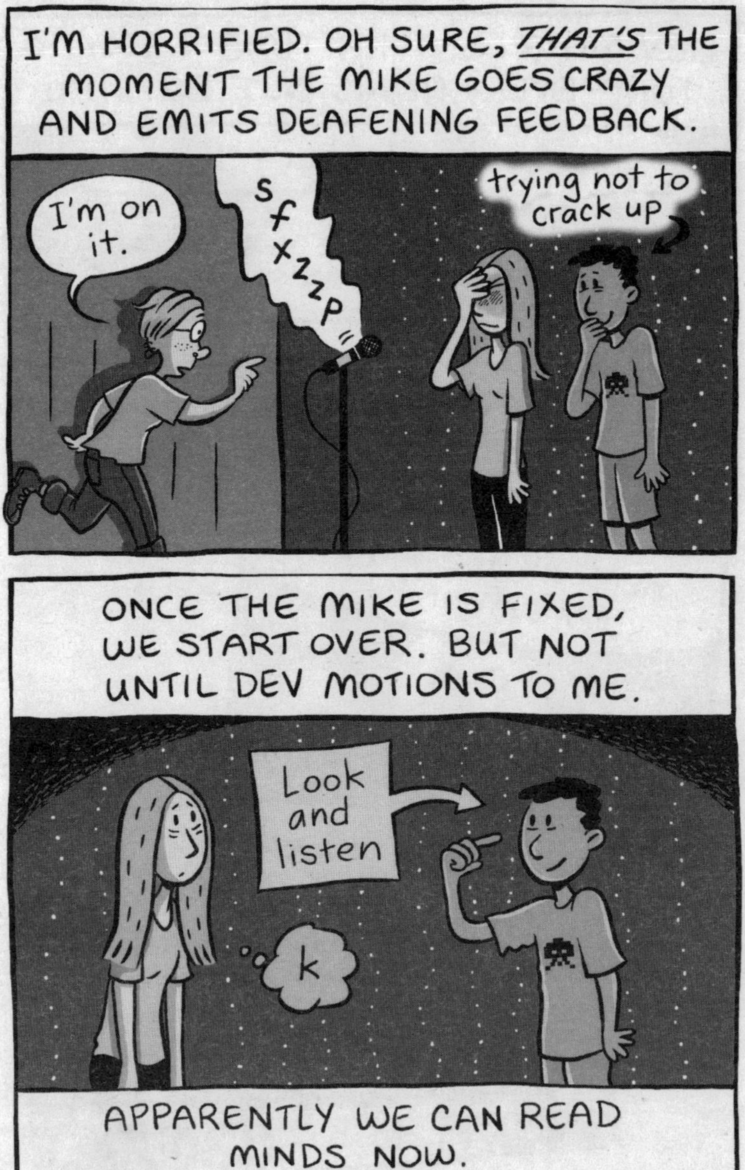
I'M HORRIFIED. OH SURE, *THAT'S* THE MOMENT THE MIKE GOES CRAZY AND EMITS DEAFENING FEEDBACK.
I'm on it.
sfxzzp
trying not to crack up
ONCE THE MIKE IS FIXED, WE START OVER. BUT NOT UNTIL DEV MOTIONS TO ME.
Look and listen
k
APPARENTLY WE CAN READ MINDS NOW.

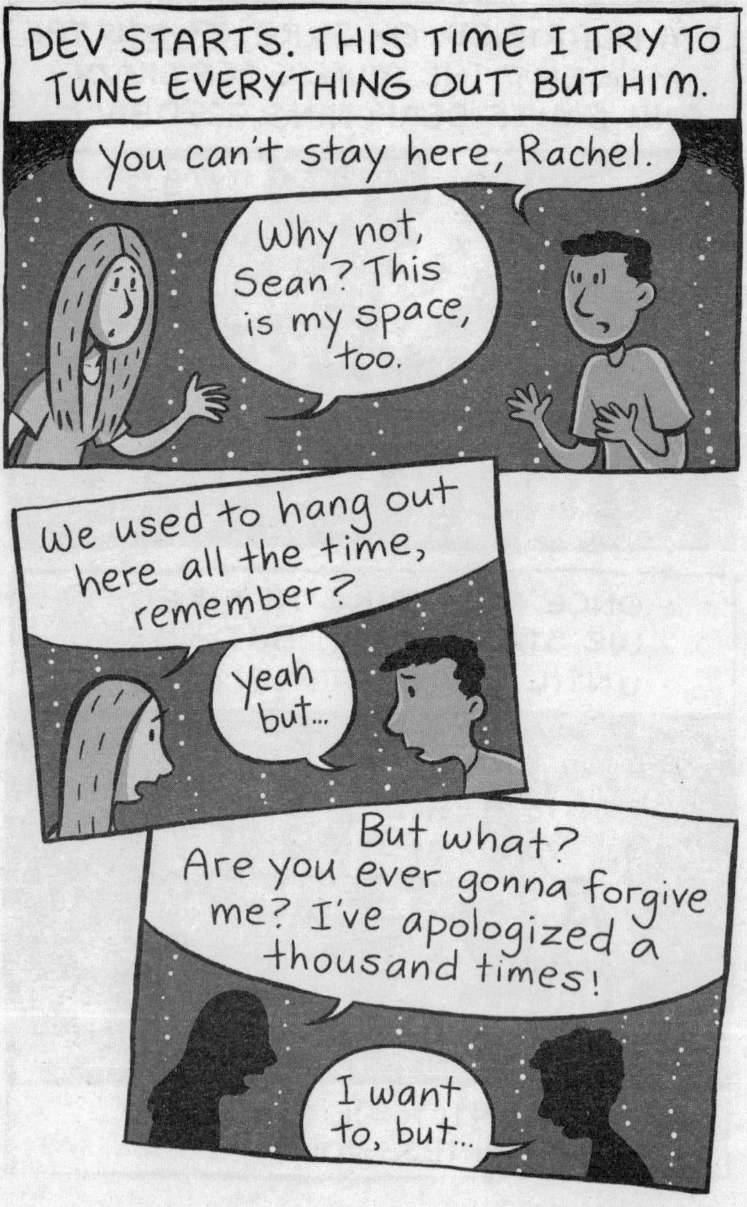
DEV STARTS. THIS TIME I TRY TO TUNE EVERYTHING OUT BUT HIM.
You can't stay here, Rachel.
Why not, Sean? This is my space, too.
We used to hang out here all the time, remember?
Yeah but...
But what? Are you ever gonna forgive me? I've apologized a thousand times!
I want to, but...

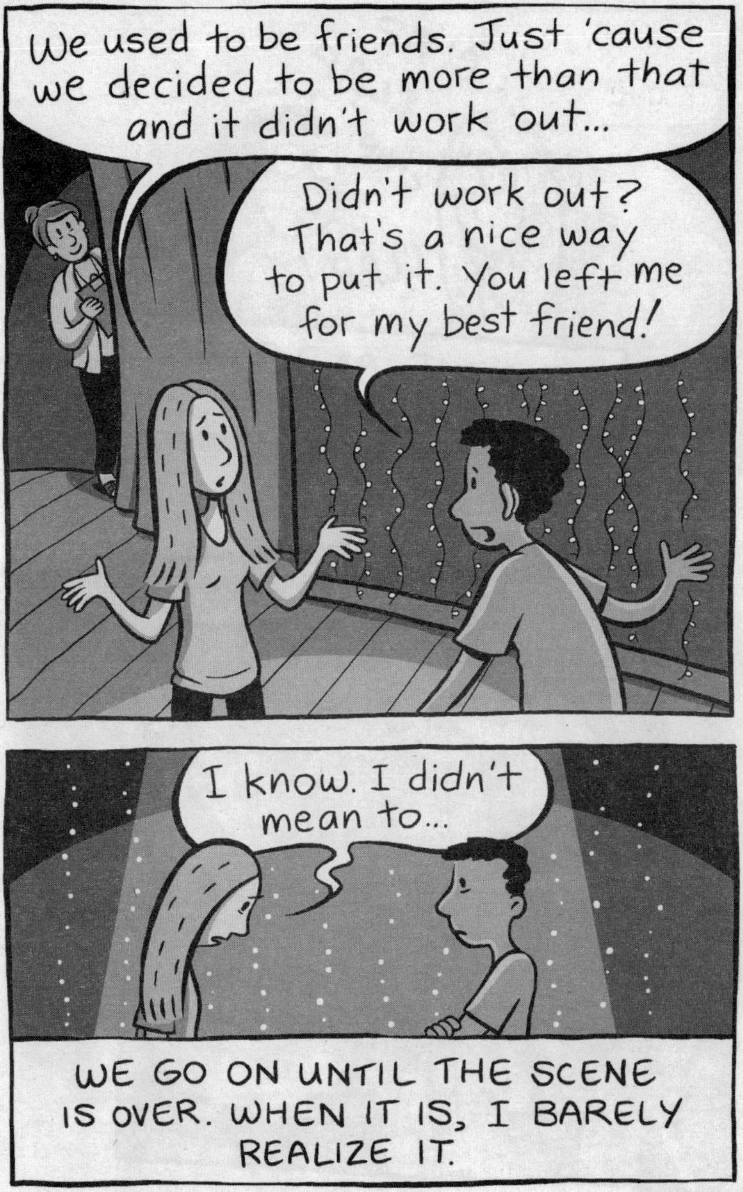
We used to be friends. Just 'cause we decided to be more than that and it didn't work out...
Didn't work out? That's a nice way to put it. You left me for my best friend!
I know. I didn't mean to...
WE GO ON UNTIL THE SCENE IS OVER. WHEN IT IS, I BARELY REALIZE IT.

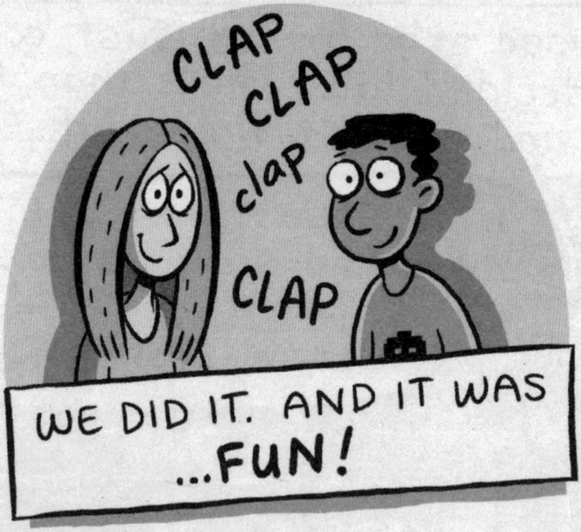
CLAP
CLAP
clap
CLAP
WE DID IT. AND IT WAS ...**FUN!**

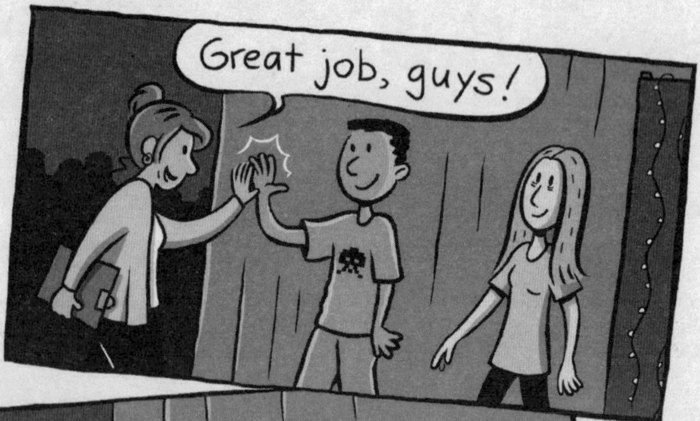
Great job, guys!

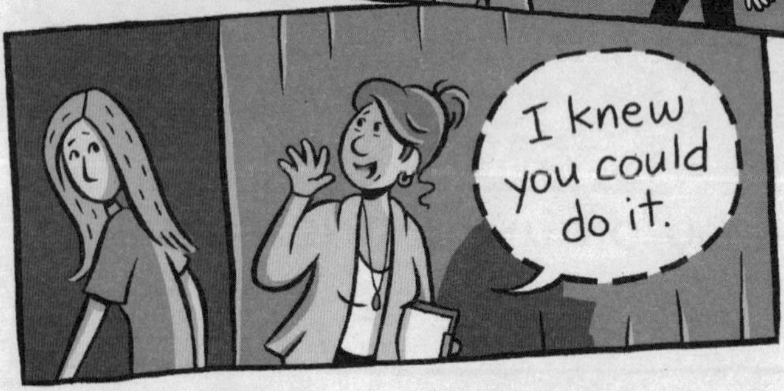
I knew you could do it.

IZZY

He won't see me behind this shed. And he probably thinks that <u>dog</u> knocked over that pile of rakes.

Oh no! The dog is chasing him!

golf ball mailbox

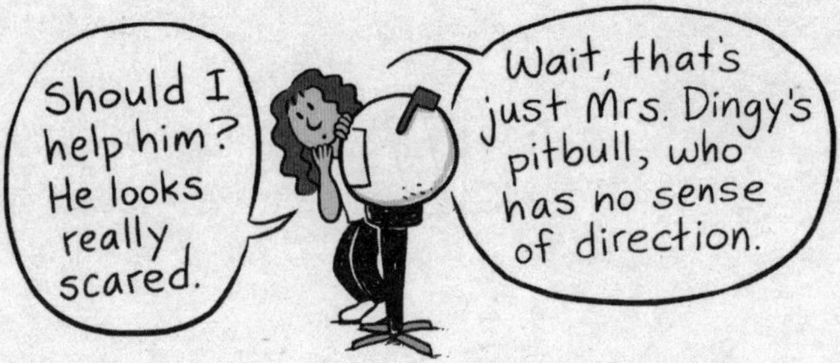
Should I help him? He looks really scared.
Wait, that's just Mrs. Dingy's pitbull, who has no sense of direction.

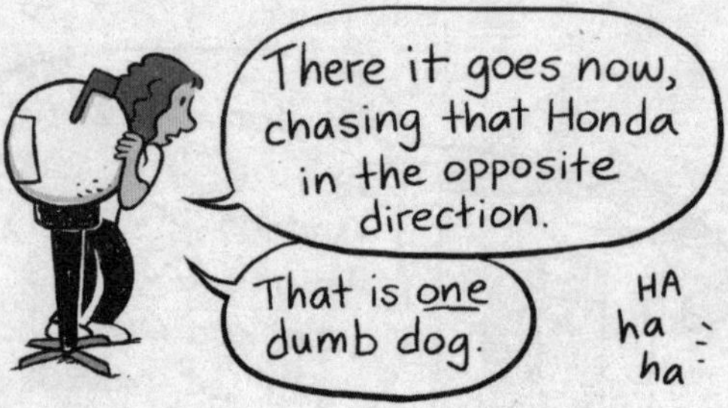
There it goes now, chasing that Honda in the opposite direction.
That is one dumb dog.
HA ha ha

I've stopped "seeing" my family and everyone else in the audience. Partly 'cause it's so dark, but mainly because I'm focused.

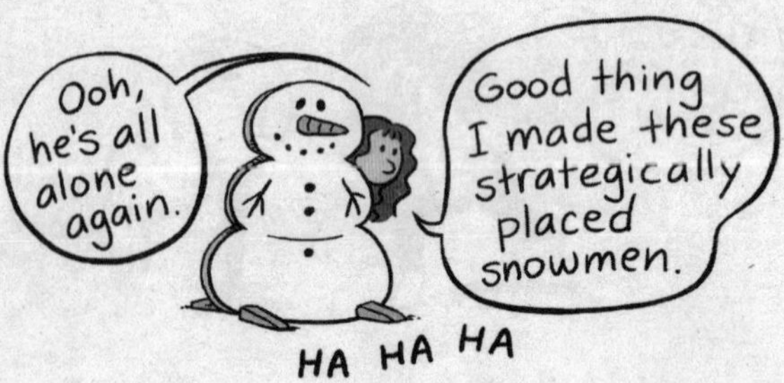
Ooh, he's all alone again.
Good thing I made these strategically placed snowmen.
HA HA HA

Somewhere out there, people are laughing. That's good. It gets me more pumped.

When I finish the scene, I get a lot of clapping and some cheers. The cheers are from my family. I'd recognize their screeches anywhere.

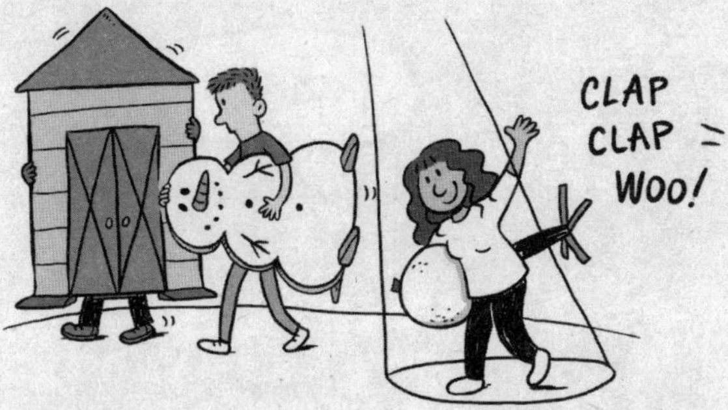
CLAP
CLAP
WOO!

I feel great, like I climbed a mountain and am floating down. I did my own thing and it made it that much sweeter.

I don't care if I **am** grounded for an eternity.

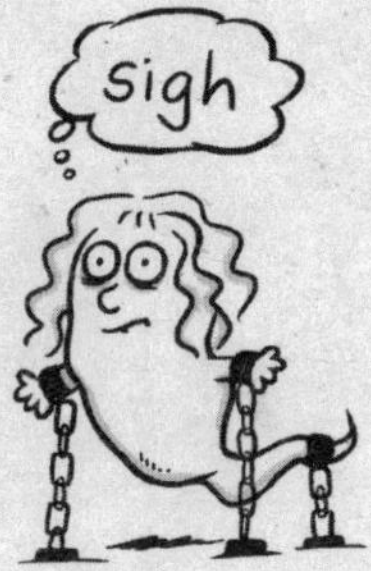
sigh

It was worth it.

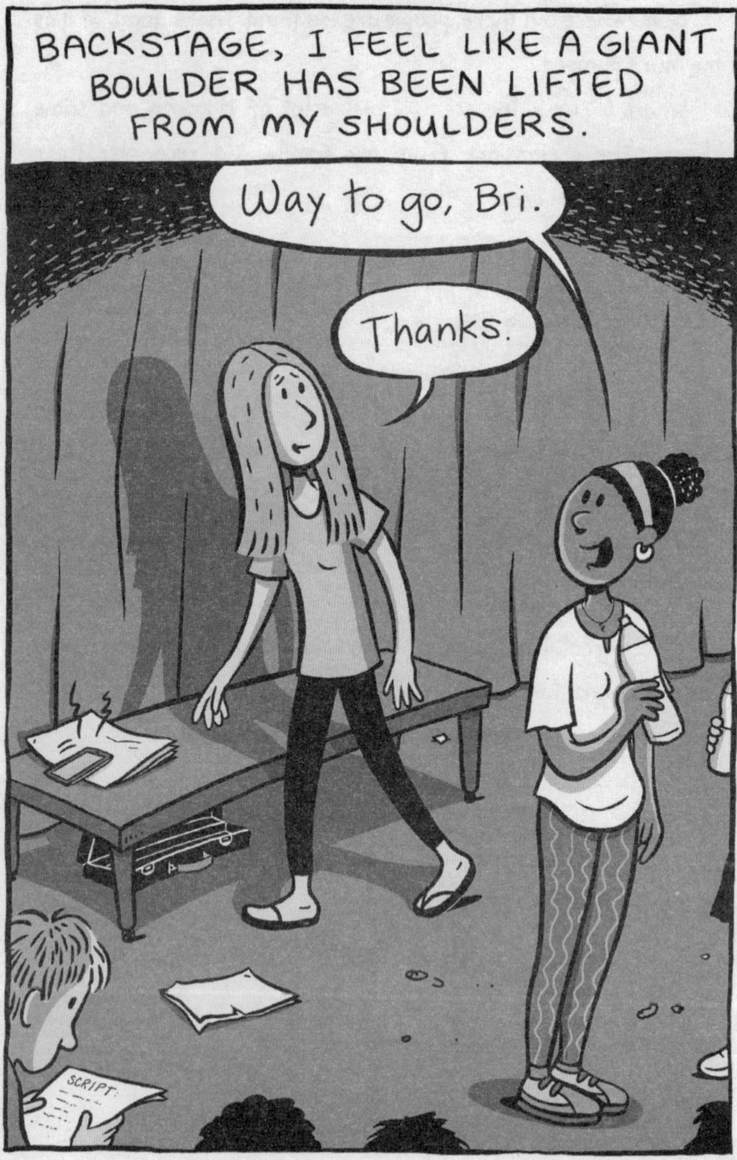
BACKSTAGE, I FEEL LIKE A GIANT BOULDER HAS BEEN LIFTED FROM MY SHOULDERS.
Way to go, Bri.
Thanks.
SCRIPT:

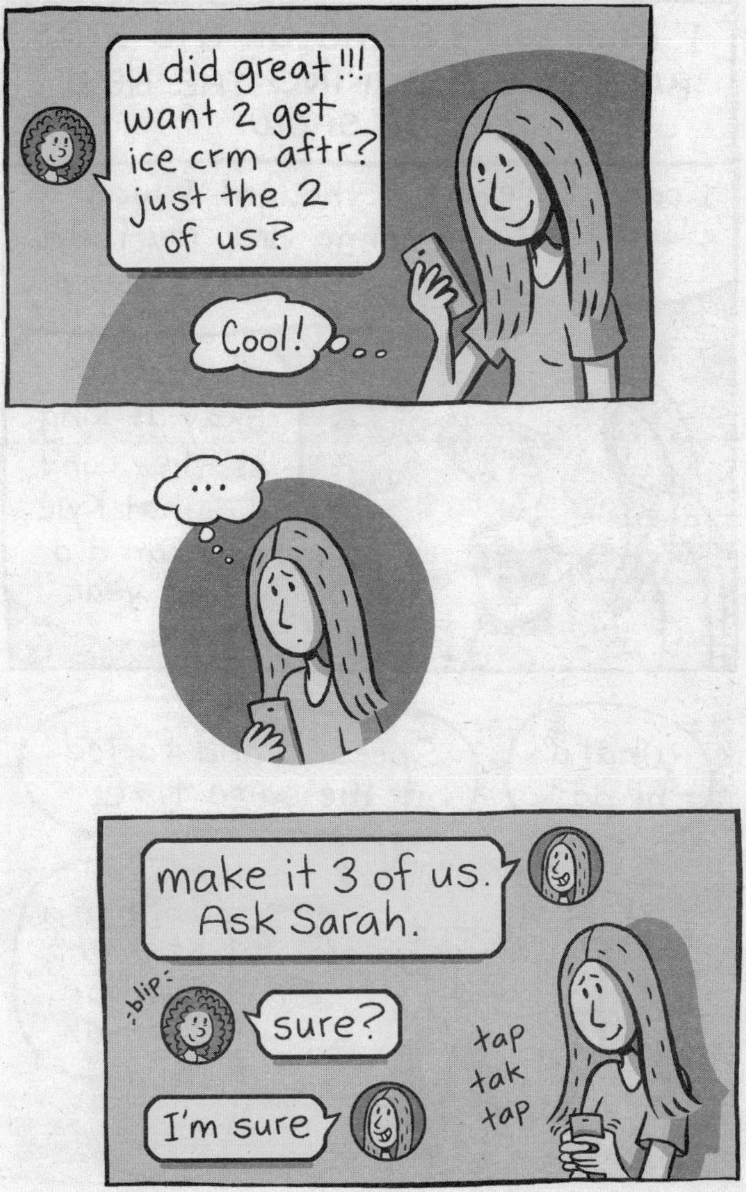
u did great!!! want 2 get ice crm aftr? just the 2 of us?
Cool!
...
make it 3 of us. Ask Sarah.
-blip-
sure?
I'm sure
tap tak tap

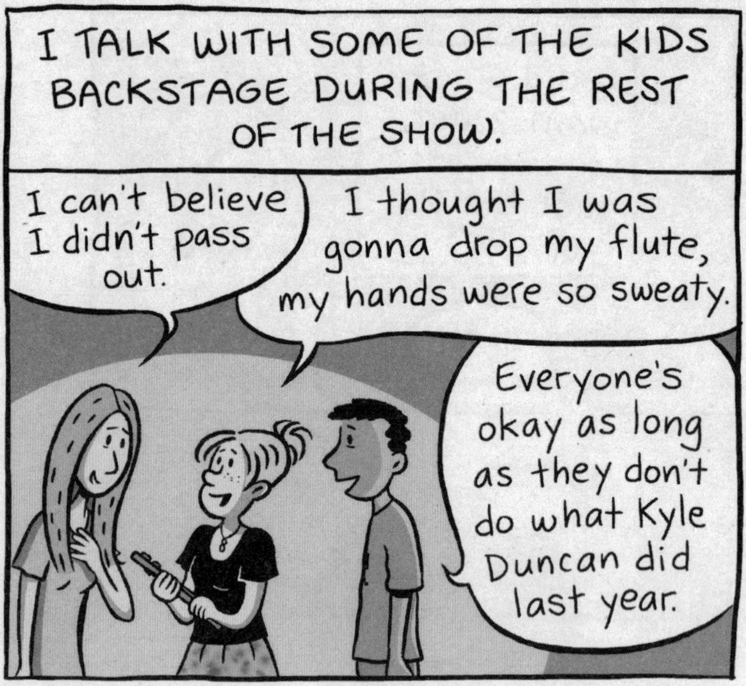
I TALK WITH SOME OF THE KIDS BACKSTAGE DURING THE REST OF THE SHOW.
I can't believe I didn't pass out.
I thought I was gonna drop my flute, my hands were so sweaty.
Everyone's okay as long as they don't do what Kyle Duncan did last year.

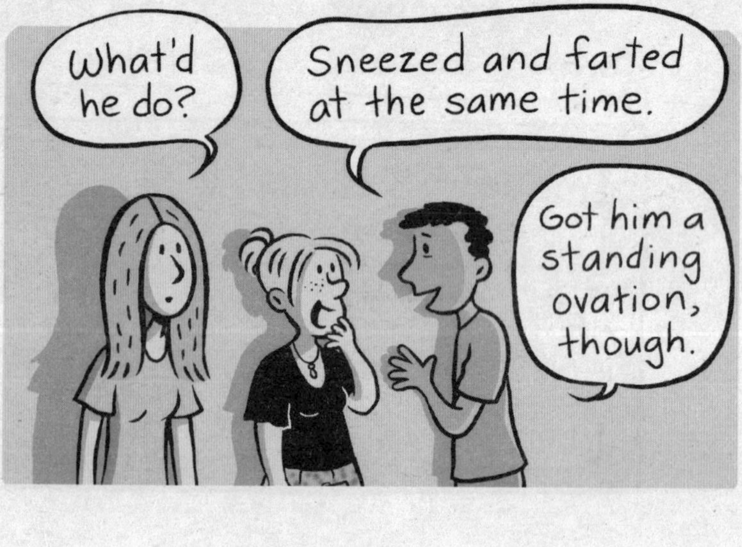
What'd he do?
Sneezed and farted at the same time.
Got him a standing ovation, though.

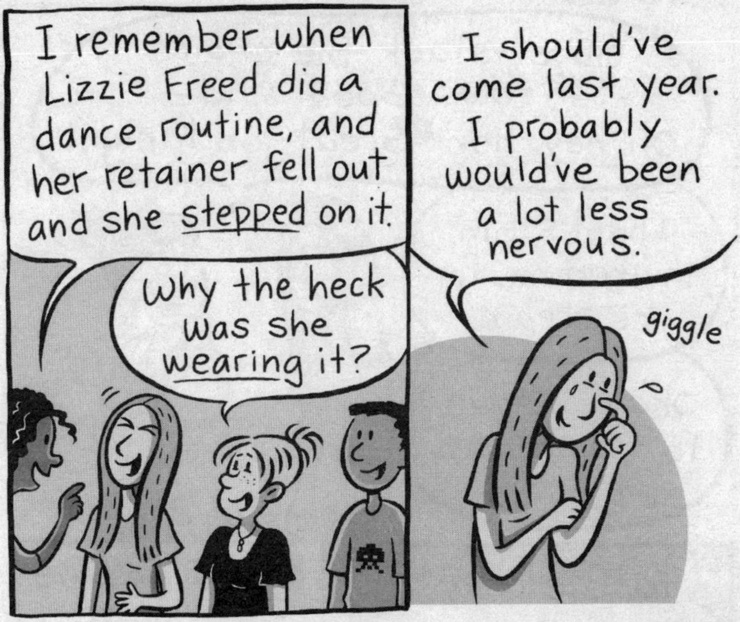
I remember when Lizzie Freed did a dance routine, and her retainer fell out and she stepped on it.
Why the heck was she wearing it?
I should've come last year. I probably would've been a lot less nervous.
giggle

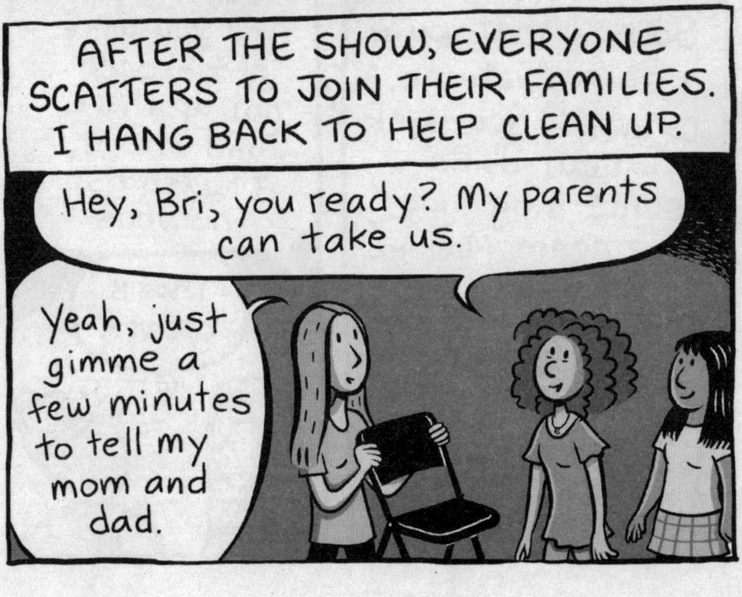
AFTER THE SHOW, EVERYONE SCATTERS TO JOIN THEIR FAMILIES. I HANG BACK TO HELP CLEAN UP.
Hey, Bri, you ready? My parents can take us.
Yeah, just gimme a few minutes to tell my mom and dad.

Guys, stack the chairs in rows. Good. And— Oh, hey, hon! Great job tonight.

Thanks. Em invited me for ice cream.

Okay. I have to finish here, anyway.

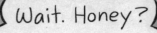

Wait. Honey?

So now that you're a stage "veteran," what do you think about doing something like this again. Maybe... drama club?

Well, I did have fun tonight. And you were right — once I got up there and into it, I wasn't so nervous.

That's great!

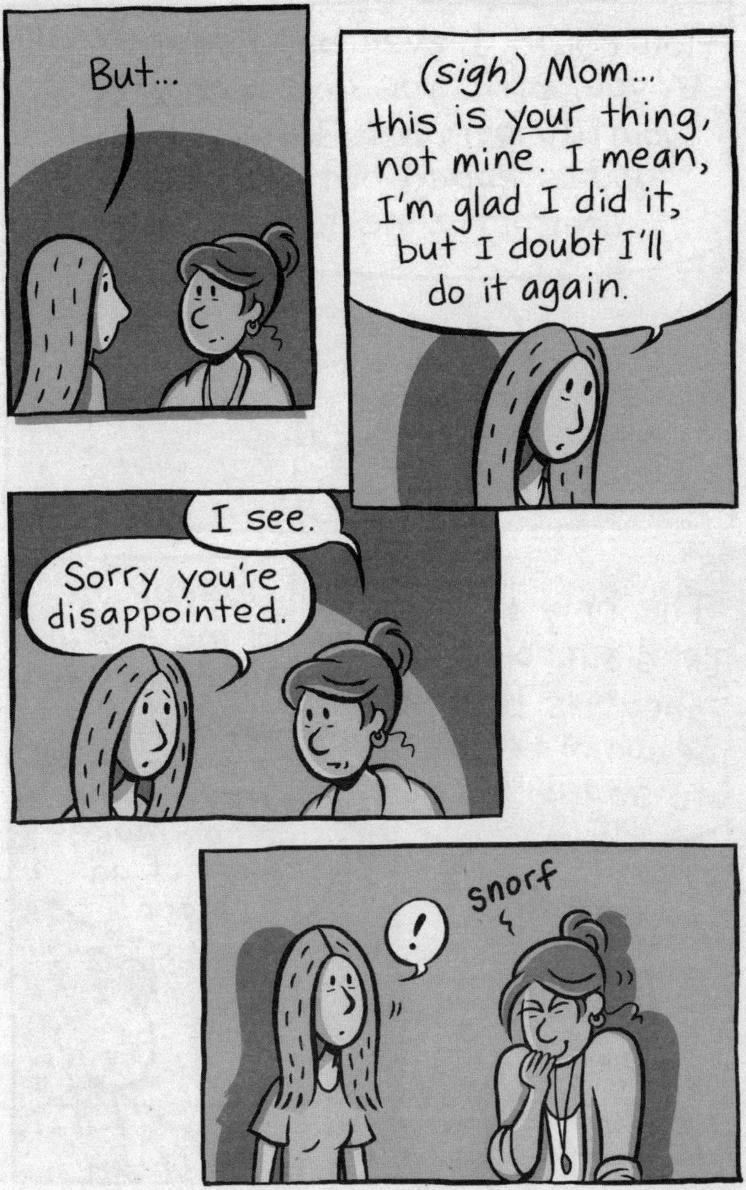
But...
(sigh) Mom... this is your thing, not mine. I mean, I'm glad I did it, but I doubt I'll do it again.
I see.
Sorry you're disappointed.
!
snorf

How could I ever be disappointed in you, Bri? You give _everything_ your 110 percent. I'm just glad you stepped out of your comfort zone for once.

The only thing I'm disappointed about is that we won't be able to share this.

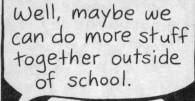

Well, maybe we can do more stuff together outside of school.

Sure. I think we can make more of an effort.

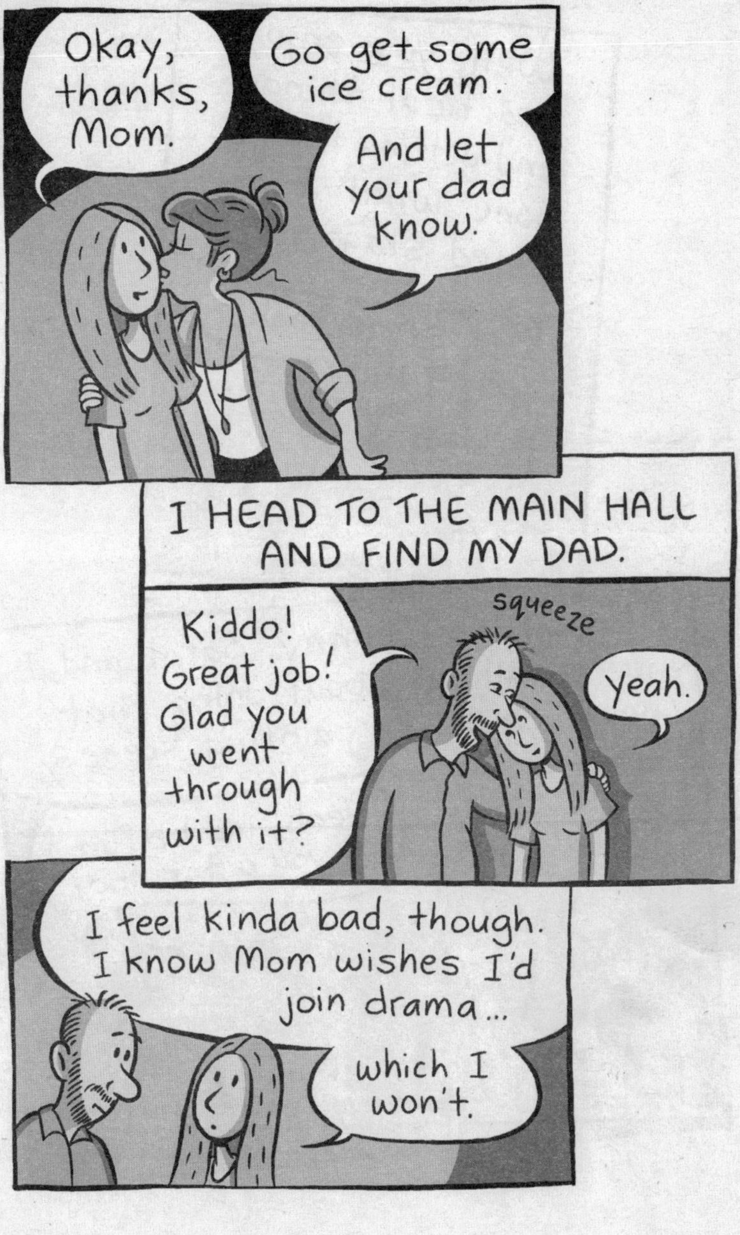
Okay, thanks, Mom.
Go get some ice cream.
And let your dad know.
I HEAD TO THE MAIN HALL AND FIND MY DAD.
Kiddo! Great job! Glad you went through with it?
squeeze
Yeah.
I feel kinda bad, though. I know Mom wishes I'd join drama...
which I won't.

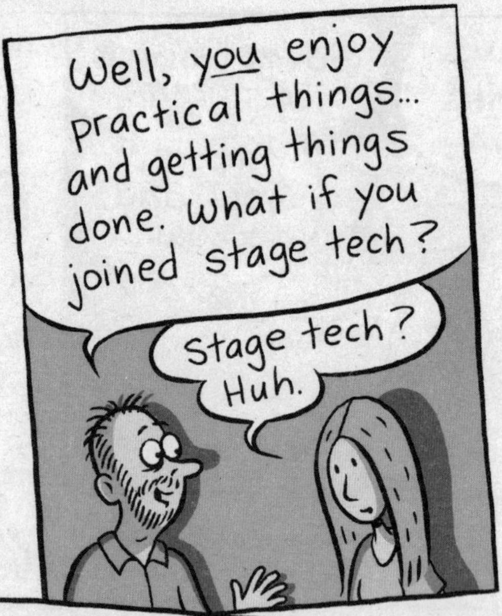
Well, you enjoy practical things... and getting things done. What if you joined stage tech?
Stage tech? Huh.

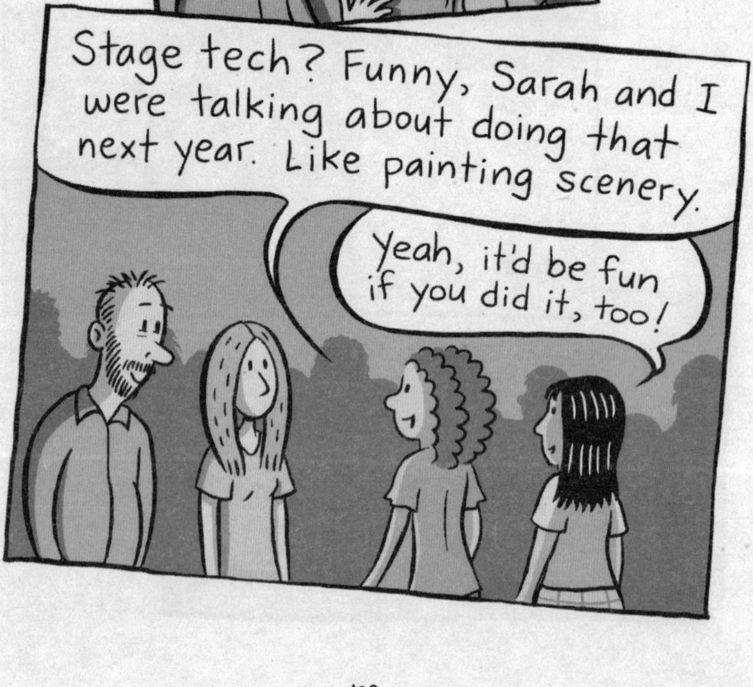
Stage tech? Funny, Sarah and I were talking about doing that next year. Like painting scenery.
Yeah, it'd be fun if you did it, too!

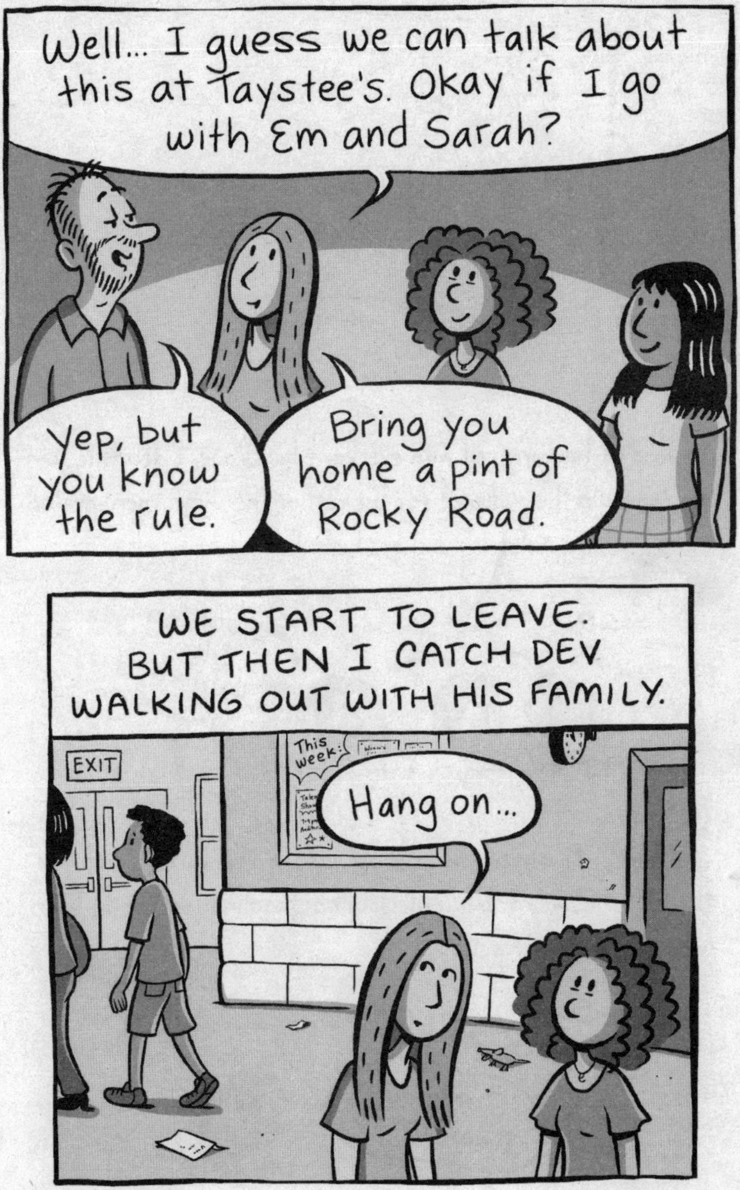
Well... I guess we can talk about this at Taystee's. Okay if I go with Em and Sarah?
Yep, but you know the rule.
Bring you home a pint of Rocky Road.
WE START TO LEAVE. BUT THEN I CATCH DEV WALKING OUT WITH HIS FAMILY.
EXIT
This week:
Hang on...

IZZY

Instead of hanging out with everyone backstage, I decide to join my family in the audience for the rest of the show. There are no more seats, so Ash lets me share hers.

looking like conjoined twins

Overall, it's a pretty good show. Lots of musical acts and skits. There's one weird but entertaining juggling act with tacos (which doesn't end well).

SPLORT

S'okay, I have more!

When it's over, we get up and start to head out. I want to say bye to my friends, but I'm pretty sure my mom wants me behind bars ASAP.

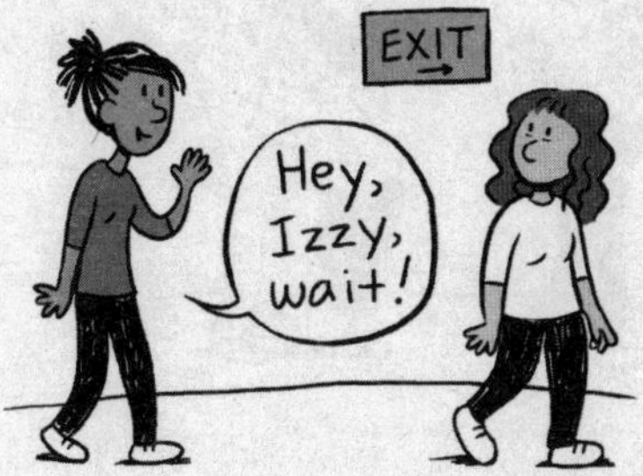
EXIT
Hey, Izzy, wait!

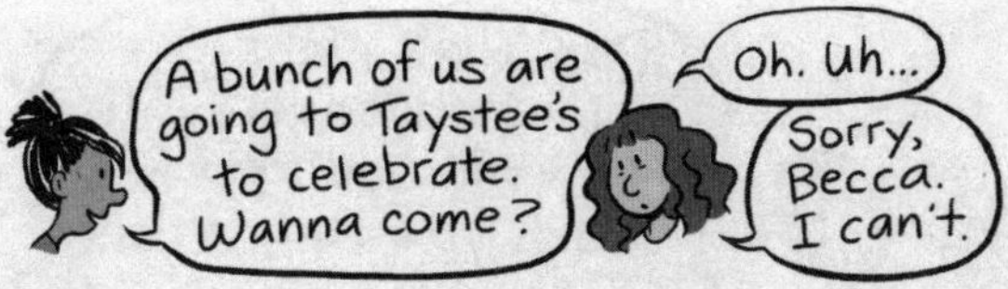
A bunch of us are going to Taystee's to celebrate. Wanna come?
Oh. Uh...
Sorry, Becca. I can't.

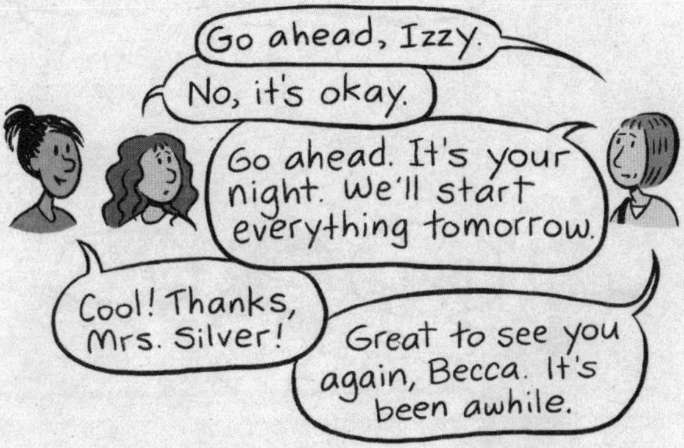
Go ahead, Izzy.
No, it's okay.
Go ahead. It's your night. We'll start everything tomorrow.
Cool! Thanks, Mrs. Silver!
Great to see you again, Becca. It's been awhile.

Meet you outside!
Thanks... again, Mom.
It's okay. Listen...
Dani was right. You were wonderful! I never realized how much you enjoy this.
And you really looked like you loved it up there.
BUT...
yeah...

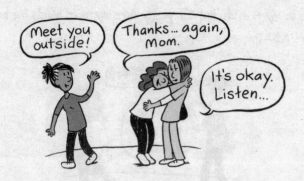

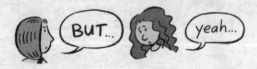

You CANNOT go to drama club until you get your grades up. We'll discuss in detail later.

Okay.

We'll also discuss your and Ashley's punishments.

gulp

Dani, Ash, I'll pull the car around. Izzy, be back in an hour, please.

Okay, Mom.

Well, at least we're in this together.

Sorta. I still have to get my grades up.

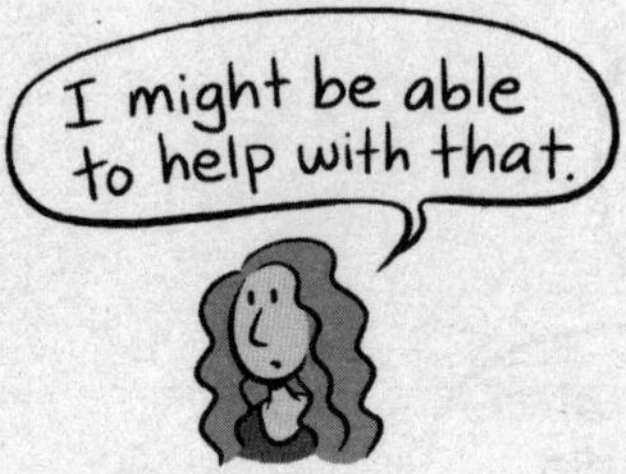
I might be able to help with that.

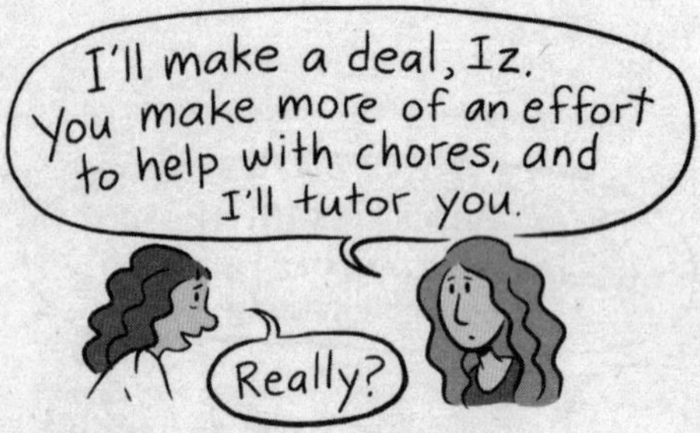
I'll make a deal, Iz. You make more of an effort to help with chores, and I'll tutor you.
Really?

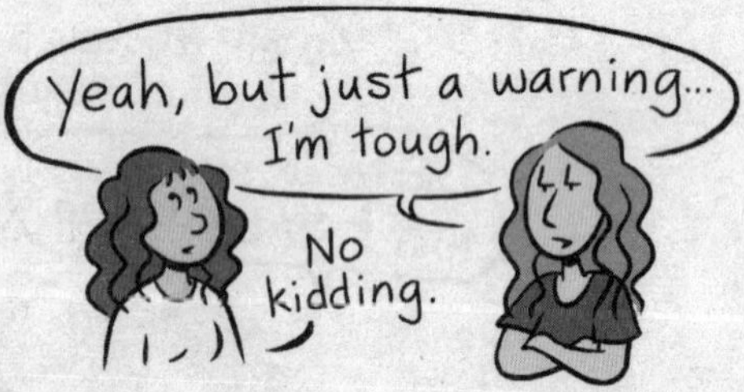
Yeah, but just a warning... I'm tough.
No kidding.

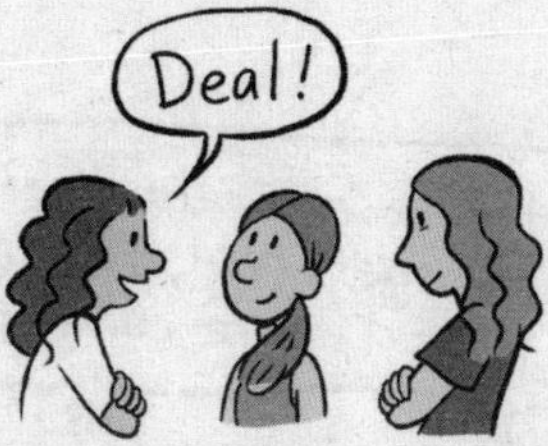
Deal!

We all head outside. Dani and Ash get in Mom's car and drive home. I walk over to Becca, who's hanging out with a group of kids.

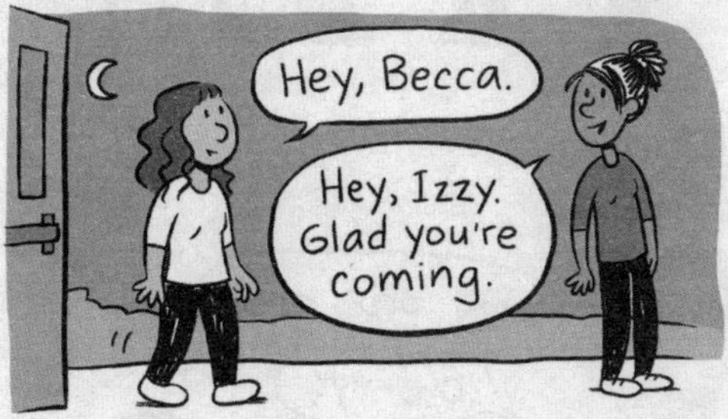
Hey, Becca.
Hey, Izzy. Glad you're coming.

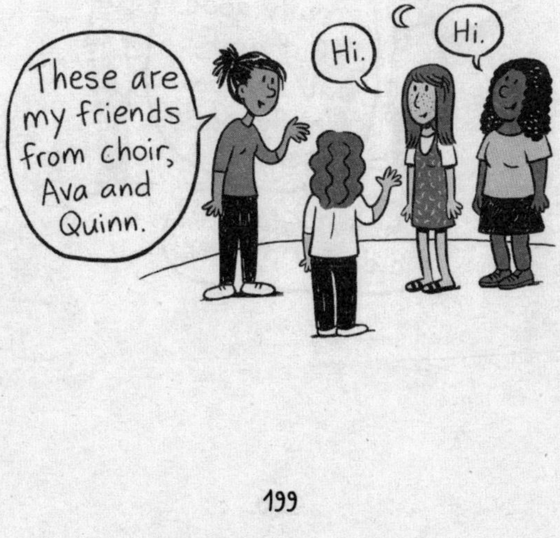
These are my friends from choir, Ava and Quinn.
Hi.
Hi.

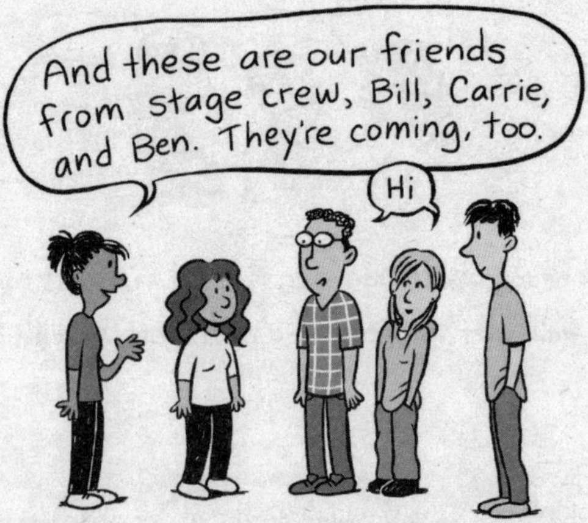
And these are our friends from stage crew, Bill, Carrie, and Ben. They're coming, too.
Hi

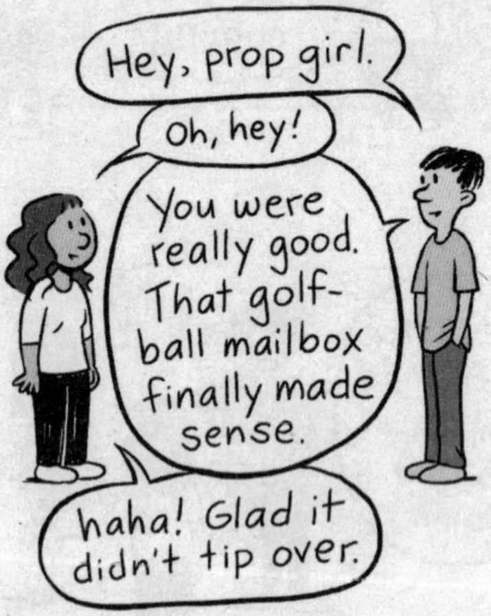
Hey, prop girl.
Oh, hey!
You were really good. That golf-ball mailbox finally made sense.
haha! Glad it didn't tip over.

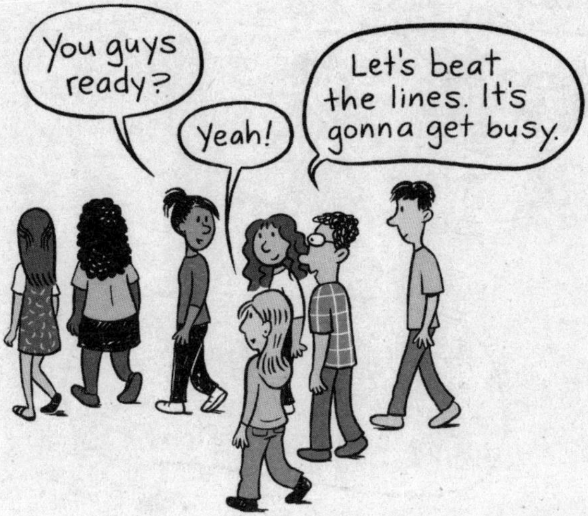
You guys ready?
Yeah!
Let's beat the lines. It's gonna get busy.

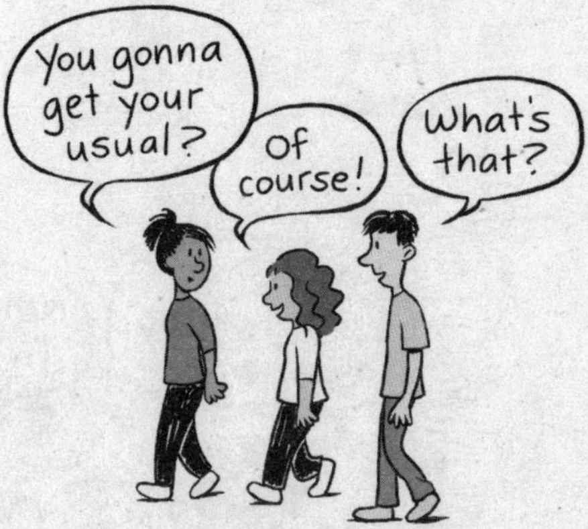
You gonna get your usual?
Of course!
What's that?

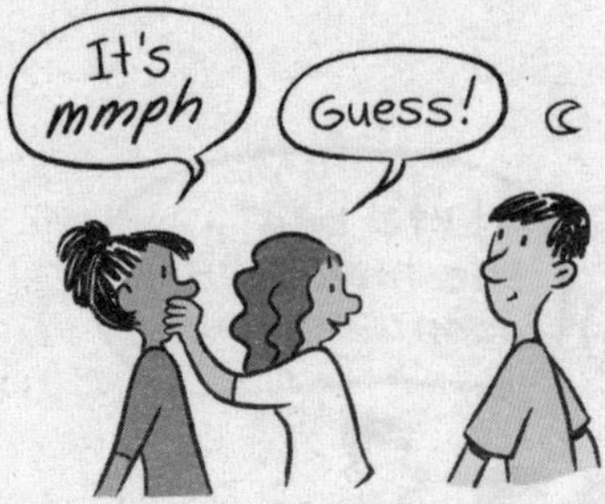
It's *mmph*
Guess!

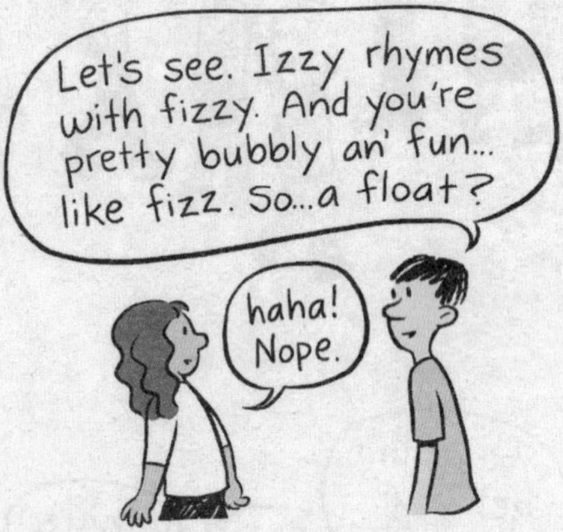
Let's see. Izzy rhymes with fizzy. And you're pretty bubbly an' fun... like fizz. So...a float?
haha! Nope.

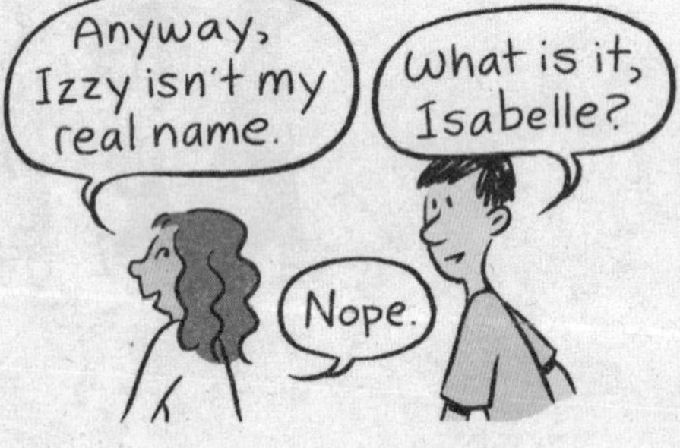
Anyway, Izzy isn't my real name.
What is it, Isabelle?
Nope.

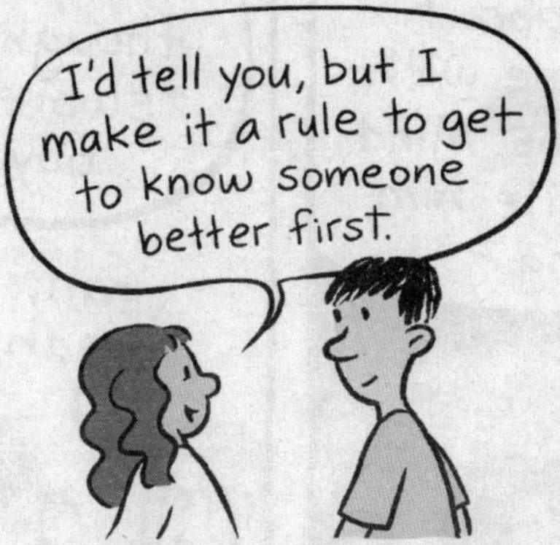
I'd tell you, but I make it a rule to get to know someone better first.

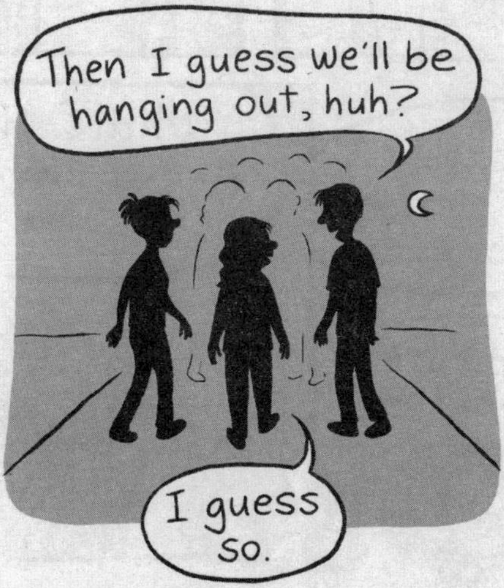
Then I guess we'll be hanging out, huh?
I guess so.

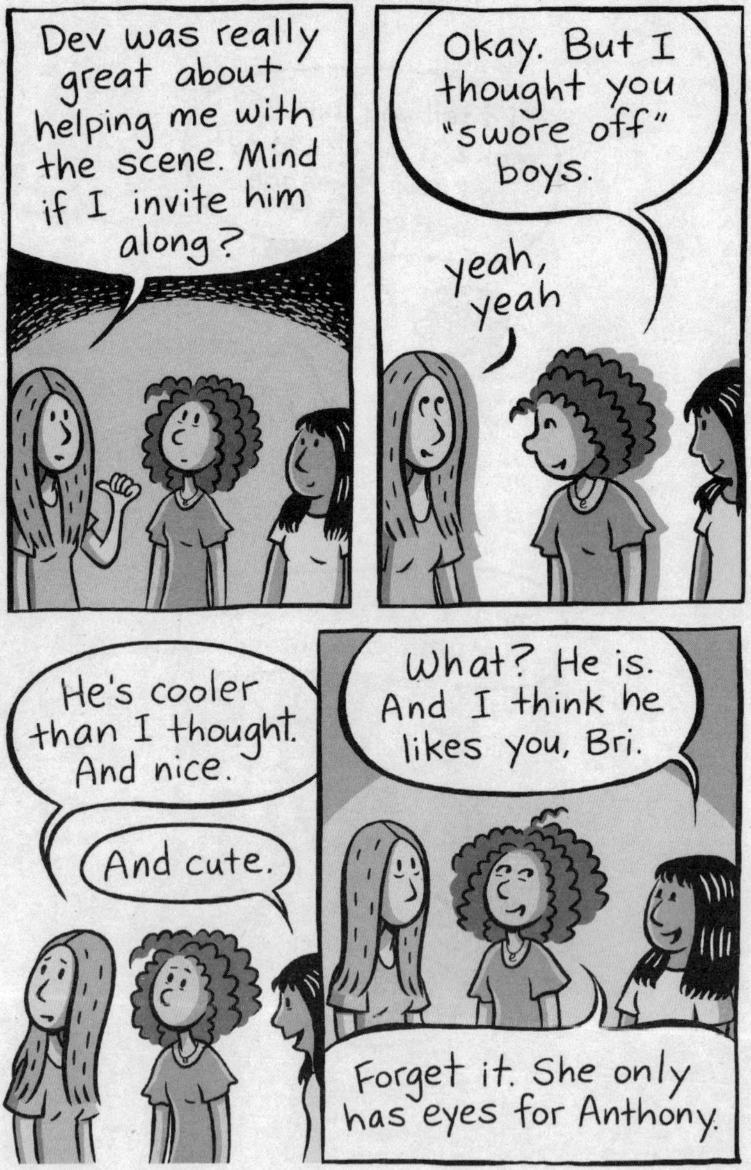
Dev was really great about helping me with the scene. Mind if I invite him along?
Okay. But I thought you "swore off" boys.
yeah, yeah
He's cooler than I thought. And nice.
And cute.
What? He is. And I think he likes you, Bri.
Forget it. She only has eyes for Anthony.

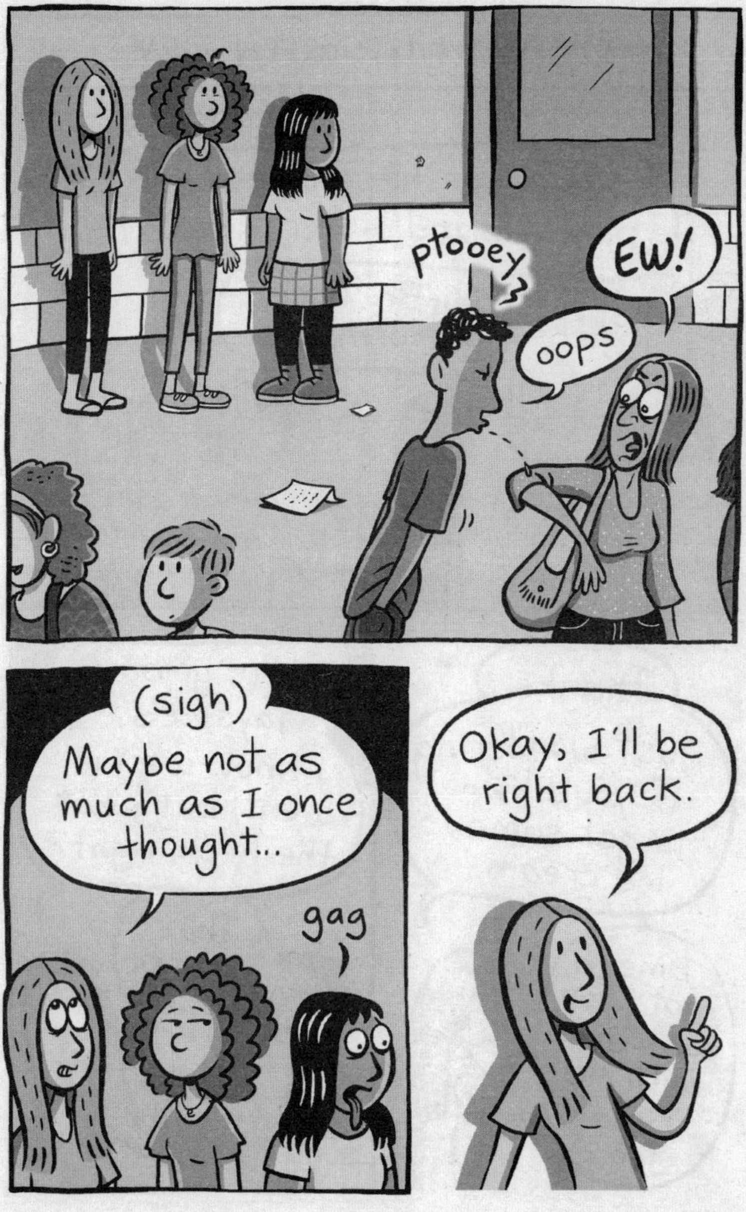
ptooey
EW!
oops
(sigh)
Maybe not as much as I once thought...
gag
Okay, I'll be right back.

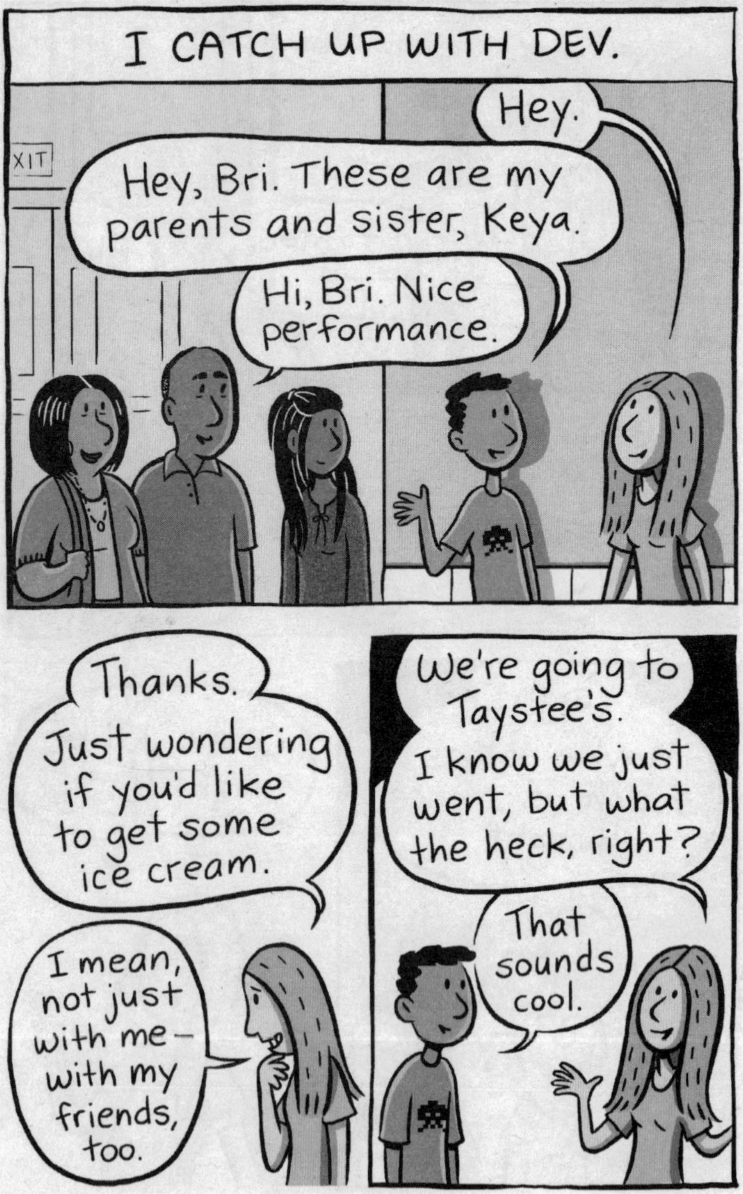

I CATCH UP WITH DEV.
Hey.
XIT
Hey, Bri. These are my parents and sister, Keya.
Hi, Bri. Nice performance.
Thanks.
Just wondering if you'd like to get some ice cream.
I mean, not just with me— with my friends, too.
We're going to Taystee's.
I know we just went, but what the heck, right?
That sounds cool.

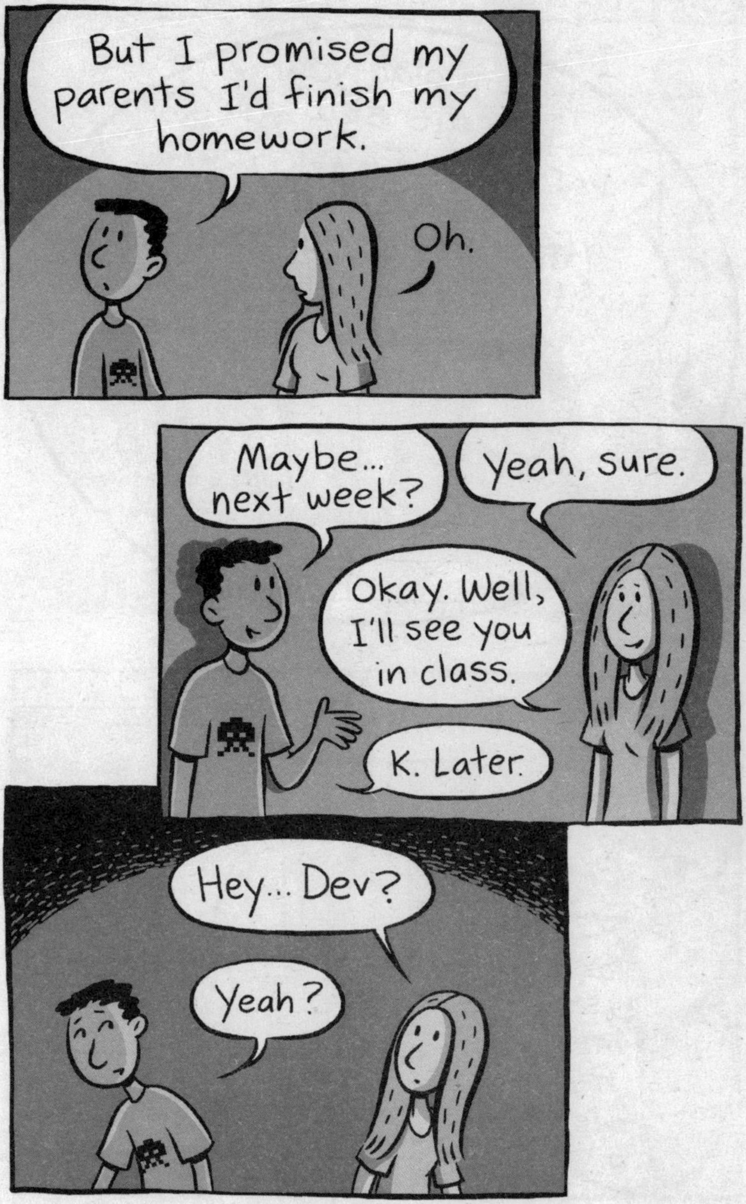

But I promised my parents I'd finish my homework.
Oh.
Maybe... next week?
Yeah, sure.
Okay. Well, I'll see you in class.
K. Later.
Hey... Dev?
Yeah?

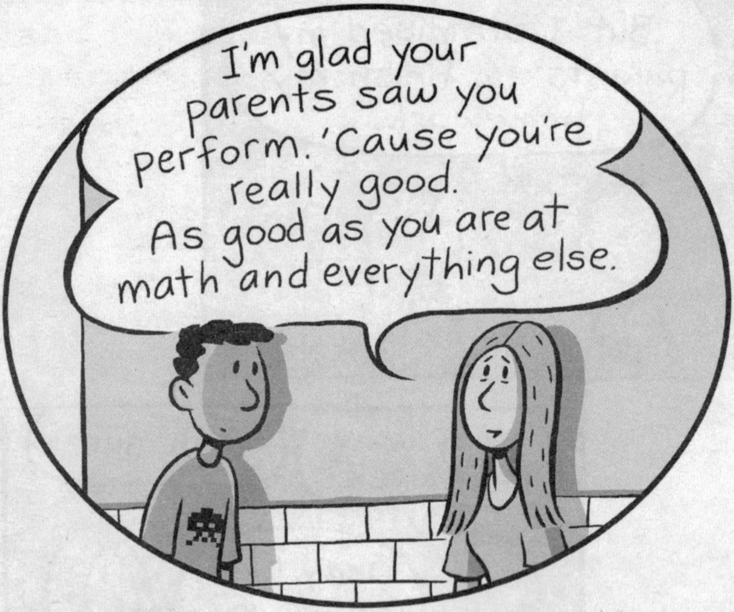
I'm glad your parents saw you perform. 'Cause you're really good. As good as you are at math and everything else.

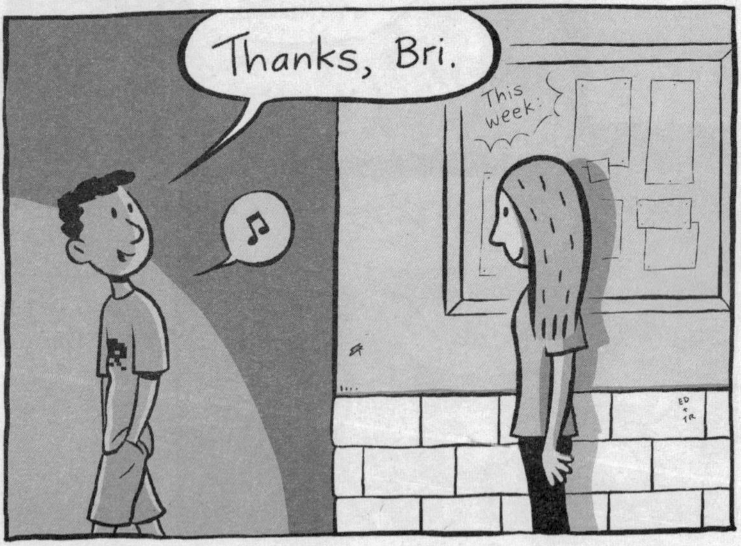
Thanks, Bri.
This week:

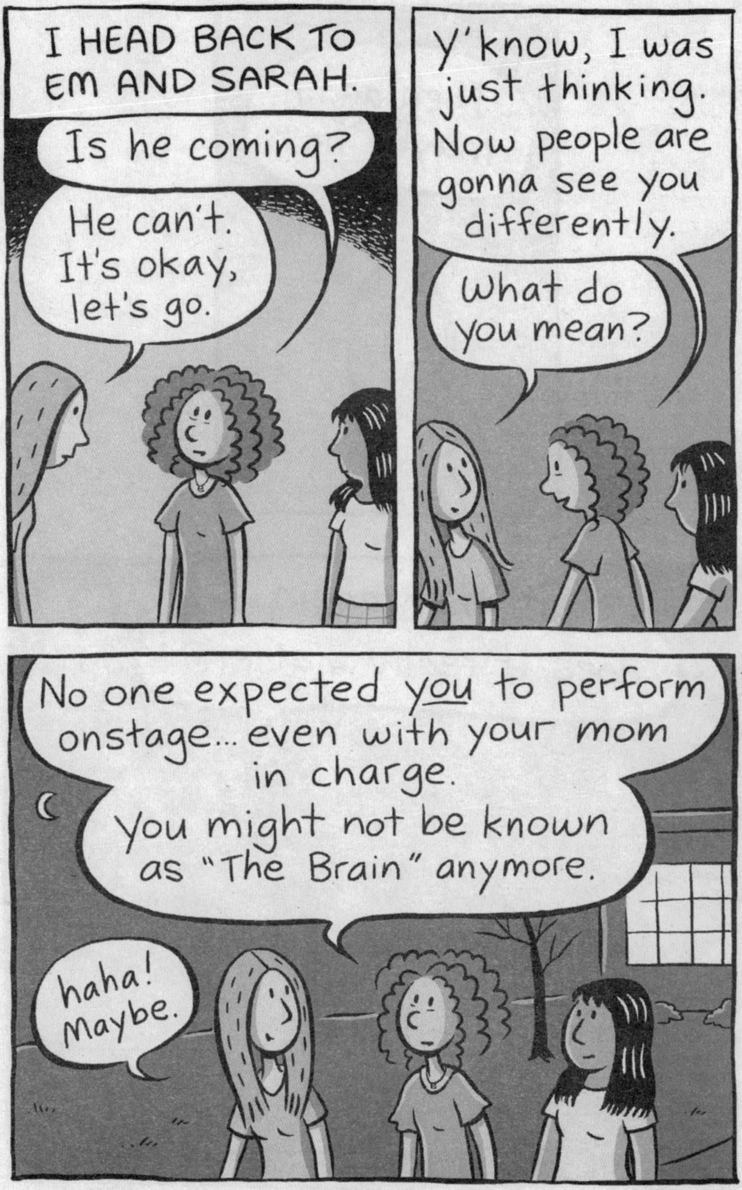
I HEAD BACK TO EM AND SARAH.
Is he coming?
He can't. It's okay, let's go.
Y'know, I was just thinking. Now people are gonna see you differently.
What do you mean?
No one expected you to perform onstage... even with your mom in charge.
You might not be known as "The Brain" anymore.
haha! Maybe.

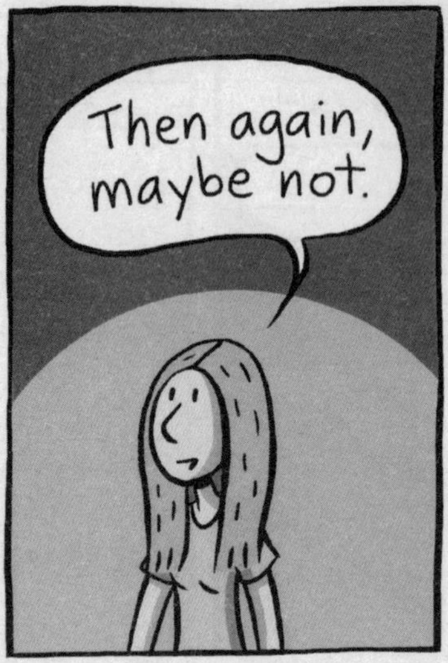
Then again, maybe not.

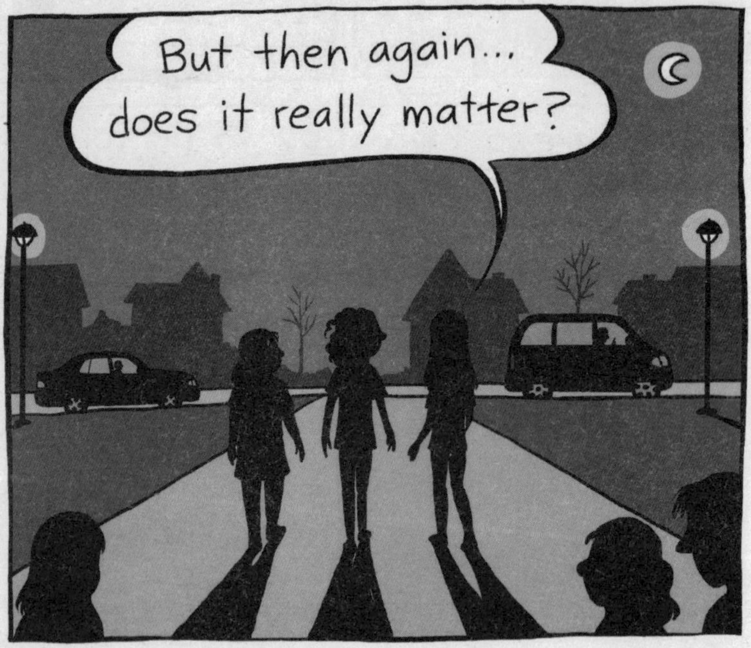
But then again... does it really matter?

Epilogue: Brianna

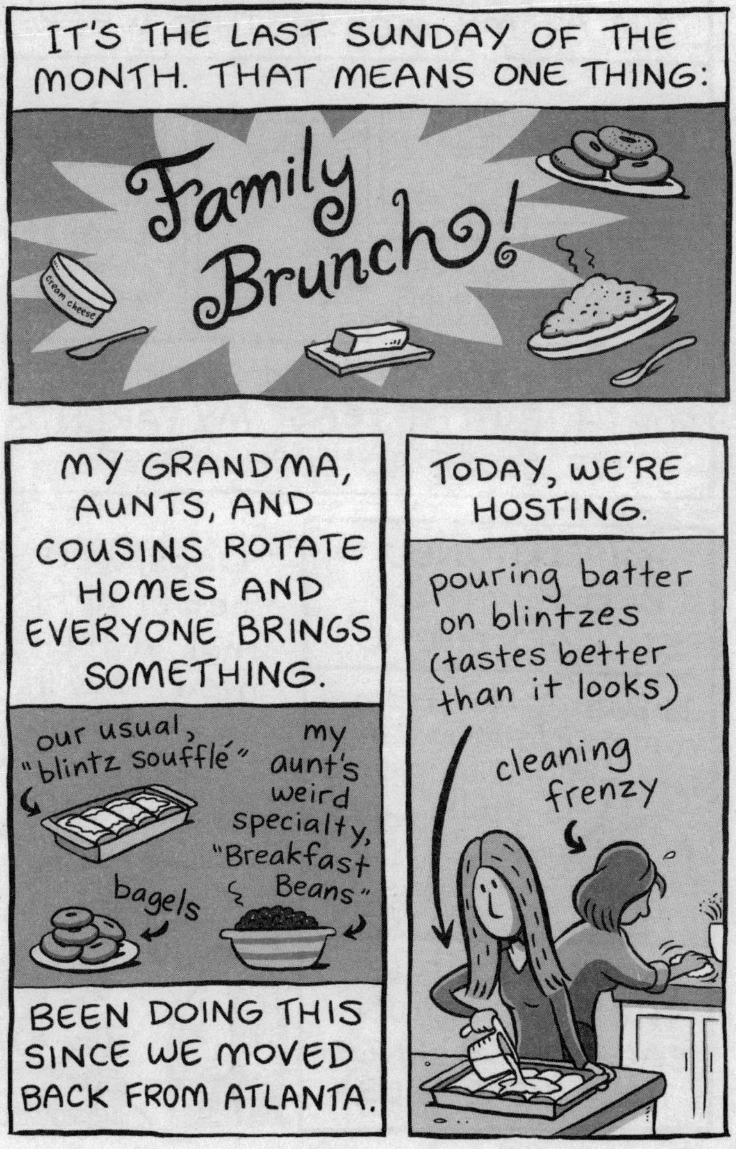

IT'S THE LAST SUNDAY OF THE MONTH. THAT MEANS ONE THING:
Family Brunch!
Cream cheese
MY GRANDMA, AUNTS, AND COUSINS ROTATE HOMES AND EVERYONE BRINGS SOMETHING.
our usual, "blintz soufflé"
my aunt's weird specialty, "Breakfast Beans"
bagels
BEEN DOING THIS SINCE WE MOVED BACK FROM ATLANTA.
TODAY, WE'RE HOSTING.
pouring batter on blintzes (tastes better than it looks)
cleaning frenzy

MY PARENTS SHARE CUSTODY.
I'M AT MY MOM'S THIS WEEK.

Dad's house

Taystee's (yum)

Mom's condo (3 blocks away)

IT'S A PAIN TO TREK BACK AND
FORTH, BUT AT LEAST MY PARENTS
LIVE CLOSE TO EACH OTHER.

I MENTIONED
BEFORE, THEY
STILL GET ALONG.

Is Dad coming?

Not today. He has a million papers to grade.

Oops, we'd better get that in the oven. They'll be here soon. Especially you-know-who.

snort

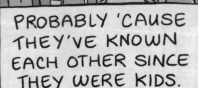

PROBABLY 'CAUSE
THEY'VE KNOWN
EACH OTHER SINCE
THEY WERE KIDS.

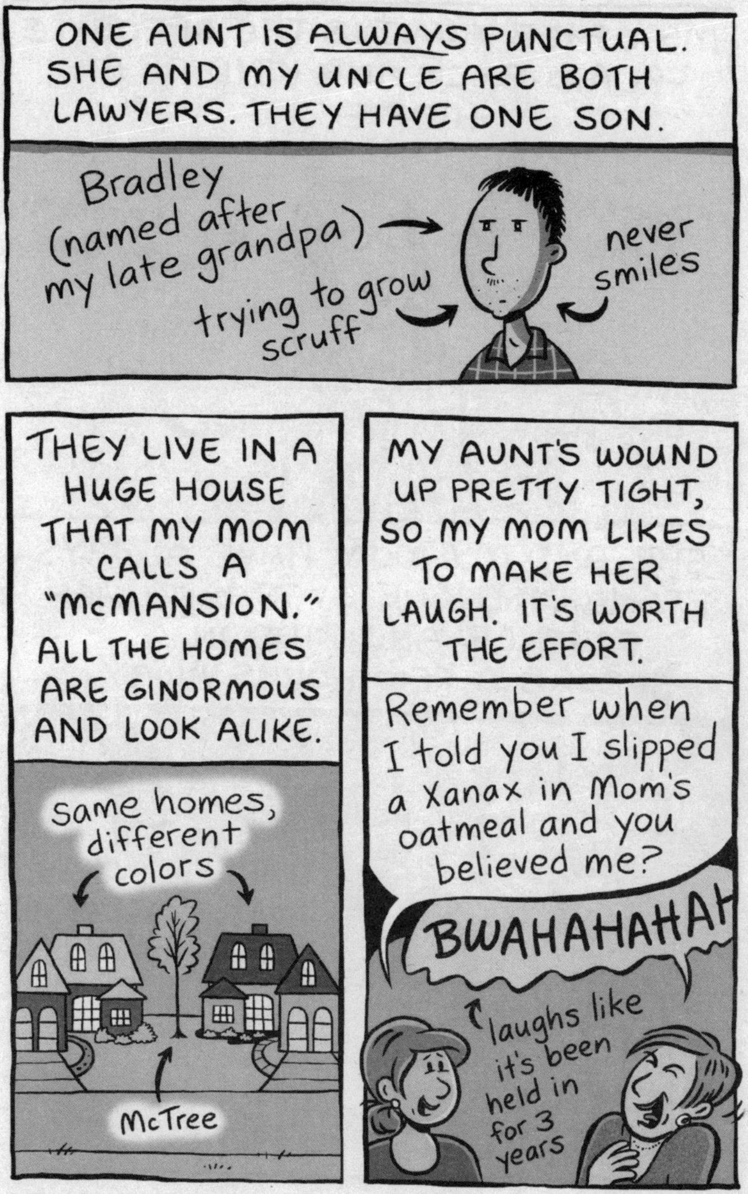

ONE AUNT IS ALWAYS PUNCTUAL. SHE AND MY UNCLE ARE BOTH LAWYERS. THEY HAVE ONE SON.
Bradley
(named after my late grandpa)
trying to grow scruff
never smiles
THEY LIVE IN A HUGE HOUSE THAT MY MOM CALLS A "McMANSION." ALL THE HOMES ARE GINORMOUS AND LOOK ALIKE.
same homes, different colors
McTree
MY AUNT'S WOUND UP PRETTY TIGHT, SO MY MOM LIKES TO MAKE HER LAUGH. IT'S WORTH THE EFFORT.
Remember when I told you I slipped a Xanax in Mom's oatmeal and you believed me?
BWAHAHAHAH
laughs like it's been held in for 3 years

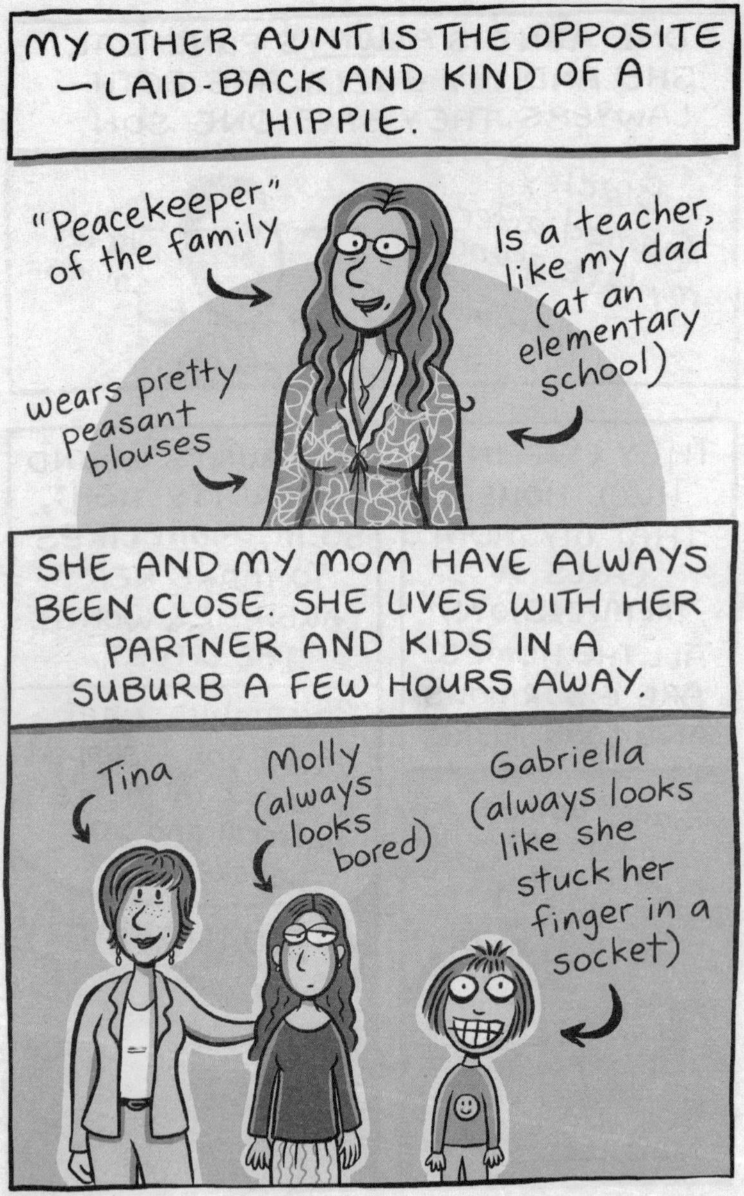
MY OTHER AUNT IS THE OPPOSITE —LAID-BACK AND KIND OF A HIPPIE.
"Peacekeeper" of the family
Is a teacher, like my dad (at an elementary school)
wears pretty peasant blouses
SHE AND MY MOM HAVE ALWAYS BEEN CLOSE. SHE LIVES WITH HER PARTNER AND KIDS IN A SUBURB A FEW HOURS AWAY.
Tina
Molly (always looks bored)
Gabriella (always looks like she stuck her finger in a socket)

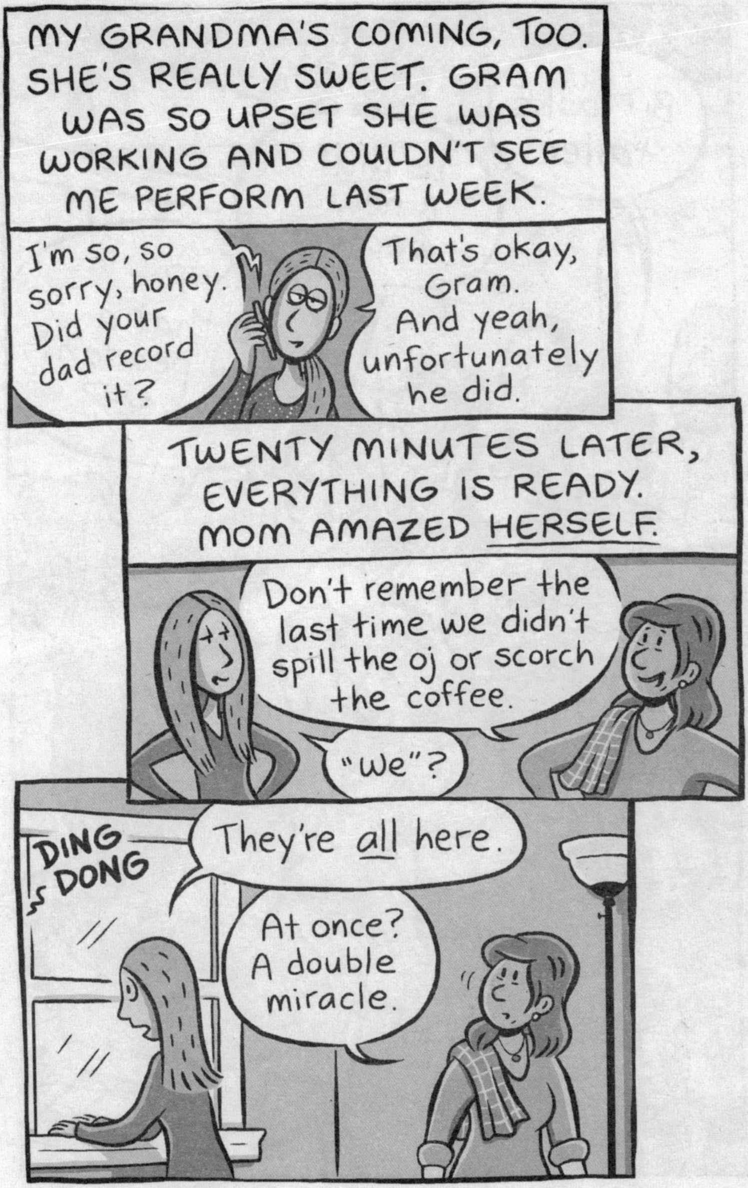
MY GRANDMA'S COMING, TOO. SHE'S REALLY SWEET. GRAM WAS SO UPSET SHE WAS WORKING AND COULDN'T SEE ME PERFORM LAST WEEK.
I'm so, so sorry, honey. Did your dad record it?
That's okay, Gram. And yeah, unfortunately he did.
TWENTY MINUTES LATER, EVERYTHING IS READY. MOM AMAZED HERSELF.
Don't remember the last time we didn't spill the oj or scorch the coffee.
"We"?
DING DONG
They're all here.
At once? A double miracle.

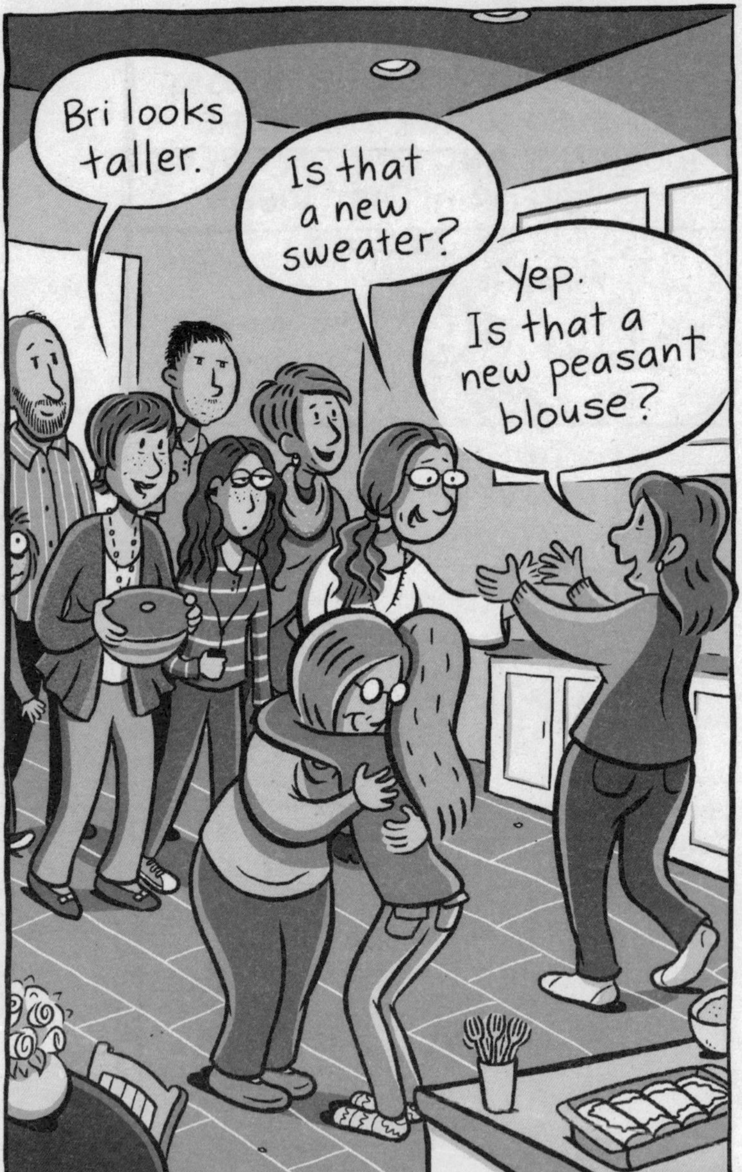
Bri looks taller.
Is that a new sweater?
Yep. Is that a new peasant blouse?

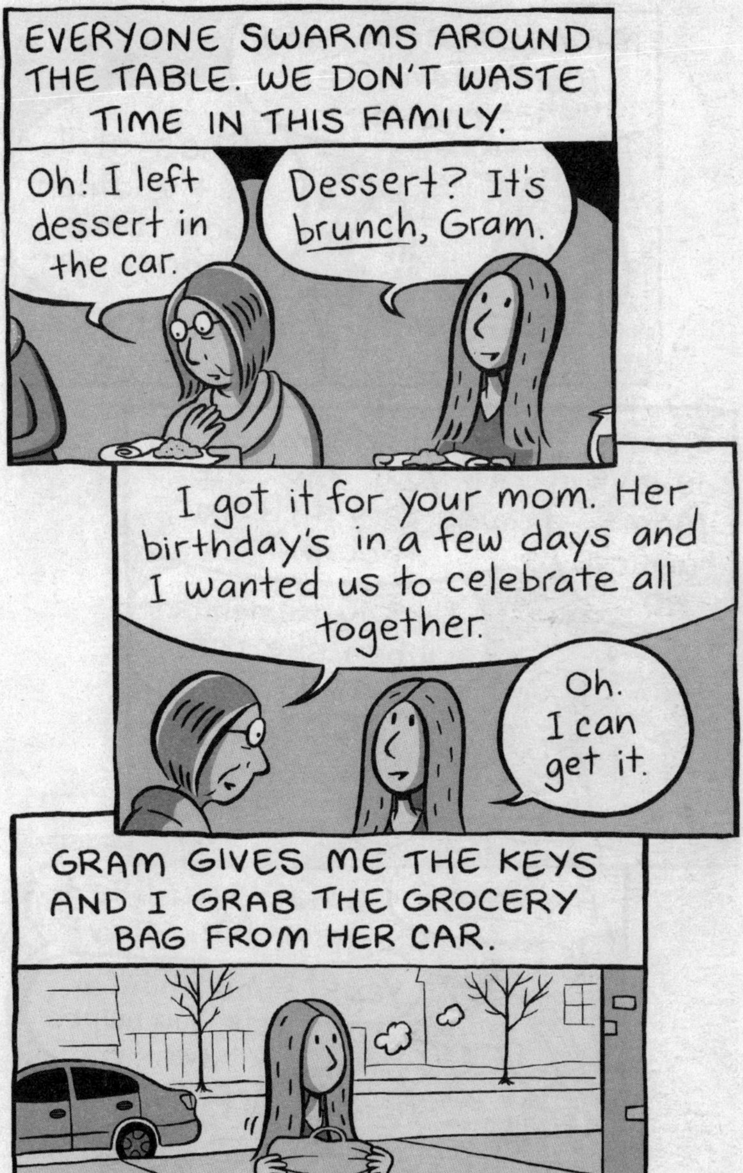
EVERYONE SWARMS AROUND THE TABLE. WE DON'T WASTE TIME IN THIS FAMILY.
Oh! I left dessert in the car.
Dessert? It's brunch, Gram.
I got it for your mom. Her birthday's in a few days and I wanted us to celebrate all together.
Oh. I can get it.
GRAM GIVES ME THE KEYS AND I GRAB THE GROCERY BAG FROM HER CAR.

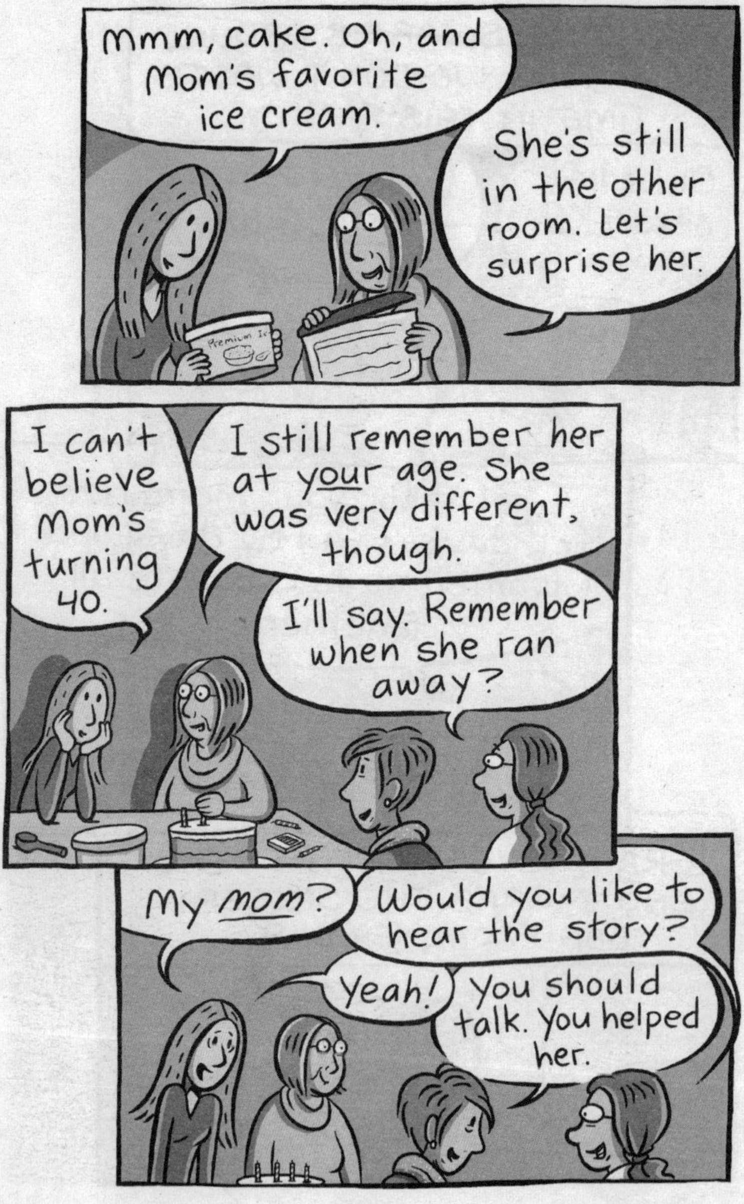
Mmm, cake. Oh, and Mom's favorite ice cream.
She's still in the other room. Let's surprise her.
I can't believe Mom's turning 40.
I still remember her at your age. She was very different, though.
I'll say. Remember when she ran away?
My mom?
Would you like to hear the story?
Yeah!
You should talk. You helped her.

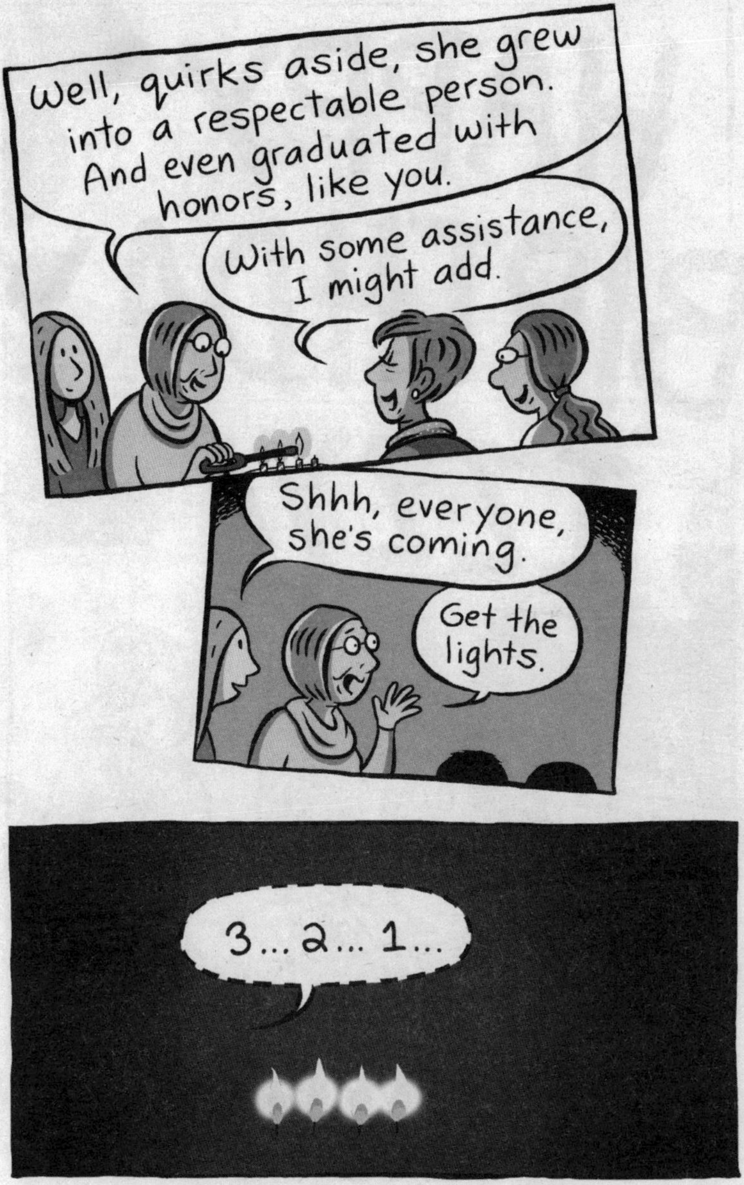
Well, quirks aside, she grew into a respectable person. And even graduated with honors, like you.
With some assistance, I might add.
Shhh, everyone, she's coming.
Get the lights.
3... 2... 1...

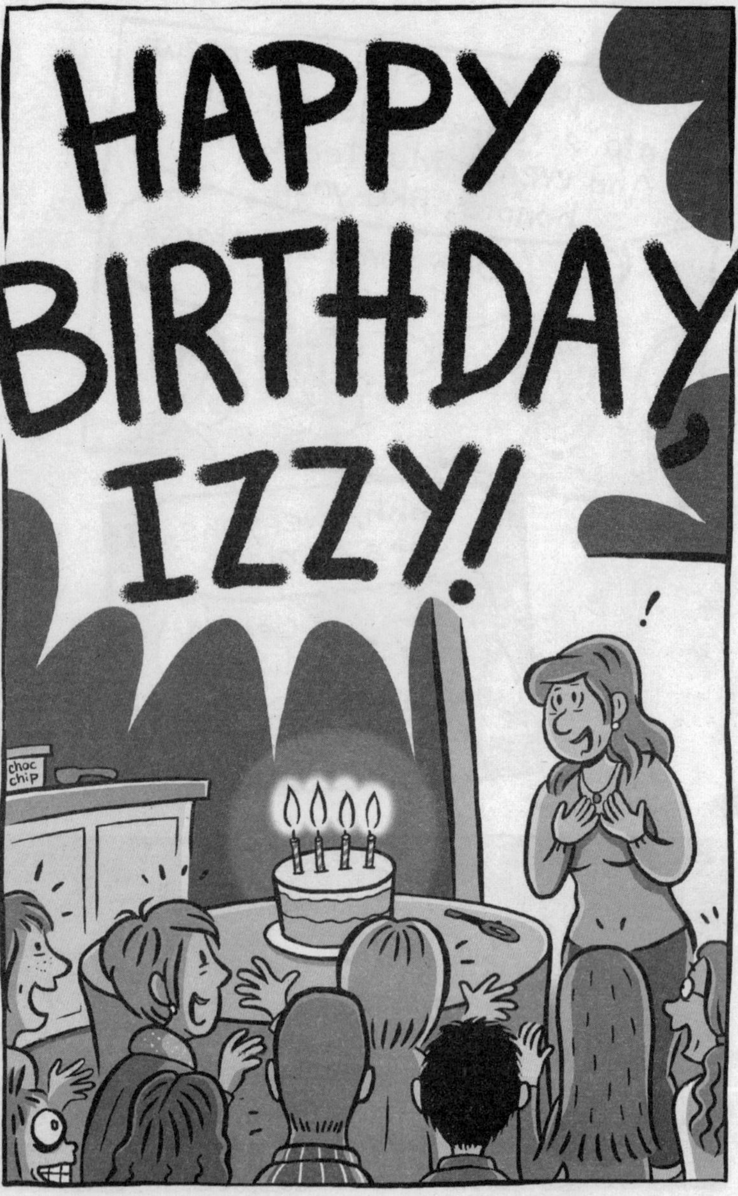
HAPPY BIRTHDAY IZZY!
!
choc chip